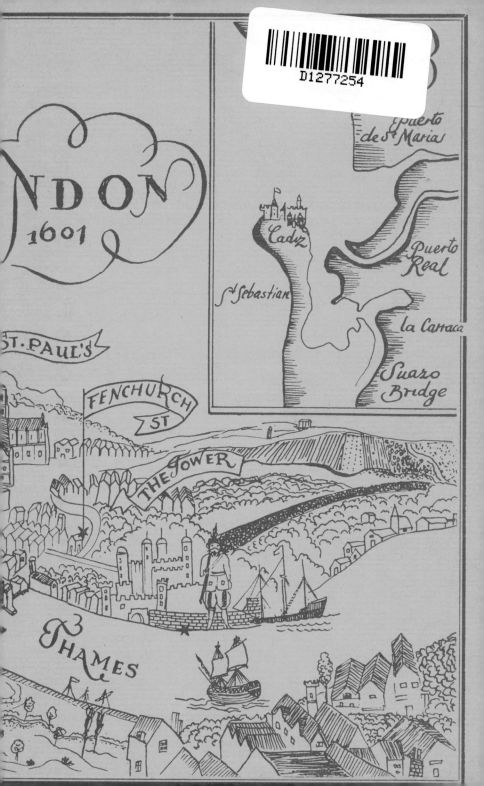

NDON
1601

ST. PAUL'S

FENCHURCH ST

THE TOWER

THAMES

Puerto de St Maria

Cadiz

St Sebastian

Puerto Real

la Carraca

Suazo Bridge

My Lord Essex

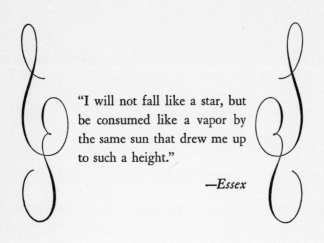

"I will not fall like a star, but
be consumed like a vapor by
the same sun that drew me up
to such a height."

—*Essex*

My Lord Essex

A NOVEL BY *Olive Eckerson*

Henry Holt and Company
New York

To my mother

Contents

Part Three: SOLDIER (1596-1598)

Part Four: REBEL (1599-1600)

Part Five: TRAITOR (1600-1601)

The Characters

ELIZABETH TUDOR, *Queen of England*
ROBERT DEVEREUX, *Earl of Essex*
WILLIAM CECIL, *Lord Burghley*
SIR ROBERT CECIL, *the Queen's Secretary*
FRANCIS BACON, *a lawyer*
CHARLES BLOUNT, *Earl of Mountjoy*
HENRY WRIOTHESLEY, *Earl of Southampton*
ROBERT DUDLEY, *Earl of Leicester, stepfather to Essex*
SIR CHRISTOPHER BLOUNT, *stepfather to Essex*
FRANCES WALSINGHAM, *Lady Essex*
SIR WALTER RALEGH, *Captain of the Queen's Guard*
LETTICE KNOLLYS, *Countess of Essex and Leicester*
PENELOPE RICH, *sister of Essex*
PAMELA BRIDGES, *mistress to Essex*
KATHERINE FYTTON, *mistress to Essex*
HUGH O'NEILL, *Earl of Tyrone*
SIR THOMAS EGERTON, *Keeper of the Seal*
SIR EDWARD COKE, *Attorney-General*
DR. RODERIGO LOPEZ, *the Queen's Physician*
HENRY CUFFE, *secretary to Essex*
SIR MALCOLM MALBY, *follower of Essex*
JOSEPH THORN, *manservant to Essex*
ADAM BAXTER, *a soldier*

Prologue

In September, 1575, Robin Devereux, afterward Earl of Essex, was approaching his ninth birthday, and Elizabeth Tudor was a woman of forty-two. For seventeen years she had ruled England, unmarried, the heart and center of her age.

Now the flush of Renaissance glory was fast rising to its zenith in England. In the next twenty-five years Drake and Howard were to make her supreme on the sea, Ralegh was to extend her colonies into the New World, and at home, a young lad of eleven, living up at Stratford, was to lift her literature to the supreme heights of genius.

Under the benign and brilliant rule of the Virgin Queen, lovingly called Gloriana, Englishmen were relatively content. With the aid of the gifted Cecils, father and son, Elizabeth was enabled to guide her country successfully through the maze of French and Spanish intrigue. The land prospered; pastures full of sheep fed the great and growing wool industry; manor houses flowered in red brick throughout the countryside; and in the towns, fast changing to cities, the children of commoners went to school.

But in 1575 Elizabeth herself was facing a fantastic future. Always the center of romantic and fascinating men, her youthful days as Queen had been dominated by the dashing Robert Dudley, Earl of Leicester, whom many people expected her to marry. Now, in middle life, she turned her eyes on his stepson, Robert Devereux, a young man thirty-five years her junior. And so began her personal tragedy.

Although she believed she had given her whole heart to the Earl of Essex, Elizabeth found she was, as she said, "mere English." When his ambition endangered her realm, she destroyed him. But the struggle killed her. She survived her one-time favorite by barely two years.

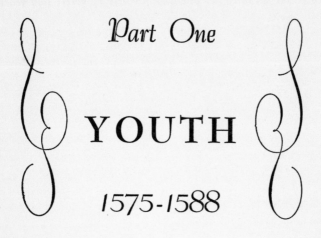

Part One

YOUTH

1575-1588

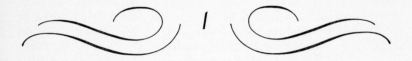

The Green Minnow

The pony stumbled and the boy rider started, tightening his hands on the reins. He had been thinking of something else or he would have seen the deep rut in the road.

"Robin! Watch the hazard." The Earl of Essex reproved his son.

Robin Devereux felt his face grow hot. How beastly to have faulted before his father, who sat so firm on his great black stallion. He heard the snicker of the page Godfrey at his back and squirmed to think that Esteban, his father's squire, whose own seat was almost perfect, must have seen too. Sweating and miserable, he glued his eyes to the road ahead, grimly alert to stones and holes in the way.

He had started the ride up to London full of the joy of being with his father, of love for Gaylight his pony, who threw up his brown head to the fair morning. The green fields were dotted with autumn flowers and on the farmlands the golden grain stood high. As he clattered down the avenue with the others, turning to wave at his mother and his sisters at the casements, he thought it the prettiest day he had ever seen. Now, as he looked to the position of his hands on the reins and pulled himself straight in the saddle, the beauty about him palled, and the gloom with which he had first awakened settled back upon him. He gave himself up to the worry of his errand.

To begin with, they had dressed him up like a popinjay, dainty as a girl, warning him to be careful of his clothes. Already he saw his light green hose of thin silk wrinkling with the friction of his pony's sides. Well, God's blood, he thought, let it, he didn't care. At sight of the gay rosettes on his tight suède shoes, he sniffed. Why couldn't they have given him a pair of boots, like his father's? He stole a look at the Earl's high-arched foot, elegant in soft brown leather reaching halfway up his shapely leg, and he blinked as the sun flashed on the glorious sword hilt. Robin felt of his own little dagger. At least that was a respectable weapon, new, and well chased with Italian filagree.

He did not quite understand why they were taking him to Somerset House, to the Queen, but he knew well what he was expected to do when he got there.

"Smile, Robin, bow, Robin, stand straight, Robin, do us proud . . ." He was to please the Queen's grace, to beguile her, to charm the gold right out of the royal pocket. It all had something to do with his father, who was Lord Lieutenant of Ireland, whose money boxes were empty. A huge sigh welled inside his chest. For his father, of course, he would give his heart's blood.

The part he hated was the dressing up and most of all, the leaving home. Back there in the country was everything he held most dear; his dogs, Penelope and Dorothy his sisters, Walter his little brother—and his mother. He wondered why his mother, so beautiful, with her gay laugh and her clever ways, could not go to London and do this thing for his father—until they told him why. His mother, the famed Lettice Knollys, was so hated by Elizabeth Tudor for her gold hair and white skin that she dared not show her face at Court.

So instead they took him. They tore him from his books and games, threw away his shabby beloved jerkins, dressed him from head to foot in light green, and now he was on his way to Court. They smothered his protests, and his mother, looking deeply into his eyes, green like her own, told him this was man's work. Well then, he would do it, for he felt himself almost a man, coming nine in November. Secretly he had made up his mind that when he was fully grown and his own master, he would go off to sea, away from all this dressing and bowing.

The wind off the river bobbed the feather on his tam into his eyes and he twitched the hat impatiently around. His father wore his peach-colored beaver carelessly, as became a gentleman, set sideways on his auburn head. Suddenly Robin's cape billowed out and he grabbed at it, crushing it beneath his thigh. He squared his shoulders and pressed his knees firmly against Gaylight's sides. Managing Court clothes a-horse-back was truly a full job.

"Winded, lad?" The Earl tipped his hat over his eyes and threw his son a side glance.

"No, sir, I thank you," he gasped. He would show that grinning God-frey, who was thirteen and who could jump the three-barred gate at the foot of the orchard, that he could ride as well as he. Godfrey, who dared to look at Penelope, forever running after her, the two of them stealing into the stillroom after the cordials and preserved fruits. Ah, home! A new thought pierced him. They had said nothing as to where he would lodge this night, and as for the subject of his return, on that they had been strangely silent.

"Sir," he addressed his father, "think you we shall lie at Somerset House tonight?"

"I doubt there'll be room, lad. The Queen's grace keeps a large Court."

Aye, he had heard talk last night of the great swell of ladies and gentlemen who would be stuffed into every available corner of Somerset, right to the steep-pitched roof. Then, if he was not to sleep at the Queen's palace, where was he to go?

At his father's nod, he touched Gaylight into a trot. They had left the meadows, and now that they were approaching the heart of Southwark, the houses were getting closer together. They overtook a crawling pair of carts laden with slimily dripping fish, and a whiff of the wind made Robin long to hold his nose. They slowed down.

"God's mercy!" A beggar pushed his revolting sore arm right under Robin's very eyes, but Esteban slashed him away, and he reeled cursing into the dusty bushes on the roadside. Robin shuddered. But the way past the fish carts was narrow and he gave it his attention, managing with a nice skill that won a smile from his father. Round the last bend they swept.

Royal London lay stewing and steaming in the sun while the glitter-ing Thames wound about its middle like a silver ribband, all bejeweled with myriad boats and sails. At any other time Robin would have thought it a stirring wonder. But now he was feeling sick. They were drawing nearer to the Queen.

"A fair prospect, eh?" His father's eye flashed toward him, and the boy nodded, turning away to hide his trembling lip.

 5

Again they slowed to a walk amongst the steadily growing throng of wagons and men a-horseback. Robin pressed his aching back against his cantle. All those gliding boats—he wondered where they were bound on this fine September morning. Oh, to be aboard and away for far places, to be a sunburned sailor, gold rings in his ears and a head full of tales from the lands of Marco Polo and the Indies! Hopelessly he gazed down the long vista of years that lay ahead, and for the hundredth time he wished he were grown.

He prayed God to save him from the Queen's fancy. Or—let God perform some miracle so that she take kindly enough to him to bestow her grace on his father, but not so kindly that she would keep the son beside her. Court was prison. It was good-by to long twilights in the meadow, to romps with Gaylight, perhaps farewell forever to dreams of the sea.

The Queen! She was an old woman of over forty, who, they said, swallowed young men like—like minnows. Green minnows! That was what his mother teasingly called him this very morning when she and the nurse were fussing over his clothes. "A little green minnow to be fed to the great royal carp." His mother's barb stuck in his flesh. Hardly aware of what he did, he guided Gaylight after the great black Saladin as they swept down the high road and onto the Bridge. The tall houses on either side shut off the sun, so that now they were in cold shadow, chill with river air and close-smelling of long-stored dampness.

He felt himself a small island in a sea of noise; he saw nothing, isolated as he was, within his own misery. On, on they went, past the shops that once had charmed him, past the chapel, midway across the Bridge. On they went, while all about them rose the cries, mingled with shrill screams, as the river traffic snarled together in the tidal swirl.

Home seemed very far away now. This was the great city, in which a man might get lost. Home! He wondered what the others were doing. Penelope would be hiding in the big tree behind the orchard wall, while Dorothy did the lessons for both of them; and Walter would be squirming in *his* place at Tom Gray's schoolroom table, while the patient tutor crammed the Greek and Latin into the baby brain. Happy, happy ones at home.

A rank, greasy odor swept down on the overhead wind and pulled him back to the immediate. He looked up, stiffened. He knew what the black shrivels hanging in the chains had been, and at sight of the long spikes on the gate tower, his eyes swam. Those spikes were crowned with brownish balls that grinned whitely at all comers, and from its perch on one of them, a large bird winged heavily away. Robin gagged and his mouth filled with sour saliva.

He coughed into his hand. At a smothered sound from behind, he went hot with anger. So Godfrey expected him to puke on his new velvet, did he? He tightened sweating fingers on his reins and narrowly avoided the edge of the last house on the Bridge as they clattered off onto the street. His sickness passed. The hazard of the turn and the small spasm of temper had saved him, and his stubborn chin went up. He swallowed a great gulp of fresher air and felt better.

But his dread returned. Lost now in the bedlam of the Strand, they forged ever and inexorably onward to Somerset House. His empty belly rumbled, but the smell of mutton pies and apple tarts on the peddlers' trays did not tempt him. He swerved Gaylight from the path of a black fellow, whose long birch brushes dripped soot perilously near the new green finery.

"Swepe, chimney swepe, with hey derry swepe from the bottom to the top!"

The cry thinned out behind them as they kept on, past the darting schoolboy, satchel in hand, past the tanner's knave with his dripping skins, past Cold Harbor where Tom Gray had been stabbed and his purse cut. No shuddery goose pimples for that now; his shuddering was for himself and for what lay ahead of him.

Suddenly Robin saw his father bow stiffly as a small glittering cavalcade, led by a rose-colored figure, magnificently astride a white charger, issued from the stable yards of Leicester House. A muscle in the Earl's cheek twitched and he made no attempt to overtake the splendid man whose irritable face, cruel and thin-lipped, was turned full toward them. Lord Dudley cut sharply off in the direction of Somerset House, where as if by magic, his way was cleared.

Why did the gentleman not stop and ride with them? He had seen the great Lord Dudley at their dinner table, where his mother laughed with him a good deal, and afterward they walked for a long time in the gallery. He stole another look at his father, whose face was fixed in stern lines.

Clop-clop! They clattered past Arundel House, but there was no sign of the Norfolk children today. Only a slender young priest turning out of the gateway and a stable knave or two.

"We arrive, Robin." His father's voice broke in. "It has been a long ride for you."

Feeling spent, Robin managed a wan smile and then they were swept, with a great press of people, into Somerset entrance. He pulled himself once more erect on Gaylight's brown back to make an entrance befitting his father's son. He need not have bothered; only a few horseboys noticed him.

A flash of brightness took his breath. Out of the drab street they had ridden into a fairyland of brilliance, picked out by the crimson velvet of the Queen's guard. How the gold Tudor rose glittered on their backs! God's body! Here was richness.

Young men in dark liveries, their shoulders bright with gold lace, teased the pretty blonde girl who hung from her low balcony to feed the pigeons. Robin thought her not so handsome as his mother. The tall young gentlemen must be the Queen's pensioners, as Tom Gray had described them, for they leaned on long golden halberds, which they poked at the birds fluttering about the girl's shoulders.

"My lord, and how goes it?" The call came from a young man, who flashed his white teeth for the benefit of the girl on the balcony. An elderly gentleman in a long cape, who looked tired and ill, raised his hat to the Earl, then moved off. Robin's head swam as he sought a place to alight.

"Essex!" A hearty voice rang out over the heads as a middle-aged man in black quickened his descent of the shallow entrance steps, calling as he brisked through the throng. "Essex! What good morning breeze brings you to us?"

"Ah! Howard!" Robin saw his father's face lighted by true pleasure as promptly now he swung down, dragging off his gauntlet to grasp the short muscular hand held out to him. The Earl jerked a thumb in Robin's direction, and the stocky man raised his brows, then, putting a familiar arm through his father's, passed with him across the yard and up the steps.

Robin made haste to alight, turning his backside to the crowd, while he felt with his toe for the ground. He staggered and all but fell into the outstretched arms of Godfrey, whose eyes were still merry.

"Curse you, let me be," muttered Robin. The green tam flew off onto the wet flags, and as the page stooped to recover it, he smothered a grin. Robin grabbed it from him and, swaying slightly, made desperately off after his father and the man in black velvet.

But where was his father? Ah, there, just within the shadow of the arched doorway, talking to the other man. Lucky they were so near, else he must surely have lost them in this wilderness of grandeur. They were now in the great hall, its high-ceilinged walls echoing to the chatter of the crowd.

So many people! Pushed and shoved about on the polished floor, he kept his father's side only by an effort. The high paneled walls stretched up and up, and his eye went up with them, past the rich portraits that glowed, soft squares of color against the dark shining wood, up past the curved and beaded border, to the fretted plaster, where against the whiteness was the brilliant blot of flamboyant scarlet and gilding of the Queen's arms: lion and unicorn and the royal cipher.

A tittering pair of pages pushed him aside and swished their rainbow satins like the gaudy flies of presumption that they were; the sword hilts clicked, and the silk-clad legs whispered. Through it all was the smell that Robin drew in through his nostrils, the smell of musk and heavy allspice, of dust and grease, and the fat warmth of gravies, succulently soaking in hot kitchens below stairs.

"Aye, bad enough it was in Ireland." His father's voice broke through, and he looked up, drawn back into his own private world. He saw his father's quick glance flick about, saw him lean to the other's ear, heard him whisper, "I'm here for further grants. How sits the wind?"

"As ever," shrugged the black velvet gentleman. He threw his grizzled head to one side, then put a kind hand on Robin, who looked up into the flat face with the shrewd level brows and the steady eyes. The man's beard and mustache were well trimmed and smelled pleasantly of pomade. His pale yellow ruff was immaculately crisp and it curved up to his ears in a strange new fashion.

He smiled down, showing teeth that were little square tags with spaces between, his lips stretched into a wide smile in which there was no mirth. He gave Robin's shoulder a tiny appraising push. "So you've brought the sprig to Court, Walter. Marry, now that I see him, I think that's good business." Over Robin's russet head they smiled.

A heavy velvet skirt whipped against his leg as a girl led a tiny Italian dog past on a blue ribband. The delicate little creature cowered and curled its thin whiplike tail under its shivering hindquarters. The girl jerked at the string and spoke sharply to the dog in a foreign tongue.

". . . doubtless you'll get in before supper." The black velvet man's low-pitched remark reached him. Supper! Robin's belly, now recovered of its swoony sickness, pained him with its emptiness. Where, in all this busy place, was there food?

"My lord Effingham, the Queen's grace desires your attendance." A

⸎ 0 ⸎

young man in cut scarlet sleeves had joined them. Despite his hunger Robin jumped. "Effingham." So the black velvet gentleman was Tom Gray's "fairest soldier in all England." He breathed short and stared at his father's friend. Lord Howard of Effingham, this quiet man then, was the Queen's fire-eating steel soldier.

But the soldier had become for the moment the courtier. "Ah, then, I must leave you, Essex. Greville," to the young man in scarlet, "Greville, the lad here looks starved. Take them aloft to my cabinet like a good man." A flick of the hand and he was gone. Robin's chest heaved.

"My lord Essex," the scarlet youth inclined his head as the Earl presented Robin.

"Fulke, this is my heir." The young man's white teeth flashed in his swarthy face. He turned to Robin, who hastily bowed, his thin legs knocking together, as someone bumped him from behind. If Greville saw the *gaucherie,* he took no notice, returning the salute as to an equal.

"You do me honor, Sir Robert."

Sir Robert! Robin was speechless. Memory caught at this name too, Fulke Greville, whom Philip Sidney loved so well. Sidney was their own friend, who visited them last summer. Together, he and Robin raced in the meadow, and Sidney, treating him with true courtesy, had *not* let him win. Ah, to be sure, there were splendid men in the world.

Pushing their way through the scented throng, grown even thicker, they followed Greville. All made way for the scarlet sleeves, but still, it was fancy work for Robin to keep after the two men up and up the broad staircase. Up the four flights, broken by great landings he toiled, panting, hurrying, till his thighs burned. God's wounds, they must be near the roof.

At last they were at the top and in a corridor, dim and musty, when a door flew open. A girl, wide-eyed, her gown half torn from her shoulders, thrust him aside and raced past. Beyond the open door, Robin caught a glimpse of a heavy man in rose-colored satin, who stood grinning before a fireplace, arms akimbo. Lord Dudley.

But Greville and his father disappeared through another door in the wall farther down, and Robin hastened after them. Just within the doorway he stopped for breath. He leaned on a table and panted; his belly rumbled and he felt entirely done for, but he dared not sit in his father's presence till given leave. He ran his fingers along the fretwork on the table edge, and looked hopefully about the room for signs of food.

There were none. The room, a small cabinet, lined in oak, was nearly empty of furniture, save for a court cupboard with a wine flask that looked to contain only dregs, a joint stool or two, and a long bench let into the wall beneath the leaded casement. The room smelled of snuff, stale Rhenish, and the soot from the smoky fire in the grate opposite. Robin sniffed. If this were the sort of room they kept at Court, he didn't think much of it.

Leaning against the plaster mantel, the Earl and Greville seemed deep in talk. Robin sighed with pain and boredom. He was sick to death of the whole business, and for one wild minute . . .

Greville rang a small brass bell. A door in the paneling beside Robin opened so quickly that he jumped. A servant's greasy head appeared. Greville gave a quick order and it popped back, the door closing on a sharp click. Longing to open it, Robin stood watchfully still. But the servant was swift and almost at once reappeared carrying a tray with a cold roasted bird and some curling oatcake. This he set on the table and went to fetch ale, which he put by the hearth to warm, and a browned tansy pudding in a little pewter dish. He had an odd swinging gait, which, in spite of his hunger, Robin noted, for he had never seen any man on land walk like it. Tom Gray had told him of Lord Howard's seamen, some of whom loved him so that they came ashore to serve his table and wait on his person. This must be one of those.

"Hast a knife, young master?"

"I have a knife, I thank you," Robin replied, his mouth watering.

His father looked up. "Sit, lad; I doubt you're famishing."

Robin bobbed his head and dragged a stool to the table. He loosed his dagger, then shot a quick look to see if he were observed. His father's back being turned, he skipped grace, and fell to.

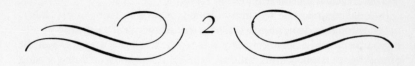

The Royal Carp

The bell of old St. Paul's was chiming the hour of four when Robin, heart in mouth, walked carefully down the slippery oak stairway behind his father. Fed and washed, brushed up, his hose tightened and his falling linen collar pulled out of his neckhole, he looked spruce and delicate. But his thin hands were cold and panic sat in the pit of his stomach. He suddenly felt the full weight of the family heavy on his shoulders. He had long since said good-by to home. The fear now was lest he fail in this thing he was to do for his father.

Truly, life was a problem. If only its perplexities were no weightier than those that kept Tonio his riding master and Tom Gray hanging over the chessboard of an evening! Why should he, Robin Devereux, be set to seek the family fortune at the ticklish feet of a Queen?

The Queen—ah, what would she do? He did not fear a woman; he could brave those at home, for there was only his nurse, whose great billow of a bosom had been familiar to him from birth, and there were his sisters, girls at best, and his willing slaves. And even his mother's beautiful mask melted at his smile.

But this was something new—different—and he did not feel like smiling now. This was no mere woman he was about to face. This was

Elizabeth Tudor, Queen of England, Ireland, Scotland, and France, Empress most mighty, by God's good grace. This was Elizabeth the Terrible, who hung men up in black shreds when they displeased her. This was Elizabeth the Tyrant, with long witch hands and white witch face, who glowered so that even the great Lord Burghley shook before her. She was the red royal carp that ate small minnows. His mother's jest had reached its full frightening force.

In a dazed dream he felt himself being pushed in front of his father, urged through a door, past two alertly still statues in steel, whose gleaming halberds sent a shrinking down his spine. Now he was in the midst of another perfumed hum, quieter, but still the same world of giggling velvet girls and silken men. His father's firm hand thrust him on.

"Oh, the poppet!" A laughing maid in light blue caught him by the shoulder and tried to kiss him.

"Your pardon, my lady," murmured the Earl, guiding his son past the pretty clutching hands, pushing him ever onward to the fatal door.

For the space of a breath Robin had that wild impulse again. He thought of begging his father to let him turn back, to run away from this devil's place with its Queens and its fortunes. For no reason that he could now name, he felt a deadly fear. But someone held open the door, beckoning them. It closed behind them, and Robin heard the arras swish richly into place. There was a buzzing in his ears, and suddenly he was fighting a thin mist through which it was hard to see.

"Step up, Robin," whispered his father.

He shook his head slightly and the mist cleared. They were in a fair-sized room with a pretty traceried window that overlooked the river. With her back to it, in a velvet X-chair, sat Elizabeth Tudor.

It was clear that something had put her out, for a sour peevishness sat on her high, pale face. Robin had a lightning impression of this, before he lost himself in a confusion of pointed chin and gauze collar, a great jewel swinging on a white forehead, and a sharp pair of black eyes that regarded him with distaste. His eye mounted to her hair and he was pinned to the spot. Brilliant, flaming, falsely red, it clustered in tiny silken cocoons to frame that white forehead. He was astounded.

With acute dislike Elizabeth stared back.

"What is this you bring me, Lord Essex?" Her harsh voice shattered the respectful silence.

"My heir, your Grace." The Earl gently urged his son forward till he stood with his shoes at the edge of the tawny velvet skirt. But he continued to stare as if bewitched. That incredible, glittering hair!

"God's body!" The oath rapped out like a bullet. "What do ye stare so for? Perhaps I have two heads?" She leaned forward so that her busk creaked. "Come, speak up. Hast a tongue in that staring face?" With the stick of her perfumed fan she struck him sharply on one shoulder.

Now he was aware that Lord Dudley, he of the rose-colored satin, was standing with one hand on her chair back, smiling, while with the other hand, he caressed the tiny curling edge of his beard. His eyes twinkled at Robin's confusion, and leaning against his shoulder was a black-haired girl, red lips parted over her teeth. They were laughing at him.

The quick blood flamed in his fair cheeks and his eyes flashed green fire. To be struck with a fan! His cleft chin went up as if she had caught him there with her jeweled knuckles. All the offended pride of the Devereux and the Knollys gathered in his slender figure, and for an instant, his Plantagenet and Bohun blood boiled. To hell with the Queen's Majesty! She was, after all, only a woman, and had he not heard her stays creak? Her breath was none too sweet, her painted face was less fair than his mother's, and under those piercing eyes the skin was finely wrinkled, like his turtle's neck.

Robin Devereux drew himself up and glared at the Queen of England.

There was a tight silence in the room. The snigger left Lord Dudley's face and the girl looked frightened. Breaths hung suspended.

A sudden cackle from Elizabeth snapped the tension. "Ah! 'Tis a lad of spirit we have here. None of your scraping nidgets, and, by my faith, I like him for it. Come here, child."

Under his very nose a hand, white, slender, sparkling with gems, was extended. Ah, this hand, at least, was as fair as his mother's. Grudgingly, he allowed her to draw him to her side. She fanned the hair gently back from his flushed face.

"Say, wilt serve me, lad? A few years, and you'll be a man; aye, if I mistake not, a real man." She smiled at him, but there was no friendliness, only condescension. She looked across him. "There is pretty promise in these shoulders, my lord."

Was her sharp Tudor temper, of which he had heard so much, dulled, and was that relief in his father's dutiful smile? She stroked his smooth boyish cheeks. He leaned stiffly away from her, an agony of embarrassment rising to engulf him. She drew him nearer, so that their two faces were almost touching. Black eyes stared into green ones, flecked with hazel. The white hand tightened on his shoulder. She was going to kiss him!

Instinctively he attempted to draw back. But now his anger was gone, consumed in the ruddy magnetism of her nearness. She was only a strange woman, trying to kiss him, and in public, too. The color mounted to his face and he grinned helplessly.

"Why, milord, he has the Devereux smile!" Elizabeth chortled. "He's touched with the fatal charm, I vow. Pretty lad! When you are a man, my kisses will enchant you. Not then will you draw back from me." She slipped one hand inside his collar and secretly tickled the warm hollow of his throat. He twitched and drew up one shoulder, laughing now.

"There!" She withdrew her fingers. "Take him, my lord, and when he is a man, bring him to me." Highly pleased, she leaned against her chair's low back and flapped her feather fan in a cloud of perfume.

His father's hand was iron on his shoulder and Robin pulled himself together. Somewhat tardily, he backed and fell to his knee. There, genius prompted him. He lifted the tawny velvet of the royal robe to his lips, then smiled again, this time straight into her eyes. He heard her draw in her breath sharply, so that her high bosom rose still higher. The great pearls rattled softly and the snakes embroidered on her bodice seemed to wink their sequin eyes. Reluctantly Elizabeth raised her eyes above the boy's head to the father, standing gracefully behind the son. She nodded.

"We will speak of Ireland after supper, Lord Essex. Bid Burghley bring you to me then."

She held out her hand for his kiss, then waved her fan again. They were dismissed. Outside the door, Robin stared at his father. The Queen had appeared content, but. . . . Lord Essex returned the stare. Then he swore.

"By the red whiskers of King Harry, Robin, lad, you've done it. You've pulled it off." He shook his head. "Lad, lad, is this how it will be? Always touch and go, always just on the fringe of disaster, scrambling out, defeat clutching thy very heels?"

For answer, Robin caught hold of his father's hand and held it tight against his chest. Then—he had not failed them.

"Keep your head, Robin, and luck's own largess will come to you."

Keep his head—and why not? Heads did fall, it was true, but what of that? Death on Tower Hill was for the great, the stay-at-homes, who dabbled their fingers in dangerous designs. When he was a man grown, he would seek his fortune in far places where there were no women, only men, and the dangers were the perils of war and high adventure.

"Your mother will be pleased."

The words brought him back to the present and the old nagging fear. Now he had contented the Queen and he would have to stay. He turned anxious eyes on his father.

"Shall I bide here, sir?"

Essex laughed. "No, Robin, no. Esteban and Godfrey will take you home. Your work is done and well done, lad. Get you started now. I doubt it will be dark before you reach home."

He drew a long breath. He had done it. He felt suddenly light and easy. He had pleased her and she had let him go. He was not to languish in finery at her heels but to go and to come again when he was a man. Ah, but then, he would be far away.

They walked the length of the hall, past the silver halberdiers, and Lord Essex stopped in the bay of a great window. The late-afternoon light filtered through the bright colors of the Tudor arms painted on the glass, and threw little spots of red, blue, and green onto the white of the plaster wall. He put both hands on his boy's shoulders.

"Robin, you have done me proud. This will mean much to me—to us all. When you reach home, go to your mother and give her—this." He stooped, tall and thin, above his son, put one hand on his head, and gently kissed him.

And this time the boy did not flush.

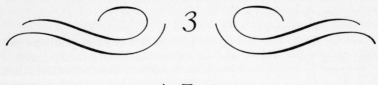

A Loss

Since seven of the late summer morning he had been up, galloping on Gaylight through the meadow with the forbidden water jump. How they had taken it, the two of them, Gaylight soaring up, up, into the clear blue, then over and down to the jolt and the long, fleet run on the surface. It was sheer ecstasy out in the fresh country air. Robin drew a long breath of pure contentment. Life was lovely and his father was due home from Ireland in three weeks.

After the Earl's departure, following the Twelfth Night celebrations, Robin set himself to work hard. He made progress with his books, the Latin and Greek coming easily now, and he had even written a little Latin poem especially for his father. Philip Sidney's sister Mary spent a few weeks with them in August, and her clever hands helped him to make a fair copy on parchment, with little flowers and birds twined about the lines.

Best of all, his riding and his archery had improved and he had saved the last target with the tattered bull's-eye as proof of his skill. He was actually beginning with the foils, and Tonio had promised to show him the new French trick as soon as he could handle himself in the first strokes. He leaned over to hug Gaylight round his smooth neck, then recollected himself and the problem that lay before him.

He now had to sneak in without being seen, either by his mother's grooms or by Tonio. He had left his riding master sleeping off a night's heavy drinking, so he was fairly sure of him. But the grooms were a different matter. They worshiped his mother and her orders about the water jump had been strict. He turned Gaylight into the long avenue, all dappled with the morning sun sifting through red-brown leaves. He would try to slip in by the back way, and Rufus, the new page, would rub Gaylight and ask no tiresome questions.

But now he heard hoofs in a sudden flurry. Someone was coming his way. Round the bend came the riding master himself, and at sight of Robin, he waved, then drew to a clattering stop. For a moment he stared at the boy, then jerked his head in the direction of the house and wheeled back. Biting his lip, Robin followed.

Something was up. He made after Tonio as fast as he could and, at the straight approach to the house, caught up with him. Ahead of them was the rosy stone front and the sparkling casements, touched up with morning sun. And there, gathered about their standing horses, stood the men, a little knot of them, in the livery of Lord Burghley.

"Tonio?" But the Italian kept his uneasy eye turned away.

"Tonio, what's the matter?"

Tonio doubled low to avoid an overhanging branch. From him came mumbled words. ". . . *la voluntia di dio!*"

The will of God. A cold fear clutched Robin's heart, and he knew without telling that whatever dread thing awaited him up at the house was already written on the tablets of time. It was something concerning his father.

Under the curious gaze of the men they alighted, and he dogged Tonio across the terrace. Burghley's men stood in a gossipy bunch among their horses, and as Robin passed the man at the end, he felt his arm caught. He stopped and the two of them stood a little apart from the others, screened by the height of the horse. Robin did not know him, but the man, with a lightning gesture, crammed a tiny object into his hand. His lips were still, but his eyes signaled caution.

"Robin!" Tonio's sharp voice rang from the doorway.

He went inside. The hall was empty, but a door stood slightly ajar, and there was the sound of voices. Without looking at it, he slipped the little object inside his doublet and tiptoed across the bare floor, as if afraid his loud heels might wake the echoes. Tonio closed the door behind him and he was alone with his mother and Lord Burghley.

The great Lord Treasurer, tired and elderly, stood before the cold fireplace, his hands clasped behind him. He faced a high-backed chair that hid all the sitter except a bright crown of hair.

"Come to me, Robin." His mother's voice was strained and low. Now he rounded the chair and saw that she, too, looked deathly ill. All the bright glitter was gone from her long eyes and her delicate color was faded to a drab whiteness.

"Robin, I wanted you first, before Penelope and the others." Her blind hand reached for him, and at the touch, like ice, he started. His mother's eyelids dropped. "Tell him, my lord."

Lord Burghley cleared his throat. "Your father," he began in a husky voice, "your father . . ." here he stopped and coughed, then went on, a little clearer, "is dead."

Dead! His head swam. He felt his mother's cold hand tremble, and the tremor thrilled up his arm. Dead! The dry voice rattled on.

"His lordship fell ill and died." Burghley placed the merest weight of emphasis on the terrible word. "He died in Dublin on the twenty-second, about noon."

The precision of those last words only added to their horror. A cold prickling ran down the back of his neck. Like a sharp blow, the word "dead" rang in his ears. He heard a long sigh from his mother.

"But—but he was coming home," he said, and his lips felt numb. The prickling ran down the back of his neck, through his chest, to flutter breathlessly in his stomach. "He wrote that he was c-coming home." He stared anxiously at Lord Burghley, who, along with his news, seemed somehow to possess the power to alter facts.

Burghley's throat appeared to be giving him trouble. He cleared it again. "His lordship was taken ill—a gastric disturbance." He turned to Lady Essex. "I have the letters here, Madam."

Fumbling in his long velvet coat, he brought out two letters, both sealed. One fell to the floor, and as he stooped to retrieve it, Robin saw the blue wax pressed with his father's cipher. He gave it to his mother, who held it loosely in her lap. The other was still in Lord Burghley's long fingers.

"This also is addressed to your ladyship. It will doubtless be from his lordship's physician, for I had one under the same seal." He lifted it close to his eyes. "Ah, yes, the same, two wings and a staff." He gestured.

"That one you have there, Madam, will be from the secretary." Lady Essex did not hold out her hand for the second letter.

Now she sat upright. "You say you had one of these letters, too? I do not understand." Tiny spots of color stained her cheekbones. "Why should Dr. Bellop write to you, my lord?"

Burghley shrugged slightly. But Robin knew. His father was public property, a servant of the state, forbidden even to—to die in privacy. The Lord Treasurer held the letter to his mother, but she took no notice. Instead she kept her head down, staring at the letter that already lay in her lap, the one from his father's secretary. What was in that other, the one from the doctor, and why didn't his mother take it?

As if in answer to his thought, she spoke. "I-I think I cannot read it now. Tell me . . ." she motioned to a chair. "Please."

Lord Burghley sat painfully down. He put his precise hands on the carved arms of the chair and chose his careful words, his head bent toward the floor. "It appears that my lord complained of pains in his head. That was on the evening of the twenty-first, as he was retiring. Yes, pains in his head, and," here Lord Burghley paused delicately, "and in his bowels. A cramp so acute that by dawn he was past all help. He expired at noon."

Cramp! To keep from crying aloud, Robin bit his lip. Almost he felt his father's writhing agony. Cramp! What had he eaten, and who had prepared his father's food? Before he was aware, he had spoken.

"What killed my father?"

The elderly statesman turned, his politeness studied. "My boy, who knows? The flux—even an onslaught of plague."

"Then there were others who had this thing?" He felt old, harsh, not a boy of ten, but a son, bitterly bereft of one he loved. Here was a stiff old man, calm and unmoved. Had he ever felt what it was to have the heart slowly torn from the breast? "There were others?" he insisted.

"Certainly there was sickness in his lordship's train," Burghley evaded.

With a silken swish Lady Essex rose and steadied herself against the chair. "Others were ill, you say? Then there is no suspicion of . . . ?" The word 'murder' hung suspended between them. Robin looked up amazed. He saw his mother's hand clenched whitely on her chair, the unopened letter crushed to a wisp. The spots were now feverish flame in her pale cheeks.

Lord Burghley rose to his own feet. "It is my firm belief, Madam, that Lord Essex died of an attack of stomach gout." The quiet finality of the words could have made truth out of the devil's greatest lie. Was it fancy, or was that a faintly relieved sound from his mother?

"It is the will of God," finished Burghley piously.

The will of God. That was what Tonio had said. So God had willed that Robin Devereux should never again be glad, should never again ride with his father, the two of them in the sweet meadow grass, while the Earl put out a gentle, restraining hand that they might hearken to the early song of a lark. He felt his mother's eye on him.

"Lord Burghley will be your guardian, Robin. We must look to him for help now that—that . . ."

With fierce dislike Robin glared at the old man. Was it for this he had been practicing early and late at his riding and fencing, to surprise his father? For this man he must now learn and perform, leaping and galloping for a man nearly crippled with gout, who sat a horse in agony. What did he know of tilting, of an arrow straightly sped? He thought of the target rolled carefully in the corner of his room, and his grief and disappointment rose wildly in him. He gulped them back. Never, never must this crippled old man guess his torment.

"We are grateful," went on Lady Essex, her hand resting on Robin's shoulder.

The old man bowed. "Lord Essex left papers with me before he departed into the west. There is a beautiful letter that perhaps later . . ."

"You mean that perhaps he guessed . . . ?" Lady Essex did not seem able to finish a sentence. Robin felt her tense.

"No, no, Madam," soothed Burghley. "I do not go so far as to suggest that the Earl had anything approaching a-a premonition. But he long intended, should anything untoward befall, that I should stand in *loco parentis,* to . . ." he gestured lamely in Robin's direction.

That man, his guardian. The lump in his throat rose higher.

"I have papers touching his lordship's education at Cambridge, and the moneys to be expended." Now on familiar ground, Burghley's voice became official.

Robin quivered. "His lordship." Why, that was himself. He was not Robin Devereux any more, he was the Earl of Essex, and only an hour ago he had been his father's son. He looked piteously at his mother, and at the unspoken pleading in his eyes, she relented.

"Well, go fetch Penelope and the others."

The briefest of bows, and he walked stiffly from the room. Carefully he closed the door, standing quite still, his hand on the knob. He felt cold and sick. He hated the sunny morning that lay in warm squares on the tiled floor. It ought to be raining heavens high.

He dragged his leaden feet up the stairs. At every step the dreadful word pounded in his ears. Dead-dead-dead. Surely the sound was outside his own body. On the landing he paused, seeing nothing, conscious only of a numbness and a light before his eyes as if he had looked directly at the sun.

Something brushed his leg and he looked down. It was the three of them, sitting huddled on the top step. He had barely avoided treading on them. Even Penelope was pale and her eyes were somber. Wordlessly he gestured them to go down, while he kept on his way upstairs. Pushing open his chamber door, he crossed the room to his bed and sank down on the counterpane, twining his arm about the bedpost. Leaning his pounding head against it, he closed his eyes.

The clock in the yard struck nine. How long the morning had been, and yet, with its burden of sorrow to unload, how short. A brief hour or so to ride, and then—this. Gaylight—he hoped someone had taken him to the stables. He thought of those men on the terrace, and then he remembered that one of them had put something into his hand.

Idly he poked his fingers into his doublet and drew out the tiny object. It was a little roll of vellum. He opened it and there, precisely drawn with a pen, was a skull and crossbones. Nothing more. He turned it over. Nothing, and yet there was something strangely familiar about the drawing. He stared at it, frowning to remember.

Esteban! On the last night before—before he left with the Earl for Ireland, the squire had been drawing for them. Grumpish as he was, Esteban could draw marvelously well, and the children clustered about the schoolroom table, watching his skillful pen. He had drawn this same design, which they had all admired. Now Robin looked at it with something like horror. This was the symbol of death—Esteban was trying to tell him something—but what?

He was too tired to think. His sick eyes rounded the room. There, propped against the wall, with his arrows and the long bow, was the target he had saved for his father to see.

At sight of it his grief gushed up and overwhelmed him.

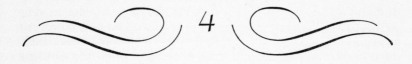

The Seasons

*H*e was seventeen. Exhausted by the head congestion that plagued him more and more, he lay on his languid pillow. One day he would be all exhilaration, then, unaccountably, be laid low. A vapory feeling as if he had seen the sun would bring flashes of light before his eyes, followed by a blinding headache.

Free of pain now, slowly recovering, he mused, while the copy of Virgil drooped in his indifferent hand. He rolled his head on the pillow and considered the few short years of his life. The English seasons came and went, and with them the delights and the sorrows. He drifted back . . .

It was spring. In a little paneled room at Cambridge, he sat with Thomas Gray. Their triform window overlooked the avenue of Trinity, where moist green turf stretched like level velvet dotted with blue and yellow crocus heads.

"Nay, Robin, construe me that once more. *'Adeo in teneris consuescere multum est.'*" Tom's good, quiet voice broke the sunny silence of the room.

"'*Adeo*'—thus training; '*in teneris*'—in early years; '*consuescere mul-tum est*'—is of great importance."

"'Greatest importance,' Robin."

Ah yes. Greatest importance. Already there were times now when he believed the only true learning to be contained in those early years with the books. How could there be anything else, when a man was grown, save to live, and use his learning for that end? Tom's good, quiet voice. *That* was another tongue forever stilled. Surely one learned early of sorrow. He turned on the pillow and sighed. The loss of Tom was still sore in him.

But while Tom was alive and at his side, how congenial was the aus-terity of college life, with the precious books, the subtle delights of Tacitus and Homer. Well-loved Trinity, and that last brief spring of his fourteenth year, dearest because he was leaving for good. He saw himself, a thin-legged Master of Arts, awkward in the billowing gown —the last lingering through the cloisters, the last mellow call to chapel. Spring, and the soft breeze in the elms, ah, would days of the future ever be so piercing sweet?

Summers had come and gone. Summer—he moved restlessly on the bed now, the pillow suddenly hot beneath his head. Once more he felt the sultry Augusts of Lord Burghley's garden at Theobalds, where he took interminable walks among flower beds, stepping over box hedges, clipped and precise as Burghley's corrective conversations. A white cabbage moth floats over the brick wall to the freedom of the kitchen garden—free, free, while he is chained forever to the fixed nature of his destiny.

"Put away thoughts of the sea, Robert, or of foreign conquest; with-draw your head from your books. You will assume your position in this world, and it is my duty to see you learned in the arts and graces of the courtier, for which you have quite enough Latin and Greek. This was your father's plan."

His father's plan. The long sigh stopped short. For his father's sake, then, he tried to find the summers at Theobalds bearable. He sweated out the hateful tasks, while young Robert Cecil, Burghley's lame son, sat for hours in the sunshine, his white clever forehead bent over books forbidden to Robert Devereux. He watched the aloof cripple, earth-bound no longer, as he boarded those frigates of escape, to wing his way along the distant miles.

Oh, the weariness of his own lot! Practicing the dance with young Horatio Vere, companion to his misery; being groomed to graceful compliance on the lute; stepping the galliard; managing the fold and hang of a cape. Bow and turn, point the foot, follow the pitiless beat-beat of the French master's cane on the gleaming floor of Burghley's music room.

A brisk bout with the foils—that at least had been allowed—then out to the terrace where the vagrant afternoon breeze was soothing. And there was the cripple. He put a thin finger to keep the page in his Horace, and turned a supercilious face to the overheated lad.

"And what is it you learn today, Master Robert? The coranto—perchance?" The pause between the two words and the final lilt were irresistible to the two Bacon youths, Cecil's cousins, who smirked openly in the rear.

"I learned the *riposte* and new Italian trick. It's fencing today, Master Cecil, not dancing." Try as he would, he could not forbear to turn his eye on the crooked back of the scholar. The shaft fell short. Cecil shrugged an unconcerned shoulder and turned back to his reading; the Bacons went down the wide steps to meet their sister; and Robin was left with emptiness and the prickle of guilt that told him he had done an unworthy thing.

Restless again at the memory, he turned and reached for the cooling tisane at his bedside. Meditatively he sipped, then lay back.

Spring . . . summer . . . autumn . . . soon it would be autumn now, and with it would come his melancholy. Always in autumn, ever since that fatherless day seven years ago, he felt the pale golden sadness of the season. His final summer at Theobalds had lengthened into autumn, with no word from home. Longing forced him to break his resolve never to write for relief.

> Madam, my mother, for God's love, I
> pray you rescue me from this childish
> Vere and the dancing master. . . . my
> eyes weary for a sight of you all . . .

And back came an imperious letter to Lord Burghley, so that in no time at all, he and Tom Gray were up in Staffordshire, galloping under the green and yellow trees of beloved Chartley to where his mother waited on the shallow steps of the terrace. God! At her shoulder stood a tall, sardonic figure—the Earl of Leicester. How nervous his mother's hand felt on his shoulder and her high voice was higher still, not gay, but betraying her discomfiture.

"Robin, my love, this is my husband, your stepfather."

Leicester, his stepfather!

Robin backed down a step and threw up his head to the arrogant figure of condescension, and behind a great puffed satin sleeve he caught sight of the angry eyes of Penelope. Why had they not told him? Surely at fifteen he was old enough to know. He felt sick with anger and dismay. Gone in a flash were all the plans for hunting with his mother, for riding, fencing, reading with them all, and worst of all, the memory of his father here at their beautiful Chartley was smirched and sullied.

His mother's whisper: "He will soon be away for Court. Please him, Robin, for my sake."

It was no use; all was spoiled. The privacy was violated by a loud-voiced stranger, and the happiness was shattered. There was now only emptiness, waiting to be planted with a tiny grain of fear, fear born of a wordless message that was the picture of a skull and crossbones sketched on a scrap of vellum. Esteban had drawn the sketch, of that there was no doubt—and Esteban never came home at all.

His father's body had arrived cased in lead. The words "murder" and "poison" stuck in Robin's mind, and although they never were proved, his heart knew his father's death to be no chance fatality of illness. No one dared to say aloud that the Earl of Leicester had poisoned the Lord Lieutenant of Ireland, but there were too many signs—all pointing to one end—for the Earl to be innocent. This would not be the first time he had used poison to remove a figure of obstruction. It was even whispered that he had murdered his young wife Amy Robsart when he found her a tiresome drag on his progress. Had he not married Robin's mother, and was he not maneuvering now, even now, to take Robin to Court with him? The grain of fear planted seven years ago had sunk into the deeper feeling of hatred.

Nay, autumns were sad. His heart throbbed. Two years old, the wound was still raw.

And winter, white and cruel, had lost its snowballing joys. It was winter that robbed him of Tom Gray. Tom was the one person who possessed the beauty of true goodness.

"Robin . . . we have had rare times. . . ." A gasping good-by, then some of the wintry whiteness settling into the gentle face, and the rest . . . silence.

It was very still in the little room. He drowsed, dreaming of the past, tired and worn by his pain, thinking not at all of the future that stretched remote and colorless before him.

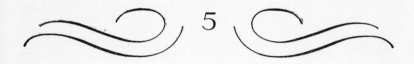

5

The Baited Hook

*F*rom an upper window in Lambeth Palace where with his stepfather he was visiting the Archbishop, Robert gazed out on a white world. He had a cold, and a slight flush lay feverishly along his cheekbones. For some time he had been sitting there in the window seat, awaiting Dudley, who chose this night for the grand cast into the stream. But Dudley did not come.

Robert uncoiled his long legs from where he was hunched, and stretched, groaning softly with relief. He stood up and crossed to the small mirror on the opposite wall. Now it could be seen that he was a good deal taller, indeed, close to six feet, more manly than boyish, at seventeen having quite outgrown the awkwardness of his ninth year. His slenderness told of fast growth and little exercise. He would never be heroic in build, like his father, nor muscular, like Dudley, who straddled about on his great calves, throwing his weight against that of lesser men. Well, tonight he was Dudley's bait, and the Earl was going to try the great catch.

He stared into the mirror. Over his upper lip he passed a finger, feeling the reddish down, colored like his curly thatch. He peered, frowning, at a small swelling on his chin, then with a sigh of nervousness threw back his wide shoulders and passed his damp palms down the sides of his body. God, would Dudley never come!

The brief winter afternoon would not wait for them; they had to get across the river, and already within the room the cold white light was fading. They were to sup at Arundel House, where the Queen kept Court, and at the thought, his bowels quivered. Strange, how the history of his life repeated itself. His head began to ache.

It was growing colder in the room. No wonder, the fire was going out. He poked it and threw on a fresh log, then gazed down into the glow. Leaning on the mantel, he fingered the sore spot; a pimple on the chin and a cold in the head. Not very promising bait for the kind of fish they were out to catch.

The door creaked and into the shadowy room came Penelope Rich. "Robin! Still mumping?" Her voice, so like her mother's, slid over the ear like honey.

He hunched one shoulder but did not reply. Now she came forward into the firelight which caught in her blonde hair and danced down her white satin and sequins. She put out one foot and wiggled it at the fire. Her brother twisted his head to scowl at her magnificence, and the brightness of her dress sent a flash of pain through his temples.

"*That* cost a pretty penny."

"Mm." Penelope nodded. "It did. And all out of Rich's nice fat purse." She spun round so that her skirt scintillated in a dizzy circle. "Like it?"

"No," he said bluntly. "I liked you better in your old gowns at home."

She had her mother's mocking laugh, but now it caught in a sigh. Folding her arms on the tall back of a chair, she considered the fire, her eyes absent. "I wish I hadn't married him, Robin," she confessed.

"Then why did you?"

She shrugged. Aye, why indeed. They both knew, and the knowledge made them bitter. Dudley's influence, used on the mother to make the daughter take the suitor with the money bags. Loving another, Penelope took him.

"Blount's home," said Robin, kicking at the log that rolled forward.

"And if he is, what's that to me?" But she could not keep the jump of excitement from her voice.

"Nothing, I suppose."

He yawned, then flung his arms wide. To the devil with women. There was his mother, who had taken the chance of a small quarrel between the lovers, Penelope and Blount, to come between them. Blount, Robin's dear friend, engaged to his sister, the two of them lost so deep in love it was wonderful to see—and the girl, driven and badgered, till she flew out at them all, and ran off with that clod. 'The rich Lord Rich' they called him, and much good it did her. Well, she repented of it now. No use to press her hand against her aching heart. She could have had Blount, handsome and loving, indeed she could have had almost any man. Philip Sidney, the Queen's golden Apollo, they said, ate out his heart for her.

He heard her sigh again. Then, "Let me look at you. It's so dark in here, I can scarcely see you." She reached up to settle the small modish ruff at his throat, pushing a loose button into its loop. "You are so careless, Robin, you don't seem to take a bit of trouble with your clothes."

"I never think of them," he said.

Now she was exasperated. "Why did you choose black? You know she hates it on her young men. I told you myself." She picked a thread from the tucked satin of his front. Then she stood off from him, her bright head on one side. "Oh, well, with your looks, it really doesn't matter what you wear."

He was not listening. "Jesus God, how my head aches," he complained.

"Too bad," said his sister absently. She slung his dagger into place and puffed out his trunks creased with sitting. Long used to women's fussing, he stood still, obedient beneath her hands. She tweaked a tiny wrinkle out of his hose, then laughed.

"Remember the last time you went to Court? You tore your new hose and everyone was furious with you." Her dark eyes softened as she leaned against his tallness, her yellow head bright against his black doublet.

For a moment both lost themselves in happy memories, with apple trees for climbing and dear days on the river, the four of them crowded into one small rowboat. Today Walter was still laboring with his books, and Dorothy, just out of her bride-clothes, was already big with her first child.

He felt her draw away. Memories were intolerable for her, too. Her mood changed. She pulled from her hair the ornament she wore. "See, I wore this for you to see. It's for her, for a New Year's gift." It was a circlet of pearls wreathed round a heart. "All the Queen's bedchamber ladies are giving her presents, oh, some of them are lovely, little gold boxes and fans. I like this, don't you?"

He took the jewel in his long fingers and turned it to the light. "It's well there is one in the family to make such fancy presents to the Queen's grace. Never could I buy the like."

She smiled shrewdly. "You'll not need presents, lad. With the Devereux looks you'll go far, but, by my faith, you'll need all you have if you're going to stand up to her."

Again he scowled. For across his mind had flashed that morning eight years before in a sunny bedroom, his mother and the nurse on their knees, dressing him in light green for his appearance at Court. What was it his mother had called him? A green minnow. He remembered how frightened he was and the relief of the ride home. Now there was no fear, only a sense of degradation, something quite different from what he felt when his father took him, a lad of nine, to make his devoir to the Queen's grace.

Desperate at the ground he had lost, Leicester was pushing him forward, hoping to catch the capricious fancy of the fifty-year-old Queen with his handsome stepson. Despite his scowling expression of the moment, Robert Devereux had the elusive gift of charm. With his smile he could bring ducks off the water, and he had a way of bending over a lady's hand that was never learned under the tutelage of Burghley and the expensive masters who had polished him. But against Dudley's plan he had set his face. It had taken his mother's pleading and his stepfather's solemn promise to take him to the Low Countries in the spring to change that. The move had been carefully planned; even Lord Burghley had been enlisted on their side and the Queen was expecting them, prepared to be gracious.

Penelope read his thoughts. "I wonder at your willingness to aid Dudley."

He kept silent. No woman could understand his longing for foreign adventure, for the sea and the far places of his dreaming youth.

She jumped to another subject. "And I still think it a mistake to wear black. She can't abide sober colors."

His face hardened, and now he spoke. "Perhaps I wear it in memory of my father. If she sees this and has the wit to remember, she'll not think so much on that drunken sot who sleeps with our mother."

"For the Lord's love, Robin!" Her hand flew to his lip and she flicked a glance over her shoulder at the closed door. Then she relaxed. "Remember, too, Philip lives in black velvet. It may remind her of our father, but it will certainly put her in mind of the Spanish spider."

"So much the better. She'll know that I too can be feared."

Now she burst out laughing. It was too much. The priceless popinjay! She rested her hands on her waist and regarded him affectionately. "She fear Philip? Oh, you have somewhat to learn, my young brother. But this, oh this, will be egg-and-pie! You with your pride and she—still, it's time someone stood up to her. But go with care, my Robin, go with care."

He went and peered out the window. "Leicester's overdue. It must be near six." He knelt on the seat, rubbing the window pane with his cuff.

"Don't!" She dragged his arm down. "You'll spoil this lovely thread lace. Scrubbing that dirty glass!"

A mellow chime carried across the river to them. Six o'clock. It was dark now. He pulled out his watch, tipping it to the fire. As he thrust it back, the door opened to admit his stepfather. With him came the cold air swirling from the passage, making the brother and sister shiver.

"Good lad!" He came briskly forward to rub his hands at the fire. "'Sblood! It's perishing!"

Two of his gentlemen stood by the door which Robert wished they would close. Over a bent shoulder Dudley eyed the girl. "Do you go with us, my lady?"

Robert saw her chin rise and he thought of what she had told him of the Earl's secret questing hand ever after her, since she was a girl of fourteen. "I?" In her high voice, she was insultingly deliberate. Then cuttingly, "Later. Rich will escort me."

At mention of Penelope's husband, Leicester grinned derisively and Robert longed to strike him. Lascivious Leicester, whose fingers slid so easily up a girl's ankle as she alighted from her horse. He thought of Blount, and wished with all his heart for him to come and carry Penelope away from both husband and stepfather. Now she swept from the room, a grand lady, ignoring the two at the door, who bowed, their wet eyes on her as she passed. Leicester kept snake men about him.

"Lord Burghley's below," said Leicester. "All is settled. You'll be presented after supper. Keep out of her eye till then. I want you to make an entrance."

Robert nodded glumly. More and more he was hating it. Perhaps he would cut and run for it after all, get abroad and lose himself in some foreign war. But the older man took his arm.

"Robin," his voice was husky, "do me this one thing. I swear I won't forget you for it. Flanders next spring, shalt go, I promise!" There was frantic urgency in the jerky voice.

Robert looked at his stepfather and saw a badly frightened man,

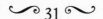

begging him, a youth, for help. It was pitiful. "How do you know she will let you go?"

Leicester winced. "She'll give me permit, I do not fear. I'm no longer the favorite. Now, if you push aside Ralegh—blast his black soul—" his teeth gritted. "Come, let's below."

Together the two Earls, the young one and the one no longer young, descended the stone staircase.

"God's death," shivered Leicester. "These clerics keep a bitter house. Cold as charity."

They passed into the lower hall, dim and drafty, and entered the withdrawing room. Burghley and the Archbishop sat together over a decanter of perry. The two gouty old men looked as thin and spiritless as the stuff they were drinking. But Robert knew that Burghley, at least, was far from spiritless. Had he not stood up to Elizabeth for forty years?

"Well, lad," he said dolorously, as Robert stood before him. "Have we Latined you for this?"

His cold eye blinked at the tall youth, only a bit younger than his own Robert, clever young Cecil. They all knew that the little cripple was being quietly groomed to fill his father's shoes. Robert gave his guardian a level look, and by the quivering of Burghley's breath, he read the older man like a book. The job was done. To the last letter of his father's wishes, the duty had been discharged. The new Earl was prepared for Court, no matter that he had no relish for it. The money, the anxious hours, all had been spent to this end. The rest lay with him.

Groaning, the Lord Treasurer got to his feet. The Archbishop warmed his ecclesiastical backside at the fire and beamed impartially on all. Leicester filled two glasses at the sideboard and gave one to Robert, who stood straight, trying to forget his throbbing head and the burning chilblains that tormented his toes.

"Here, our guts will need warming before we cross that infernal river."

Robert downed the drink, felt immediately better. They wrapped themselves in warm cloaks that reached unfashionably down their legs; damn the mode in this weather. High boots replaced their velvet house shoes; sable tippets and fur-lined gloves were designed to guard against the cold. Burghley's aquiline features were framed in a hood cap lest he take a chill, and he seemed unnaturally tall in his cork-soled pantofles.

They went outside and a paralyzing blast cut the breath out of them.

"Pull your cloak about your throat," gasped Leicester. Robert obeyed and they climbed to their saddles. He was the bait; he must not freeze on the hook.

London was a white fairyland of ice and snow. Winter left his breath, congealed into a glittering film, on roof and tower. Westminster loomed, high and pallid, amidst pale shadowy trees, and the palace at their backs lifted frigid battlements into the air.

Not since the winter after Harry the Fifth beat the French at Agincourt had there been so great a frost. The river was frozen over so that their horses stepped out upon a glassy floor seven feet thick. The air was dry and a powdery snow silently descended.

It was completely dark and the river was picked out by torches that streamed crazily onto the frosty air. Dotted about were little worlds of light where folk huddled, blinking about their bonfires. A puff of sweet warmth swirled past the riders as they swerved to miss the chestnut sellers. Tumbling down the Southwark Stairs, hanging onto each others' coattails, a yelling line of boys, shrieking for joy, slid far out on the ice toward them. Robert's horse shied.

"Steady, lad," he murmured. He pressed his thighs against the horse's ribs. "So-o."

"Hold him up, Robert," snapped Leicester. "And keep your mouth shut, you'll get worse cold. Curse the fate that struck you with this rotting head." Another blast came gusting along the ice. "Be-Jesus! It's enough to cut the flesh off a man!"

Pressing his lips grimly together, Robert sniffed, and the action seemed to clear his head. He glanced at his stepfather, whose profile beneath the down-pulled brim of his beaver showed plainly in the light from the fires. The Earl was looking blotchy about the jowls and he wheezed perceptibly. Gone was the slender elegance of his youth; only a blurred outline of the Queen's idol now remained.

Drawing farther away from the south shore, they picked their way through the crowd. The going was slow, and despite the cinders spread on the ice, they had to take care lest their horses slip. The whole river resembled a fair ground, for down the center was a jumble of tented booths, where Londoners bought ermine tippets or country eggs. Burghley gestured: the bear ring, where a crowd pushed, fighting for a chance to get close, their wet shoes freezing to the river. But Leicester was not interested.

From a nearby brazier the smell of roasted flesh, delicious on the frosty air, reminded Robert that he was hungry. Over there behind the winking lights of the great house was warmth and supper. His spirits rose. The stopped-up feeling was leaving his ears and even his frost-bitten toes throbbed less sharply.

They mounted the bank and clattered into the yard of Arundel House. The chilly moon had risen, streaked by snow clouds; and the dark shape of the immense house stood out bold and clear. Cressets flamed through iron baskets to light the way, and threw a glitter onto the slippery iced flags of the court. As they alighted, the wind came screeching past the halberdiers at the door.

"In with you," urged Leicester.

They passed into the light and warmth.

6

The Catch

*I*t was a brilliant night. To the last moment of his life he never would forget it. Could ever there be so glorious a scene; could delight reach a higher zenith? Gone was the sulky mood, vanished with the first sight of his friend.

"Robert!"

"Charlie!"

They grasped hands, laughing for joy. Blount was superb in a foreign suit, the Italianate polish of the Grand Tour fresh on him, to the pearls in his ears. Together the young men passed into the perfumed maze.

"Penelope?"

"The Continent?"

They plied one another with questions. Grinning, they sat in a recessed window, their long legs drawn out of the way of parading feet. They blinked at the glitter. The spectacle mounted in splendor.

"I've seen nothing more glorious abroad," confessed Blount. "It's incredible."

Multicolored pieces on a great chessboard, the figures grouped and gossiped, gathered into a sort of wonderland whose fiery heart was the red-crowned goddess in orange, moving remote and distant from the two youths.

A hearty burst of laughter came from Ralegh, jesting with his silver cronies; a glistening vision of white was Elizabeth Throckmorton, loved by many, loving none. There went the Queen's Moor, Walsingham, all dark elegance; and the man with the pearls large as peas, roped through a buttonhole, was Sir Henry Lee, who set the mode for all at Court.

"I envy him his style," said Blount.

"I don't," said Robert. Clothes were of no account to him.

The bent shadow in purple, Bishop Aylmer, gave his princely hand to Penelope's kiss, whose satins creased on the floor as she curtsied. Then she escaped to them, her color matching Blount's as he took her hand.

"Come to supper," she smiled. "I know where there are good places."

In a dream Robert followed his sister and her lover. Seated at table, he could not eat for looking. Marchpanes, gallandines, all went drifting by. Loving sweet music, his ears were ravished by strains from the gallery where men played on viols of fine dark wood, inlaid with ivory and nacre, on golden harps and sackbuts of chased silver. He could not eat for listening. Forgotten was the lordly pose of seventeen years. He stared.

Lord Rich, already a bit tipsy, ate with drunken gravity. He stabbed a sharp-pointed knife into a tiny carrot and held it aloft.

"Good fresh roots," he observed, "fresh from garden—all new and fresh." Poking his neighbor with a sharp elbow, he said, "I like my roots fresh from garden. Bed to pot, bed to pot."

He sniggered lewdly, while his neighbor, dressed in churchly garb, looked down his long pink nose, and Rich laughed the harder. If Penelope heard, she gave no sign. Running about was Arno, the Queen's clown, a rainbow monstrosity, with a chattering ape on his shoulder. The little creature darted out an arm and tweaked the jewel in Rich's ear.

"God's death!" He sprang halfway up in his chair, one hand to his burning cheek. "May the devil blast you, dwarf!" Muttering now in complete ill-humor, he subsided to his food.

"Art a spoil-sport, my lord," observed Penelope.

Robert had seen Rich in the tiltyard push a man off his horse, so that he broke a leg, whereupon Rich roared, thinking it a side-splitting joke.

Yet, when he looked at his young wife, shedding her blonde loveliness on Blount, his eyes were pitiful.

A scream from the far end of the table. Katherine Fytton, one of the Queen's maids, was trying to repress her shudders. Arno had allowed his monkey to coil a long silky tail round the girl's throat.

"Enough!" called the voice of authority, and one of the girls threw the little beast a sugared cherry.

Everyone was eating casually, as if well used to the plenitude of rich food on gold and silver plates. They plied their new-fangled forks and dipped their fingers in rose water between courses. The Queen's hounds wandered hopefully about, but none threw them bones. That was no longer done. Robert saw a few old-fashioned folk who ignored their fringed napkins and wiped greasy hands on the cloth.

Sitting near him at table were men to take the breath. Sidney, the Golden Apollo, pretended to eat, while watching Penelope laughing with Blount. Someone stooped, whispering, over one of the diners, who laid down his napkin and leaned stiffly back. Why, the diner was Lord Howard of Effingham, a little grayer than that day at Somerset House. He inclined his head to the whisperer and showed the square tags of his teeth; once again it struck Robert how mirthless was the smile on the flat face of the Lord Admiral.

Blount nudged him. "The dark brothers," he whispered.

Ah, yes, the Bacon youths. There they were, grown up since those summers at Theobalds, and dressed now like twins in cut velvet. They sat flanking their cousin Cecil, all three looking as if snipped from the same pattern. Cecil was pale, and he picked at the wing of a pheasant, while the brothers delicately ate shad roe, bending narrow faces above their little forks. How the piercing eyes of Cecil darted about as he saw and seemed not to see!

A withered old woman in magnificent emeralds now addressed Blount. "Tell me, my good lad, you have recently been to Italy, is it true that the Venetian ladies wash their golden hair in dog's urine to keep it bright?"

The ready blood rose in Blount's face and Penelope looked demurely at her dinner, though her brother saw her eyes were merry.

"Well, don't ye know?" persisted the old countess.

Blount thought it was so.

"I heard the same when I was in Spain," she chuckled. "I heard more, too. 'Tis said that Philip has the French sickness." Greedily she gulped her wine.

Penelope giggled. Rich was more French than English, and if not too drunk, was bound to resent this last remark. He was not too drunk. He glared at the countess, who lifted a greasy face from her wine cup. She broke into a bawdy grin.

"Contain yourself, my lord Rich. True it is we call it the French sickness, but then the French call it the Spanish sickness, and the Spanish call it the Italian. But we English know what it comes from and that's enough."

"It is, indeed," affirmed an Irish lord devoutly. Lord Rich sent a gusty sigh onto his food.

Robert now addressed himself to his meat, but a new commotion stopped him. High over the pages' heads the swan, a snowy wonder, sailed on a lake of blue jelly, its roasted sides golden brown, and red currants for its eyes.

"*Ciel,*" murmured Blount.

"Pooh," sniffed the countess. "Swan makes a rare show, but it plays hob with your stomach."

A louder cheer now! Two strong boys staggered in with a great silver pie dish, the crust all crenelated into little turrets and cones.

"Sing a song of sixpence!"

The Queen's butler was busy; there was a cluster of heads round the dish, lowered to the Queen's table, so that the youths could not see what passed. A sudden twitter and a frightened rush of wings, and a hundred larks burst from their prison and went whirring to the top of the room.

The clapping drowned the shouts. The tiny birds were terrified. One flew so straightly up that it struck its head on a rafter and fell, a dazed little lump of feathers, on the golden cloth. Round and round swirled the larks as into the hall stepped the Queen's falconers.

"Ah!" Penelope's black eyes grew cruel.

Unhooded now, the fierce little short-winged hawks sat blinking in the light. Then up, up, went one soaring after its prey.

"A hawk! A hawk! Twenty angels on the speckled one to bring down the first!"

The larks, frenzied, flew here and there, until one by one, marked by the hawks, they fell, so that the floor, the tables, even the gay company were sprinkled with their blood.

"Lord!" Another shriek from the excitable Katherine as a dead bird fell onto her plate.

"Zounds!" A fat lord, caught under the chin by a hawk leash, gave a strangled gurgle. The two youths laughed hysterically.

But now majesty, having eaten nothing, was pleased to signify that she had had enough, and the whole company trooped to its feet. Robert, too, had eaten nothing. Strolling at the edge of the crowd, he caught sight of Dudley, a long way off. In his tallness he towered over the heads, and he sent a searching glance about for his stepson. Catching Robert's eye, he beckoned.

The long night had faded, and now he was alone. He lay in his cold bed, trying to compose his whirling thoughts to memory of the scene.

They brought him to her, and once again, their eyes met. Majesty and beauty, each secure in its own, faced each other. He felt himself, tall and black contrasting with her, as arrogant and orange, she looked straight at him. Her painted mouth was closed in a firm line, but her eyes drooped, softened, glittered strangely in the candlelight.

Down on his knees he went, needing no firm hand's prompting, and he kissed those long fingers, quivering as he did so, at the scent and the soft hush that hung over the scene.

What did she say? Ah, he knew not. She smiled, keeping her thin lips together, so that her flat cheeks widened in a candid confidence as she leaned to whisper some nonsense into his ear. They danced, and he was astonished at her spring and lightness. Someone put a lute into his hands—was it Dudley?—and he struck an attitude, one knee bent, and sang.

Ah, those long summers with Burghley's music master! What did he sing? An old tune of Tom Gray's, one they sang in the meadows of his boyhood. But the words, they at least, were his own, a flash of inspirational genius. He made her a little verse, the rhymes popping neatly into his head as he went along, the whole improvised, so that she knew it done on the spur of the moment. And she—cradled as he knew her to be in French lyric and Italian harmony—clapped her exquisite hands for joy.

Now it was over. Now he lay wrapped in delicious reminiscent languor, and the whole night swirled together in one delirious, diamond dream. Lightly he thought on Dudley, flushed and eager, looking tonight almost young again. But it was not for Dudley he had triumphed; for himself he had won the difficult cast into the stream, and for him was the prize. The Low Countries in the spring, and then—ah, what could he not draw into his eager net? If the fond looks of tonight meant anything at all, he was made—gilded and crowned for success. He had won.

He stretched his legs to the bottom of the bed and felt the cold melt out of his feet. He felt light as air, snugly warm, his thoughts floating. Suddenly drowsy, with a smile on his lips, he fell asleep.

7

Royal Thanksgiving

"Aah, hum!" In her ugly carved bed, Elizabeth yawned. Outside her window a glorious wintry sun rose redly over the square tower of St. Paul's, to shine on the wet slates of Somerset House. Stairs below, the great house had long been stirring.

Elizabeth yawned again, then fumbled at the bell rope. Before she could jerk it, Mary Ratcliffe appeared with a little silver bowl in which there was a posset, spiced and warm.

"Good morning, your Grace."

Elizabeth buried her sharp nose in the tempting warmth. Noisily she supped, then looked up, a little trickle at one corner of her mouth.

"What sort of day?" Her voice was harsh with sleep.

" 'Tis a grand November day, Madam."

"Humph! No November days are grand in London." She drank again. "Foggy, is it?"

"Not more than seasonable, your Grace." Mary turned the shift that hung on a clothes horse before the fire.

"Seasonable!"

With the infernal mist coming off the river, and an icy wind to blow into the nostrils and throat. Ah, the sun was getting up, that was something. A thin shaft of light suddenly glowed on the plaster wall and touched up the portrait of her father, King Henry, that hung over the shallow fire arch.

Propped on her pillows, Elizabeth sipped her drink and regarded her father. Masterful he looked with the stubborn little ear set back on his great thick neck, and that buttoned-up mouth beneath the red fringe of his mustache. Smart, too, in the dove-colored suit slashed over a fine white shirt. A Tudor, like herself.

"The sun becomes my father, Mary. Ah! *He* was a man, with six women to sleep in his bed, Mary, and God knows . . ." she checked herself. Even to Mary she would not speak of a king's mistresses. She smiled sardonically. Of all the marrying and mating, she was the only one left. And she? The smile grew bitter. A barren stock, she was. There had been Robert Dudley and now for four years there had been Robin Devereux, her young cavalier—and what besides? A new wig, and Henry's pearls for this day of days. The smile had quite gone now.

"Here, girl! Me guts are warmed. I'll get up." She swung a pair of high-arched feet over the side of the bed. Clutching the flannel night-rail to her, she stalked stiffly across the floor and put the gray hair out of her eyes. Through the window she peered at the day.

"Ha! I thought last night the King of Spain's prayers must have reached the courts of Heaven and today it would rain on us."

Steam was rising from the sun-struck cobblestones in the courtyard, and beyond lay the Thames, coldly a-glitter in the morning rays. The steep-pitched roofs and spires were shining and smoke from myriad chimneys rose into the early air. The Lord God of Hosts was sending them especially fine weather for the occasion. She pushed open the casement and the mellow voices of a hundred clanging bells swirled into the room. London was early celebrating. Down at Paul's Cross they must be gathered by hundreds for the great English victory over the Spanish Armada. Shutting out the sound, she turned.

"I shall honor the day by washing my body all over, so tell 'em to look lively there with some good hot water." It was a dangerous thing to do in winter, but nevertheless, she would do it.

They came scurrying with sponges and buckets of hot water and warm towels. Ah, that was good! Damp and steamy, she stretched her foot to the bathing woman and flexed her toes to have them dried between. Now! On with the thick yellow silk stocking, clocked in gold. Not every ankle could stand a stocking like that.

"Pull it straight, fool." Her woman pulled the stocking up under the golden garter ribband. She stood, naked save for the gaudy hose. Next came the fine lawn shift and the tight busk, laced to show the figure.

"Come on! Tighter! I can still breathe." She rested her hands on her hips and gasped. Not one of those girls of hers should boast a straighter back nor a waist more slim.

Mary wrapped her in a warm dressing robe and she sat before her mirror. In came her barber who deftly combed the gray hair back from the high forehead and hid it with the resplendence of a new wig. Real titian hair, from the heads of young girls, and so cunningly matched that all seemed to belong to the one head that now wore it. There went her father's pearls, twisted in two great loops.

"How well my hair sets them off." She was affable to the spidery little barber.

Blonde Mary now returned with two tire-women who bore in their arms the white satin robe of state, jeweled and slashed and furred, and they put it on the bed, with the long train of purple and silver samite where it lay, a tumbled waterfall of beauty.

Elizabeth took a hand mirror and stared into it. A long, pale face, with thin cheeks, and a firm pointed chin. She reached for the rabbit's foot and touched her sallow cheeks with bloom. Sharply now she glanced at Mary, who stood at her shoulder, the lace ruff in her hand. Mary's cheeks were flushed with hurrying and dawn and—youth. Elizabeth sighed heavily and scrubbed a little more rose onto her face. She was beginning to be really afraid of her glass, with the searching eyes of Essex so near these days. Was it possible that four years had passed since the youth of seventeen had captured her fancy? Yes, there were crow's feet around her eyes, faint wrinkles at the corners of her mouth.

"Well," she remarked to her image, " 'tis certain you'll never have a pair of chins like old Winchester. God will spare you that." She would always be paper-thin, with her own particular elegance; but—fifty-five, and Essex, her heart's darling, was—twenty-one.

Mechanically she submitted to her women. They tied and laced and buttoned her into the rich clothes. She stood mute, thinking of herself and Essex. Strange that she felt these qualms only when alone in her rooms. Out there in the blaze and glitter, she glowed, a royal jewel in its proper setting. Here, in her privacy, she was entirely a woman. She drew in her breath and a little tremor shot through her.

Into the ruff sank her chin; blessedly softening, the gauzy dream rose about her like woven air in which her face was framed as in a portrait. She began to feel better. Today she was to appear as a goddess regnant, a triumphant prince among her people, tasting with them the sweet fruits of victory. On with the play!

At last all was done. They had given her wine and a piece of oaten cake. Now she stood before her long mirror, magnificent, calm, her pulses beating strongly. By Heaven, she would show them all this day how to wear a state robe! No flinching, no staggering at the drag of leaden skirts, heavy with pearls and silver thread. Already her neck felt stiff from the effort of keeping her head erect under the pull of the head-dress; her ruff was chafing on her throat a thin angry line; her modish square-toed shoes pinched abominably; but she was gorgeous.

Now they were putting on her gloves, and she held out her hands proudly. White as snow they were, exquisitely untouched by the years. The gloves were a lovely fit.

"My fan!" A perfumed whisper, it was put into her hand. Over her shoulder she peered at them, fumbling with her train. "And now, for God's sake, let us go!"

Into her role of Gloriana she stepped with a fine Tudor flourish. Now, out into the hall to her obsequious ladies and gentlemen, down the wide stairs . . . pausing to rest her jeweled glove on the newel post while she caught her breath.

"Ah, Hatton, a very good morning to ye." The stately Lord Chancellor dropped to his knees. She spotted her Chamberlain. "Carey, the King of Spain will have to do the watery weeping today, since Heaven is disposed to be dry, and we shall not wet our shoes after all." She gave a grating laugh.

On through the hall, to pause again in the doorway for them to catch up with her. Out into the courtyard, and at sight of her, tall and regal, the cheering on the walls began. She drew a deep breath. By God, this was good, this was worth living for. These days of rejoicing were the vindication of all she stood for, majesty, power, divine right, England! She *was* England today; English hearts were her heart, and in the hollow of her hand she held their loves.

The cheering rose, swelled. Ah, this was better even than her famous journey to Tilbury, and she after that, riding down to Plymouth in a steel breastplate, to nerve with fiery words her troops about to meet the Spaniard! The Spaniard! Her cheeks burned beneath the rouge as she climbed into her coach, the kaleidoscopic pageant swirling about her. Men-at-arms grounded their halberds, her trumpeters, fantastic archers, shot their arrows of silver sound into the air, and gentlemen pensioners by the score marched in spangled velvet beneath a forest of golden battle-axes. The bells of London shook their carillons to the clouds, and through it all thundered the heavy banging of the ordnance. But she would not start yet.

"Where is Essex?"

The cheering rose again, then patted away as a cream-white palfrey, led by two pages, came daintily through the gate. Before it, in the full pride of his majority, walked Robert Devereux, the Queen's infatuation. Head high, a flushed smile on his lips, he strode the world on air. The delicate coat of the horse was not more immaculately white than the young Earl's doublet of silver-shot sarcanet, cunningly sewn over with brilliants in the Italian fashion.

Straight to her he came, dropped on one knee, and gently kissed her glove. Elizabeth gave him an enchanted smile. Again her pulses beat, madly, wildly. But one moment only would she allow for the private pleasures of a Queen. With the back of one gloved hand she touched his cheek.

"My white and silver knight," she murmured.

He stepped back, bowed, and slipped the velvet halter of Eleazer over one arm. Then he turned to walk behind the chariot as became the Queen's Master of the Horse. Throwing up his head, he encountered a savage scowl on the features of Sir Walter Ralegh, Captain of her Majesty's Guard. A rigid silver statue he stood at the head of his troop, hearing and not hearing, seeing and not seeing. At the choking admiration in the Queen's voice, his black brows rushed together.

Out in the streets through yelling lanes, Elizabeth waved her hand imperially from under the fringed canopy, and the people waved back, their holiday faces red-cheeked from the river wind. It whipped the women's heavy skirts and flicked off the caps of little lads, held high in their father's arms to see the Queen.

Essex held his head high, too. He wondered how it would feel to be the heart and center of all this adulation, to wear the royal purple and ermine, to be the instrument of power and majesty. His heart beat fast at such a thought.

The bells of the city were mad. Brazen and silver-throated, they clanged and clamored their paean of praise for a sovereign who had nerved a country to victory. An old woman, withered face close-coifed in snowy linen, hobbled between the guards to lay a tiny nosegay of rosemary at the Queen's feet.

"Give ye godden, your Grace!" From her slowly moving chariot Elizabeth tossed a gold angel, but a small boy had it before ever the aged eyes saw it, which was a pity, for Elizabeth was chary with her gold angels.

The brilliant cortege wound its way down Fleet Street and there at Temple Bar were the city musicians playing for their very life one of her favorite airs. Hah! "Greensleeves!"

A flaming blot on the clear landscape was the Lord Mayor and his aldermen, solid and deferential. Now the procession entered a lane of city companies, clad alike, a long blue sheath through which the bright blade of magnificence thrust itself to the church steps. In her coach Elizabeth drew breath again.

"My God," she thought to herself, "but these shoon pinch cruelly. I must make shift to walk without faltering." She moved her sore feet, then descended, her glove on Essex's shoulder.

Used as he was by now, at twenty-one, to the brilliant pageantry of Elizabeth's public life, he could not help blinking a little at this particular show. There was color, color, everywhere. Gold and silver sent flashes of light through the eyes, already dazzled by the sun off the river, and in the midst Elizabeth walked, calm and steady, the presiding genius of it all.

Again he felt that exciting stab of wonder; what, what would it feel like to be where *she* stood, now, at this moment, to have the power of command over all this strength of color and deference. At her side he walked up to the church, feeling for the moment as if he were indeed her consort and not merely her favorite lord-in-waiting.

Unaware of the burning thoughts of her favorite, Elizabeth felt her burning feet and forced her attention to those about her.

Old Aylmer, Lord Bishop of London, backed by his Dean and the other princes of the church, was bowing to the ground. God's teeth, Aylmer was old and decrepit, with his seventy years looking more like ninety as he tottered on ahead, his purple cassock whipping his thin shanks. For John Whitgift, the Lord Archbishop, her "little black husband," she had a special smile, as she swept into her tiny oratory.

They drew back. With some difficulty and a secret creaking of knee joints, she knelt in private prayer. To herself and God she mumbled a word of thanks, for royalty must abase itself outwardly before the Lord.

But practically, she always held to the theory that God helps those that help themselves. Use your wits; then think of God.

"Amen," she muttered, and rose, Robert Devereux at her elbow. With him she turned into the long aisle where among the rising strains of the *Te Deum* red and yellow banners of Spain waved overhead.

"They make a rare show, Robin," she whispered, pressing with her hand his outstretched arm.

"Aye, that they do. Better here than where they were," he murmured in her ear. Together they crossed the transept, walking in a gentle swell of organ sound, and then she and her robes were seated on the opposite side. Essex knelt beside her, facing the chanting boys, whose clear, piercing sopranos followed accurately the beat of the music master's thin finger.

"We praise Thee, O God, we acknowledge Thee to be the Lord."

Sweet little robins, chirping to God. She glanced down at *her* Robin, beside her in bridegroom white, the light from the transept window touching his curls with soft red and violet fingers. Heaven above! Essex was handsome and charming enough to turn any woman's head. How she loved his beautiful hair with the auburn tinge; and his nose, with the distracting little curve in it that gave the face its elfin look. He flicked up his eyelids at her, and she caught a flash of clear young eyes, green, shot through with little hazel flecks. She dropped her prayer book and he bent his tall head and handed it to her. Over the dainty enameled thing their fingers touched, brushed lingeringly. A fluttering breath rose in Elizabeth's chest, but she swallowed it away and braced herself to her duty.

Dr. Pierce, Bishop of Salisbury, was clearing his throat. God's peace, let him not be long-winded today. For today she would not stop him, however long he took, bearing to the uttermost for her people, a willing martyr to the intolerable weight of state robes and state panoply.

Round at her company she shot a look, as they stood solidly massed in the nave. Chief among them was the white-haired William Cecil, Lord Burghley, her prop and staff, his fine, intelligent face mildly aglow with the exultation of his thoughts. Ah, he had brought up her young cavalier; with a twinge she was reminded of the Lord Treasurer's dislike of his ward, of his unspoken disapproval of her wild affection for the youth. At that moment Burghley raised his head proudly.

"He doesn't need to look as if he thought *he* had done it all. Some of my bold-legged lads had a little to do with it, I trow."

Her bold-legged lads were scattered among the congregation. Ralegh, the black-browed Devonshire man, out of whom she had made a knight and the Captain of her Guard; and Lord Howard of Effingham, her brave Admiral—ah, there was devotion.

"Effingham's the best of all the Howard lot; I must see if I can reward him. An earldom, I wonder . . ."

Who was this, coming in late? Drake, fresh up from Plymouth. She had feared to miss him on this great day. He came, with the salt sea in his eyes, treading the nave as if it were the deck of a ship. He slipped to his knees beside Frobisher, her long Yorkshireman. Two men after her own heart, though she liked Frobisher, the proper man with the quick temper, best.

She moved her feet more comfortably on her hassock. Pierce had worked around to her soldiers and sailors, congratulating them. No need of that, she would do it better than he, when her turn came. So he thought God had done it, did he? Well, there could be two minds about that. Proper homage to God should be paid, but to her doughty commanders, their ships and their men, a full meed of praise should go. No Queen was ever more superbly served on sea and they should hear her say it.

Ha, at last! Pierce had arrived at the Spanish King. This was better. With a satisfied gleam in her eye, she smiled at Essex. By the blood of God, Spider Philip must now sit in his Escorial and spin new webs. What gnawing of fingernails when he learned the full horror of all that had befallen his Armada at English hands! Over half those ships which so proudly set sail from the cheering harbor at Lisbon, under that incompetent *hidalgo,* Medina Sidonia, now lay rotting on the bed of the North Sea, or were piled up in broken hulks on the rocks of the Irish coast. Some were riding at anchor in her harbors, while others were black charred fragments floating ashore on incoming waves. By every courier came fresh tidings of the grisly fate of the Spanish Armada.

And where were Philip's haughty grandees and his fierce *soldados?* They, too, were rotting heaps on the Irish and Scottish coasts, where it had pleased a Protestant God to put them, that their whitening bones might serve a warning to all who tried to overthrow Elizabeth of England. Their corpses strewed the beaches all the way from the Giant's Causeway to Blasquet Sound.

"Ay, weep, wide brown eyes along the Spanish shore,
Your dark-haired lovers shall return no more."

A proud smile curved her lips and she swept her fan softly toward her. The purple cloud that was the Spanish threat had rolled away, at least for the time being, some believed forever. . . .

It would soon be time for her to rise. She was aware that Burghley was whispering to Walsingham. How dreadfully ill the Secretary of State looked today. What was it they said tormented him—stone in the kidney? She had never liked the man, with his somber Puritanism, but he had a good nose for plots, and he served her faithfully. Perhaps she had been a bit too hasty that time she threw her slipper in his face. But the man was a fool; said the Spaniards would never attack. Without doubt he was silenced now. And so, praise God, were the Spanish. Her sea hawks had brought the vulture down, gutted and bleeding; the rest did not matter, and as for Walsingham, she would send him home to bed after service.

Now they were singing. The immortal Old Hundredth of Louis Bourgois rose to the vaulted roof.

"All people that on earth do dwell,
Sing to the Lord with cheerful voice."

Elizabeth gripped her fan, gave her prayer book to Essex, and rose to address her people.

They brought her back to Somerset House. Dinner at my Lord Bishop's had ushered in the early winter twilight. With torches and singing they escorted her, their Queen and Goddess, riding in her plumed coach like a triumphal Caesar. To the last she kept her head erect, to the last she waved her hand at a delirious London. Finally it was all over and she had done her duty. A vile headache and a heavy stomach were the results.

By the time she had dragged her aching body into the great hall of her house, she had had more than enough of the day. But not yet was she ready to give in. She would rest and revive her fierce Tudor spirit that was only drooping. She had ordered a feast and a ball and she meant to reign over the merry scene in true style. She tottered into her room and fell into the nearest chair.

 49

"God's truth! But today I have given of my heart's blood. Well!" to her gawking women, "get me out of this hellish harness! My stays are killing me and you stand there like a lot of dying monkeys!"

Terrified, they clustered about her, unlacing, unbuttoning the splendor. She grunted. God's blood, they should be used to it by now; thirty years she had queened it over them.

"Ah! Delicious!" She kicked off the silver shoes. For an hour she had been looking forward to that. Now, off with the busk, and then scratch, scratch, up and down her aching ribs.

"Mary, scratch my spine . . . higher . . . ah, there!" She took deep breaths and bent under the soothing tickle. Suddenly she thrust an exploring finger beneath her curls. Was this new wig becoming lousy already? In truth, if there were nits in it, someone should jump.

Then she caught sight of herself in the mirror, breasts sagging under her shift, red wig awry; it was the reflection of an old, decaying woman. Her face grew stiff with rage.

"Clothes!" she screamed. "Bring back my stays! Damn your eyes for a lot of worthless idiots! Any prince is better served!" She looked about for something to throw.

Mary Ratcliffe came and knelt on the floor. "Will it please your Grace to drink this?" In her hand she held a small Venetian glass of gold filagree. For a moment Elizabeth looked at the girl as if to strike her. Then something in the blue eyes conquered her. Never could she resist beauty, even in a maid, and of late she had permitted herself to love Mary a little.

Grudgingly she took the delicate little cup. Without asking, she drank; Mary was clever with cordials and knew how to soothe a woman's fraying nerves. The drink was cool and refreshing. She leaned back and closed her eyes. On her throbbing head Mary's hands were comforting.

Soon she was laced again and wrapped in a dressing robe. They had smeared a fragrant salve on the angry red line at her throat and her feet had stopped aching. They carried away the white and silver, and she was left with the quiet of the dusky room. She lay in her chair and let the warmth creep over her. How good it was to be safe and warm! Childish nights spent in freezing bedrooms, thanks to her father's parsimony, and days spent in fear of her suspicious sister, Queen Mary, were far memories.

"Never," she murmured, "will I brook discomfort when I am

Queen." Slipping into that borderland of asleep and awake, she thought she was a young maid again, talking to her governess.

Now she was listening to Tom Seymour's teasing laugh, as he courted her stepmother, but chased after her. She was running from his eager hands. She ran faster, faster . . . ah, he was gaining . . . gaining . . . he had her! But his face had changed . . he wore a white suit . . . It was Essex who came and, taking her hand, led her through her dream.

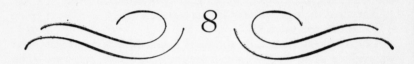

8

The Queen's Pawn

*I*t was only a little golden pawn from the Queen's chessboard, but at sight of it, Robert felt his temper rise. It hung from Blount's shoulder, where he had tucked it out of sight; but as he leaned over the cards, the bauble fell out of a slit in his velvet, and now it lay between the two friends.

Essex was tired with the Armada celebration, and his steady losses at the gaming with which they whiled away the waiting for the Thanksgiving supper did not improve his mood. Now the sight of the jewel stabbed him with a jealous twinge. Blount looked up from the board to encounter his friend's fixed stare, and he blushed.

Robert caught the rising flush on the fair skin, and his anger flared. Deliberately he flipped the hanging trifle with his finger and drawled, "Now I perceive that every fool about this Court must wear a favor."

Blount's smile froze. "I need not take that, Robert." But his voice was even.

"No," retorted Essex, "not while you have the Queen's grace in your favor!"

Carefully Blount tucked his little jewel into its velvet nest. Then he looked once more up at his friend's angry face. "Come, Robert, if you are bent on quarreling with everyone whom her Grace delights to honor, you will have your hands full. Mark my words——"

"Then it is true! You do mean to supplant me if you can!"

The royal hand had bestowed on him such honors; that same hand lingering on the cheek of another—the thought drove him mad. Ah, Gloriana liked the red blood flushing softly beneath fair skin!

"They told me right! It is true!" he repeated.

"What can you mean?"

"Christ's blood, Blount, do you think I and the others have not seen you sucking up to the Queen and the Cecils, and now, and now—" he gasped, as his rage mounted. "You wear gold favors as a matter of course! No doubt the pretty campaign is laid for conquest!"

Blount laughed lightly, though his very lips were pale. "Certes, Robert, your passion runs away with you!" Then he too lost his composure. "You are a greater donkey than I could have believed, despite what I have heard!"

"Zounds!" Essex sent his heavy chair crashing to the hearth. "I'll not take that!"

Grabbing at his dagger, Blount scrambled to his feet. "Shall I cut it into you?"

For a second there was silence in the little paneled room, silence broken now by furious soft breathing. The fire crackled. Then the door opened and the long, inquiring face of Burghley obtruded itself onto the scene. Close behind, peering over his shoulder, was his son, Robert Cecil.

No one moved. "My lords, what is this pastime?" Burghley's dry voice broke in.

"Pastime," Cecil's murmur was skeptical.

Blount's color returned and he snicked his dagger back, while Essex lounged to the far side of the fireplace, to bite his lip and stare at the flames. He heard Lord Burghley.

"Sir Charles, you are wanted. Please to come."

Essex heard the door close, then across the floor, the precise heels of Cecil, who stooped, turned up the chair, then sat on it. The silence continued. At last Essex looked round. Robert Cecil was eating cloves. He closed the lid of his little silver box and slipped it away, then popped the spice into his mouth. Cloves, always chewing cloves; Essex had come to hate the spicy scent, so mindful to him of the little man. Cecil sucked a moment, then gestured up at the wall.

"I have always thought that painting did poor justice to my father," he said mildly.

He pressed his crooked shoulders against the velvet back of the chair and with Essex, he contemplated the Lord Treasurer's portrait. It hung against the plaster, a noble study of a noble man. William Cecil, Lord Burghley, had been drawn in his robes of office, one fine hand grasping his staff, his wary face looking out at them from the canvas as if to utter one of the familiar portentous reproofs. A hundred times, as he grew up under Burghley's tutelage, had Essex seen that look.

He raised one shoulder, but did not speak. Cecil was only hanging about to learn what lay between the two of them, himself and Blount. A sudden clatter out in the courtyard drew him to the window. Cecil followed and together they gazed below.

A few of the Queen's gentlemen pensioners had ridden in a flurry among some men-at-arms, dicing on a heavy table. Table and all lay on their side, the men scrambling about, while the laughing riders swept off to the stables. It was the usual winter brawl, nothing more. A beautiful bay cantered into the yard. The freshly lit torches of the cressets glittered on the man's breastplate as he alighted. He flung his gauntlets at the horse boy's head and flicked the mare on her cheek. She tossed her head and he smiled, then puckered his lips in a whistle as he shouldered off through the indifferent crowd. Beneath the shallow arch he disappeared.

"Ralegh," observed Cecil.

"Pushing squire." Essex could not keep it back. He had to say it. It was Ralegh who only a few months back had dealt him the well-nigh mortal blow. Pulling a slight rent between Gloriana and her favorite, he carried the tale, and Essex was suddenly facing ruin. It had taken some quick dodging to miss the stroke. Ah yes, Ralegh stood high on his list of hated enemies, second only to the Cecils.

"I note that few speak to her Majesty's captain," said Cecil meanly. "It seems he is not popular at Court." He paused. "It takes a belted earl to catch people's fancy."

Aye, thought Essex, not a lousy knave without a castle to his name. But this time he was silent.

Cecil turned away. "I must leave you, my lord." Then just short of the door he paused. His quiet words fell exactly on the still air. "By the way, I hear there is talk of sending Ralegh to Ireland." The door closed behind him.

Ireland! Ralegh to Ireland! The long-necked skipjack to wear the livery of her Majesty's Lord-lieutenant!

"No," he muttered against the window. "She'd never do that."

Still, worse men than Ralegh had gone to that Irish grave. Perhaps the perils of the accursed land were not too good for this soldier in fancy armor. His own thoughts broke—soldiering! What had become of all his own high hopes of glory in the foreign field? He was now Essex, silken dandy, matcher of wits with small, black schemers, beating against the bulwark that was Burghley.

Once more he became aware of the bustle below. A young ostler skillfully gentled a horse as it shied and whinnied past a glowing brazier of sea coal. Essex watched, his heart warming to man and beast. The simple life—that was it—he had really never wanted anything else. A rough young ostler, a stable hand, forsooth, led a better life than Essex, gilded darling of Elizabeth Tudor's Court. Envy of the young fellow swelled his heart as he watched him through the gateway.

Depression flowed over him and deep under this was the tiny prick of nerves, a warning voice against he knew not what. How much higher dare he climb before he feared to look down, lest at the height he become giddy and fall screaming to his ruin? With a guilty twinge he remembered his feelings as he escorted the Queen to church.

He considered his rise, pointed out as the meteoric triumph of the age. Knighted at Zutphen after glory in the Low Countries, then the Garter, and Master of the Queen's Horse, at fifteen hundred pounds the year. So had the great Dudley begun *his* career—and where was he now? Forgotten, in a molding grave. Now, richest prize of all, was Gloriana's present of the farm of the sweet wines, as she filled with a generous hand his coffers, gilding the sign of her favor with real gold. For the sweet wines revenue he was thankful, held as he was beneath the dead weight of his debts. All this was dangerous enough, he knew, and in the fertile soil of his fortune his enemies flourished. He was nearly at the top—from whence there was no move—save down.

Again the door opened and this time a girl's head came round the panel. He turned. Ah, chestnut hair and bold blue eyes—Katherine Fytton. Only Kat would come opening doors and poking about for sight of a man.

"I was sure I would find Charles Blount with your lordship." The husky voice was petulant. "I have a message for him."

Essex turned back to the window. He was feeling rude and petulant too, and Christ's blood, the world was a-dust with girls. Katherine came in and closed the door firmly behind her. She was not looking for Blount; she had found the man she sought.

"Lord, does that fire like me!" Shivering, she made for it, dropped on her knees, holding out her hands with the long rosy nails. Under lowered brows, he watched her. The firelight caught in her hair, softly glowed on the swelling bare breast and white neck. Over her shoulder she smiled. " 'Tis turned to a foul day, my lord."

Still he preserved silence. He must be careful of this chestnut filly. She was not like all the others, willing to spend an hour with him in a dark room, and then forget it. He had tried them all, redhead, blonde, black-haired beauties, all eager and palpitating to his strong caress. He knew Gloriana shut her eyes, for was she not her father's daughter, who knew that a man had his burning hours, and what was a girl in a closet, more or less? But this one was different. She would clutch and hold—to keep. He would take care.

She crouched by the fire, an assured red smile on her lips. Aware of his narrow watching, she held up an arm to fasten a bracelet.

"Art struck dumb, my lord?"

"What brought you, Katherine?"

"I told you. I was looking for Charles Blount."

Two of them after Blount. Had the Queen . . . ? "What did you want with Blount?"

She tossed her head and laughed tormentingly, throwing up her chin and showing the scarlet tip of her tongue.

"What with Blount?" he repeated.

Her laugh was shrill. "My lord of Essex! Jealous of a poor girl, for whom you care naught——"

He was at her side. His iron hands grasped her shoulders as he dragged her up. For a second he shook her wildly, then his fingers closed loosely round her throat and slid down the bare flesh inside the low neck of her bodice.

"Chestnut baggage! Jealous, is it?" His teeth now gently pinching the creamy skin, he mumbled against her neck. "Why, in God's name, should I be jealous? If I wanted you, I should take you. Be merry with that, my wench."

He pushed her away. Panting a little as her blue eyes snapped, she kept her temper. She caught up her curly hair, sank on the hearth, and picked up her jeweled combs. Then she smiled. "I think, my lord," she said coolly, "you would not take me—unwilling."

A step sounded in the corridor, came closer. Katherine's eyes narrowed as she froze, the comb in her wary hand. The sounds died and she sighed. She finished her hair, hooked her bodice, and rose to her feet.

A clock in the courtyard struck six. "Ah, God! I'm on duty in the tiring room. Fare you well, my lord." In a heady flash of musk and heliotrope, she was gone.

He hardly felt her go. His mind was still busy with Blount—and Ralegh. Ralegh was his avowed enemy, and now, was Blount to be among them? More words like those of this afternoon, and they would be fighting. Even if dueling were not forbidden to the Queen's young men, he could not fight his sister's lover.

Suddenly he started away from the window. He would lay these doubts at once. He would find out if the Queen had sent for Blount. And at the same time he would relieve his mind about Ralegh. He went out into the long silent corridor, up shallow flights of back stairs, down a wider hall to the Queen's apartments. His steps rang on the stone flags, lost in the sharp grounding of the halberds. With the flat of his hand he pushed open the door and came face to face with Ralegh standing negligently outside the Presence Chamber.

For a moment the two stared at each other, then Ralegh raised a comic eyebrow.

"The white and silver knight himself! And in such—unseemly haste." He ran his eye over Essex's collar which hung open, his jeweled order dangling all askew.

"Announce me." Essex was short.

"Her Majesty may not be disposed—" drawled Ralegh.

"I will be judge of that." Essex took a step forward. "Announce me or——"

"Prithee!" A quick burlesque of fear flashed over Ralegh. "Prithee, upset me not. I am on duty, good milord."

Essex flushed. "To the devil with you for an insolent varlet. Do you mean that I should strike you from my path?"

Ralegh's grin set into a sneer. Their faces were a scant ten inches apart. Essex raised his hand, and in a trice Ralegh had slipped his silver halberd across the door. They measured each other with flaming eyes and panted a little. The door behind them opened. Mary Ratcliffe came out and narrowly missed striking her white forehead against the shaft of Ralegh's weapon.

"What's amiss here, gentlemen?" as she put aside the pole. "Has my lord of Essex threatened you, Sir Walter, that you must brawl it outside the Queen's door? Fie, for shame, the two of you!"

Both men softened as they looked at her. Gone for the moment was their feud. A pretty picture she made in her smoky blue velvet and thick white lace. The torchlight made a little glory of her fair hair.

"Sweetheart, announce me to her Grace. I have urgent need of speech with her."

Ralegh's dry laugh jabbed the quiet. Essex turned quickly; in a moment the air was tense again, but Mary was quicker.

"Announce you to the Queen? Like that, milord?" She giggled and flicked open the hanging collar and he flushed and fumbled with the buttons. "Here, let be. I will do it." She stood on tiptoe and quickly did it up for him, slinging his pendant into place and anchoring the V of the ribband under a pearl button.

"You're a pretty thing, Mary," he whispered. Lightly he touched her round breast with his forefinger. Mary looked up and smiled.

"She's about to dress for supper, my lord, but I think she will see you. Please don't tire her, though."

She turned and he followed. With a wry smile Ralegh watched them go, then grounded his halberd viciously between his feet.

Elizabeth was standing by the fire, one shoe pressing into a low hassock. Her fiery wig was undimmed by the velvet and ermine splendor of her dressing gown.

"The Earl of Essex, Madam," murmured Mary, and left them.

"How now, Robin!" she called in her high voice. "Still lolloping in your cathedral clothes? Aren't ye cold, lad? Come here, to the fire."

They stood opposite each other, scarlet and white, lambent in the fire and candle glow.

She held out her hand, and he dropped to his knees. She did not care to know what had brought him to interrupt her dressing. It was enough to have him here, at her feet, where he belonged.

Softly he kissed her fingers. "It is never cold where you are, my Queen and my lady."

"Pretty words."

She seemed to have difficulty with her breathing and pressed her hand to her side. She tipped his chin into her palm and her searching eyes were bright with love.

"If only all my men would talk to me thus."

"That, your Grace, adoring you as I do, I could not endure." His

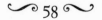

58

clear gaze was candid. "Though all the world worship you, as why should they not, only I would talk to you—thus." The deep whisper was a caress that left her tingling.

She stroked his cheeks and with a fingertip traced the light line of his brows. "Why are you so heartbreakingly sweet, my Robin?" She sighed reminiscently. "I remember the first time I saw you. Your father, a fine tall man, brought you to me. God's death, was it twelve years ago? How time flies, at my—" she bit back the word.

"You were dressed in light green velvet; some woman's loving care, no doubt. Your father presented you to me, and I was enchanted. I meant to kiss you, and you——" she pulled a short curl gently, "you flushed and ducked away. I pretended to be highly angry, but secretly I thought you were bonny." She laughed. "You do not duck now, my Robin."

She sank into her chair. "Sit here beside me for a moment, and then I must send you away. Tell me, why did you come?"

But he felt that suddenly it did not matter why he had come. What had Ralegh's sordid little affairs to do with them? Or Blount's? He laid his lips to her hand. No elderly woman, this, but an exciting goddess, moving in a mysterious atmosphere of romance and passionate color. How thrilling to be so near to her who held in her pale, clever hands this intoxicating power!

"My beloved," he murmured, "I could not stay away so long. Out of your presence I starve and languish."

At the extravagant words she glowed. Then she smiled. Where had she heard the very like before? Leicester! She sat bolt upright. "My God, Leicester! I was going to say a prayer for him in the church, Robin."

Privately she shuddered. Was it possible that the man who for so many years had been her favorite, on whom her doting affections were entirely fixed, could have slipped so utterly from her mind? And he but a few months in his grave. The thought was frightening. It meant that old things were passing away, and worst of all, it meant that she was getting old.

Seated on the hassock, Essex stirred uneasily. At the mention of his stepfather, he was embarrassed. Dudley it was who had forced on him the part of pawn in the game of political chess, and for this, more than anything, he despised Dudley. He was glad the man was dead. He would lead the Queen onto another subject. He decided, after all, to speak of Ralegh.

"Is it true, your Grace, that Ralegh is being considered for Ireland?"

In the shadows Elizabeth's eyes grew keen as hawk's. "And who has been saying that?"

"I—have heard it, your Grace."

Elizabeth pulled his ear. "I, too, have heard something of the same. Fear not; when I make Ralegh my Lord Deputy, I will ride naked through Cheapside. Claim it of me."

So much for Ralegh.

"Long before he died, Leicester warned me against such a move. Heigh-ho! Many's the merry time we had together, and all the world wondering why we did not marry. Well, *he* settled that, with Amy Robsart, and then your mother. Robin, you had no love for your step-father, did you?" Her hand played softly in the curls above his ear.

"I loved my father," he said quietly.

How could he speak to her of his hate, who had poured over Leicester the same bright warmth that now was his? Ah, but he would play his cards better than Dudley. He might even climb to a seat beside the goddess herself. He gave her a sidelong look, fearful lest she read his thoughts. But she was smiling to herself, and there was strange mischief in her smile.

"You're a bonny lad, Robin, and you've a silver tongue in your head. Tell me, I have seen you with my maids, Mary Ratcliffe and Katherine Fytton, do you use it on them? I sense some practice in your flatteries." With her hand she smothered his hot answer. "No, never mind." Her lip lifted. "You'd have to say 'No' because I am the Queen. Is it not so?"

She threw his face from her and rose. Regal and nervous, she swept across the floor. In three strides he was after her. He seized her by her narrow back, he swung her round, and now his hand was on her bosom.

"You are my beloved mistress. Could I lie to you?" His gaze compelled her. "Could I?"

He slid his hand inside her bodice and crushed her to him. Together they stood, mingled scarlet and white, loving protagonists in a desperate game. For a moment, under his insistent stare, her eyes widened as if they saw something beyond his love that frightened her. Then his lips were hard upon her painted mouth.

For both of them the world shook, then settled slowly into stillness. The masterful arms of young Essex embraced a Queen; a woman quivered on the breast of her beloved. Gone were petty fears and vexations; together they stood, ah God, together, in the perfumed dusk of a Queen's private chamber.

He ran his lips softly down one white cheek. Gently now he dropped a kiss under her ear.

"My goddess."

"My beloved."

9

A Rival

*D*own to supper she swept, in gold banded with sable. Down, down, into the blazing color and warmth that was Somerset House, decked for a Queen's great day. The bitter night outside was for halberdiers, shivering silver sentries under frosty torches; inside all should be light and warmth.

She waved a hand. "There's a draft on my ankles. Find it."

She coughed. A tall, old-fashioned figure in a long black velvet houppelande, came forward. Dr. Roderigo Lopez, her Portuguese physician, held a small cup in his yellow hand. "Majestee," after seventeen years in her country, he had still his accent, "will it please your Grace to try this cordial? It is both useful and pleasant."

"Hum!" She sipped and smacked her lips thoughtfully together. "Vile! 'Tis neither useful nor pleasant, for I am as hoarse as before and the stuff has a sickly taste. It likes me not." She thrust the cup at him and turned away.

She sniffed the savory odors that filled the warm air. "Scotch collards, if I mistake not. Has Pilchard the wit to cook me some tonight?" She loved the little delectable morsels of flesh, roasted on skewers and served with mushrooms. Again she sniffed. "Ha! Unless I am mistaken, there is eel broth in the wind. How my stepmother, Anne, doted on eels! A good Flemish cook, my Dutch stepmother. Pity my kitchen knaves are not so nimble. All show and no flavor!"

She grinned round at them all, then led them, fainting, into the banquet hall. Graciously she bowed to Monsieur de Chouart, five years at her Court, his nose still superciliously in the air at Tudor magnificence. Her maids, a pink cloud at her back; her beautiful hall festooned with evergreen looped about the scarlet and gold shields quartered with her arms; great fireplaces to throw a ruddy glow on jewel and velvet; and the candles, bunched in glittering bouquets on the walls, burning steadily with their hundred tongues of flame; all this was splendor, and the French Ambassador should admit it, by heaven.

Dinner over, she singled him out. "Ah, monsieur," she called, "have we shown you anything marvelous today?"

Now! Let him acknowledge her four hundred knights, her yeomen and her ladies in velvet and lace. Let him speak respectful awe of her fifty princes of the Church, sublime in ecclesiastical dignity.

"Well, monsieur?" with a proud smile.

As if in ecstasy, the Frenchman closed narrow eyes. *"Mais, oui, majesté, c'était un spectacle merveilleux, comme les nuptials du dauphin——"*

She flinched, stiffened—what was the frog saying? Her plucked red brows rushed together over the high bridge of her nose.

"Dauphin? What Dauphin?" She knew very well whom the French Ambassador meant, but she was not going to acknowledge the dead French husband of whey-faced Mary Stuart. *That* one had so many husbands that the sorting of them out was a task! And now she, too, was dead, and the thought of English steel upon that small neck was disquieting.

She turned a pettish shoulder, but not before she had caught the faint smile on the Frenchman's lips as he bowed away. She resolved to send him home as soon as Burghley could concoct the letter.

In the shadow of the dais stood Frances Walsingham, Sidney's dark-eyed widow. Demure and shy, she was only lately returned to Court, out of mourning seclusion for her noble husband. Essex caught her eye and winked. Elizabeth saw. Unaware of the scrutiny of his mistress, Essex looked fixedly at Frances. He was attracted by her grave beauty in the gray half-mourning. She bore herself well; indefinable marks of breeding were in the pale face and quiet hands.

Elizabeth tossed her head, nodded to the musicians, and gave her hand to Blount. After a moment's hesitation Essex crossed to Frances, who greeted him with a delicate lifting of brows. He bowed and offered his hand. Her rosy flush delighted him. She placed a hand like a snowflake on his arm, and they stepped to the middle of the room.

The dance over, Elizabeth summoned her.

"My lady Sidney," her loud voice was lost on none. "It is a scant two years since my lord, your late husband, entered his tomb. Strange that his widow could so soon forget him in thus disporting herself."

Frances gasped. Mourning periods at this Court were short, since Elizabeth disliked being reminded of the unpleasant facts of mortal life. Hers had been unusually long. For a whole year she had worn her cypress, seeing no man alone, truly mourning her noble friend and husband. For another year she had kept to herself, entering the world now only on her mother's urging.

Under level brows she looked at the Queen. What she saw was terrible and for a moment her spirit quailed. Then she remembered that she was, indeed, Sidney's widow. Her chin went up.

"Your Grace," she countered clearly, "my late lamented husband was a man of happy humor. I scarcely think, if your Grace will forgive me, that he would wish me to sink myself in sadness forever."

Down the spine of Essex a tiny thrill crawled. Devil take it, the girl had spirit, and she expressed herself well. It would do her no good, poor lass. Gloriana swooped, a fierce hawk dropping like stone on the gentle dove.

"Nevertheless, we consider it unseemly and a bad example to our Court. I recommend that you retire to your father's house. He is, I hear, ailing."

Frances bit her lip and withdrew.

"And now, Robin," said Gloriana, turning with brittle gaiety, "we shall see which one will tire first, you or I."

He bowed and led her to the dance.

Swords in hand, Blount and Essex faced each other in the great shadowy hall. This was earnest now. The afternoon quarrel had flared again.

The evening done at last, the Court off to bed, the two brushed elbows. Now the golden pawn hung in the open, for all to see. Essex caught the flash and his pent-up irritation boiled over. A drawling word, Blount's instant retort, and their daggers were bared. But someone snatched a pair of rapiers from the wall and a few eager hands cleared the space as the two squared back for the clash.

Lips tight drawn, eyes set and wary, their muscles tensed, they might have been the deadliest of hereditary enemies, instead of two friends, ruffled to the point of violence. They crouched, and Essex struck. Blount parried; his was the stronger wrist, steel, like his blade, flexible as the controlling brain. His point flicked forward, but Essex was quicker. Blind with anger, the two aimed automatically for the breast. The handful of watchers did not breathe. The two beat about, then Essex, back to the stairs, sprang lightly onto the rise.

"Holy God!" Rounding the top of the staircase, Katherine Fytton saw them and screamed.

Essex started, turned slightly, and stepped aside too late to avoid Blount's point, which caught him above the knee. He staggered a little and crimson dyed his silk. Blount's wet point drooped to the floor and he turned paler than Essex. Robert panted a little and clenched his teeth against exquisite pain. The stroke had severed a muscle.

As they carried him off he saw his friend's rueful face, and somehow he found strength to laugh, for there was no anger now. What a pair of fools they were!

Into the foggy morning air the Queen's maids stepped and crossed the courtyard to the river steps. The wind had died and a thick mist rolled in off the river. Drawn up to the steps was the royal barge, its slim pennants limply dangling against their poles in the dull atmosphere, the watermen standing among their little forest of upended oars, stiff at attention.

Now that the festivities were over and majesty had done its duty by the London public, Gloriana could indulge herself in more congenial surroundings. They were off for the country. A small consequential knot of gentlemen hovered about the landing and with them Derby, the Lord Butler, looking as if he had not slept, eyes red-rimmed and his nose a cold blob on the bleak façade of his face.

In clammy silver Ralegh and his men stood beside a chilly crowd of ladies and their men, muffled to the eyes, the gentlemen softly stamping the cold out of their feet. Here and there moved the gallants, their gaudy plumage somewhat draggled in the morning mist. In the warm light of last night they strutted, colored cockerels, but this morning they presented a subdued sight, spirits low and a bit of the sparkle rubbed off.

"Way there! Way for my lord's litter!" A closed stretcher, curtains drawn, now appeared, borne on stout shoulders, fellows whose breath flew in short, panting puffs. Half running, they disappeared onto a lower landing where a barge waited, flying the Essex colors.

"Who's that?" Mary Ratcliffe craned her neck.

"Sh!" snapped Katherine Fytton, her pretty face sullen. "Here she comes."

Gloriana was in a vile temper. She came down the steps, her long greyhound nose elevated, walking with a slight limp. Her ulcer was bothering her.

She stopped. "Where is Essex?" Silence. Her nostrils flared angrily. "Well?" De Vere knelt on the slimy stones. "Well? It's a mortal cold morning to keep a body waiting."

"Madam, there has been a slight accident," De Vere apologized.

"What? Accident? Come to the point."

"Your Majesty, after your Grace retired, the Earl and Blount— they—" Vere threw out his hands, "they had words."

"Words? What words?"

"Your Majesty's favor, the little gold chess piece that Blount wears— my lord resented—high words—and early this morning—they—er— had it out."

"Are you trying to tell me that two of my gentlemen fought? After what I have said? God's death! I will have no brawling here. Where are they?"

With difficulty Vere suppressed a grin. "The Earl, Madam, has retired to his house. His litter has just left."

"Where'd he get it? In the neck?"

"I regret to say, Madam, that the Earl was slightly wounded in the left knee. A mere trifle. He craves your Majesty's pardon."

"Humph! Let's hope it won't mar his dancing. Send my physician to him, and when he is mended, let me know. As for Blount," she looked around, "he is commanded to keep his house."

She grabbed fiercely at Derby's outstretched arm and stalked down the water steps. "Dueling," she muttered, "what's the world coming to?"

Behind her warm curtains she settled herself and clasped her filagree ball of hot coals to her stomach. The heat comforted her and she leaned back. Privately she was delighted. Two of her gallants dueling, and over her. She would see they redressed their difference, and she herself would give them a good going-over. But—a duel—and her two pets, the handsomest of her young cocks! By God, the news should run across the Channel to the French Court, where Catherine de Medici should hear that a duel had been fought over the Queen of England.

She did not think at this moment of Essex. And he, groaning in painful discomfort, did not think of her. He thought only of himself and he cursed his foolhardy heat. The small flurry and the subduing wound had quite purged his temper, and now there was left only regret.

He honestly wondered, as he lay on his bed, where his fortune lay. If here, in silken elegance, then he must play the part better than this. If Gloriana wanted her golden courtier, he would set his mind to the task. He would say good-by to youth and its small follies; this sort of thing belonged to them.

And if he played his part properly, she might find other uses for his sword. Meanwhile there was the business of getting well, and the patching of the rift between himself and Blount.

Part Two

COURTIER

1590-1595

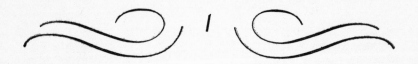

Marriage of a Favorite

*L*ying on his bed, Robert thought constantly of the dark eyes of Frances Sidney. As soon as he was partially recovered, he presented himself at Walsingham House. There, amidst dark paneling, shyly she received him.

He was charmed. Under flickering candlelight she played to him, while in the shadows he lounged, watching her. The satin ribbands of her lute lay lightly against her cheek, velvet soft. Her body, slightly ripened with the two children Sidney had given her, swayed erect, slender, infinitely patrician. As he watched, little nervous tremors shot through him; he thought she was everything he most desired in a woman. But though she made his pulses quicken, there was no having her outside the marriage vow, that he knew. As to that, why should he not marry her?

Frances lifted her eyes from her lute strings and smiled at him. The blood rose in his face. He swept lute and cushions aside and seized her. At arm's length she held him off, but gently.

"Sweetheart, marry me."

"Yes," the word was smothered beneath his kiss.

Did he vow eternal devotion? She did not think of that. Madly in love, she was eager as he to rush into marriage. No need to wait. Indeed, better to hurry it up, the quicker to get the storm over.

"I flatter myself that the Queen will not receive the news unmoved." He grinned at his betrothed. But to his mother and Penelope he confided, "The Queen's rage is a compliment I would fain forego."

Lady Leicester said nothing, but her eyes sparkled maliciously. If Robert could give Gloriana the long-overdue lesson that a man must live out his life in his own way, so much the better.

Arrangements went quickly forward, and on a midnight early in the New Year he and Frances knelt in the small chapel of Walsingham House and were married. The light from altar candles bathed their bent figures, tall bridegroom and bride, slender in a dove-colored gown. The nervous bishop botched the service, now and then glancing apprehensively over his shoulder as he proceeded.

Smiling behind her fan, Lady Leicester stood and enjoyed the thought of Gloriana's rage. Nearly as much she enjoyed the sight of the bishop's discomfiture. He looked as if he feared a long white hand reaching from the shadows to strike him down. With satisfaction she regarded the bridal couple. The narrow back of her new daughter-in-law pleased her; Robert had chosen well.

Penelope Rich also stood in the shadows, holding hands with Blount. Her eyes were on her brother, but Blount's were on her. She pulled her scarf over her yellow hair and turned to him with her slow smile. Sighing, he drew her closer.

Tall and somber, Lady Walsingham, the bride's mother, watched the ceremony, and her gray eyes were bright with the tears that fell onto her black weeds. All too soon upon the heels of death, into this Puritan house of mourning, had come the sweet bustle of the marriage. But young people had better marry than burn. Still, it was a perilous match for a beloved only daughter to make with this handsome Devereux. She too sighed.

And so the furtive, half-frightened affair was concluded. England's favorite and his bride were bundled off into the country, and the news of the marriage trickled quietly into the eddying stream about the Court. Away in the green country the wedded pair stayed, Frances blind with happiness, Essex keeping a wary eye on the post. The Queen came down to Richmond and the two, husband and wife of a month, fled back to Essex House. The weeks there slid by and there was no news. Was it possible she didn't know?

Then one day a messenger rode in with a letter from the Queen's secretary. Essex snatched it open and sank upon the window seat of his study, drawn into the fine spidery web of Cecil's script. To the end he read of Gloriana's rage, undiminished by Cecil, right to the final bit.

. . . and so I trust, my lord, that being of a worthy disposition to her Grace's pleasure, you will put it about to amend without delay this rash and temerarious attachment. . . .

Amend the attachment! Then the Queen actually expected him to put Frances aside, undivorced but unacknowledged, placing her in the wretched anomalous position endured by wives of favorites. And . . . if he refused?

From across the dining table in their private cabinet he faced his wife. In his pocket was Cecil's letter. To his happiness and well-being it administered a severe check. He had seen what a furious Elizabeth could do, especially to those who had shared her loves. He looked at his bride and considered.

As for Frances, she was still overwhelmed by her marriage. Hardly over her excitement at being Lady Essex, she was whisked to this great town house with its dizzy bustle, so unlike her quiet widowed state at Walsingham. Here there was no rest, no chance to become decently acquainted with the man she had married. She lived in a world of crumpled bridal finery, in which she saw her husband only in bed.

Couriers were coming and going at all hours. The secretaries, Reynolds, Wootton, and Cuffe, seemed never to sleep. She had no idea of how many rooms divided this Gothic pile of which she suddenly was mistress, nor how many people lived under their roof, serving her husband and eating at his expense. Although they had been married near two months now, she had had less than a dozen meals alone with her husband. Well, they were together now. But now they sat silent, too silent.

Idly she reached out and took a tangerine. "Henry Cuffe says there are letters from Richmond." She started to peel the fruit. Every morning she wakened with the same frightened feeling, every night she went to bed with it. *What will she say when she knows?* Both of them lived with this burning matter which they did not discuss, a matter which lay acutely between them. If there were letters from Richmond . . .

Essex frowned. He wished Cuffe would keep his mouth shut. "Yes, Fran. She knows."

Frances went a little pale round the mouth. "What did she say?"

"Oh, the devil's in it. She's furious. It's my stepfather's business all over again."

Ah, yes, when Leicester married Robin's mother, there had been a fearful scene. "Who told her?"

He laughed bitterly. "They got the little hunchback to do the job. I fancy he did it rather well." He slipped his hand into his pocket and felt the letter. Mentally he rehearsed the precise phrases. Between them he could read all too well those things the Master Secretary did not say. How speak of the heaving bosom of fury, the crashing of crystal decanters, the fishwife oaths? He could imagine, and as he mused, he sank into a brown study.

Frances put down the fruit and looked earnestly at him. How she loved him! In his arms, for the first time, she had lost the lonely regret of Sidney's death. Home from Zutphen she brought dead Sidney, the laurel wreath resting on his cold heart. Hers was frozen too, but Robert had warmed it. New, beautiful warmth, born in the beloved embrace, had brought her back to life. Now she was shivering, clutched in cold fear.

"Wouldn't it have been wiser to send one of your own friends, Robert, someone to put the case more—sympathetically?"

Essex shrugged. *He* had not chosen the messenger. He stared moodily at the dinner service, chin sunk on his hands. Between the eyes of Frances crept a questioning crease.

"Robin?"

Without looking up he reached across and patted her hand. "She's so infernally unreasonable," he complained.

"Robin." Now he raised his head and looked at her. "I don't regret it, do you?" she said.

His eyes dropped to the tablecloth. "N-no."

A wild pain shot through her. So he *did* regret it. Delirious days were soon forgotten and the delicious secret of their marriage now sank to a tiresome necessity. She struggled to keep her voice even.

"What are you going to do?"

There were two things she knew he could do. He could return to Court and brazen it out, forcing the Queen to accept in her offhand way the fact that her favorite was married. Or he could retire to Wanstead and live the life of a country squire. She drew a long breath. Life in the country with Robert could be exquisite. They could travel when the quiet life palled. Their children would grow up with her own little Elizabeth Sidney. Wistfully she gazed at him, holding her breath for his answer.

"Do? How can I say? I cannot return to Court until I put you away." At her stricken look he went on to add hastily, "But that I shall never do."

She leaned limply back against the high carving of her chair. So that was it. She was to be buried in the country, bearing children to a phantom husband, whose visits would be hastily snatched delights haunted by uneasiness. Her lips felt numb but she forced herself to remain calm.

"Perhaps it would be better if I—retired for a little while." At his sudden jump her heart sank.

"Sweetheart, it would be for only the shortest space of time, that I swear. Just—till I can bring her round."

The room was very still. A large fly buzzed against the windowpane and went humming off to light on a tapestry on the opposite wall. Watching it, she followed the embroidery of a little bunch of flowers in the slender hand of one of the needlework ladies. Her eye went round the delicate cup of the flower, down the stem, round the pointed leaf, and back up the stem again.

She heard her own voice saying, "If that is what you wish, Robin."

Oh, why was he so charming, and why had she given in so easily to his charm? She feared the terrible circumstantial hold that Elizabeth's power gave her over young ambitious men. She ached with exasperation at her husband that he was not man enough to break that hold.

Through a fog of pain she heard him, "Let me do things in my own way, darling. I'm sure I can work well to our fortune."

Already he was over his initial anger at the Queen, that she saw. And now he was thinking, not of their love, but of their fortune, *his* fortune. She had married a man who was in love, but not with her; he was in love with success. How far would he go to achieve his goal?

She rose. Eager now in courtesy, he rose too and came toward her with open arms. She went into them. Under her cheek she felt the thudding in his chest. Oh, he *must* love her, he must! But how reconcile this love with the other? Something womanish in her made her say, "Are you relieved that I didn't make a fuss?" He should see that she was different from that tempestuous termagent down at Richmond.

"You make a fuss?" He tilted her chin up. "You couldn't make a fuss. You are my gentle little sweet and I adore you, beloved."

Helpless now, she let herself be drawn into the sweet mesh . . . his urgent hands were at her throat.

Kneeling on the window seat, she watched him ride away, his man Joseph following. Joseph Thorn was a small, crooked figure, always at her husband's shoulder, a devoted shadow both abroad and at home. Watching his dogged progress after Robin, she felt no jealousy, only envy. If only she could put on breeches and ride with him, even into battle. He turned to wave his plumed hat . . . he was gone.

She sank back against the wall. Her bodice gaped open and her smooth hair fell from its pins. Her lips burned from his kisses. So this was what it was like to be married to a Devereux. Now he had gone down to Twickenham to see Francis Bacon, to pick those wily brains in planning his campaign of return to Court. It might be weeks before she laid eyes on him again. Mechanically she tidied herself.

To his suggestion that she go down to Wanstead she replied quickly, "No, Robin. I'll bide here in London with my mother."

She was not yet ready to face his family in her new role of discarded wife. Crookedly she smiled. How oddly things turned out! Married so young to Philip Sidney, he only a boy, in love with Penelope Rich. And now she was again a wife, this time to Penelope's brother. In some strange way her life was bound up with that of this woman with the witch's eyes and the moist red mouth. *She* would be down there with her lover, and their child, and she would gloat over Gloriana's newest victim. And there would be Robin's mother, too, with her sharp innuendoes, pouring them like salt on the new wound of her daughter-in-law. At thought of the Countess she quivered.

"I can really talk to you, my dear, She's stolen both our husbands."

No, dear God, she was not steeled to that as yet. She would go home and try to bury her trouble in comforting her mother.

"Mama, has Uncle Robin gone? Henry Wootton said he rode away out of the yard."

At the sound she jumped. Little Elizabeth Sidney stood in the open door, her clear child's voice breaking like a silver bell on Frances' gloom. Elizabeth came to the window and leaned against her mother. Frances drew her close and sniffed deeply of the silky warm curls. Elizabeth was her father's true child, with his blond beauty, with the poet's mouth and the eyes already at seven a little dreamy.

With an effort she roused herself. "Yes, Uncle Robin's gone. What have you been doing?" She wiped a speck off the small nose and smoothed back the fine yellow hair.

Elizabeth heaved a sigh of remembrance. Shuttlecock and sugared apples, prayers and letters said without a mistake, made up her small day. "And I did not get my shoes muddy, though it was ever so wet when we took our walk." She held out a tiny buckled foot.

Suddenly Frances decided to go to Penshurst. To see Elizabeth running in the strong breeze off the downs, her skirts and hair flying, seemed the most desirable thing in the world. The little girl was to have gone to her grandmother Sidney at the old family place, but Essex said easily, "Oh, let her stay with us." With a tightening of her pain she remembered that it was his tenderness to her child that first won her to him.

"Elizabeth, should you like to go to the country?"

"With you, Mama?"

"With me."

"And Uncle Robin?"

Without answering, Frances drew her close. "No, with me. Should you like it?"

Elizabeth pressed her hands together. "Oh, yes, Mama! Then, I should see the baby lambs!"

Frances smiled. It was what the seven-year-old Philip Sidney would have said. Like all the Sidneys, Elizabeth was gentle. With them there would be quietness and healing in the fields and dales of Penshurst. For one guilty moment she thought of her mother, alone and grieving in the great London house. Well, she would go to Walsingham later. But now—she shook the tear from her eye and sent little Elizabeth to fetch her nurse.

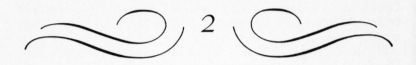

French Venture

The year 1590 had wasted to its end and once more it was November. People hugged their fires and in the shadow of the river bridges, children died of the cold. In the land across the icy channel, great Parma thundered down through Picardy with his Spanish troops, and another of Philip's armies entered Brittany.

Scurrying into London with letters from Henry of Navarre, the new French King, came Viscount Turenne. He delivered them to the Queen's Secretary and the French Ambassador, and put up at Essex House. Over tankards of mulled ale, he and the Earl, back at Court, his marriage partially forgiven, unofficially talked out the problem of English aid to France.

With the news that the Spaniards were swarming into Brittany, Elizabeth's nerves jumped. Essex watched her fly at Burghley.

"Why was I not informed that Philip was at our gates? Is England to be sold to the Spaniard while old men sit on their backsides at the Council table and pass laws regulating the sale of beeswax in country towns?"

Essex smothered a grin and Burghley sighed as he passed over his mistress' fantastic summary of the activities of her Privy Council. "Madam, his Excellency the French Ambassador has been waiting these three days to see your Grace."

"Christ's blood, what's to-do here? Is the Queen to be the last to be informed when someone desires audience for matters of import?" She gesticulated with the pomander she was sniffing. "Well, fetch him!"

Monseigneur came gravely in, his face carved into lines of worry. Essex knew he had seen Turenne and heard the worst. With him now he brought letters from the Prince de Dombes, the King's general, begging for help.

Elizabeth gave her hand to be kissed, then snatched the letters. Rapidly she skimmed through the flowery French, then threw the papers onto the table.

"Your king, Monseigneur, where is he in this?" Apparently Henry of Navarre was ignorant of the fact that his general had appealed for aid. Elizabeth was amazed, and said so.

Monseigneur believed that his royal master would soon be sending letters of similar import to her Majesty. In the meantime . . . ?

"How near are these Spanish vultures to our shores?" asked Elizabeth sharply. No use getting excited if there were no immediate danger.

"Madam, Don Juan d'Aguilar landed last month with three thousand troops in Upper Brittany where he met the Catholic League Commander and they are now quartered at Hennebon."

"Hennebon?" She gestured and Burghley put a yellowed map into her hand. "Ah, Hennebon!"

A port, but a good seventy miles south on the peninsula. Essex leaned with her over the map. Still, it *was* a port and if the Spaniard were not watched—he tapped the coastline with a finger. "He could whip round the point there and come coasting along the Lizard to Plymouth," he said.

She looked up at the Frenchman. "You say they had to capture this Hennebon? There was hard fighting? Ah, then, they will lie there for the cold months." She moved away from the table. "We shall do what we can, Monseigneur, and in the meantime there is Sourdeac up at Brest. He is loyal to your king, he must hold this Don Juan de Grandioso till the spring."

The Frenchman sighed and took his departure. *Tiens,* these English! It was like moving Mont St. Michel itself to get them to make up their minds to anything.

In the room Elizabeth turned to Burghley. "Today is Tuesday, milord. Council meets tomorrow. You shall tell them that I favor aid to Navarre, but only when the need becomes acute." Then at last she turned to Essex with a grin. "It is time these French frogs learned that we English do not come running every time they croak."

The French dilemma fired Essex. He called on his friend Francis Bacon in his fine new house in the Strand. The table in Bacon's study was littered with papers, among them the fanciful new masque for Gloriana, but half done, and intended for the summer fetes. Essex propped his long legs against the stones of the fireplace and the flames of the sea coal burnished the wrinkled leather of his high boots. He slapped a glove against his thigh.

"Francis, I've the itch to see Rouen and get a whack at Parma."

Bacon regarded his friend with cold gray eyes. So Essex had the old bee in his bonnet, did he? Aloud he suggested, "And if you are killed, Robert?"

Essex laughed lightly. "My lady is breeding down at Wanstead. We expect an heir in the spring. There'll be another Devereux to guard the name."

Across Bacon's somber face flitted a slight smile. "And if it is not a son?"

"The women have consulted the astrologers. They guarantee a son." Essex bent to kick a hot ember into the fire. At the other's silence, he raised an inquiring brow. Superstition! "You and your advanced school. My beliefs are simpler. I have a wife and shall have a son."

"He that hath wife and child hath given hostages to fortune," said Bacon ironically. "But that's beside the point. So you are for Rouen and French Henry, are you? That's bad, Robert, bad."

Essex moved restlessly. "Man, I'm rotting here like a dead tree. I've got to have action."

"But not that way, not that way." In the Earl's desire to be gone, Bacon felt a shifting in his own fortunes. With Essex abroad or killed, his own chances for promotion were indeed slim. "I counsel you against going to France."

"What then?" demurred Essex.

"Your destiny lies here, Robert. It is your task to persuade the Queen that you are another Leicester or Hatton. Let those who do not matter do the fighting and the racketing about. Or, if you must go to foreign wars, let others command. In that way you are free to come and go as you please."

Impatiently Essex lunged to the other side of his chair. The level voice went on.

"Your genius is that of the courtier. You are at your best here at Court."

"A foppish peacock!"

"A royal favorite."

"Train bearer to a crusty old woman. She's old, getting older, full of megrims and intolerable whims. I've got to get away. I can't breathe."

Bacon's gaze narrowed. He studied the face before him, the adventurous hazel eye, the high brow, the slightly crooked nose that lent such charm to the countenance. He looked at the lips, full and chiseled, then at the chin, too soft for resolution or for aught but a stupid stubbornness. How persuade this hothead to stay where he might be of use?

He tried again. "Leave the scene of your greatest triumphs and you play into the hands of your enemies. Seek glory in the field and you ruin yourself at home."

"Why not glory when I return?" persisted Essex. "If I am successful in the field, the Queen will see that I am a force to be reckoned with, and will therefore accede the more readily to my wishes."

Bacon threw out a nervous hand. "That, Essex, is what you must *not* covet. The peculiar kind of fickle glory that springs here at home from military success is most dangerous for you. Win the adulation of the people to the Queen's hurt, and you destroy yourself."

Essex smiled. "That is a risk I am well prepared to take. If I win the people to me, I need fear naught. After all, the Queen is a woman, and the people tire of a female monarch. England needs a king. And besides," his eyes crinkled, "I have a friend in the North, a Scottish friend."

The scalp on Bacon's head crawled. So, it was out! Here, indeed, was a fool, who did not stop at the deadliest crime of all. As for himself, here, in his own house, to be made privy to such madness. He felt his lips suddenly cold.

"In God's name, Essex, watch your tongue!" He glanced hastily over his shoulder. "Most of my household I can trust, but there may be a prating knave . . ."

"Pish!" Essex laughed lightly again. "Fret not. I do not talk treason."

"Try proving that in Star Chamber."

"Star Chamber! Ha! Now do I perceive that you have been too long at your books. Man, where is your sense of humor? They'd never try the Queen's pet in the Chamber, no matter what he did. I am secure."

"Better heads than yours, my lord, have rolled on Tower Hill. I mind that a king's own uncle . . ."

"Somerset? Pooh, he needed beheading." He rose and stretched. "I'm off. Off to Court to get Gloriana's blessing and permission to try to kill myself." He grinned at his friend and left.

"Mad with pride and sure-footed on the brink of disaster," muttered Bacon, watching him go.

With the cold wintry weather there came a rise in Gloriana's spirits. She commanded concerts and masques at which her loud laughter rang out above all others. She feasted with her nobles and kept a sharp eye and a heavy hand on her maids. She celebrated Christmas with gusto and outdanced them all. She held audiences and rated Burghley so that he went grieved and quivering from her presence.

Christmas turned and the snow swirled past the windows of Greenwich. The Queen walked nervously about her private cabinet and behind her, Robert Cecil at his elbow, Burghley scratched at his everlasting papers. Down the hall, in another room, a gentleman of her Court pulled on fur-lined gloves, his face black with fury.

It was Essex. For two hours he had knelt before her, pleading to be sent with the four thousand men who were going to the aid of Navarre and his Huguenots. For two mortal hours the pair of wills contended, and hers, being a woman's, proved the more stubborn. At first Essex knelt on the soft rug to spare his bones, but as time passed, and she remained obdurate, he pressed his knees to the bare boards and never felt the hardness.

"I will not! I will not!" she shouted. "Do you never learn, Essex, that I do not intend you for foreign service? You are but a rash youth and to send you to that addlepated Navarre would be to court disaster. I tell you plainly that you waste time, so ask me no more!"

"So your Grace does not intend me for foreign service? Can it be that your Grace does not intend me for foreign glory?" he observed nastily.

"You impudent bellwether! How dare you!"

So he was beginning to think himself as high in the people's graces as their monarch, was he? Here was a forward cock whose comb needed cutting! She lifted her hand to strike him, then clenched it, and let it fall.

"Get out of my sight!"

He jumped to his feet, smothering his oath. With the smallest of bows, he withdrew and stamped to his own quarters. "To the devil and his dam with her," he muttered. "By God, it's time there were a man to wear the crown!"

He tore off the light doublet and called for riding clothes. He thrust his arms furiously into the sleeves and flung out his legs to Joseph for the boots. He pulled on his gloves and snatched up a cloak and hat.

Joseph was running bowlegged about. "Where be we going, master?"

"Wanstead, Joseph." He stuffed some papers into a square pouch. "Come on, stir your stumps. We don't draw rein till we get there, not though our bums freeze to the saddle."

Bidding his barber follow the next day and answer no questions to anyone, he and his servant stole away through a back entrance, alert lest they be stopped. Then out onto the river road, their horses' feet crunching the snow into hard little cakes that flew into the air as they raced off.

Frozen and blue with the bitter cold, they arrived at Wanstead Park to find Lady Essex and her maids putting up Twelfth Night greens in the great hall. A pretty sight the girls made, standing on stools, gracefully handling the long swathes of fir and bunches of gay red berries. The Earl stood in the doorway of a great carved screen and looked about for his wife. Frances was above in the minstrels' gallery, looping a swag of green about the wooden tracery. She was unaware of her husband's arrival.

Little Elizabeth Sidney saw him first. She was sitting on the hearthrug, her arm about the neck of Rafe the boarhound, who snoozed in the warmth. At sight of him she bounded up.

"Uncle Robin!"

He swung her into his arms, the hound barking in welcome ecstasy. Essex looked up into the pale face of Frances that appeared between the slender spikes of fretted oak. Her cry was lower than the child's, but as she turned to come down the stairs, her heart was in her eyes. She came slowly, her body heavy and unwieldy with its burden. He set down the child, and at sight of her drawn face, his heart contracted.

"Robin, my darling!"

"Sweetheart, you should not be up those slippery stairs. How are you, beloved?"

She could not speak, but turned her lips against his cold throat. She drew him to the fire and gave a rapid order for a hot drink. They sat looking at each other. Essex held Elizabeth on his knee, and he rubbed his still cold nose among the curls on her little nape till she shrieked and shuddered with delight. The noise brought in the Countess whose high voice broke in surprise at seeing him.

"I forbid you to rise," she said, as he kissed her hand. She spread her skirts into a chair. Despite three marriages and several children, the Countess of Essex and Leicester, now Lady Christopher Blount, was still beautiful, with her high color and her high breast. She chattered her amazement at seeing him from Court at the merry holiday season, holding up her hands and throwing back her head to show her pretty teeth. Into Frances' eyes came a look of fatigue.

"Well, lad Robin," his mother said at length, "and what have you done now?"

Elizabeth and her megrims were old knowledge in this family, where the men were constantly coming and going, in and out of her shadow. When they visited their homes, it was a sure sign they were in Gloriana's black books.

Essex laughed bitterly. "Why, Madam mother, I have merely asked her Grace's permission to go to France with the others."

"Robin." Frances made a small unhappy sound.

"Don't worry, Fran, it seems she has other plans for me."

His mother clicked her tongue. "You'll learn someday, my lad, that your Gloriana is a whip dog that holds fast. She's too much Harry Tudor's daughter to do otherwise." She poked the dog with the square tip of one shoe. "You'll jump when she calls and you'll lick that long white hand of hers and you'll like your servitude."

He held Elizabeth to him and rubbed his chin on her round silky head. "That I'll not, by God."

"Ah," insisted the Countess, showing her teeth like a white fox, "you think to stand up to her, do you?" She shook her head. "She's got you where she wants you, tied to that damned thin waist of hers, to be draggletailed wherever she likes."

Her green eyes, so like his, sparkled, but her chin was hard. Years of standing up to the Queen had taught her much, gained her but little. It took a stout heart to withstand the steely onslaughts of royal rivalry. If she could goad her son to finish what she had started, so much the better for all of them. Under the prodding, she saw him flush.

Frances, too, saw her husband's color rise. She could not know the thoughts that raced through the older woman's quick mind. She only thought it too bad of his mother to bait him when he came home so seldom. Why could they not be happy—from her chair she caught his eye and smiled wanly.

The Countess saw and was irritated. That girl! What Robin needed now was a good back-stiffener, not a drooping wife, pregnant, and no earthly good to him in bed or any other way. She rose to leave the hall.

"Stay here for a few weeks, then when she sends for you, go, but take your time. Let her know you fear her not. Remember!" With a vixenish look she left them.

For the next day or two he was moody and irritable. The severe hail and sleet kept him indoors and he found the hours spent with his ailing wife and young stepdaughter well-nigh intolerable. His mother, with her high chatter and sentimentous remarks, bored him. He read much, his favorite Tacitus and some parts of a new poem by his friend Edmund Spenser, sent to him in manuscript from Ireland. It was a sensuous nuptial hymn, and in the exquisite peal of bridal music, he forgot himself and his misfortunes.

He wrote letters to Francis Bacon and received one that threw him into a pet for twenty-four hours. Bacon with his cold opportunist philosophy—Bacon was as bad as Cecil. Both invited his disgust.

Then one evening when the wind had stopped and the long shadows of the leafless trees showed blue on the still snow, Charles Blount came riding into the yard, Penelope Rich at his side. She was mounted on her black and silver Spanish jennet, and she wore a green velvet habit and her sable hood. Out of this Christmas frame her golden hair and cold rosy cheeks were charming.

It was not until one saw the voluptuous black eyes that one remembered how the charms of Penelope Devereux had called up the unlawful passions of at least two men. First Sidney, then Blount, to say nothing of the husband whose coarse ardors she fled. Now, riding with Blount, she glowed. Any other young woman would have braved the winter in a coach, with charcoal heaters to keep cold from fingers and toes. Not Penelope. Her delicate beauty was a hardy flower that no wind could beat down, no hot sun destroy. Her constitution, like that of her mother, was resilient to the buffets of fate and weather.

Blount swung her from the saddle, and, lifting her habit daintily, she mounted the shallow steps into the house. Blount and Essex were firmer friends than ever. It seemed impossible that they had ever drawn steel against each other. Perhaps the black eyes of Penelope drew them close together. She kissed her mother and brother, bowed mockingly to her sister-in-law, and tweaked one of Elizabeth's curls. Then she glided to the chair nearest the fire, and threw off her hood. She leaned her yellow head against the high back and smiled slowly at the two young men.

"Tell him, silly."

Struggling with numb fingers, Blount unbuttoned the middle of his doublet and drew forth a letter.

"Ah!" said Essex's mother.

Frances leaned forward painfully. Essex took the letter, broke the wax, and shook it open. Then he gave a short laugh and tossed it over to the Countess. It seemed that Gloriana would agree to anything, only Robin, her rash, beloved fool, must return at once to her side.

That night Frances lay beside him and tried to smother her feeling of desolation. In two months her child would be born. Would he be able to come and see it? Before the memory of childbearing, the blood and the brutal tearing, her brave spirit quailed. The very sight and sound of a husband helped one through the worst of it. At the birth of Elizabeth, Sidney had been devoted; but when they tore her tiny dead son from her body, there was only the comfort of her mother. For then, Sidney was dead, too.

She listened to the faint snoring of her husband. Now that the dearest wish of the moment was about to be granted, he lay sleeping with a light heart. When would he leave for France—would the danger for him be great, she wondered. Men were so selfish, they exposed themselves so recklessly. She thought of the stupid, chivalrous death of Sidney. She had given one husband to England; she could not spare this one.

"Let him not be killed," she prayed.

Her back was aching and she turned clumsily in bed, carefully, so as not to disturb him.

In the gray of early morning they all stood in the cold hall to see the two young men off. The Countess urged Robert again to wait until the Twelfth Night fete was over at Wanstead, but he was all fire and impatience to be away.

She shook her powdery head at him. Never since her marriage to Leicester had she been close to this older son of hers. Walter, the younger, was soft and malleable to her counsels, but Robert was different, wild and heedless of destruction.

"You're too eager, Robin," she admonished.

He laughed and pinched her chin. "Madam, my mother, I shall have the Queen's patent for France before the week is out, and in proof, I shall send you all a present." He tossed Elizabeth, still in her night-rail, up into his arms, and set her down with a light smack on her small bottom. "Be a good lass, and Uncle Robin will send you a pretty for Twelfth Night."

He turned to Frances. She stood sideways and let her head droop against his shoulder. "Try to come again, Robin," she whispered.

Penelope came down the stairs in a trailing night robe of crimson satin. Her yellow curls hung on her shoulders, and her black eyes held a drowsy languor. The four watched her descend. Essex and the women knew that Blount had spent the night in her bed and she knew that they knew. She smiled sleepily at them and gave her soft hand to her brother.

"Give her the devil, Robin," she murmured. She put her hand to Blount's lips and gave him a gentle push toward the door.

"Go," she said. "I'll live till your return."

Next day at noon Essex stalked into Elizabeth's little paneled cabinet. He scarcely waited to be announced. Straight up to his royal mistress he strode and seized her in his arms. Through closed white teeth he grinned at her.

"So you couldn't do without me, is that it?"

"That is not it," began Elizabeth with asperity. Then their eyes met and she stared into the fascinating green depths. "So stubborn, so proud."

"Aye. Even as you are, my lady, stubborn, proud, but somehow glorious, my Gloriana." He pressed his lips to the velvet over her breast. "Whose kisses have you had in my absence?"

"None, you fool, none. There is only one kiss for me, and damn you, well you know it."

He laughed. Then he kissed her roundly and nibbled at her ear. "So you are letting me go to Henry, after all?"

She stiffened, then leaned limply back into his arms. "All right, all right, go, witless idiot, get yourself killed, and then see. Has that whey-faced girl presented you with a son yet?" She grasped a handful of hair at his temples. "Never mind! I'm not interested in breeding and bearing. Never was."

She tramped across the room, then whirled on him, hand at her hip. "Look at me, Essex! I tell you, England is my husband, and Burghley and the others are the midwives, and from me springs the greatness that is England's heritage. Do you see now why I have no time for lesser things?"

He stared at her, admiration curving his lips. What a magnificent creature! She was right. What time had she for lesser things? On his knees before her, he lifted her dress to his lips.

"You are marvelous, my Queen," came his husky whisper.

On the eve of Twelfth Night there came a messenger to Wanstead bearing gifts from the Earl for his family. In the box that was strapped to the saddle lay a tiny pair of blue satin shoes for Elizabeth Sidney, and a cameo set in fine pearls for her mother.

A letter to Frances closed with the following:

Sweetheart, I go to France, but when, only God knows.

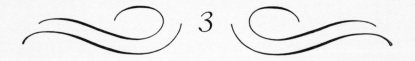

3

First Command

*I*t was not till June that a move was made to send the Earl to France. Two more excited months succeeded, with Essex dashing about, gathering romantic young men to his standard. Walter Devereux threw in his lot with them and went down to bid farewell to his family. As for Robert, he could not get away even to take leave of Frances, at Chartley now, with their baby son.

But the Queen found time to knight Robert Cecil, and Essex, his eye on Rouen, kept his temper.

Hot August dawned over England. Elizabeth set off to Cowdray in Sussex, to escape the plague and graciously to allow Lord Montague to spend a vast sum of money on her entertainment. Essex accompanied her on the first stage of the journey. Till early evening she bumped along the roads, Essex riding forward out of the dust of her coach wheels. She loved to travel through her country to see for herself the progress of life in the fair meadows and fruitful expanses. They passed fields of corn where reapers binding sheaves gaped at the royal cavalcade, and Elizabeth waved her hand to them from her coach and called a blessing on their labors.

Catching sight of a buxom farm wench with a great stone jar on her shoulder, she sent one of her pages to ask what was in it. Sweating and stumbling, the girl came barefooted up the hedge, face set in amazement at the silken splendor that suddenly had burst upon her.

"What have ye there, my girl?" shouted Elizabeth from her window.

The girl mumbled something, at which the page called out, "I think she says it is cider, your Grace, but truth to tell, 'tis hard for me to understand her noddle-pated talk."

"Hold thy tongue, poppet," ordered Elizabeth. "I'll have a dram. Good sweet cider is a treat here in the country."

They brought a pewter cup which the girl wiped out on her apron, then up-ended her jug and poured the Queen of England a draught of the clearest, sweetest cider in all Christendom, stone cold, and sparkling like wine.

Gloriana drank with relish. "More," she commanded. Then, "Try it, Robin. 'Twill comfort you." But Essex, lounging near his horse, refused the drink. His stomach was queazy, and he had his old trouble of head pains upon him.

Then the royal coach went on its way through the lanes and over the hills. They passed old abbeys that since Henry's time had been converted into rich manor-farms with great thatched barns and pastures for flocks of sheep. Elizabeth looked with love on the land; she almost forgot the proximity of Essex, riding in the dust at her wheel. It had indeed been a warm August and beneath its breath the landscape drowsed. Sussex at this time of year was almost as lovely as Surrey, she thought. She eyed the manors; not many of the old-fashioned half-timbered houses being built any more; everyone, lord and squire alike, favored the new red brick. She was proud of her country gentlemen, with their educated sons. Indulgently she smiled at the thought of these landed men, who now left borough and shire to flock into the Commons. They were feeling their power, all right. Always urging her to do something, this or that, marry—choose an heir—anything, good Lord, except raise taxes. Her smile widened to a grin and she fanned herself.

So on they went into the long English twilight that held until the Queen's entourage arrived at the bridge on the edge of Lord Montague's estate. A midsummer charm held the scene and the grass lay soft and languidly green under the beeches. There was the sweet smell of early hay in the air, and over the downs a little vagrant night breeze stirred.

It was here that Essex took his leave.

Framed in her crimson coach window, Elizabeth looked out from her summer splendor of quilted muslin sprigged and tied with green. Green satin was looped in her hair, and a light veil protected her white neck from the road dust. Regret sat in her eyes.

She laid a wrist on his hand. "It seems I am committed to a French war and I like it not. You are victualed for two months only, so remember it. Do what you have to do and come back to us."

She gave him a green stone to give to the King of France. "Tell his Majesty that the stone will endure so long as he break not faith with us."

Hat and gauntlet swinging from one hand, he bowed. The short ride had tired him, but he was alert and eager to be off. With a queer look in her black eyes, she dismissed him.

Tossing in the Channel, Essex had a moment of misgiving. Had he done right to fly in the face of Bacon's counsels and leave the home field to his enemies? He seized pen and wrote to Elizabeth:

> . . . if another in mine absence should rob me of your gracious and dearest favor, I were in his case, *qui mundum lucratus perdidit animam.**
> . . . I wish your Majesty's joys to be as infinite as your worth and my fortune to be as everlasting as my affection . . .

To this she replied: "Maintain your affection, my lord, and your fortune will follow."

He landed in France and news of his progress trickled back home. Facts, good and bad, well twisted with rumors, were skillfully woven by Cecil and the others into a strong net for catching him, should he prove unwary. His army, they said, sat down, awaiting the French King; he was piddling around instead of getting on with the job; he was finding difficulty in reaching Navarre; his army was eating its head off, and nothing done.

Most of this, unfortunately, was true. Then something occurred which sent Elizabeth into fresh rages. Essex accepted an invitation to go to the King, through dangerous country. Accompanied by his lancers and voluntary gentlemen, he headed for Compiègne. As for his army, it sat back on its heels and waited while its commander paraded in orange velvet before the round astonishment of the French.

---

* (One) who, gaining material elegance, loses his soul.

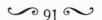

It was the velvet that infuriated Gloriana. "Tawny velvet!" she shouted. "By God's most precious death, what does he think this to be? A May Day fete? Bones of Christ! I send four thousand men to Normandy, and my general turns it into a rantipoling picnic!"

She sent for Robert Cecil. "Tell that cock-a-hooping fool that when two months are up I recall both him and his army. Bid him get on with the siege of Rouen and leave off practicing his pretty horsemanship. Tell him—here!" She snatched the pen and wrote:

> I have come here from Cowdray, where I lie hourly expecting news that you have found that sense which I did believe you to possess. In God's name, my lord, what does the French King that you are so tardy to perform that for which I sent you? Since you met his Majesty at Noyon, I have received nothing of your venture that could content me. Of late I have had no word from your hand. I do desire you to escort the French King to me here in Portsmouth where I may be assured of his good intent.
>
> Elizabeth R.

And this reached Essex at Arques where in his tent he lay, burning with fever. With it also, to salt the wound, came the half-dictated letter to Cecil. Groaning with the pain in his head, he dragged himself to his table to write of his sickness and grief at her harshness. He closed:

> . . . and as for me, I will not weary till my last hour, what wrong soever you do me. Your Majesty's servant, miserable by his loss, and afflicted with your unkindness.
>
> R. Essex

But a worse loss befell. Leading a skirmish before Rouen, Walter took a ball through the head. They carried the long corpse, a prone white shadow of the laughing fellow who had shouldered him as they sailed out of Plymouth, to his tent, and Essex, weak with fever, cried. The blood had been washed from the small hole in the side of the skull, and under the damascened breastplate they had put the captain's field uniform of white silk. At his feet lay his fine polished morion.

That night Essex sat long, gazing into the dead face. So ended Walter's life. Never too close, nonetheless they had shared many things: rides through hawthorne hedges, gallops over moors. Both had loved their father, their sisters. Now another Devereux life was flung away in

England's service. He rolled himself in a blanket and dreamed of home.

Recovering from his grief, Essex allowed himself to be persuaded by Henry's general, the brilliant and resourceful Biron, to take Gournay, a vital garrison to both French and Spanish. But the council was unimpressed by this new maneuver, and as for Elizabeth, she peremptorily ordered him home. Daringly, he remained sulking in France.

By Carey, his aide, he sent letters, angry, sweet, persuasive, all tending to enforce upon his mistress the necessity of Biron's strategy, attempting to infect her with the exciting vitality of the French commander.

Just in from hunting, Elizabeth stood with one booted foot on a low chair, a dainty whip balanced across her knee. In silence she read. "So!" She seized her whip and turned a terrible look on Carey, kneeling at her feet. "So! You are come in place of your master. God's wounds, you are brave."

Carey kept his head meekly bowed. This was not the moment to say anything.

"So he has taken Gournay, what then? I am not greatly pleased by this intelligence. What's Gournay to me that English blood must be spilled in its taking? The job they were sent to do was Rouen." Furiously she slashed at her skirt. "Why does not Essex return? Does he not know that I will be obeyed?"

Ah, now was the time to speak, now that military strategy was, for the moment, set aside, and the more pressing matter of the Earl's return brought forth. "Your Grace," murmured Carey, "I beg you to consider what this may do to his lordship. He will return at your Majesty's command, it is true, but in what case, Madam?"

"Well?" She was relenting.

"How is he to show his face at Court if you heap upon him such glowing disgrace? Believe me, Madam, when I say that it is the Earl's intention to bury himself in the country there till he die, which I can assure your Grace will be right speedily."

Elizabeth tossed her head. "I do not doubt that we shall be able to tempt the gentleman back to our side."

Carey shifted his weight to the other knee. "Madam, you do not know how worn is the Earl's spirit. He is sick of the fever, and his mind is low and continuously torn for his brother. That—and now this, Madam, will break his heart."

She turned and looked at him there on his knees. She felt an intolerable weight at her own heart. Essex grieving in his tent, and Carey, here, pleading for him on his knees. This was not how she had planned it at all. She had never intended there should be aught between herself and Essex but love and kindness and gentle, sweet discourse.

"Oh, get up and go to dinner, my lord Carey," she gestured pettishly and Carey fled.

Elizabeth flicked her skirt gently now. So she was like to break his heart, was she? Walter's death was a grievous thing, indeed, but it would never have happened if they had not been acting the goat before Rouen in that skirmish. Still, it *was* an only brother; perhaps she had been a little harsh.

She forgot her last imperious summons, sent just before Carey's arrival, which not even Essex dare ignore. She wrote him a kind little note, promising nothing but not commanding his immediate return. He never got it, for already he had started on the homeward journey.

But before he started, he rode up the hill and sat there, gazing out over the landscape. In the distance was Rouen, ancient and gray, shrine of the Maid of Orléans. The winding roads lined with yellowing poplars marked the way he might not take, and before him lay the sea, restless, like his spirit, waiting to bear him back to servitude. Sighing heavily, he wheeled back down the hill to bid farewell to his thinned troops, lined up to await him. He knighted twenty-four of his gentlemen and tried not to see the pity and regret in the eyes of his men. This was scorching fire on his wound.

He cleared his throat. "My soldiers," his high, clear voice carried well over the quiet ranks, "I am recalled to England, and, to my regret, I must leave you whom I love with my whole heart. Would that we might have taken Rouen together. . . ." There was more, touching the dead, lying buried here on French soil, and finally, the bitter resignation of his command to the replacing officer. "God save the Queen!"

They cheered him as he went on board his little ship. On the tiny deck he stood, his heart like a stone, his face turned toward France that slowly retreated from his gaze.

He found the Queen in a cold mood. She was just up from Oatlands where she had gone to recover from the shock of Christopher Hatton's death. The loss of her Chancellor had shaken her badly; at the pull of the old tie, breaking away, she was low and depressed. Restlessly she braved the plague to return to Whitehall, where Essex found her. She kept him waiting a day and a night before she summoned him.

He came heavily into her presence and knelt, his face tired and worn.

Hot reproaches rose to her lips. But she caught sight of his eyes and they died away.

"You are pale and fever-wracked, my lord." Then, gently, "What has that damned France done to you in so short a time?"

Startled, he looked up. He had expected a high, rating voice to rasp his nerves. Instead there was a soft concern that sent a strange thrill of pain to his heart. He put her hand to his lips. "I thought I was grief-stricken, but it has all melted away in your loving-kindness, my lady."

It was her turn to be surprised. She, too, had braced herself for a proud defiance, and in its place there was only Robin, her Robin, kneeling to her as he used to do before that blasted girl forced her way between them. She leaned over him, kissed his forehead, and pushed back his hair, keeping her white hand on it as she smiled down at him.

"What of Walter?" she asked softly.

He drew a shuddering breath. "A soldier's death," he said in a low voice.

She patted his hand abstractedly. "I wish you hadn't gone, either of you."

They forgave each other and both forgot for the moment the deaths that had so devastated them. Hatton had a great funeral, and services for Walter were held down at Wanstead. The Countess wept on Penelope's shoulder.

Essex attended the Queen and they hunted and gamed. But his heart was not in it. She saw that he had left it in France with his men.

She sent him back. By the middle of October he was on his way. Letters came fluttering back along his trail to her:

. . . most fair, most dear, most excellent sovereign . . .

Now there was hard fighting around Rouen. The English and French gained very little ground; relations between them became strained.

"These Gallic warriors," growled Essex, "their ladders are too short and their deliberations are too long. This is a coil I would fain escape."

"*Ces Anglaises,*" sneered the French, "they and their elderly mistress!"

The war dragged on till the end of the year. Wild with impatience and longing for action, Essex flung himself into a trench outside the city with his men and narrowly escaped death. He walked about, dragging a pike behind him like a common foot-soldier. The men worshiped him.

At last news of Parma's approach came through. Elizabeth ordered her troops home.

"It is enough, in God's name!" she cried. "That idiot, Henry, has no money and he spends ours as if it were water. We have already lost more men than we can afford, and I trow there have been a multitude of sad hearts at home this Christmas tide. The Leaguers are too strong, and for my part, they can have Navarre in a pot, and welcome they are to him!"

She wrote a letter that Essex dared not ignore. Truth to tell, he too was sick to death of the whole venture. Henry played at war as if it were a merry game for which his friends could well afford to pay.

Essex relinquished his command once more and stepped aboard his ship; in sight of his officers he drew his sword and kissed the hilt. The soldiers cheered as before, and he waved them a farewell salute.

In silence he went below to his cabin. He shut out all his friends. He sank into a chair and let his head drop on his outstretched arms. He was deadly weary.

This was failure at its bitterest. It was not enough that he and his friends knew themselves well out of this French caper; that there was strong rumor that Henry of Navarre was thinking of making peace with his enemies, then turning Papist. Common sense dictated the withdrawal of the English. But Essex knew what celebration his enemies would make of all this.

This was his first command; it had ended in humiliation and stalemate; in failure.

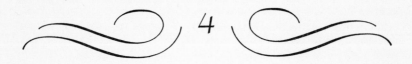

The Queen's Portuguese

*I*n his comfortable house at Holborn, Dr. Roderigo Lopez, the Queen's Portuguese physician, told his servants that he did not wish to be disturbed. He was entertaining his old friend, Antonio Perez, and he anticipated a pleasant chat with his fellow compatriot.

They made a strange, almost bizarre picture in the candlelight, as they sat over their decanters of fine Spanish wine. There was the Doctor, with his long yellow face above somber velvet, and Perez, who wore the fantastical colors of his native Andalusia. Above the gay silks, his dark visage was twisted with suffering, for beneath his doublet he carried the mark of rack and rope. Sitting opposite him in the shadows, Dr. Lopez marked how the soul within had been twisted like the body, for Perez could not hide his hatred of Philip, whose torturers had made him the strawny cripple he was.

"You passed a pleasant evening yesterday with the Lord of Essex, I trust," observed Lopez, as he filled their glasses. "*Por dios,* there is a hothead for you."

"Hardly would I call him hothead," smiled Perez, "that sits better on

Señor Ralegh. My lord Essex has the hasty heart, but I have known him to be wondrous cool-headed on occasion."

Perez had not come merely to chat with the Doctor; he had come to learn what the Queen's leech knew about Essex. All unknown to Lopez, Perez had been these many months in the Earl's service. And he had come for another purpose, deeply hidden from the Doctor.

Had Dr. Lopez been present at Essex House on the previous evening, he might now have shuddered to see this Antonio Perez sitting fraternally at his own table. For, as the yesternight wore on, and the Spaniard's tales of the dark bloody ways of Philip's Court began to pall on Essex and the Bacons, Perez dropped a brick.

"We speak of Spanish plots, *amigos*," he said easily. "But one need not go to Spain to uncover them. Here—" he paused. Essex tensed in his chair and Francis Bacon allowed one eyelid to droop over an eye.

"Well?" prompted Essex. What was the fellow getting at? Obviously he had something to say. Plots were everywhere, that much was plain. Else why did all men high in power employ their own small rings of spies; indeed, plots were in the very air one breathed. There was nothing special about such a remark; it could hardly be that Perez had something definite. He waited.

"Her Majesty the Queen walks on thin ice these days," went on Perez.

Essex shot a look at Francis Bacon, who sat imperturbable as ever; it would take a very keen eye to catch a whitening of the knuckles that lay half hidden on his knee. Nevertheless Essex saw it. Anthony Bacon was blank.

Francis broke the silence. "All monarchs live close to peril. What is unusual about the thin ice beneath the feet of the Queen's Grace?"

"What is remarkable?" repeated Perez. For an instant his tired eyes flickered sideways. "Must I point out to you, gentlemen, that when a Queen's life is so closely threatened as the Majesty of England, it is entirely remarkable that she shall live so long?"

"Now, by God's death," swore Essex softly. "If you know aught, Perez, you shall make it ours."

"I!" shrugged Perez. "I know only that he who would uncover this treachery must look close to the Queen—veree close." He drank up his wine. "That, señores, is what I know." He would say no more.

Soon after that the Bacons took themselves off, and Essex and Perez had a nightcap together. At parting they leveled each other with steady eyes. Perez then pulled on his gloves. Again he looked at Essex.

"I sup with the Queen's physician on the morrow," he said. "Shall I convey your lordship's felicitations?"

"Yes," said Essex slowly. "Yes, señor."

White teeth flashed in the sunken face of the Spaniard. "I bid your lordship good night. *Vaya con dios.*"

Homing to his lodging with a lanterned page, Perez groaned as the cold found the misery in his injured bones and tendons. In his own mind he was sure that Philip II had hired Dr. Lopez to poison the Queen, and he yearned to see the Doctor brought to torture and death. Torture! He clasped an aching shoulder. Ah, well, tomorrow night should uncover to him further useful evidence.

As for Essex, he sat on, bemused in his empty room. Was it possible that Perez had uncovered a trail that should lead to the Queen's Portuguese? Lopez was a yellow devil; Essex paid him in vain to gather information, and he knew that the Doctor sold and resold it to others, even the Queen. But—high treason—a drawing and quartering affair! He shuddered.

Now Perez sat opposite the Doctor here in his beautiful house in Holborn, drinking excellent wine after the finely cooked dinner. He would apply the pump to his host. He promised himself by all the saints that before he left he would take with him a full meed of news for Essex.

"Your family is well, I trust?" Perez knew Señora Lopez, who wore her lace like the wife of a grandee, who had not appeared this evening, and at various times he had seen the handsome Lopez children, a son at Winchester and two or three olive-skinned girls. Lopez bowed. His family, it appeared, was in excellent health.

The door opened and a yellow-faced gentleman appeared, his cheek badly swollen and tied up in a cloth. The Doctor rose. "Ah, my good friend, how goes it this evening?"

The gentleman answered with some difficulty, his words thick and his voice somewhat weak. "I feel myself much improved, good Roderigo. I came to pay my respects to our friend here."

Perez rose to bow, his heart jumping with excitement.

Esteban Ferreira, here in the house of the Doctor! It was not generally believed that this Portuguese was a paid agent of Philip, but surely everyone in London knew that he was an ex-servant and bitter enemy of Don Antonio, the Portuguese Pretender. Don Antonio was a guest, however unwelcome, here at Elizabeth's Court. What was his enemy

Ferreira doing in this house? Perez felt every nerve on the tingle. The scent grew warmer.

"I grieve for the señor's indisposition," said he, with a concerned gesture in the direction of Ferreira's face.

"A rotting tooth," explained Lopez. "I have treated him with my drugs, but he should have the pincers put to it as soon as may be."

Ferreira winced, and behind his silky whiskers, Perez smiled gently.

"I have had him here for this week past," went on the Doctor. "Soon we shall have the surgeon and all will be well."

Perez smiled more openly now. Ah, fortuitous toothache, so to cover up the deeds of two treasonable dogs! So Ferreira feared the pincers, did he? A swift memory of the rack seared for an instant through his brain, and fury filled his heart.

Pleading a headache, he soon left.

He lost no time in letting Essex know what he had seen at Holborn, and the latter frowned as he digested this fresh bit of news.

"Christ's wounds," he muttered. He sent for Bacon and the two considered the matter. Swiftly they made their next move.

Returning from a professional call, Dr. Lopez was informed by his servants that his house guest had been quietly arrested and taken away early in the afternoon by two unknown men. Furious, baffled, and vaguely uneasy, the Doctor made inquiries. At length he learned that Ferreira had been returned to the household of his former master, Don Antonio. More ominous were the sealed orders bearing the Lord Treasurer's arms that had accompanied him.

Lopez knew it was worse than useless to follow the matter in that direction. Tapping his long yellow fingers on the arm of his chair, he sat and pondered the small calamity. Ferreira would henceforth be held in close and sharp custody and no letter could get through to him. He knew the Pretender of old.

Don Antonio hated him, Roderigo Lopez. He envied him that favor which, as the Queen's physician, he enjoyed, and which the down-at-heel nobleman could never hope to gain. Elizabeth regarded Don Antonio, as he haunted her Court, with cold disdain. Barely tolerating him in England, she found it difficult to forget how she had sent men to be killed and ships to be sunk, all in his interest, and how he had made a fiasco of the whole thing. Accordingly, the Pretender smoldered with jealousy in the shadows, while his countryman walked serenely in the light of prosperity. No, the Doctor knew he would get no quarter from Don Antonio, and any attempt on his part to aid Ferreira would only make matters worse for that unfortunate. The more Lopez thought about the matter and the Lord Treasurer's part in it, the more uneasy he became.

Then something happened to throw him into a real panic. His letters were intercepted and copied. Distracted and thoroughly scared, he went to the Queen. She received him indifferently.

"Majestee, my friend Señor Ferreira is not to blame if he no longer prefers the service of his former master. That one was a man notoriously unkind to his servants. Majestee, he had not paid them for years, he was of a monstrous ungratefulness to all who did him kindness, even to your Grace."

Elizabeth was illuminating a manuscript. She threw down the brush and looked up at the yellow old man. "And what if this Ferreira prove to be a Spanish agent?"

"Ah, Majestee, he may prove to be so, but in any case, does it not have to *be* proved?" For the space of a moment, as he stood there, head inclined to one side, he looked incredibly cunning.

"True. What then?"

"Madam, if he be proved guilty, let him suffer. But I solemnly swear to you that I believe my friend to be innocent of aught save good to your Grace and to England."

Elizabeth examined her hand. There was a stain of vermilion on it. Absently she wet a finger and rubbed it on the spot.

"Madam, if you will order Don Antonio to release Ferreira, I will be earnest of his conduct. But now a thought occurs to me. Might he not be used as a valuable agent between the two kingdoms? Surely your Grace desires peace above all earthly things?"

"I do not see this Ferreira an agent of mine," she said shortly.

The Doctor's shoulders went nearly to his ears. "Then, if your Majestee does not desire this course," here he coughed discreetly, "might not a deceiver be himself deceived?"

She glared at him. Evidently he meant that Ferreira should go to Spain in double capacity, serving her while seeming to serve Philip. Suddenly in her mouth she felt a sour taste. What was she doing here on this winter afternoon, discussing plots with her physician? She regarded his yellow neck, his long hands with their predatory nails. Disdaining to answer, she waved him away.

Lopez left, feeling that he had done neither himself nor his friend much good. How thankful he was that he had not mentioned the tampering with his letters. *That* might have led to God knows what?

As for Elizabeth, sickened by the unsavory episode, she picked up her brush and dipped it into the scarlet paint. But her hand, which even when she was calm, had begun to lose its cunning, trembled now more than ever. With an oath she tossed the parchment into the fire, where it crackled and writhed into a scorched roll.

"Plots, plots," she muttered wearily.

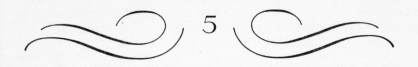

Plot and Treason

*N*ow Essex was once more riding high. For nine months he had sat as member of the Privy Council. Seriously he threw himself into the business of government. Using Anthony Bacon's cleverness and connections abroad, he began to build up a system of espionage that bid fair to rival that of Walsingham, his dead father-in-law.

Now actually a part of government, he felt his power strengthening. In a burst of self-confidence, he made Francis Bacon a daring promise. "I'll get you the Attorney-Generalship. 'Tis soon to fall vacant."

Aye, Francis knew that, and his own hopes soared. He had made no mistake, he felt, in taking Essex for his patron.

Accordingly, the Earl laid siege to Gloriana. She promptly let him know that she and the Cecils favored Sir Edward Coke, her brilliant arrogant Solicitor-General. The two argued, quarreled, and nearly came to blows.

"I shall be advised by those who have more judgment in the matter," she declared.

"So you might be, Madam. But I speak as one who is for your service, not as one who speaks for private ends."

She flared up. "Indeed!"

Heedless of the gathering storm, he plunged on. "Perhaps I lack judgment to discern between the worth of one man and another, but the world is fast teaching me where merit lies." With his earnest need to make his point, he spoke stiffly, with a pompousness that was more than she could bear. "I lack not for followers, wiser and more honest than I, who hold me in esteem. I cannot be so great a fool."

As always, when he spoke of followers, she was pricked by a small pinpoint of anxiety. She forced herself to remain calm, concentrating on the single chilly word, "Indeed."

"I advance the claims of my friend Bacon from a just opinion of his true worth. Those advisers whom your Grace trusts leave out such a man as he, and others too."

Her self-control cracked. She set her teeth. "I will have no backbiting curmudgeon about me, Essex. Full well do I know to whom you refer." Her little eyes bulged, black and glassy. "And let me tell you, rash youth, Lord Burghley is more to me with his counsels than you or your Bacons will ever be."

She clapped her hands. "Sir Thomas Heneage and my chessboard." He was dismissed.

But next evening he resumed his suit. She should not think him beaten. They were at Greenwich, and after supper she commanded his attendance in the long gallery. Disposed this night to be chatty, she talked of many things as they paced to and fro. She spoke of her father, of his gilded youth and his brilliance. Essex listened idly, wondering how to steer the conversation round to Bacon. Ah, she had done it herself.

"Only one of my courtiers used to remind me faintly of my father. Old Nick Bacon, father of those two friends of yours, Robin. What a grand old fatty he was! Pity he had to die." She threw him a sidelong glance.

He could not ignore the chance. "His sons are worthy bearers of his name, Madam, especially Francis, who, I swear——"

In a flash she whipped round on him. "In God's name, are you at that again?" She glared at him. "If you can think of naught else, begone to bed!"

"By God, Madam, I will!" In a towering hig, he left her and locked himself in his room. For two days he sulked, while Henry Carey, Blount, even Robert Cecil, sent messages. To all of these he preserved a surly silence. On the third day he emerged, pale but calm.

As for Gloriana, she was friendly, but with teeth outward. Something was happening to make her more determined than ever to oppose the Essex scheme.

Parliament was meeting and she was nervous and irritable. Only seven times in her long reign had she summoned the houses to sit in deliberation over the finances of her realm. Now her eighth parliament was debating another royal request for money.

"I would this were over and done with," she confided to Burghley, who came to report progress. "I fear the Lord Keeper has not sufficiently emphasized the acute need for moneys with which to meet the foreign peril."

Burghley was soothing. This was only another of the many nerve storms through which he had seen his mistress. They would weather this one. "The Commons, Madam, have upheld their precedent and have agreed to revote the subsidy. Even now the bill is being drawn up."

The Queen gnawed at her lip and the caked rouge came off on her tooth. "But tomorrow, my Lord Treasurer, tomorrow is what keeps me on the anxious seat. You will ask for three subsidies payable in the next three years and Commons will object. I know them."

She was right. Shrewdly she put her finger on the sore spot, the matter of prerogative. Commons resented the Crown's dictating to them the terms of the grant, and on that basis they opposed it. To Essex, equally nervous and restless, she kept a close mouth, but to Burghley she admitted that Commons was rapidly pre-empting her power.

"God help my successor," she said grimly.

Intuitive for once, Essex awaited the outcome with unnatural tension. And well he might. Something was in the wind. Bacon the calm, the wise, the opportunist, had made a false move. He opposed the Crown in this matter of money grant and championed the people. He spoke eloquently in the House.

"If this short term of payment were adopted, it would go far toward the ruining of us. For gentlemen would have need to sell their plate and farmers their brass pots to meet their just taxation." He was roundly applauded, and continued. "But let the moneys be paid over a period of six years, rather than three, and we shall all rest happy in the venture." Commons rose and cheered.

Ralegh and Cecil kept their dignity and rose to measured opposition. But Essex was aghast. Bacon had made a capital error in their joint plans for his advancement. Was this the man he had chosen to support? No need to tell him of Elizabeth's rage.

She raved. What did this fool Bacon know of the needs of government? Wait till *he* had squeezed the very juice out of his brain, if he had one, trying to make the money stretch over mountains of expense. Even with the money set to come in within three years, they would be hard put to it to finance their affairs.

The debate raged on for three weeks, and on the twenty-fourth day the bill was passed on Bacon's plan. The money would come dribbling in over a period of six years and the Queen and the Privy Council could ride the rack, stretching themselves along with the money.

"Bacon my Attorney-General!" raged Elizabeth. "I'll see him boiled in a pudding cloth first!"

But once again Essex tried to reason with her. In the midst of her furious pacing she stopped and leveled him with a look. Would he never give up? She clenched her jaw. "One of us must yield in this, and your lordship knows full well which one it will be!"

Harshly she ordered him on pain of banishment to remain silent.

In silent chagrin Bacon retired to the private recesses of his house. And now, as the holiday season approached Essex became absorbed in something else. The Lopez affair had flared up again. and this time he was convinced that he had uncovered a plot to assassinate the Queen.

Late one night Perez came to Essex House with some truly startling news. Another Portuguese, one Gomez d'Avila, a former neighbor of the Doctor's, had been arrested as he was returning from Flanders.

"Myself, I saw it," declared Perez. "There he stood, a perfect picture of guilt, shivering and shaking, while they took from him his letter pouch. And this—this is what they found." He threw onto the table a letter.

Strange reference to musk, amber, pearls, in quantity, to be delivered to an anonymous dealer. The letter smelled of treason.

"What said he?"

"Ah," smiled Perez, "just as they forced him onto a horse between two soldiers, he saw me in the crowd.

" 'For the love of God, tell Dr. Lopez of my plight.' Those were his words, milord."

Dr. Lopez again! The damned Portuguese was in every circumstance that came to light. Essex frowned. "Still—" he hesitated, "suppose this man Gomez is innocent?"

"That, señor, is hardly likely, with letters in code."

Essex dismissed Perez and went to his writing cabinet. Cuffe and

Wootton were wrestling there with code messages from abroad. And here came a messenger from Reynolds, down at Eton, where he was conferring with Don Antonio. In cipher the message read:

Dr. L. has received word from Ferreira warning him to prevent the return of one Gomez d'Avila to England, lest he himself be undone without remedy. Dr. L. replied that he had sent thrice to Flanders to prevent the arrival of Gomez.

A smile lit the tired face of Essex. "Send for Ferreira," he ordered.

In the dead of the night they brought the Portuguese under guard to Essex House. The Earl was not ready to let the public into his secrets. There were whispers of course, in the streets. London knew that the Earl of Essex was employed in the unraveling of a plot against the Queen.

Still pale, but no longer swollen in the face, Ferreira was shown into the small cabinet, where the Bacons and Essex, with two secretaries, awaited him. There was a fire burning in the grate and in the light of a two-branched candlestick on the heavy table, the English looked the conspirators rather than the Portuguese. The two Bacons had thrown their heavy cloaks over their chair backs, and their gloves lay on the table beside them.

With no ado, Essex handed Ferreira the messages that had been decoded and copied on a fair sheet of paper. In silence the other read and a muscle in his cheek twitched. Otherwise he remained calm. Then he looked up and encountered the piercing gaze of five men.

"What does this mean?" he asked.

Instantly the two secretaries bent to their scratching, quills flying harshly over paper.

"It means," said Francis Bacon, who had had much experience interrogating prisoners, "that your Dr. Lopez has betrayed you and all the others."

"Madre de dios!"

Across Bacon's face a pale smile flitted. Ferreira saw that he had already made a mistake. He moistened his lips. He must think quickly.

"Is it possible, gentlemen, that you do not know the Doctor to have been in the pay of Spain for years?"

"Possible," asserted Bacon dryly.

A contemptuous sneer curled Essex's lip. How these fellows ratted when driven into a corner. What in God's name did this yellow Portugee think of them that they would tolerate a known Spanish agent in their midst, to go unwatched? Bacon threw him a warning glance.

"And the Doctor is to do what?" he said persuasively.

Ferreira shifted in his chair and looked about him. The candle flame flickered on two down-bent brows intent on their papers: the secretaries. It touched two intellectual faces lit by the cold glitter of reptilian eyes: the Bacons. It threw into deeper shadow the tired lines on the high-bred face of Essex. Ferreira swallowed and felt the palms of his hands grow moist. He must be very careful.

"There is a plot," he said lamely. Silence. He went on. "Don Antonio's son is to be bought over to the interests of the Spanish King. Dr. Lopez—the Doctor——"

Bacon leaned forward and pinned the stammering Portuguese with his eyes. "Dr. Lopez is to be the agent?"

"Yes, yes. That is it." He looked about for a sign that they had done with him. He received none.

"Continue." The implacable voice of Essex prodded him on.

"Andrada, Emanuel Andrada—you remember him, no?"

"We remember him, yes," said Essex, without humor.

"He was arrested, you remember, three years ago, on suspicion of espionage, but was allowed to return to Spain. You do not forget, I hope, that Dr. Lopez was responsible for his release?"

In grim silence he was at last dismissed to the custody of his guards, and as he went, his scalp prickled with a foreboding of evil.

As for the wretched Gomez d'Avila, he was dragged into the Tower. Down the wet stone steps he went to a damp cell under the river. All night he shivered with cold and apprehension, till morning brought Francis Bacon to question him. Cool and quiet, Bacon brought with him his own secretary and one of the Earl's.

"We will see the prisoner in the interrogation room."

They brought the terrified Gomez, knees knocking together, pushing him into the gloomy stone chamber with its low, groined roof and massive pillars. Round one of these they went into a large recess lit by a heavy lantern, where Bacon, still in his hat, leaned in easy elegance against a small oaken table. Gomez shot a convulsive look at the terrible machinery that lay beyond the table. Then he fixed his eyes fearfully on his questioner.

"You are now going to tell us everything you know—for instance, the meaning of the letter we took from you." Bacon was almost pleasant.

The Portuguese was a little man with a round bullet head and bright eyes like a squirrel. Like a small paralyzed animal he stood and said nothing, not from stubbornness, but because terror had taken away his voice.

"We are aware you know a good deal," went on Bacon. "You are not the ordinary messenger that is employed in errands of this nature." The little man gulped. "We are patient, but we shall not wait too long."

Still Gomez remained silent. Bacon made a weary gesture, and the two guards at the back of the prisoner laid heavy hands on the skinny arms. With a quick movement they jerked him backward onto a long bedlike frame and secured his arms and legs. Bacon watched them at work. He was bored at the prospect of having to resort to torture. It was always better to get willing confessions. Admissions wrung from agonized lips or from men about to lose consciousness were not apt to be accurate. The two had finished strapping Gomez to the rack and now they stood aside. The man's eyes rolled and his head moved weakly from side to side.

Bacon made another gesture. "Wait a minute." The man was verily about to die of fright. They were defeating their own ends. "Now," he leaned over the man, "do you understand what I am saying to you?"

Gomez gasped and tried to speak. He nodded his head feebly. "Now, do you talk, or do we tear out your arms?" Bacon did not raise his voice but the little man heard. He nodded his head again and his eyes spoke for him.

They released him and he sat on the edge of the frame, large tears rolling down his cheeks. Suddenly his knees buckled and he groveled on the floor before Bacon. He began to sob. A flood of Portuguese now issued from his mouth, and Bacon made out, between the gasps, that he would talk, if they would give him a moment's time to recover himself.

Bacon leaned back and began to play with a gold tassel that hung from his front. Gradually Gomez took heart and at last he said plaintively, "Señores, I weel tell everything, but everything." Bacon nodded.

"I am—how you call eeet—intermediary—and I take letter to Ferreira from man in Brussels weeth name, Tinoco. He is Spanish agent." He paused.

"The letter we took from you. The musk and amber—what was that?"

Ah, the musk and amber was code for rewards and bribes to be conveyed to Don Antonio's son by Tinoco and Ferreira. Yes, it is quite true, señores, there is a plot to buy the son of Don Antonio with a bribe of fifty thousand crowns. There is also good reward for Dr. Lopez, who is to poison the father of the young man, Don Antonio himself."

Bacon hurried to Essex. They re-examined Ferreira. Coolly he admitted everything but his own part in the plot. Ah, so it seemed the Doctor was sheltering himself behind his friends? Ask the Doctor, offered Ferreira, ask the Doctor about a diamond and ruby ring that he had from the King of Spain. The Doctor was the pivot round whom the whole black mass turned.

Bacon and Essex drew satisfied breaths. Soon they would be ready to make an arrest. Even if Dr. Lopez fled, they could easily bring him back, convicted by his own flight.

Essex was now relentless in his pursuit of the Doctor. The Queen's physician had spread unsavory tales of certain treatments he had carried out on the Earl's ailing body. It was even whispered that Essex had the pox. Fresh insult, added to the injury of treason!

And then came a letter from Brussels, from Tinoco himself. It was addressed to Lord Burghley, of whom the writer begged a safe-conduct to appear before the Queen with vital information touching the safety of the realm. Burghley and his son conferred with Essex.

"We shall draft the reply prudently," decided the elderly lord. "We shall allow safe-conduct for Tinoco into England, but—" he paused. Cecil was meticulously taking notes, but Essex, lounging in his chair, said nothing. He was absorbed in watching this cat-and-mouse game the Cecils played so well. The younger one now returned his father's glance. A smile curved his bearded lips.

"I see."

Tinoco would have a cleverly worded permit to enter the country at will, but not one word would be said as to his leaving it. The trap was expertly baited; the fox put his foot in and the jaws closed.

They brought the young Portuguese to Essex, who decided to conduct the interview in French, for he guessed the prisoner to have an imperfect knowledge of that language. At first Tinoco was glib and ready with answers. He had come to warn the Queen of a Jesuit plot against her life.

And just what was the nature of this plot?

That Tinoco could not say. He had information from a source he was not at liberty to reveal, but he hinted that it came straight from Madrid. Essex nearly laughed in his face. Did this young fool think they were so easily to be fobbed off with so transparent a tissue of lies? The prisoner continued, little knowing that they had d'Avila and his own correspondence in their grasp. Gradually Essex wore him down. He began to stammer. He doubled back on his tracks; he denied, contradicted, and tangled himself in the meshes of his own story.

He was taken to his cell where he at once wrote, protesting to Burghley. For answer, a double guard was placed and strict incommunicado was clamped down on him. For some time he was allowed to rot and then Essex visited him again. He was broken. Not all the miseries of his four years of Moorish slavery could equal this refinement of torture. He babbled to Essex.

"In truth, señor, I entered what I believed to be a Christian land where at least some of the people were civilized. *Cuerpo de dios,* what have they done to me? I am shut up like a common felon."

"Perhaps you would care to talk to me, señor?" suggested Essex.

Tinoco felt in his surroundings the taste of death. So innocent-appearing were they, with the gentle comfort of cushions, fresh air at the windows, and good meat for eating; the contrast of all this with the steel guard in the passage terrified him.

"But yes, señor. I shall be happy to tell what I know. For that I have come to your country."

Mariá de los dolores! Anything to get a hearing and try to strike some kind of bargain with his jailors.

When Essex left the Tower, he was satisfied that they were near the end of their goal. In his pocket he carried a signed confession from Tinoco in which the old Jew was completely implicated. It was obvious. Else why should Lopez write that incriminating note to Ferreira, touching Gomez d'Avila abroad. Thrice he stood accused; Ferreira himself, the miserable little Gomez, and now, Tinoco. All had named the Doctor the ace of spades in the pack.

On New Year's Day they arrested Dr. Lopez at Holborn. Lopez was in his study when a servant told him a pair of gentlemen awaited him below. He went to the head of the stairs and looked down on the two men in his hall. They stood with their backs to him, loitering, obviously impatient to be away. Two wore long cloaks, and there were two others, men-at-arms, on whose doublets were the Devereux arms.

Señora Lopez drew her husband back into his study. "Rigo!"

The Doctor was calm. "Be of good cheer, *querida,* I am not alarmed."

"But—two soldiers—what does that mean, my husband?"

"It means that strange and sinister things have occurred, but they cannot touch us. I shall confer with his lordship and return to you before sunset." He kissed her hand and went quickly downstairs. Courteously he was requested to accompany the gentlemen, and he took his flat velvet cap and departed with them.

They proceeded to Essex House in silence. The two gentlemen took the coach with the Doctor, and the yeomen escorted them on horse. The Doctor looked out the tiny window at the busy London scene that rolled past. It was a dull day and the houses, with their overhanging stories, the fronts striped with half-timbering, seemed to frown on the little cavalcade. Curious folk, well used to such sights as these, nevertheless suspended their small matters to stop and stare at the Devereux arms.

Lopez's mind flitted busily about. Since the other two did not speak, he was left to his thoughts. Where were they taking him? D'Avila, he knew, was in the Tower, and Ferreira still in custody of Don Antonio down at Eton. Was it possible—no, they would not imprison him, the Queen's physician, especially when he was innocent of any of these black matters that so absorbed the Earl of Essex these days. The Tower? *Dios,* he was no great lord, to be singled out for those dubious honors passed out on Tower Hill by the Queen's headsman. He was a poor doctor, who had done only his duty. He ventured to relax against the cushions and preserved his calm.

They drew up at Essex House and clattered into the courtyard. The Doctor alighted and followed his escort into the house. He faced the Earl and the Cecils with an air of polite curiosity that had in it not the faintest trace of embarrassment or guilt. To all their questions he was courteously attentive with satisfactory answers. Even when they told him he might not return to his house, he was not alarmed. He prayed permission to send word to his wife.

After a couple of hours Lord Burghley suggested that the Doctor be allowed to retire to an apartment on an upper floor. Pale but steadfast, he followed a servant from the room. When the door had closed behind him, the Lord Treasurer put both his veined hands on the arms of his chair and bent his snowy brows on Essex.

"I think, my lord, that we shall draw blank here. The Doctor's answers are good."

Essex's eyes flashed then narrowed. He puffed out his lips with annoyance. "I cannot agree. When we have searched the house at Holborn, you will find that we have the right pig by the ear."

"Possibly, possibly. We shall see. At any rate, be sure to send word to his wife that the Doctor is remaining here."

The younger Cecil departed with his father. Through it all he had not said a word. Now, straight to the Queen he went, losing no time, knowing full well that Essex would be on his heels.

She was indignant. What was Essex trying to do? Make a mark of an old man whose worst fault was his inability to cure her racking headaches?

"You have an opinion, Cecil?"

"A mare's nest, Madam. The Earl has an anti-Spanish obsession. He sees plots and spies behind every door."

At this moment the Earl himself was announced. One look at Elizabeth told him he had been forestalled. His mistress promptly opened the ball.

"Well, my lord," began the high voice. "It seems that you have bitten off a larger piece than you can swallow. Do you not take shame so to abuse one of my most faithful servants?"

Essex glared at Cecil who sat quietly at the table corner, eyes downcast and fingers drumming on the polished surface. Damn him.

"Down!" ordered Gloriana, and obediently he sank to his knees. "Now. You have brought against this man most cruel slanders that you cannot hope to prove. Is it not so?"

He set his teeth. "Madam, I shall prove everything to your Grace's complete satisfaction."

"If what I hear is true, you will have your work cut out for you." She stared at him, her eyes stormy. "I am much displeased with you, my lord. Well do you know that my honor is at stake in this matter, and I will not have it said abroad that we hound innocent men to their graves. There is enough of that at foreign courts. There'll be no de Medici practices here. Do you mind me?"

She took him by one shoulder and shook him, but not roughly.

"Madam——"

"Peace! It is malice and nothing else that has hatched this affair. Out of personal spleen you are scourging this poor creature. How can you, my lord?"

He shot her a baffled look. How much, in God's name, did she know of him and all else? "I tell your Grace——"

She cut him off. "I'll hear nothing, Essex. The man's house and papers have been searched to no avail. What would you? That I should do to death a man who has offended you?"

Ah! Then she knew the tale of the pox, too. It was too much.

"Madam!" he shouted, scrambling to his feet. "There is a matter of a diamond and ruby ring that you would do well to investigate. Is there nothing in that?"

She stared back at him. Having delivered what he felt to be a Parthian shot, he craved permission to retire. The door closed sharply on him. Elizabeth raised her eyebrows at Cecil, who pursed thin lips and held his peace.

In black despondency Essex shut himself up. He was cruelly embarrassed by the raking he had received in the presence of Cecil. Frances, with her soft breast and comfortable hands would have soothed him, but she was down in the country, tending their second child, who was ailing. It took all the patience and persuasion of Lord Howard and Henry Cuffe to make him relent.

He agreed to return but not abandon the scent. The affair of the Doctor was no longer a matter of treasonable guilt to be resolved to a just end; it was become a personal struggle for the vindication of his honor before the Queen and those accursed Cecils. He *had* to prove the Doctor guilty. Skulking in his chamber would not achieve this, with Council meeting without him, and the Cecils up to God knows what.

Lopez must suffer.

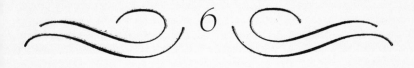

6

Penalty

*F*or the moment the Lopez affair rested. In the flush of restored favor, Essex renewed his suit for Francis Bacon. He and Gloriana went for a brisk gallop in the morning air, and then there was a new play by William Shakespeare, that clever fellow from up in Warwickshire. It was a satire on the French and Russian courts, and Elizabeth was pleased to be amused at the ridiculous masque in the last act.

"And do you think, my Robin, that love's labours are all lost?" In high good humor, she tapped his violet shoulder with her little fan.

"Madam, I cannot tell."

Elizabeth made a *moue* and her eyes sparkled. She knew what he meant.

The supper was excellent with spicy sausages and round sea fish cleverly cooked in milk with sweet herbs. For the Queen's special delight there was a delicate new cake covered with a thick crust of toasted almonds. Warm and full of content, she and Essex sat down by the fire to chess. Soft music from the gallery soothed them and there was a softer hum of conversation from the painted throng that eddied quietly to and fro about their little table. He let her win, but not too easily, and with a grin of joy, Gloriana leaned back in her chair and pulled her skirts halfway up her legs to get the warmth of the fire.

This was the moment for which he had waited throughout the long day.

"Has your Grace given further thought to Bacon's appointment?" He put the question almost casually.

But she was not to be caught by any approach, however artful. "I thought I forbade you to mention the subject, Robin."

"Madam, you did. But time has elapsed, and—"

"Robin, I will tell you why I shall not give the appointment to your Bacon." At her words his heart sank. "It is simply that he is too young. I cannot allow that a man of thirty-odd years has the experience for so heavy a task. Nor shall you use the Crown for the rewarding of your friends. Come, now, we will not speak of this again."

Alone with Cecil, she said, "My lord is determined to force Bacon upon me for Attorney. Lay that hope forever. I charge it to you."

In bitter silence Essex gave all his grim attention once more to the case of Dr. Lopez. He worked Bacon hard upon the investigation. If he could press it to a satisfactory close, surely the Queen would revise her opinion of the lawyer's youth and inexperience.

The shadows closed around the Doctor and early in February he was removed to the Tower. To his distracted wife he wrote reassuringly; he was certain to be exonerated. His apartment was furnished for comfort with a small grate and chairs and table. In an inner room was his bed and a small *prie-dieu* with a crucifix hanging over it. He asked for some books, which were brought to him.

At a little after six on the following morning, in the cold chill, he was aroused from his bed to receive a visit from Essex and Sir Robert Cecil. He could not control a shivering in his old limbs as he paced his outer cell, trying to warm his sluggish blood. Now that he was an inmate of this frowning pile from which so few men came back to life, he felt less sure of himself. Six weeks' confinement at Essex House had shaken his nerve. He was an old man and he was beginning to feel confused.

Essex, too, was cold, wrapped as he was to the chin in a heavy cloak and gloved in fur. Between his high shoulders, Cecil's face was its usual ivory.

They began with the diamond and ruby ring. Yes, gentlemen, admitted the Doctor, assuredly he had received it from Spain, but it was intended as a present from King Philip for the queen's Majesty. Yes, he had taken it to the Queen, who had refused it. No, he admitted, it was not likely that the Spanish King would send so valuable a present to his hated enemy, Elizabeth of England, but the Doctor implored them to remember that Philip was an old man, and weary too of bloodshed. Was it not possible that in his declining years he could contemplate friendly overtures to the great Queen of England? And after all, did not her Majesty desire, above all things, peace for her realm?

Essex moved irritably. Talk like this would betray them surely into Spanish hands. What was needed was a bloody military victory, forever to lay the strength of Spain in the dust. All this babble of old men who would save English blood at the price of English honor! He looked with loathing at the Portuguese.

Cecil coughed now and veered onto another tack. They would like to know, he said, about those letters that had been smuggled into the country to the Doctor.

Ah, the letters. Those, gentlemen, were quite harmless to England and concerned Don Antonio only.

But there were the signed confessions of Ferreira and Tinoco. What about those?

Then the Doctor became excited. His old eyes glared. Those men were liars, perjured villains! Did not the gentlemen see what they were trying to do? They were shifting the attention to himself, larger game for the net, the Queen's physician-in-chief.

But what of Andrada, of whom Tinoco swore that he had received embraces and gifts from great Philip himself, to be handed on to Dr. Lopez? Why should the mighty King of Spain trouble himself with such small fry as a Jewish doctor? Was it not possible that Philip knew the Doctor to be close to Elizabeth, so close that it would be the easiest thing in the world to poison her?

No! No! A thousand times, no! The sweat sprang out on the yellow forehead and the Doctor stammered agonizingly in his efforts to speak.

Essex now took the lead. He pressed the Doctor with searching questions. The old man denied everything, wildly calling on his saints to witness that he spoke truth. What was his connection with Andrada? He was not going to deny that he had worked for the release of a known agent of Spain, was he? Trembling now in every limb, the Portuguese admitted that he had lent his name to a plot.

So! There *had* been a plot! And what was the Doctor's interest in the matter? Surely something beyond the mere service to the realm?

The old man faltered that he only wanted to gull the King of Spain and get a little of his money.

Ah, was that all? Had he not promised to take note of secret preparations of England's army, of how many ships the Queen has at home and abroad, the names of her captains, and to note the forts and weak places and send it all to Philip?

No! No! The Doctor screamed his denials.

"Then, why," persisted Cecil, "did the Count Fuentes send word from Madrid that since the Doctor had daughters, they should not want by this for good marriages?"

The Doctor shook his gray head. His enemies were too much for him, he groaned. All this which looked so bad upon the surface had in reality a pure motive. But he was old and muddled and he had forgotten the answers to the questions.

They gave him no rest. Mercilessly they closed in on him. This ingenious story of a peace overture conducted by Walsingham, what of that? Did anyone else know of this fantastic mission?

No, the Doctor moaned, only Andrada and Walsingham, himself, and he was—dead. As for Andrada . . .

"Andrada!" the Earl snapped his fingers. "His word is worth exactly nothing. Can the Doctor think of no one else who knew of this?"

Dr. Lopez sat silent, his eyes vacant. Essex shrugged and set his lip.

In their net the Doctor writhed and twisted and looked about with staring eyes for escape. With a sinking heart he realized that he had failed to convince his judges. He knew that he was speaking the truth, that he had indeed been employed by Walsingham in the very plot he had tried to describe. But unfortunately for him, so many had learned the art of counterfeiting the ring of truth that no man in his senses would believe a statement that could not be proved.

In despair he sank down on his seat and hid his face in his hands. Thus they left him.

Essex had done his work only too well. He had begun the case as a chapter in his feud with the Cecils and perhaps to pay off a couple of old scores with Lopez. Now, to his surprise, the Cecils, of their own free will, had abandoned the Doctor. This was in no deference to his judgment, that he well knew; they had their own dark reasons for turning narrow backs on the wretched Portuguese, and were now highhandedly leading the chase as if Essex had no part in it at all. In any case, the Doctor was now doomed.

The two men walked out together into the pale February sun. In silence they entered their coach. Essex was full of the scene he had just quitted; not so Cecil. Mindful of the Queen's recent injunction laid upon him concerning Bacon, he resolved to speak now to Essex. He made an innocent remark.

"My lord, the Queen has resolved before five days pass, without any further delay, to make an Attorney-General. I pray your lordship to let me know whom you favor."

Essex stared at him. What was this? "I wonder, Sir Robert, how you can ask that question. You already know that my strongest favor lies with Francis Bacon."

Another game of cat-and-mouse.

Cecil moved his head downward. "In my turn, I wonder how your lordship should go about to spend your strength in so unlikely and impossible a manner." With this, Cecil crossed his thin legs and looked out of the coach window. They rumbled over the cobblestones of the Strand. Essex preserved an indignant silence.

Cecil continued pleasantly. "Now, if your lordship had spoken of the Solicitorship, I should not have been surprised at the choice of Bacon."

Essex found his voice. "Digest me no digestions, Cecil," he said harshly. "I am not deceived. You and the Queen may set yourselves against me, but I warn you that the Attorney-Generalship for Francis I will have, and I will spend tooth and nail, annuity, power, might, and authority to get it for him." As he said them, he bit his words into little pieces.

The secretary shrugged. It was his way when he preferred not to answer. Essex continued. "I can but think it strange of both you and my Lord Treasurer that you prefer the claims of a stranger against those of a kinsman."

For answer Cecil reached for his little silver box of cloves. Then he spoke. "It has never been my way, my lord, to allow personal feeling to influence my service to the Crown. Such is the policy of our family." Cecil spoke blandly and proffered the open box of cloves.

Blindly declining with a wave of the hand, Essex now exploded. "God's death, Cecil, do you come the pompous ape with me? I have not dwelt at this Court without learning that a man's first consideration is his skin, and second, that of his family."

Cecil popped a clove into his mouth and snapped the box shut.

"But," went on Essex, "I will pass over your treachery to your cousins, and merely point out that if you will compare the merits of your two competitors for this favor, you will find those of Bacon outweigh those of Coke."

"Possibly." The secretary's mild answer was borrowed from his father. The coach stopped outside Cecil House. "Here I leave you, my lord."

The little man stepped out at his doorway, made over his high shoulder a courteous signal which Essex barely acknowledged as he drove away.

Shortly after this the three Portuguese were brought to trial. London was aflame and great crowds gathered in front of the Guildhall while the deliberations were taking place. Inside the building the accused men faced an imposing array of judges and the men who had hounded them to this pass.

Lopez was quiet but his hands and lips trembled; his bloodshot eyes stared out of wrinkled lids. The other two were still, both pale, Ferreira from pride, Tinoco from amazement. They had not saved themselves by their lying incrimination of the Doctor.

In summary judgment all three were convicted and sentenced to the traitor's death. They stood bareheaded while the details of their punishment were solemnly read out to them. To be half-hung, then cut down while life was still in them. Castration! Ferreira felt the cold blood race down the backs of his legs. He glanced at Lopez but the old man was staring trancelike into space as if he neither saw nor heard. They were then to be disemboweled and quartered. God save the Queen!

They were led back to their cells to await her Majesty's pleasure.

But Elizabeth hesitated. She could not bring herself to authorize the death of the Doctor. About the other two she had no feeling, for she was amply convinced of their guilt. Still, hardly could she put them to death without sending the Doctor with them. And she was not able to rid her mind of the thought that he was innocent.

The people clamored for the blood of the Jew. A dark foreigner, a convicted poisoner, a plotter, a receiver of stolen monies, a Jew! Away with him! And cheers for the Earl of Essex who had shown himself true Englishman in bringing such a reasty villain to justice. The Earl could not step out of his house without encountering a little group of loiterers who cried out with joy at the sight of him.

The months slipped by while the prisoners died the slow, agonized death of waiting; and still the Queen hesitated. It may be that she hoped for something to come to light in Spain or Flanders to exculpate the wretched Doctor. To her, he seemed no more than a pathetic old man who had blundered into a morass of intrigue through ill advice and poor judgment. For, as she said, he did not appear to be fashioned of the stuff that makes for traitors.

Then, one sunny day in June, she yielded to the urging of her ministers, among them John Whitgift, her Archbishop. She threw out one long hand in exasperation, then drew the paper toward her. The pen scratched and over the bent red head, the eyes of her councilors met.

"Now, in Christ's sweet name, leave me in peace!"

Bowing, they took the paper. The news ran down the corridors, out through the doors into the courtyards to the men-at-arms, to the ostlers, to the tradesmen who surged about the back precincts, out to the streets.

"The Jew dies tomorrow!"

Raised above the heads of those about him, Essex sat his horse and watched. To his companions he said nothing, but sat with his bridle hand on his horse's neck, the other resting negligently on his hip. He felt restless and irritated. The Lopez execution was being disgracefully mismanaged. Idly he watched them securing Tinoco and Ferreira heavily by the arms, then turning them to face the scaffold and watch the Doctor's death, who was to go first. Their ghastly pale looks did not move Essex, who thought only of the dark bloody work to which the two were committed, and of the Spanish money that had bought them. A grim smile crept over his lips.

How ridiculous the Doctor looked as they plucked him from the gaping, jostling crowd, pushing him up the rude wooden steps. In his crude yellow smock, uniform of the condemned, he was a grotesque figure. The rough frieze robe, hanging like a sack on his spare frame, had a hole at the top, through which poked the scraggy neck and waggling gray beard. This moved the people's mirth, and when the old man attempted to speak, they roared and shouted.

Essex jerked impatiently. Did the hooting rabble intend to make a picnic of this execution? Evidently many did, for there was a plentiful smell of cold sausage and garlic on the morning air. Whole families milled in the crowd, and children were hoisted onto shoulders, the better to see. Tyburn Hill was fair on this June morning, the grass about the place was very green and the air breathed warmly of summer. It was not often there was such good weather for these occasions.

Over a slight lull the old voice quavered. "Good people, I pray you with my dying breath——"

"Get on wi' it! We'll come do Bloody Dick's work for him, an he start not soon! On! On wi' it!"

Yes, by God, thought Essex, on with it. Cut short the scandalous breath in the old throat and put an end to scorching gossip as well as treason and plot. He was as eager as they to throttle the Portuguese.

Still the Doctor tried. "I do swear that I love my mistress better even than Jesus Christ!"

"Aye! But ye'll not tup her again this side of Hell!" The crowd roared at its own wit, and those about Essex smirked behind their gauntlets. But a curt order from the sheriff put the rope quickly about the corded neck and they strung him up. They finished him, castration, disemboweling, and when flesh could feel no more, quartering. Dripping, Dick rose, wiped his hands and arms on the smock he had stripped from the doctor, and signed to Ferreira's guards.

In his saddle, Essex shifted. Two more. Already he was exhausted. Idly he watched as Ferreira died hard. Did the Portuguese think, in his agonies, of the aged Doctor? For it was his testimony, more than anyone's, that had tightened the noose about Lopez. Ah well, there were now two less to trouble them. With Tinoco done for, the affair was closed, and England's Earl Marshall had done what he could for England.

Now it was Tinoco's turn. Essex watched him closely. What a young fool, so to bring down ruin on his own head. The other two were of no importance, but this young man had most of life before him. With clenched fists he stood, muscles tense, while they put the noose on him. Swinging in the air, he held his breath, and when they cut him down for the finishing, he staggered to his feet. Catching Bloody Dick off-guard, he fetched him a lusty blow behind the ear and felled him. The crowd went wild. This was something more than they had expected. They hitched their belts and surged forward.

Essex groaned and beat his clenched fist on his pommel. What a brawl! The crowd cheered the naked young Portuguese, rope about his neck, desperate power in his arm. Bloody Dick closed with him, but Tinoco drove his fist beneath the other's belt and doubled him up. A rough ring jumped about the two, cheering them on.

"Christ's bones!" Essex rose in his stirrups. He gestured sharply, and a lieutenant cut and slashed forward into the crowd to reach the furious captain. Under their orders, the yeomen strove to break the ring about the strugglers. Below, the people screamed their disappointment at not being able to see. Essex could just make out the two, crouched, their heads bobbing about as they feinted and dodged. What, in the name of ten devils, was that captain doing? He saw Bloody Dick stagger, bellowing with rage, as his men caught him and prevented his fall. Then Tinoco was down, felled from behind. With a howl, Dick seized his knife and fell upon him.

White with rage, Essex turned his horse, and threaded the throng, his face screwed into distaste. The whole thing had turned from a grim display of justice into a humiliating farce. Mingled with his anger was a vague discomfiture. Who had really won in this affair of the doctor? Had the Cecils triumphed after all, with their hounding of the three traitors to the scaffold, whose ceremony, with its intolerable bungling, had been left to him? In silence, among his friends, he rode home.

Back on Tyburn, empty now of the trampling crowd, all was still save for the small twittering of little birds that hopped about the stained grass. The bodies were there but the heads were gone. Mounted on pikes, escorted by the happy people, they were carried off to Tower Bridge. To the three Portuguese had fallen the honor of being executed for an attempt on the Queen's life.

Late that evening Elizabeth sent for the older Cecil. The June day had turned cold and the light drizzle that now fell found the age in old bones. Wrapped in a warm robe and sitting in her high-backed chair, she sipped at something in her small porringer and felt out of sorts. She shivered as a knock came at the door.

"Come in, come in, Burghley. I'm having some slops. Stomach's queasy." She heaved a deep sigh. "Well, my lord, Justice has this day been done on Tyburn, and I cannot say I feel better for it." The old Lord Treasurer stood by the fire, one velvet-slippered foot resting on the hearth. "Sit down, sit down."

She never permitted Burghley to stand or kneel in her presence. Long association had bred in her a deep respect for her old servant, and however harshly she might deal with him on occasion, she felt for him something like affection. Besides, it pleased her to pamper him in his old age, made her feel almost—young.

He held a small box in his hand.

"What have ye there?" Across her shoulder she peered, moving her stiff neck gingerly.

With a bow he handed it to her. "For your Majesty," he said quietly.

"Ah!" She knew. She opened it. There lay the ring, its diamonds blazing softly, its rubies like blood. Again she shivered. Damn Essex, damn him. He stops at nothing. "I cannot help but think the poor man was not guilty as they said." Uncomfortably she looked at her old councilor across the hearth. In her eyes he read a pleading for comfort. Straight back at her he gazed, his aged light blue eyes slightly milky in his lined face.

"Madam, I am an old man, and I am beginning to believe in fate. I feel sure it was the Doctor's destiny to die today on Tyburn, and that neither you nor I could have prevented it."

She stared at him. She was not reassured. Fate! Did not God help those who helped themselves, and was it not their duty to have helped the Doctor out of his dilemma? Fate! Then she veered round.

"You are a good man, Burghley, and I know you desire to help me." For a few minutes she contemplated the fire. "It is of his widow that I wish to speak. She must keep his goods and chattels, the house at Holborn and all its contents. She is to have all. See to it." Her hand closed over the little box. "And now, good night, Burghley. You and I have seen much in our time." It was the only concession she would make to age.

Alone before the fire she slipped the ring onto her finger and sat looking at its brilliance in the light. This, more than anything, had killed the Doctor. Gold, diamonds, rubies—the price of an old man's life. Suddenly she recalled that windy afternoon when the old Portuguese had disturbed her at her painting. She had spilled red paint on her finger. She looked at the rubies.

"Fate," she murmured.

And Essex, she wondered what he was thinking. She supposed he felt a grim triumph at having brought a miserable old Jew to justice. Perhaps he thought he had beaten the Cecils at their own game for once. She smiled, but in her smile there was no mirth.

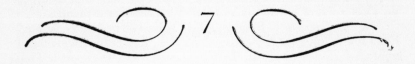

La Reine S'Amuse

*I*f Essex felt any triumph at all over the Lopez incident, it was short-lived. His success in saving the Queen's life had apparently no weight with Elizabeth, for not a month after the drama of the doctor, she suddenly gave the post of Attorney-General to Coke.

Essex beat his clenched fist against his head. "Francis, I vow I will get you the Solicitorship. Never despair."

But Bacon was crushed. Too late he saw how he had destroyed his chance, if indeed, he ever had one. To Anthony he wrote, "No man ever received a more exquisite disgrace." And to Burghley, "It is finished. I shall retire to Cambridge, there to live out my days in solitude and meditation." He felt a sudden nostalgia for the quiet cloisters and cool rooms of his old college.

As for Gloriana, she was delighted with herself. She had rapped Bacon sharply over the knuckles, and so was avenged for his interference in the matter of the Parliament grants. Perhaps another time he would watch what he did. Her appointment of Coke was a master stroke, for he was brilliant and hard, polished with solid endowments of brain and experience, a fit man to serve a Tudor.

He was one who would bring to the Crown all the resources of English law, who would pursue with relentless thoroughness those whom the Crown accused of treason, sedition, or invasion of the prerogative. Gloriana smiled slyly, and looked about for a like Solicitor to take the place vacated by Coke. Her eye lighted on a gentleman named Fleming, a man greatly inferior to Bacon. She twirled her fan and considered.

Mindful that blood was thicker than water, Burghley for once pitied his nephew; he and his son set themselves tactfully to advance Bacon's suit with the Queen. But the mere mention of Bacon's name sent her fleering from rage to rage, and brusquely she ordered them all to leave her in peace.

To Essex, who continued to press her, she snapped, "By God's most precious blood, Essex, if you do not leave me alone in this matter, I shall undo both you and your friends. Let there be an end."

Bacon became pale and ill. Hopelessly, he sent a rich jewel to the Queen, an enameled button set in pearls. Gloriana thanked him and returned it. To Burghley he wrote that he was going abroad, and through his uncle he sent his respectful farewells to the Queen.

Gloriana snarled. "Burghley, *I* say who shall go abroad and who shall stay at this Court. Tell Master Bacon to cool down."

Bacon's nerves wore thin. Spitefully he wrote to the Lord Keeper Puckering:

> I do see well that I cannot hope to succeed at Court so long as my cousin, Sir Robert Cecil, is in her Majesty's loves and favor. That little man does work ill to me on every and all occasions. I shall forthwith abandon my service and give myself over body and soul to contemplation. I have said the same to Lord Essex, who, God knows, has caused much disquiet to himself on my behalf.

Essex was appalled. Even his own hotheadedness was wary when it came to writing his mind about the Cecils. "Francis, you will get nowhere villifying the Queen's pets. Where is your philosophy? It seems you must eat some of your own advice at last."

But Bacon stared bitterly out of his study window and did not answer.

The Queen put the matter into the back of her mind and gave herself up to the enjoyment of summer. She refused to see how Essex sulked in the background of all the gay scenes about her. She was so pleased with a new tune written for her by Bull that she rewarded him with ten rose nobles and sent his wife a pair of grey satin sleeves richly worked with jewels, the gold thread shaped into little square notes. Then down at her lovely Richmond she whetted her appetite with a small storm over her favorite maid of the moment, who had dared to marry without her permission.

While the young men stood about the tennis court in their silk and sweat, and the silent maids clutched nervously the garlands they were weaving, she whipped up her passion. The weeping bride was banished to Somerset House, and the young groom was sent to the Tower. There also lay Walter Ralegh, who, in consequence of having married Elizabeth Throckmorten, languished in severe disgrace.

Still in a tight rage, Elizabeth ordered the Court to Whitehall, giving sharp and elaborate orders for the entertainment of the new French Ambassador. She meant to impress him with a show of English merrymaking, and the bearkeepers and houndsmen threw themselves into a mighty bustle.

Tom o' Lincoln, sufficiently recovered from the grievous wounds of his last fight, was now ready to be torn anew, and in the early dawn was brought from his den across the river. Shackled to a great iron post driven into the deck piece of a heavy barge, he lolled sullenly on his chain. He shambled ashore, his four keepers poking him with long steel-shod pikes, and a crowd of idlers and young lads greeted him with delight. Nearly seven feet when reared up on hind legs, his coarse coat was literally covered with scars, some half healed, others gleaming white amid the heavy fur. His long black muzzle was torn in twenty places, and one of his ears, now dark and leathery, flapped in shredded ribbons. He was almost as famous as great Sackerson, who had finally died with one little eye left, and most of the fur torn away from his brave neck.

"Aye, there, Tom o' Lincoln!" The little boys, bold on their perches atop the railing of the landing, called to him. They threw the shells of their hazelnuts at the monster.

"Ah, there, ye murtherin' limbs o' Satan," growled Paddy O'Connell, the Queen's Irish keeper. "By the black beard of old Nick, ye'll run if I turn him loose o' ye!"

At this the little boys laughed the louder. Tom o' Lincoln would have to kill his keepers first to get loose, for he was great and precious to the people as well as to the Queen, and well they knew it. He was taken away to his underground quarters to await the afternoon.

Whitehall looked gay in the cool breeze off the river, with the royal barges, brave in scarlet and green and white, hung with green garlands of the maids. Above the steep-pitched roof of the palace the royal standard flaunted brilliant checkers to the sun, while within all was hum and savory commotion.

Rich fruity bouquet of wines; heavy spice of sweetmeats. Suddenly the Queen was pleased to signify that dinner was over. Stifling belches behind fans and lace handkerchiefs, the Court trooped off to the galleries for the bearbaiting.

Already in the center of the courtyard, Tom was collared to his stake with a goodly length of chain to allow free movement about among the dogs. Restlessly he padded about on all fours, snout to the ground in search of choice titbits among the apples, nuts, and sweets that were showered upon him. At a signal from the Master, two boys came as close as they dared, long rakes clawing back those bits they could not reach. Tom could not fight well on a full belly.

Slender trumpets now announced the approach of royalty, and to a sprightly air Gloriana, brilliant in egg-yellow barred with scarlet and silver, her red wig shimmering with a thousand crystals, took her seat in the center of the royal pavilion.

Essex stood in her shadow, arms crossed on his chest, a lowering scowl on his face. Sunk in spiritual gloom, he wore black striped with peacock green to emphasize his mood. Gloriana ignored him.

On leashes, four to a man, the hounds were coming into the yard below, jumping up at their masters with short, excited barks. They were mastiffs, with short noses and powerful jaws for gripping. Two clutches of them were now turned loose on Tom, who backed against his pole, lips lifted in a wary snarl. He made a sudden sortie out to the dogs that scattered, barking furiously. Raging and growling, they circled closer. Full to his rope's length lunged the bear, and they skittered back, their claws rattling on the brick paving. At last one fellow, more reckless than the rest, shot in to seize Tom's muzzle. In a flash the bear grabbed him, howling and snarling, and squeezed him viciously against his great barrel chest. The mastiff gave a sharp yelp, then dropped limply to the ground, where he lay still.

Paddy O'Connell swore in his beard. The mastiff, Brown Boxer, was one of his favorites. The other dogs went in by two's and three's, batted back by Tom, who sent them rolling over and over in frenzied bundles of flying legs and tails.

Up in the galleries the betting grew as reckless as the dogs. How many hounds would Tom kill or disable before the Master called an end? Blount and young Christopher, his brother, leaned far over the railing, yelling to the dogs to fight. And on the other side of the pavilion the French Ambassador smiled at his suite, then looked down his long nose at *ces fêtes sauvages des anglais*. The new effeminate coterie in France, to which he belonged, viewed such sights with disgust. A masque or a revel would be more to their taste.

Gloriana swept her fan of yellow plumes against the flies and gave a crisp order. "Tell them to get those dogs in or take the brute back to his den."

She was not enjoying herself, not with Essex skulking at her shoulder. A prickle ran up her back but she shrugged it off.

A fresh lot of dogs was brought in, animals of fiercer character than the others, and they charged Tom, hackles rising on their swelling necks and shoulders. At a shout from the Master the whole pack flew at the bear, and there was suddenly a swirling mass of forms, biting, roaring, tossing, tumbling. The bear clawed them off and fought his way out, a mass of blood and saliva. Four dogs lay motionless or feebly twitching, necks and backs broken, while two others limped out of reach of those terrible claws and great yellow teeth.

Again the dogs flew at Tom and fastened themselves, tearing and snatching at his flanks, where he could not reach them. He rolled over on the ground, crushing the life out of those not nimble enough to jump before the enormous weight flattened them. The others ripped and slashed at the thick brown hide.

Essex took little heed of the spectacle. He was busy with his own thoughts. He had half a mind to clear out for Wanstead and his own womenfolk. Not a word had Gloriana vouchsafed about the Lopez plot. But she wore daily the diamond and ruby ring that flashed accompaniment to her barbed remarks to others about Bacon. He seethed.

Pah, what a lot they were! Mistress Elizabeth Vernon was sliding her eyes his way now. She was a delicious small thing, with her pouting mouth and cloud of silky hair under a net of pearls. At his frown she shrugged and turned back to the delights below. Kat Fytton jested with two men, one in ox-blood velvet, the other in gray. Gray damask took his pearl earring and pressed it into her hand as they wagered on the dogs. Then he shouted with laughter at her as he won. He plunged his hand down between her breasts and brought up a lacy kerchief which he threaded through one of his finger rings.

But now it was plain that Tom was getting exhausted, and in order to save him for a public fight on the Monday, the Master called an end to the baiting. Seven dogs had been killed outright and for several others, only shooting remained. Everyone save the French Ambassador, the Queen, and Essex had had a most enjoyable afternoon.

Also a certain one of the Queen's maids, who complained of dizziness and sweating, but none paid her any heed. The Master of the Revels announced a water carnival for the morrow, and Elizabeth smiled sarcastically to herself. Her sharp eye had noted the Frenchman's distaste. Ah well, tomorrow they would show him fol-dols enough.

The Queen's maid was put to bed with a rising fever and swelling in her armpits.

The palace clock struck eleven. Newly released from the Tower and forgiven, Ralegh was gambling with some cronies in the Presence Chamber. The Squire of the Body, on duty for the evening, was in terror lest Elizabeth, just retired, should hear the shouts. Southampton and a young hanger-on, the former losing heavily, were cheek-by-jowl with Ralegh; all three were tipsy.

The squire grew desperate. "For the last time, gentlemen, disperse. Shall I call the guard?"

Ralegh swept another trick off the board. He did not look up, but Southampton turned irritably. "Shut thy babble," he ordered.

"I have my duty—" began the squire.

"Oh, to the devil with it," drawled Ralegh. He pocketed his winnings. "I'm off." Only just back on the fringe of favor, released by one of Gloriana's whims, he was not anxious to find his way back into trouble. He picked up his feathered hat and thrust an arm through that of Southampton's young companion, guiding him out the door.

Southampton sat on heavily and let the cards slip idly through his fingers. In a moment he looked up to see the two back, Ralegh solemn, the other pale as a winding sheet.

"God ha' mercy on us," the young man whispered.

As if struck, Southampton held the cards above table. "What's that?"

A bleak smile flitted across Ralegh's face. "Mayhap, my friend, my winnings did me no good, after all. There's plague upstairs."

The silence was stupid. Southampton, still drunk, only half comprehended; the youngster crossed himself and fumbled out a rosary; the squire sat weakly down.

Ralegh recovered first. "Cheer up." He was dry. "If plague is for thee, 'twill get thee. Down in Devon we have a prayer:

> 'Fram ghasties and ghoulies
> And lang-leggitty beasties
> And things that go bump! in the night—
> Good Lord deliver us!'

And I say, add plague to that, and sleep with a light heart."

The others were still pale.

"Buck up!" repeated Ralegh. "It's the hangman or the headsman for the likes of us. Aye, 'tis born in upon me this night that I for one, am destined to be beheaded, which is the proper death for a gentleman rogue, who is not allowed to die decently in battle. I shall die a noble's death, by gum! No gasping out my end in a dark hole. Try such consolation, my lords. You will find it wondrous comfortable in time of plague." He grinned at them.

But grim panic held the Court fast. The Queen's maid was worse. At ten of the clock the old midwife who tended her had uncovered the swellings, and a maid holding a basin of vinegar at the bedside dropped it and ran screaming from the room. The news spread like smoke.

Plague! How it stalked through a city, reaching a clammy hand to garner old and young, rich and poor alike, into its ghastly harvesting. Why had the Court come to London just now, when the dead carts were overflowing with rotting corpses, when sulfur fires burned day and night at every crossing, when dozens of doors were chalked with the deadly sign of the double red cross!

Shivering with fear, the Court paced about the halls, afraid to go to bed. Lord Burghley came in, limping cruelly on his gouty foot. Ralegh and Essex gave him curt greeting.

"Have you told her Grace?"

"No," replied Essex. "By now she is sleeping; we cannot alarm her."

Burghley frowned. "Little do you know her Grace, if you think to alarm her, even with plague. But it is urgent that she move. You've told Derby?"

"No."

Contempt shone in the old eyes. These young bloods were no good in a crisis. "Gentlemen," he was short, "it would seem that this shock has undone you entirely. I shall take the responsibility." He limped toward the guard. "The Queen's maid," he ordered.

Pompous old geck, thought Essex.

"When you have lived to my age, gentlemen," Burghley was now sermonizing, "you will know that it is very difficult to alarm the Queen. You will have but one fear, which is of anything that imperils the royal safety." A sudden flash of pain knitted his brows. He rested one hand on the back of a chair. "Sir Walter, inform my lord Derby that her Majesty will be wishful to take barge in the morning, possibly at dawn. And you, my lord," to Essex, "will remain within easy call. The Queen may have need of you. I pray you, oblige."

Mary Ratcliffe came in. "Her Grace is awake. She wishes to know what goes forward at this hour of the night."

Burghley smiled knowingly. "Take me in," he said. Essex followed.

In her favorite high-backed chair sat the Queen, reading a Bible by the light of a small lamp. Above her dressing robe of black, her face was ivory.

"Madam, Madam," remonstrated Burghley, "your Grace has not been to bed."

"I'm not so old as you, Burghley," was the dry rejoinder. "I cannot sleep, and you—I suppose you do not need to sleep." For a moment she looked beyond him at Essex, but did not address him. She closed her book, first marking her place with a ribbon, then rested her hands on it. "I cannot sleep, my lord," she repeated, "even when I would. What's the matter with Essex? He looks scared. Have the Spaniards struck, or is it the plague this time?"

Essex stared. She was uncanny. Always she asked for it straight off; bad news she gulped down at one dose, like a sour physic.

"The plague, Madam. The poor young lady is even now, I believe, *in extremis.*"

The sharp eyes softened. "Poor wench. Poor, poor wench. We'll leave. Tell Derby to get 'em up at dawn, we'll go down to Oatlands." She rose and shook out her robe. "As for me, I shall go to bed. I have seen too much, my lords, to let this thing level me. Call me in three or four hours. The girl, meanwhile——"

"She will not see dawn, your Grace."

"Amen." She was silent for a moment. "So be it. She is Papist, is she not? I shall pay for her masses. See to it. Letters shall go to the family from Oatlands." She turned to Essex. "Get to bed, Robert, and take Burghley with you."

In a high attic chamber the Queen's young maid lay dying. They had dosed her with dragon-water and mithridate, to no avail. Death crouched at the door, waiting to claim her. Everyone had run away except an old crone who had recovered from a light attack of the sickness eighteen months before. She sponged the girl's burning head with cold water.

"If I had some egg yolks for a poultice," she muttered. She turned the moaning patient on her pillows. She tottered to the door and peered out into the narrow hall. All had fled. In their selfish terror they had left the stricken woman to die; the aged nurse knew it was no use to try her old legs on the stairs to go for help. It was five flights down to the kitchens, where, like as not, she would be thrown into the street. And the girl might get out of bed in her delirium and wander off.

"She's dying, belike. Ah me, weary's the world, weary's the world." She went back to the bed, her worn slippers scuffling on the stone floor. The girl had stopped turning and groaning and was lying still and lethargic, her flush gone, a pallid greenish hue spreading over her drawn face.

" 'Twon't be long," murmured the nurse. Indeed, the girl was sinking into the coma. "A priest, a priest, her soul should be shriven."

But the sufferer was past all spiritual help now. For an hour or more she lay thus, while the nurse nodded and dozed, and finally roused herself to feel the sick girl's head. It was wet and deathly cold. Suddenly the lips parted and a blackish fluid issued from one corner of the mouth. The features shrank and lost all semblance of life. A spasm passed over the face and down the limbs. She was dead.

The lovely dawn was just flushing over London when the Court gentry, subdued and quiet, stole forth from Whitehall as if they feared to rouse the plague to follow after them with grisly steps. Then gentlemen took horse and the girls and elderly men trooped down the long narrow covered way that led to the water-steps, the maids reaching fearfully for each other's hands in the gloom of the passage.

In a hushed silence the boats waited for them. The royal barge with Elizabeth glided away with no sound save the soft lap-lapping of the little waves and the ordered splash of the oarsmen.

At the same moment a shrouded figure wrapped in a long white sheet was carried feet foremost out of a back entrance and hurriedly bundled into a cart. The girl who a short week before had been beautiful in the springtime of her youth was now a loathsome corpse, already blackening and marked for a grave in the common pit outside the city walls.

Around the little cupola of Whitehall the ravens slowly circled, and from a chapel nearby a bell began to toll in measured and sorrowful accents.

Failure

*A*nd so, with death and delight, joy and sorrow, the year grew older. Summer lingered with soft showers and long, warm days. Autumn succeeded and all the beeches turned copper red and golden yellow before they dropped their painted leaves among the flaming bracken. The barns were full of sweet hay, and the harvest moon shone down on revels rich with great piles of fruits and nuts and greater sheaves of corn and barley.

Down in London town Thomas Nashe wrote: "Autumn hath all summer's fruitful treasure," and Edmund Spenser brought his Irish bride from County Cork to see the wonders of Elizabeth's England. He also brought some books of a strange allegory that he was dedicating to England's Faerie Queene. It was a very fantastical legend that he was composing, and he spent long nights reading it to his young wife, whose eyes grew large with imagination.

The Faerie Queene herself flitted from Oatlands to Richmond, from Richmond to Greenwich, and thence back to London, where she declared herself too restless to endure life.

She knew Essex was sickly, shut up in his town house with Joseph and Frances, who now was with him since little Walter had died down at Chartley. The whole house was in mourning; it was as if the older Walter had died all over again.

Elizabeth pushed painful thoughts of her favorite into the back of her mind. She fretted and fumed until Lord Burghley suggested she come down to Theobalds and see his new gardens.

She took her maids and a few young men and went rumbling off in her coach to the country. Riding grotesquely at her window was Robert Cecil. That hand in the suède gauntlet, which was all she could see of her secretary from her curtained window, ought to have been Essex's. She sighed, leaned back, and closed her eyes. She felt sixty, but she did not feel ready to acknowledge her years. Devoutly she hoped her neuralgic toothache would not begin again, or her racking afternoon headache. By God, she thought grimly, I feel as queasy as if I were with child.

Bareheaded, looking incredibly frail, Lord Burghley awaited her at his gates. The breeze parted his beard in feathery fronds on his chin. She greeted him cordially, though the jolting had brought on the headache. She gave him her hand and together they walked up the avenue of late-flowering trees, through the gate in the inner garden wall to the stately entrance.

Elizabeth raised her thin nose. "Already the air refreshes me, my lord. I shall sup in my room tonight. Come to me later, and we will discourse. Let this lot of zanies," she waved her hand at the score of ladies and gentlemen, "amuse themselves for once."

The gentle ministrations of Mary relieved her, and after a light supper with only a couple of her young men to serve her, she sent for the Lord Treasurer.

"Let us take a turn in the garden, my lord. It will not be dark for an hour or two."

Mary threw a light cloak about her shoulders, and Elizabeth stepped out onto the terrace and down into the garden. The evening air was full of the scent of Burghley's flowers, as together the Queen and her old minister paced the tidy walks. Somewhere in the back of the house there were laughter and lights, but the garden was theirs alone.

"You have made a fair place." With appreciation Elizabeth stopped beside an exquisite fountain, a miniature retreat closed by a latticed wall. The blue tile lining the delicate marble dyed the water indigo, and the swan that glided among the small white ducks wore about its neck a little golden collar.

At the conceit she smiled. "Are you bringing back Chaucer and the Early Ages, my lord? My gallants will not approve that. 'Forward' is their watchword, though in truth," here she sighed, "I fain would wait and look about me while I may. Here in this garden time has verily stood still. I like it."

The summerhouse with its tenantry of pallid Roman busts pleased her, too. "Tomorrow I shall sit here out of the sun, and see if I can speak to these dead monarchs in their own tongue."

Burghley showed her his mild wonders. There was a fine carib from the New World. "And Ralegh tells me the sugar bush from Florida is like to thrive under glass. I mean to try it soon." The flat voice droned comfortably on.

"Remarkable," conceded Gloriana.

But neither was thinking of the garden and the wonders of the New World. In the depths of his wily mind Burghley had buried his speculations about his nephew Francis Bacon, and the new bid for him to have the Solicitorship. Sad as it would be for fate once more to pass over the fortunes of his nephew, he privately longed for another stiff check to be administered to the prestige of the Earl of Essex. For two and a half years the struggle had lasted, with Essex determined to win; with a flip of the royal finger he could be sent back into a dark corner, his hopes on behalf of his friend forever blasted.

Burghley glanced at the face beside him. The thin profile was a delicate cameo, cut against the dark green of the trees. Above the rich fur the white face and flaming hair glowed in the early evening light like jewels. The Queen's step was light and elastic, marvelous for one turned sixty. Her expression was quiet and withdrawn.

She, too, was thinking of Essex and Bacon and the whole lot of them. What a precious parcel of rogues they were! She knew they hung about her only for what they could get, their daggers loose in the sheath. She knew, too, how the old lord beside her figured in all this, as he moved the principal figures about like men on a chessboard. Did he think she was going to give the Solicitorship to his nephew, that dry lawyer? Aye, no doubt he did, because of Essex. And she felt the heat rising in her face. With a kind of mild anger she thought how the affair of Essex had caused embarrassment between her and her faithful old minister. After all, Burghley was one man whose good will she valued.

"You amaze me, my lord." She broke the hush. "God has permitted you to outlive most of the great men of our day; you have outraced them all, and by my faith, I think you will survive me."

"Hardly, Madam," protested Burghley. "I am hard upon eighty, and I grow deaf and miserable with my years. I should not care to outlive your Grace; for me the light will go out when Gloriana ceases to rule England."

At that her loud, familiar laugh echoed through the trees. "God's truth, Burghley, art becoming a courtier at the last? I pray you, my lord, leave the pretty speeches to the young bloods and those who must needs flatter me to hide their brainlessness. Aye, me," again she sighed, "I can forgive an addlepate if he hath a silver tongue. Perchance that is my weakness, but if it be so, 'tis too late to do aught about it now. The pattern must continue to the end." With a quick look she pierced him.

Burghley threw out a hand. "I am too old and feeble to serve you well," he began, but she cut him short.

"Never deprecate yourself, my lord. You have served me well, and well do I know it." In silence they paced on. Her mood changed. "Live, Burghley, don't leave me. You are the last link with the past. I could spare Hatton and Walsingham, aye, yes, and Leicester," here she grew hot again, thinking of Essex, "I could spare all those, for they understood only themselves, and that but darkly. But you, my faithful friend, you know me better than I do myself." She picked a glossy leaf, twirling it between her fingers. "Heigh-ho!" she tossed it away. "Many the witches' brew you and I have concocted to dull the sense and dim the eyes of our enemies. I have trusted you, Burghley, and you—you have failed me not."

In the dusk she smiled sentimentally into his face, as he stood, his head respectfully inclined at just the correct angle for an old and confidential servant. Then he raised his white brows and they looked into each other's eyes. Sharp little black eyes, lit with reminiscence and the tiny sparkling fire of malicious amusement, and steady old light blue ones, mild with age and wisdom, but behind their milky mildness, a wary look.

The first chilly wind of night swept the garden. "Let us go in," said she. "The evening air is bad for your gout, my lord."

In her chamber she sat thinking of the garden and Burghley, and of Essex, the thought uppermost in both their minds. Of the Earl they had not spoken a word. How the old lord detested and feared her association with her favorite! Truly, in this thing she was alone, with no one to help her; with it she must cope unaided.

Burghley had powerfully reminded her this evening of the passing of time, yet he no longer irritated her. Now she regretted the times she had sent him stoop-shouldered from her presence, his eyes moist from her harshness. Lately she had come to lean on him as if she took a peculiar comfort in his being, feeling in him some safeguard against an austere future that frightened her. So long as Burghley lived, she could find strength to go on, even though she must walk some paths alone.

She called Mary to read, and the girl settled herself into the lamplight. She opened a slender volume, bound in violet and powdered with tiny gilt flowers.

"What have you there? Ah, Ronsard. Very well." She leaned back and closed her eyes.

The fresh voice lingered over the ardent lyrics of the Frenchman. Soothed by the rise and fall of Mary's reading, Elizabeth lay back, half listening.

> Ah, time is flying, lady—time is flying;
> Nay, 'tis not time that flies but we that go,
> Who in short space shall be in churchyard lying
> And of our loving parley none shall know,
> Nor any man consider what we were;
> Be therefore kind, my love, whiles thou art fair.

"'Time is flying,'" murmured Elizabeth, laying her hand on Mary to stop her. "Robin, Robin, why do we waste the years in wrangling?" Languidly she moved her head against her cushions. "'Be therefore kind, my love, whiles thou art fair.'"

She motioned Mary to go on; but she did not hear. Her thoughts were away with Essex. She called his image to her mind, her heart softened, and she resolved to be more gentle with him.

And while she lay in her chair and drank in the beauties of poesy and the summer night, the Earl, up in town, lay on his bed and wooed elusive sleep. He thought of his sister Penelope and of her dead admirer, Sidney. What was it he used to say of sleep? "The prisoner's release"? He moved restlessly on his feverish pillow. God's death, what a warm night for September.

He rose and went to his casement, pushing it open to the night. The harvest moon lay calm upon the Thames and touched with silvery light the familiar skyline of London. Essex sat and cooled his hot head and his hotter heart at the window. He leaned his arm upon the sill and rested his head upon it.

He was sad and depressed over the loss of little baby Walter, named in hope and joy for his dead brother. Now the firm hand of the older Walter had reached out for the tiny one of his little namesake and together they had gone off into the shadows. The old melancholia moved from the brain to the heart and he drew a sobbing breath.

He had many things to console him, yet he was restless and unhappy. Never could he resist the desire to torment himself and the Queen with importunate demands for favors which it was against her grain to grant. Why did they so disquiet one another with the perversities of their natures; why did he insinuate his desires upon her, then cling so tenaciously to his intent? In early days they used so to delight in each other's company that they were never apart. Now, although a strange attraction drew them together, they never could meet without that clashing of their wills which drove them frantic.

And yet—the passion of admiring worship possessed him again—yet, she was still Gloriana, a fascinating creature of silk and steel, vibrating with color and forever unexpected in her fantastic resources. Ageless, indestructible, she made all other women beside her seem pale and lifeless. Ah, she was his glorious mistress; he was still her favorite. His lip lifted in a half smile, and he closed his eyes.

And thus Joseph found him, sleeping peacefully, with the London night in his hair. Horrified, he tried to close the window, but the Earl was fast in slumber, lost in the matchless mazes of his dream.

Near the end of October, Elizabeth gave the patent for Solicitor-General to Fleming. When Cecil broke the news, Essex could not believe it. Matters between Gloriana and himself had been silken smooth of late, and it was like old times. He had been so sure now that she would grant him his wish. In that content he had relaxed, bringing forth in his assurance the full dazzlement of his charms.

He smiled bitterly at the little secretary. "For myself I can get anything; for my friends, nothing."

Half stunned, he took horse from Richmond and went down to Francis at Twickenham. He strode into Bacon's study where he found the lawyer absorbed in a new globe.

"Well, Francis, it seems you possess the world in little today, and that, by God, is all."

Bacon looked up, his pale face a shade whiter than before. Essex nodded. "The Queen has denied me a place for you, and has given it to Fleming." The other gave a slight groan. "God's blood, I know, Francis. The truth is, you've chosen the wrong one to back you. I'm a curse on what I touch." He bit his lip and scowled at the floor, his eyes bright with angry tears.

Bacon got up and in his agitation took a short turn about the room. He put his fine hands behind him.

Essex saw them clench the nails into the palms. "Francis," he offered, "you'll not suffer, that I promise. I've a fine piece of land, well worth eighteen hundred pounds——"

Bacon stopped pacing and shook his head. Essex threw out his hand and grasped the other's arm. "For God's sake," he cried passionately, "don't add to my bitterness by refusing me this favor!"

Bacon sank into his chair. He was afraid of accepting a gift of such value. As matters stood now, he was not within an obligation to the Earl; quite to the contrary. Would it not be better to stay clear of the necessity to repay a favor?

"I am minded," he said cautiously, "of the Duke of Guise. He sought to bind men to his service by gifts and obligations."

Essex laughed shortly. "When I ask you to be my man, body and soul, Bacon, you may sell me to my enemies." He dragged out a chair and threw himself into it. "I am no Duke of Guise, though verily, I believe the Queen has more love for him than she has for me, and God knows, she has many times wished *him* dead."

Bacon was not comfortable. These constant quarrels with the Queen would someday force a real crisis in which the Earl's friends would be called upon to take sides. He had no intention of ruining his future by a romantic alliance with a losing cause. For the Earl he had no sentiment whatever. Too often, of late, it had been increasingly apparent that the Queen's favorite spent chances as recklessly as a gambler who wagers money he cannot afford to lose.

Bacon had hoped to climb to power on the shoulders of his patron; it now appeared that Essex was a mere child in the eddying whirlpool of political intrigue, an immature hothead who, far from assisting the success of another, bid fair to destroy himself. Bacon grimly promised himself that if and when a trial of strength arose between Gloriana and the Earl, he would take care to be on the right side.

Aloud he said, "I much prefer, my lord, that we hide the matter in forgetfulness."

Disappointment clouded the other's face. "I will not be hindered in this. You shall take the land, Bacon, that I vow."

Take the land . . . well, why not? But first, he would have to think carefully about it. "Give me leave to consider for a space of two days, my lord, and I promise you an answer then." By then he would have thought of a way whereby he might accept this handsome gift while retaining his own integrity.

Restless and upset, Essex refused to stay the night, but galloped off to Wanstead. Three days later one of Bacon's couriers brought him the following:

> My lord of Essex,
> I see you mean to force this issue to your own satisfaction. To please you, then, I accept. But I beg you to be very clear in your mind that I can be no more yours than I was ere I took to myself this pledge of your lordship's munificence. My first duty is to the Crown; that much is clear. But should I grow rich in time, grant me leave to give this back to some of your lordship's unrewarded followers.
> Your lordship's in all obedience,
>
> F. Bacon

Essex drew a deep sigh. Since his failure to succeed for Bacon, his conscience had bothered him. Perhaps this gift would plaster the wounds of both of them. With this he had to be content.

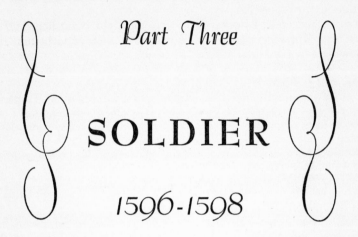

Part Three

SOLDIER

1596-1598

Spanish Assignment

The Spanish were besieging Calais and all day long Dover and the coastal towns were shaken by the sullen booming of Philip's guns. His general had slipped down from the Netherlands and was determined to get the prize. The English port governors waited for the welcome news that Elizabeth, up at Greenwich, had decided, once again to send relief to Henry of Navarre. They listened to the guns and the gooseflesh rose on their necks. As for Henry, he stood on his Normandy beach, his eyes fixed seaward, looking for the help that did not come.

In Dover six thousand men leaned on their English pikes and watched the ships straining at their hawsers in the harbor. And still Elizabeth waited. Mindful of Rouen, back in '91, she felt no trust in Henry. She felt still less trust in Essex, who was to take the relief expedition across the Channel. Why should English blood be spilled and English gold be spent for something that Henry might do alone, if he would bestir himself? She sent polite letters but no men. Her ministers importuned her. Still she delayed.

The guns continued to boom, to the rising panic of the port officials. It would be less than comfortable to have Philip's generals within spitting distance of Dover.

Then an ominous silence settled on the French town. And just as Elizabeth determined to send relief, word came that the town had surrendered. The citadel of Calais was in the hands of the Spaniard.

Essex bore the heavy news to Elizabeth. This was a worse calamity than when English Mary lost Calais to the French. If his eyes did not convey to her the reproach he felt, it was only because he felt no personal loss. This Spanish coup would make no difference to his protracted mission abroad. For when the French voyage was concluded, he was to go to Cadiz. Now that there was no need to go to France, his departure for Spain came that much closer.

Elizabeth received him coolly. She felt the Calais disaster a mortal blow, but she did not let him guess it. In the sunlit room Burghley stood beside her, and it was to him that she turned.

"My love and gratitude to the loyal counties that have stood promptly by," she said. "It seems that their help will not be needed." Burghley bowed and turned to go, but she signed to him to stay.

Fine words, thought Essex. He marveled at her composure. Aloud he said, "And what of the people who will surely rise and growl when they learn what all men must know within the next few days?"

Elizabeth stiffened, and a savage look crossed her face. Highstomached knave! Bitingly she spoke. "Essex, I have grave doubts of your competence in this new venture. Open your mouth a little wider, and you may be sure that Cadiz will never see you!"

Then, at his wounded look, she softened. "Can you not trust me to devise some balm to the hurts of my people? Robin, what a poor prince you must think me that cannot look after my subjects in so small a crisis as this."

He swallowed the retort that rose in him. After all, this was a small affair, and he must keep his mind on the larger issue of the Cadiz venture. He was soon to take ship for Spain. He must be careful or she would stop him. He looked at her and forced a smile. She touched his cheek with a finger and dismissed him.

To Burghley she said heavily, "God was on the side of the Spaniard this time. What to do now?"

"Calais is past recall, Madam. The immediate problem is the people."

"Naturally." She was irritated. "Don't be profound."

Burghley raised his hoary brows and his eyes were owlish. In silence she returned his look and softly she tapped her fan on the chair. She had committed a major error; that they both knew. The task was now to cover it. Between the Queen of England and her minister a delicate tendril of thought was putting forth into the light.

Elizabeth broke the silence. "Now, had Henry been forthright, we might have committed ourselves the sooner. But his vacillation—" she paused.

"Reassurance of French strength did not come, Madam," agreed Burghley. "Now they have failed and it is God's mercy that we were not abandoned to Philip's guns or worse."

He spoke gravely and no smile crossed Elizabeth's face. But both knew how flimsy was the fabric that they planned to stretch between the people of England and the unkind truth which was their mistake. Inwardly she sighed. Oh well, it was a mistake, but not an irretrievable one. Burghley would attend to it so that faces were saved. Meanwhile, she would think of other things. Robin, for instance. She paused before she put her next question.

"What think you of my lord of Essex for the Cadiz venture? He seems overyoung for the job."

"With your Grace's permission, I should say, let him go. There will be Lord Howard to keep him in line, and other responsible gentlemen. Ralegh, if you will."

She flung back against her chair. So Burghley was for Essex and Cadiz. And if Essex failed—she read Burghley like a book. If Essex failed, so much the better for his enemies, and for Burghley's son, Robert Cecil.

"Pooh! Ralegh's no soldier; he's an explorer. Haven't ye found that out yet? And if you have forgotten Essex's prancings at Rouen, I haven't. I wish to God we had Drake here. A thousand curses on that fool's errand in the Indies!"

"But if Drake and Hawkins return with treasure, Madam, as there is every prospect of their doing—" began Burghley tactfully.

"Yes, and if they do no better than my adventurers have been doing lately," retorted Elizabeth, "I shall be bankrupt, and that right speedily."

Then she let Burghley go. He was glad to retire to the peace of his little cabinet, where he could compose his all-important letter in quiet. That document should not be entrusted to the bungling of a secretary, even his son. The letter was to go to the Council, there to be read by them. Thus would England and the world learn that Calais had been lost to Spain, not by English defection, but by the double-dealing of Henry of Navarre, who had hung back for them to pull his chestnuts out of the fire.

When all came out, Essex smiled sardonically. How cleverly the Queen had squirmed out of the tight box into which her shifting resolution had shut her! With what dark skill had she lightly disclaimed all responsibility in the matter, declaring her own course to be open and sensible. The episode left a sour taste in the mouth of more than Essex.

But a speedy end was put to his impatient yearning for action when the Queen sent for him to receive the last instructions for Cadiz. Losing no time, he and Sir Francis Vere, veteran soldier of Elizabeth's campaigns, hastened down to Greenwich. Her Majesty was pleased to be disagreeable.

"I would I had not consented to your going, my lord," she began.

His heart sank. She was giving way to her usual revulsion against his leaving her for a more dangerous climate. Should he have to go again through all the tedious business of persuading her to consent to his going to twist the forked tail of that devil Philip?

He threw a glance at Vere. That gentleman was gazing studiously out the window. The Queen tapped the arm of her chair, her long eyelids cast down in thought.

Essex shifted to the other foot. "I shall be back ere you have missed me." He tried to keep eagerness out of his voice.

She did not hear him. Fretfully, she went on. "There is fear in my mind for your success. So many things can go wrong. Adverse winds, surprise attacks, unexpectedly strong resistance from the enemy, lack of energy at the crucial moment."

"But, Madam!" he cried. "Surely you do not question the ability and prowess of those gentlemen whom you have honored with this command!"

Elizabeth tossed her head. "Howard is well enough, for he has sense to take advice from his betters." She bent her eyes on his companion. "And you, Sir Francis, are seasoned, God knows. But you, Essex," here she whirled out of her chair and round onto him so that the skirts of her farthingale swung like a bell, "how do I know that you and Ralegh will hit it off? There can be no wrangling between you and your officers. I should not fear, were Drake or Hawkins here—damn that black day ever they sailed for the Indies!"

Essex was scarlet. How intolerable, here in the presence of Vere, his inferior in command, to be scolded like a boy! What was she thinking of?

"Madam, your soldiers will never fail in their duty to their Queen." His tone was stiff.

"My knight-errant," scoffed Elizabeth. She heaved a theatrical sigh. "Well, *che sarà sarà*. It seems I am to trust to God once more."

On both of them she heaped the strongest injunctions to carry out the terms of the expedition to the letter. Essex was irked afresh. Did she think that he, as joint commander with Howard, did not know every syllable of their instructions, down to the last comma? He and the Lord Admiral, aided by Ralegh, were to destroy warships and stores in Spanish harbors, to capture and burn towns on the coast, to seize booty from these towns and to watch for prizes.

"And remember," she warned finally, "there is to be no unnecessary slaughter of the enemy, and no killing of women and children and civil men. That I expressly forbid. We will show these Spanish butchers that we can make war in as humane a manner as possible, though," here she shuddered, "war is never humane, and why men love it so, passing even the love of women, only God knows."

Then she dismissed Vere, keeping Essex for the last word. Although it had come to the parting, neither could put away inner exasperation at the other. Thought she: why does he strain so to get away from me? Does he wear that long face to fool me into thinking him sorry to be going? Thought he: why does she humiliate me before others whenever she can? Is she not wise enough to see that never can she chain me to her side with such bonds?

With a cool caress they parted.

Alone once more, Elizabeth paced softly about the beautiful room. She looked at the lacy carving surrounding her coat-of-arms on the wall, but she did not see it. Instead she saw the Devereux arms, and a foolish young man, thirsting to be up and away on a harebrained scheme. What if Philip *had* made an abortive raid on her Cornish coast? He had been scared off and little harm done. She had small faith in this plan to retaliate by spoiling him of his fair city of Cadiz. It was one thing to get a town; it was quite another thing to hold it.

She drew a bowl of early daffodils toward her. The yellow blossoms caught the spring sunlight from the tall colored window. There were flowers in Spain, too—and women. Her mouth twisted.

"Why is he not content to stay here by me?" For the fiftieth time she asked herself the same question. "I have made it worth his while and can continue to do so. But he seeks adventure on foreign shores. New places, new faces, new loves."

Well, God's truth, they might succeed, but she felt nervous and worried as always when he was about to set forth on a hazardous adventure. She would never forgive herself if he were to die on some far-distant shore in England's service. She had not forgotten what she felt like when Sidney threw away his young life at Zutphen, and *he* had meant less than nothing to her.

If only they brought home rich booty, perhaps the glut of the war party would be slaked for a time. God knew she needed money, with her officers in Ireland calling for more men and supplies to keep the Irish rebels in check. And that Henry of Navarre, who after all, was her first line of defense against Philip, *that* one swallowed money as a whale swallows little fish.

Thoroughly disturbed now, she rang a little silver bell and summoned Master Nicholas Hilliard, who was painting her miniature. She would sit to him a while and compose her thoughts, which were beginning to torment her. The artist came in with his delicate brushes and pots and set about his minute business. She watched the refined bearded face with its absent eye, the clever quick hand, and forebore to interrupt his hushed absorption.

She did not want to talk. She tried not to think. She reached for a book, thought better of it, and withdrew her hand. It was no use. It would come, the deep, stabbing little fear. Push it down, down into the secret dark of the heart, it still was there. She was afraid of a victorious Essex, who might return, gilded with triumph, to stir the imaginations of her people. There was room for only one ruler in England; perhaps she had been too free with her favors, too plenteous in her assignments to the Earl.

She had meant to send him to France, to try him once more with Henry. If he bungled again, as in '91, she could recall him. With Council at her back, and more gold to plaster the wounds of her young Earl, his place would be more than ever secure at her side. Now the disaster of Calais had changed all this. It was a severe blow, and worst of all, it had put Essex nearer to his sailing.

She twitched in her chair. It was all so heart-sickening. If only they could be happy together at home, without this eternal yearning to be up and off. She drew a long sigh and her face hardened into sullen lines. Perhaps she would not let him go, after all. She was still the Queen, and without her patent he couldn't stir a foot on his way. She could still stop him.

With Alva on her very doorstep now, she might have need of them all here at home, before so very long. Perhaps the Cadiz adventure would never take place.

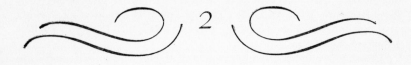

Plymouth

In a light April rain Essex rode down to Plymouth. He was accompanied by a straggling few of his followers and his body servant. He pushed himself hard on the last day, as if terrified of the clutching hand on his ankle, pulling him back. As he neared the port town, it seemed that he could not put the miles between himself and Greenwich fast enough. At last he arrived, bone-weary but of high heart. He had covered the first lap of his journey.

Outside his headquarters he swung down and went in. His spine, well used to the saddle, cried out when he eased himself into a chair, holding out his long legs to Joseph, who pulled off the boots, caked with little mud splotches. He smelled of sweat and his horse, but he did not wait to do more than throw some cold water at his face and gulp down a glass of wine before calling for pen and ink. He would write to Cecil the news of his arrival.

The light of a small lamp threw new shadows on his face, furrowed with fatigue. Impatiently he frowned at the paper. Should he tell Cecil of his farewell to the Queen? Should he admit that he had ridden with fear crouching on his back, fear that at every step a rider would overtake him with a letter ordering him back to Gloriana's side?

No. He would not write of the fears and dashed hopes of that last meeting. The Secretary should believe that all was well, that there was no rift between him and Elizabeth, to be cleverly widened in his absence.

A night's rest improved him and he was up with the sun, new verve and energy for his schemes filling him. There were thousands of things to be done, and who knows, any day now the final license to depart might arrive from Greenwich. He refused to think the license might never come.

He was very early abroad that first morning, to see Lord Howard of Effingham, his brother officer. Reports to receive; dispatches from the Queen to her Admiral to deliver; so off he went to Howard. After a short interview he came away, determined to keep his temper with a man whom he cordially disliked. If he recalled those halcyon days of his boyhood, when Lord Howard was Tom Gray's hero, and his too, he dismissed memory with a shrug. He was now grown up, surfaced with cynicism, old in knowledge, secure in royal favor that placed him shoulder to shoulder with the great soldier.

He rode down to the wharf, Henry Cuffe at his heels, to see the busy tangle of activities there. It was a capricious April morning, with little ruffles of wind to lift the skirts of the waves and show some white beneath. Plymouth harbor was alive with ships, some lying at anchor at a distance, their masts and spars tilting with the tide. Others were drawn up alongside, decks swarming with dark-faced sailors, busy with tar brushes, caulking seams.

The fleet was gathering; vessels of the Royal Navy, proud with Tudor colors, brave ships of the City of London, merchantmen for cargoes and troops. A few of the promised Dutch warships had already arrived, while Mynheer van Duvenvoord, the Netherlands Admiral, was due any day now.

At sight of the ships Essex's heart lifted. There was his own *Due Repulse,* flaunting his orange-tawny Devereux pennant at her masthead, his arms quartered on her mainsail, furled, but showing a great medallion of color in its middle. High above, on the crosstree, straddled a stout young fellow, putting all his brawny strength into tightening lines.

He looked down on the Earl, far beneath, tall and straight, gazing up at him from the quay.

"Ahoy there, my lord!" The man smiled freely and waved a red stocking cap.

"Ahoy yourself, my man!" called Essex, his white teeth flashing. "What do you do up there?"

"Making a noose for the Spanish King!"

"Make it stout and tight then!"

"Aye, that I will!"

A great roar of delighted laughter went up from the crowd of men on the wharf.

"Cheers for my lord of Essex! Confusion to the King of Spain!"

Essex laughed with them. The stalwart rope-tightener slid down the rigging and jumped to the deck. Essex beckoned to him. He liked the man's cut. At the signal the young fellow, panting a little from his breathless slide, came over the side to the wharf. He doffed his red cap.

"Your name, my man."

"Adam Baxter, may it please your lordship."

"It pleases me. Where art from?"

"From Sheffield, my lord. I was born on Yorkshire moors. People are bakers, but I cut and run to sea at fourteen."

Essex liked the way he stood, head high, the moor and the sea wind in his eyes and a good up-country ring in his voice. "Stay close to me," he said. "I have use for you on this voyage."

"Aye, aye, sir." Baxter touched his forelock and returned to his work.

Lord Howard now stepped out from a small knot of men. A frown puckered his forehead, and Essex guessed he had overheard the small display of friendliness between himself and the sailor. Howard looked irritated. Hah, thought Essex, he thinks me still the boy of Somerset House, small and subdued at my father's side. So he objects to a friendly gesture in the direction of a deck hand, does he? Hell's fire, deck hands swallow smoke and blood as well as gunners, and are as good for dying, too.

Howard and the other officers were admiring the Admiral's flagship, the renowned *Ark Royal*. A noble sight, she rode proudly at anchor, towering above the merchant barks, hoys, and pinnaces. She was getting a new coat of paint on her twenty-year-old bulk, a covering for the old Armada scars, long stripes of Tudor green and white, and under the bowsprit, a lithe fellow clung, touching up with gilt the royal lion that reared itself on the beakhead. Long red cotton strips, drying after the spring shower, would be stowed aft till needed to conceal the men from gunfire.

"By God, she's a handsome sight," said Essex, as he joined them, and at praise of his ship Howard flushed with pride.

"Verily," he said, "she's fit even for an island venture, should I fancy the trip. Her whole keel and bottom are sheathed with lead. The Indies worm would have a cruel time boring through that."

Howard was entirely happy with his ship. She carried a full quota of culverins, sixty-pounders, and lighter guns. A good dose of lead for Philip's boys. And his gunners he placed second to none. With ball coming straight at them, they would work, fight, and never turn a hair.

"I only hope that my *Due Repulse* will prove maneuverable as your *Ark,* my lord," said Essex. "Never shall I forget how we ran up to Medina and cracked off his oars like twigs from a tree. Prr—ing!" All save Howard laughed.

"As to that," Howard was sententious, "a good warship should trust to sails alone; it was our sails as much as anything that saved us in '88."

But Essex was not listening. He had spotted Charles Blount emerging from a shed, and he whistled and ran, vaulting casks and piles of rope, to reach him.

"Robin! Well met! When did you get down?" They clasped hands, clapped each other on the shoulder and laughed. In a close group of young men they moved off together.

With Blount here to share the excitement of preparation, Essex was now in a new flurry. They inspected the warehouses where the provender for the troops was piled in great hogsheads; they dashed off to the drilling grounds to watch the military review. There they ate camp dinner and under a merciful dry sky, flecked with clouds, they watched the regiments go spanking past.

A thousand glittering spines pricking the blue air, the great pulsating porcupine that was the pikemen flashed by. Tall, rangy chaps from Cornwall, Devonshire lads, ruddy Yorkshiremen, and some fellows from the fen lands, half-savages with beetling brows and shaggy hair; all had come to get more than their halfpence coat and conduct money. They were in it for a fight, and spoiling to get at the Spaniard.

The cavalry was all red and green, with St. George's cross sewn to the back of every jerkin, and the sun glanced off the stout steel helmets pulled down on the heads. Essex pitied the Spanish force that would be the object of one of their battering charges. With their officers in fine corselets and open helmets of chased silver, they were magnificent.

"Give them plenty of cannon and ammunition, and nothing in God's world can stop us," rejoiced Blount. "Essex, we are in for success this time."

In the midst of the preparation bustle the commanders continued to wrangle. White with wrath after one encounter, Essex snatched a joint letter to the Queen and signed his name above that of Howard. Howard took a penknife and cut out Essex's name.

Elizabeth held the mutilated epistle dangling in air, and snorted. "By God's wounds, if these two do not patch up their difficulties and that right speedily, I shall recall them both. It is disgraceful."

To Cecil she was even more caustic. "I blame Essex," she said. And the sour remark reached Essex and drove him to bitter words.

. . . I did not think, Madam, to stand so poorly in your Majesty's good graces . . . I can but assure your Majesty that I am ready to surrender my command if such be the royal will. . . . Be pleased, most dear Queen, to be gracious to one who loved you above all else on this earth, and so you shall bestow all those happinesses which a man might wish this side of Heaven. If I may hear your Majesty is well and well pleased, nothing can be ill with your Majesty's humblest and most affectionate vassal,

Essex

As for Howard, he received from the Queen a reproof that brought the sweat bursting out on his brow.

"Burn my liver!" he cried to Clifford. "I'd rather drown than get another letter like that."

At the urgent advice of their friends both men made a stronger effort to command their tempers.

In the town the men grew restless and sharp discipline had to be preserved. After the hanging of one murderer and the drowning of another, tied to the corpse of the man he had killed, the madness died down, the restlessness subdued.

And so April melted into May, which continued fair, with good winds from the north to make the commanders groan at the waste.

One night an exhausted rider slipped into town with secret dispatches for the Earl. Essex had gone to bed, but he threw a gown about his shoulders, lit the candles himself, and, before he would hear a word, poured the man a drink. His hand was not quite steady as he poured the wine; he dreaded what he might have to hear.

Making sure that the corridor outside his door was empty, he drew a chair close to the messenger and awaited the news with desperate quietness.

"My lord, I bring you news from the Indies. They are both dead. Buried at sea."

Essex stared, unbelieving. "No, not Drake, not Hawkins!"

"Their crews are sick and starving, my lord, but they are arriving. Troughton in the *Elizabeth Bonaventure,* Winter in the *Foresight,* Nicholas Baskerville in the *Hope.* Straggling back, and 'tis feared that more will put in here at Plymouth. I was to bring you intelligence in secret lest they cast down the spirits of your men in their adventure."

"But the Admirals—what of them?"

"My lord, it is said they fell sick of the fever and that Hawkins died first in Dominica in November, then Drake in January in the *Defiance.* Their bodies were put into lead boxes and they were buried, Hawkins off Puerto Rico and Drake in the waters of Portobello."

Under the gold and emerald waters of the Spanish Main. "Well, God rest their souls." Essex bowed his head. Then, quickly, "Then the venture is a failure?"

"My lord, little is known of that as yet. But it is feared that only a scanty harvest of gold and pearls will go toward melting the cost of the expedition."

Essex shook his head. Now, more than ever, it was vital that he should not fail at Cadiz. The Queen would be angry enough at the loss of her two greatest seamen, and furious at the financial failure of the mission. No, they could not fail now.

For some hours he sat brooding. The messenger had gone to eat and sleep, warned to keep out of the taverns and to keep a close head on his news. Essex was left with it. A fitting memorial to these two gallant men was the continuance of the fight against Philip. Why, in the name of God, did the Queen not send word?

Letters, letters, and more letters went posting off to the Queen, to the Council, to Cecil. By now, Lord Howard had the tragic intelligence of Drake and Hawkins, and he fumed at Burghley, whom he suspected of sending the messenger to Essex, throwing a bone between them as if they were two dogs. He fretted at the Queen's keeping them dangling. But remembering that corrective letter, he held his peace. Essex did likewise.

Then the word came. Yielding finally to the storm of entreaty from both minister and commanders, Elizabeth sent Fulke Greville, wild with excitement, the license to depart buttoned close in his breast. He clattered into Plymouth to find the Earl and Howard peacefully at dinner with their officers.

At last! Essex flung down his napkin, going himself to give the order. Then, and only then, did he give his full attention to Greville.

"Never was man more welcome, Fulke!" He clapped the Queen's envoy on the back so that he choked over his fried fish. "It puts new heart in us. And hark ye, Greville," he smiled ingenuously, "I shall have letters for the Council, but on your life, see you deliver them after we have been a full week at sea, and there is a complete meeting of the ministers. No more bungling; this time I mean to succeed."

The word to embark ran like fire among the waiting troops. It touched off a spark here and there, till it kindled in the stout fellows a blaze that warmed their hearts of oak. That night the taverns of Plymouth town, open for the celebration, roared with sea chanties, and mariners swaggered over the cobblestones before the buxom lasses of the south country.

Down in the *Blue Whale* Adam Baxter sat, a well-padded wench a-straddle on his knee. He cupped his hand over her firm, pointed breast and gently shook it to and fro.

"Honey dugs, what shall I bring thee from Spain?"

Her grin widened to show coarse, pointed teeth. "I wants a necklet of beads and a basket o' Spanish plums."

A tipsy roisterer, tankard slopping in his hand, lurched against them. "I can tell ye what she doesn't want and that's a dose o' the pox! So mind what ye do!" His hiccough was drowned in the general roar.

Tales of booty and streets paved with gold rang through the town, but for the most part the adventurers were wildly thrilled at the prospect of facing Spanish soldiers.

"Drake singed Spanish Philip's beard! We'll cinder it off his ugly face!" A man from the west country banged his hand on the board. "By Cod! We'll make him show his backside. It takes Englishmen to do that!"

Then someone struck up a rolling ditty.

> "English lord, German count, and French marquee
> A yeoman of Kent is worth all three!"

The others took it up and yelled until the *Blue Whale's* roof rang.

As for Essex and Blount, like many a brother officer, they sat in their lodgings and wrote to the women they best loved. Lord Howard wrote to his wife, thanking her for the ivory crucifix she had sent him and promising to observe all her tender admonitions about his care of himself. Blount sent to Penelope Rich, his beloved, his final reassurances of devotion, and a brooch set with pearls in which was his portrait in little. And Essex sent a gold chain to the Queen and a tiny pocket compass to his son at Chartley.

The adventure had begun.

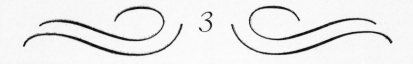

First Blood

June the first dawned brilliant and clear with a sufficient wind from the north to enable them to work their vessels out of the harbor. Essex was aboard early, standing high above his captain to view the splendid sight. All the town turned out to see them off, and the local militia escorted the Queen's gentlemen officers to the water front, then lounged in a bright uneven line among the wharf crowd.

Essex's eyes narrowed in the bright sun as he swept the harbor. Seventy transports and victualers rode in the center of the war squadrons. The crimson flag of Howard burst from the top of the *Ark Royal,* there was a gust of cheering and beating of drums, and she slowly left the landing, her squadron gathering behind her. Under his feet Essex felt his own deck tremble as the wind caught his great sail and his *Due Repulse,* sleek and tawny, rode from her moorings like a queen.

His heart swelled with pride and gratitude. This, this, was the true meaning of life, for never was Englishman so much in his element as on the sea, bound for high adventure. For this he had played the gallant at Gloriana's court; for this he had danced to delicate tunes, and affected a concern in the cut of a coat. For a time he feared he had overdone it and tethered himself forever to his mistress with this fine strong chain of his contriving.

He turned to look back, and there behind him was Lord Thomas Howard, with his *Mere Honour,* decked out in vivid blue, and Ralegh in the snowy *Warspite.* Following in their rear came the *Neptune,* a beautiful little vessel of four hundred tons, under the command of Jan van Duvenvoord. High on his quarter-deck he stood, legs braced apart, his flat face turned to his commanders, whose ships, like the others now filled the graceful line.

One hundred and fifty of them, heavy with guns, swarming thickly with men, sailors and fighting foot soldiers, and all this going to bring Spanish Philip to his knees. A booming salute from Howard's master gunner, and like a beautiful dream, the fleet moved out of the harbor.

"By God!" exulted Essex, "the Queen should be here to see this. Her fears for the expedition would melt like snow in the sun."

All day they beat steadily southward, the strong wind pushing them nearer to their goal. As evening came on, the wind fell off somewhat; trumpet calls and loud ahoys now rang out across the gently undulating waters. The Lord Admiral dropped anchor and four other flagships did the same, while the rest shortened sail. Out from the *Ark's* masthead bellied the arms of England, and a warning shot boomed. The commanders were summoned.

Essex mounted the steep-pitched ladder to the Admiral's cabin. It towered above all, its little Gothic panes glittering in the rays of the setting sun. There on high, he stepped forward to the balustrade of the poop deck, rested his hands on the carved and gilded arms of England. He unrolled a heavy parchment, crackling and glinting with scarlet and gold.

He cleared his throat. "In the name of her Majesty the Queen, the high and mighty Empress Elizabeth Regina, Queen of England, France, and Ireland, and of Virginia, Defender of the Faith."

Heads bared, the great ship's company sank to the deck below. A tinkle of arms, a creaking of leather settled into stillness. Light salt breezes ruffled the Earl's chestnut hair as he shook out the parchment and tilted it to the fading light.

"Her gracious Majesty has been pleased to send us from her own hand a royal prayer to the Almighty God that He may prosper us upon our adventure."

This was Elizabeth's command, that the message be conveyed to the

Admiral's company on this their first evening at sea. It was Essex's job to read it; and avoiding the sarcastic eye of Lord Howard, he lent his mellow English voice to the task of speaking for Gloriana.

The men on their knees below him paid but small heed to the words of their sovereign, lost as they were in admiration for this fine figure of their commander. Lord Howard, all soldier now, his fine courtier's posture abandoned, was itching with irritation to get on with the job. It was going to be no small task to curb Essex to prudence; to keep Ralegh, nearby, sardonically twisting his mustache, in line; to subdue Cadiz and bring home the treasure that was expected, nay demanded, of the expedition. Tired, he shifted his weight, listing a little to the tilt of the deck beneath him.

"'. . . To these devout petitions, Lord, give Thou Thy blessed grant. Amen.'"

"Amen," responded four hundred voices.

Essex looked up. Automatically he said, "God save the Queen!" and kissed the scroll.

So, blessed by Gloriana, they departed, each to his own ship. The Lord Admiral's galleon blossomed with soft golden lanterns and the others silently followed in his wake. With the dawn, rosy-pale, they scattered, lest a chance passer-by give the alarm to the Spanish.

Within two days of Cadiz, they picked up an Irish barque, bound from the Spanish port for Waterford. Courteously but firmly her captain was invited aboard the *Ark,* and he came, reluctantly, convoyed over the side by a small, gleaming escort of Howard's men. Into the great cabin he straddled on bandy legs in ill-fitting hose, a resigned look in his wary Irish face.

To their questions he was glib. "Faith, gentlemen," in a strong south country brogue, "'tis the advantage ye'll be havin' of me."

"We shall be obliged to you for information touching the strength of the town." Howard's polite tone held a touch of iron.

Among the hated English, the Irishman knew himself trapped. His tiny yellow eyes shifted from side to side, glancing among the empty faces. He squirmed in his effort to tell enough to escape the persuasion of a tight cord about the head, and not to tell enough to help his captors. Upon his long top lip a light sweat appeared.

"Well," drawing out his words, "'tis little information an ordinary seagoing man like meself would be havin' concernin' the strength, as ye put it, of the town o' Cadiz." At a glint in Howard's eye he went on hastily, "But I hear that the Spanish king is sick in his bed and is not after keeping his eye on the likes of you at all." He ran his tongue over dry lips.

There was silence in the cabin. Then Essex suddenly flung down a small bag before the captain. At the chink of gold the Irishman started. "Now that I remind meself, as I came through the Roads, I see with me eyes a monstrous big fleet o' merchant ships, outward bound, they said, for the Indies, and some of the king's own galleons a-waitin' to escort them."

"Ah!" Now the English started. All but Howard, who sat stolidly against the back of his chair. "And you have no knowledge of the strength of Cadiz," he persisted.

Eyes on the bag, the Irishman said, easily now, "Sure, 'twill be easy as pushing over a baby. I'm told they're the weakest o' garrison—and the Spanish king—ah, but I mentioned that before." Hanging now on his heel, he eyed them expectantly.

"Our men will return you to your ship. And—thank you." Howard was stiff.

The Irishman snatched up the bag, bowed hastily out, and nearly fell his length crossing the threshold of the cabin.

"He will have a new opinion of English—pirates," grinned Christopher Blount.

Essex was ablaze. "Now, it would seem that the Lord God is with us. Gentlemen, what's to be done?"

"I shall call a select council at once," decided Howard.

The first wrangling of the expedition began, as the leaders, huddled in Howard's cabin, argued and disputed. Impatiently the other ships lay off and on, the whole sea dotted with English craft. Below the cabin Essex's men lounged, ears strained for news from above. Through an open pane Howard's voice, raised for once in loud relief, came clearly.

"Then that's settled. Essex, you will land the army and assault the town." The men below felt their hearts leap. "But first, we shall inspect for landing places. I shall attack the Spanish ships or at least confine them within the bay. Captain Alexander Clifford, you will prevent those galleons from annoying us while we do the job."

A heavy scraping of chairs, a creak of an opening door, and the officers poured down to the deck below, their feathers rippling smartly in the wind.

This fair wind continued, hearts already high leaped higher, and on

Sunday morning, nearly three weeks after they had set sail from Plymouth, they sighted the fabled town of Cadiz. And there, great Heaven, was the Spanish fleet, anchored half a league off San Sebastián, at the west and of the high town. What could be more to their taste? The English praised God and cheered.

The English ships had been sighted, too, and all along the heads of the mainland people were gathering to marvel at the fearsome display of the morning sun on the sails of one hundred and fifty vessels.

"Madre de dios!" exclaimed the Prior of San Sebastián, crossing himself. He then bustled inside the Priory to send a priest to hide the golden candlesticks.

Cadiz lay, a glittering prize in the dawn, her spires and battlemented turrets crowning the head of a long L-shaped island, the top or haft of which pointed roughly northwest. At the base of the L and over to the east was her only connection with the mainland, the Suazo Bridge, a chunky little strip of pointed roofs and conical towers spanning the water. Baxter, straining over the shoulder of his lord, gazed eagerly at the land, while Essex's thoughts sprang busily forward to the marching victory that would soon be his.

He turned and smiled freely at the other. "See that?" he gestured toward an old castle that guarded the entrance to the channel. " 'Tis Matagorda, or what Drake has left of it. I'll wager the Spanish are screaming that El Draque has returned." Suddenly he felt a twinge that Drake, indeed, would never return.

The stocky little captain of the *Due Repulse* also stood at Essex's back, his hand cupped about his squinting eyes. "Little sign of fortification there. Now, if the Lord Admiral can cripple the galleons, the landing will be child's play."

"Mm," grunted Essex. "Seems little sign of military activity." He shifted his weight to the ship's list. "There'll be some resistance, I pray, from the fort garrison. I should not like it said that Cadiz fell like a ripe plum to our picking."

Now they made out the little moving specks that were people on the cliffs, and in the harbor they could separate and count Philip's galleons that clustered like great alarmed birds, hugging close to the safety of the land. The Spanish ships were alive with tiny animated doll figures, running about on the decks and into the rigging.

Up on his quarter-deck, Essex's captain signaled to the mate, who was bawling orders through a long iron horn. With a grand majestic sweep the *Due Repulse* followed the others into the harbor. Behind them English ships poured into the outer bay, while Philip's galleys and galleons shrank close to the eastern shore under cover of the fort's guns.

With a deafening clatter of chain, the *Repulse* dropped anchor; the men on deck shouted, and the happy excitement in Essex's throat all but choked him. At last! His hour had struck.

"Entramos!" he cried, and cast his plumed hat into the water. "The longboat and barges. Over the side with 'em!"

With a wild cheer the men filled the first two. The wind was rising, the waves ran high, but with reckless disregard the boats were swung over the boiling trough. They crashed down on the water and immediately capsized.

Screams, choked cries for help, oaths, and the sea was suddenly full of men, plunging frantically back to their ship's all side. But few sailors could swim, let alone foot soldiers, and dripping and gasping, they were hauled aboard by down-flung lines, and a quick count was made. Fifteen were missing.

In a towering fury Essex raved at the survivors. "What wanton fools have I brought with me!" Above the wind and confusion his sharp voice was steel. "Is life so cheap, you clumsy swine, that you can throw it away before the Spaniard has smelled you? If you must spend your worthless lives so freely, spend them for England!"

The next boats were carefully lowered, the men watching and taking the chance. At this point a smart little pinnace came up, Ralegh in the stern. Lithely he scrambled up the lines and sprang down onto the wet deck. A heavy military cape whipped his shapely legs.

"My lords!" he shouted. "It is well-nigh impossible to land, unless the weather abate a little. The garrison is mustering in numbers, and you would be at a great disadvantage to attempt to run in under their fire."

"That is a chance we are well prepared to take," cried Essex.

Ralegh's black eyes snapped. "My lord, the galleons are leaving the northeast, and it would seem they purpose taking up a position dead to the east of the town to cover our attack on that portion." He gestured toward the *Ark,* heeling to the strong wind. "It is the Lord Admiral's plan to attack the fleet, but he wishes to call a select council on the matter."

With a muttered oath Essex sprang into the shrouds and, shielding his eyes with his hand, saw for himself that what Ralegh said was true. If they attempted a landing in this complicated sea under the very noses of the garrison, they would be picked off like gooseberries.

Hell and thunder, he thought, fifteen dead men, and now the silver popinjay to salt the wound. He jumped to the deck. "As you will, Ralegh," he said grudgingly. "Delay is my meat these days. I am used to it, though God's wounds! I have little stomach for it, and I grow more squeamish with time." He pushed past his men as Ralegh disappeared over the side.

That night saw English plans perfected. The English leaders counciled on their move of the morrow, while outside, the walls of Cadiz blazed with cressets, and on the Spanish ships, silhouetted against cabin lights, little black forms showed now and then. Among the Spanish, all was ceaseless activity.

The English agreed that an immediate attack on the Spanish ships was indicated, that once the galleons were disabled, the town would be an easy capture.

"I claim the honor of leading the attack on the ships," though Essex was quick, Howard was quicker, and his hand fell like a stone.

"My lord, I cannot permit the placing of our three flagships in danger together, for I gave her Majesty my solemn word that their care would be my first consideration, that it should be above all others—" here he hesitated, and Essex flushed. The ships must be protected, he well knew, but Howard's significant pause meant also that the Lord Admiral was under strict orders to protect Essex, too.

The attack, then, was assigned to Ralegh and Vere. Grumbling would do no good, that he also knew, for Howard was in supreme command on the sea.

"So long as we float," Essex told his captain glumly, "we are at the Lord Admiral's word. But once on land—by Heaven, we shall see!" A muscle in his thin cheek twitched.

"Our orders, sir?"

"To lie back with the others." To himself he muttered bitterly, "While the silver fox draws first blood."

But morning brought a new calamity. With sleep still in their faces, the commanders came out on deck to see the Spanish fleet away from its anchorage, moved further back into the bay.

Under cover of the dark, the merchant ships had crept up behind the warships into the inner bay, where they took refuge at Port Royal, set comfortably back into the land. There they were, securely bottled up by the others that formed a broadside chain of protection. Four great galleons, newly built by Philip less than a year ago at Genoa and named for four of the twelve apostles, lay ranged right across the gap, with the smaller galleys filling up the spaces between them. So narrow was the strait that less than a dozen ships could pass abreast. On one side was Fort Puntal, on the other, the mainland.

And so they waited for the English.

Like a snowy eagle Ralegh in his *Warspite* swooped down upon them. Longing to follow, Essex watched, envy in his heart. He marked how Ralegh maneuvered into position, the gun ports that swung back as the long cannon nosed forward like giant eels, gliding out of their dens to rend the enemy. Then, of a sudden, Essex caught his breath; Ralegh had anchored too soon and was out of range.

"Now hear him curse and tear that black beard of his," he muttered. Vere went dashing past Ralegh, anchoring within culverin shot of the enemy, and the *Warspite* raced up past the other, only to mask his fire. Essex nearly wept.

"By the foul pit of hell," he swore to his captain, who was almost as upset. "Fine veterans these, who cannot measure distance, and must needs get in one another's way. Go it, Vere! Blow the damned explorer's head off. Up, and get alongside!" He was dancing with impatience.

Soon the two ships were abreast, and now their broadside shot took deadly effect on the Spanish. In auxiliary position, their squadrons closed up the rear. Behind Essex and Howard waited the others, holding their breaths and praying that they would be needed.

Essex strained his eyes at the fort. How the Spanish must be feverishly working to get their guns into action. No answer as yet. Ah! Boom! The first of their cannon spoke, but the ball whistled wildly into the sea. This was followed by a muffled roar from the Spanish again, but there was no shot fired. Had a Spanish cannon burst then— why did not the Spanish reply?

Now the *San Felipe,* over in the inner bay, rained clumsy blows at the two light English ships. The two merely shuddered a little and bounced back, bruised but unhurt.

"Come on! More! More! We like it. By God, we are no pinchfists! We'll give it right back to ye!" Essex pounded the rail in his excitement.

As if in answer to his cry, a blasting hail from the *Warspite* tore through the *San Felipe's* sides and smashed into the men aboard her.

"Ah!" Essex turned to the fidgeting captain.

"My lord," pleaded the little seaman, "could we not join the cannonade?"

Essex chuckled. "So you think Ralegh needs a hand? We are two of a kidney. But—did you not hear our orders?" He measured the distance between themselves and that part of the channel where the fight was thickest. Then back at the captain, his boy's eye twinkling. "We'll chance it!"

The *Due Repulse* crept up the channel and poured fire into the enemy. The noise was deafening. Essex was in ecstasy. He ran down the short companionway to his lower gun deck. He slapped the backs of his men and yelled at them. Soon his face was black as theirs from the powder smoke and he coughed as it tickled his lungs. Crash! Reload and fire. Crash!

With a wild scream a beardless boy hurtled from the rigging, jarred by a Spanish ball. He splattered into a tangle of men, bearing all to the deck. A thin stream of blood followed him as they carried him off. Soon more blood began to flow as here and there enemy shot found its mark. One man had his legs crushed as a cannon broke its moorings. He lay and moaned horribly.

"Take him below," ordered Essex above the din. He was borne off to the surgeon, who gave him some drowsy syrup to deaden his pain until he died.

There was a lull. "At any rate," commented Essex, "our fellows die nobly, not like yon chained Spanish rowers, poor devils, whose chests are crushed and whose arms are torn off as they lie in their slave trap."

For three mortal hours the banging and crashing went on, till every man's ears rang like a churchbell. But for the most part the men on the *Due Repulse* were unhurt. The sun crept to its meridian; the wind died down. It began to get warm, and as yet the long summer day was scarcely half over.

"My lord," begged Adam Baxter, "you have not broken your fast this day. You must eat—that is, I pray you, sir, take some food."

Essex laughed and gave him a bat with the back of his dirty hand. "Smoke and fire's my meat today, lad. Get yourself something and bring me a handful of biscuit and a dram. 'Tis all I want."

By now the Spanish were badly shaken. It showed in the panic as Ralegh's terrible *Warspite* made for them. The *Due Repulse* crept closer to the kill, and now Essex could hear the high Spanish voices above the din.

"*Por dios!* Let the *Inglesi* have a good dose of iron! Do you wish to serve out your days in an enemy prison? They will tear out your tongue and put live coals to your eyes!"

Red dribbled from the enemy scuppers. "They must be wild," muttered Monson. Again came the voices blown through sound and smoke.

"Madre de dios! The cables—cut them!" The clear Spanish of the *San Tomàs'* captain was music to the ear of Essex. He guessed the intent, as the officer smelled the disaster that was upon them. They would try to escape. For Port Royal! "Hurry, you sons of devils, hurry!"

But it seemed that the captain had reckoned without the incoming tide. The *San Tomàs* and the others drifted onto the shore of the mainland, where they made good eating for their enemies. Gone was discipline; in vain the captains cursed and screamed their orders. The prize galleys were surely doomed.

The *Due Repulse* shivered and heeled a little away as the four Spanish helplessly grounded, first the *San Felipe,* then the others, striking with terrible shocks. They canted nearly onto their sides, while the men poured from their ports like pease from a bag. The water cut off feeble screams and mercy prayers. In vain they called on their saints.

"Fifty gold pieces!" A wave choked one man, but he fought up to the surface. "Blessed Santa Teresa, save me—" another wave stopped him. His head broke through. "Fifty gold pieces!" he screamed, "that I vow—" the third wave hurled him against the side of the ship and smashed him like an egg.

By two's and three's the Spaniards sank. Those that drowned were lucky. For the *San Felipe* struck higher up on the beach and her men fell into the sticky mud and were held there by the weight of their body armor. While they cursed and struggled, up came the Dutch, blue eyes blazing with murder. In light, maneuverable boats they rowed ashore, sprang out, and drove their daggers deep into Spanish throats. Memories of Parma in their own homeland gave strength to their arms. Many a burned Dutch home and violated girl were avenged that afternoon on the muddy flats of Cadiz.

Then with a booming flash the *San Felipe* blew up. Those of her men left on board were hurled skyward like puppets. Arms and legs, streaming blood, flew into the water, and a flaming body sizzled as it hit the wet. The *San Tomàs* was set afire by her own crew, and roaring flames licked high into the shrouds and sails while her cannon burst with great shattering growls. Timbers cracked like fireworks, and sailors catapulted into the water, swam piteously about, blackened and scorched, trying with charred hands to cling to floating spars. Again the Dutch bore down upon them and relentlessly did them to death in the water.

"For God's sake!" swore Essex, "what are we—butchers and cowards?" Her Majesty expressly had forbidden wanton slaughter.

To his relief he now sighted Ralegh and Howard in their pinnaces, rounding the hulk of the *San Tomàs,* and soon the Dutch boats sheered off back to their own vessels.

The sea fight was over and the way for the land attack was now clear.

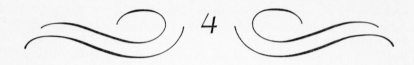

Dubious Victory

They took Cadiz with small loss of men, finding it almost too easy. Cowed by the loss of their galleons, the Spanish offered but poor resistance. Sidney's sword in his hand and Drake's memory in his heart, Essex cut, thrust, and carved a glittering path through the defenders for his men to follow. By evening the town had surrendered, and the English commanders were quartered in the Town House. As for the Spanish, they crept within doors, fearful of the throng of Dutch and English that choked their squares and alleys.

Staggering with fatigue, Essex and Christopher Blount approached the Town House, austere and oriental, with twisted pillars and fancy stone work. A tired silence had fallen between them, which Essex now broke. "I sent to the Lord Admiral a suggestion that he go to the treasure ships and nail them, while we did the work here."

"Refused, of course." Blount's voice was drugged with fatigue.

"Refused," sighed Essex.

"Could not Ralegh go?"

In spite of himself Essex laughed. "Ralegh! And leave the sack of Cadiz? Christ's teeth, Christopher, when did you see that one afield when there is game to the hand?"

"But—the treasure?"

"Ah, yes, the treasure. Well, we'll not lose those ships if I can help it. There's more treasure there than we'll ever squeeze out of this town."

They entered the Moorish colonnade, threading the English guards to mount the steps of the entrance. Behind them in the deep dusk a fellow was lighting the long row of wrought-iron lanterns that hung like dark flower buds against the night-gray walls.

Inside they found Ralegh and the others. Despite his forty-three years and a slight leg wound, Ralegh managed to look jaunty. His uniform was dusty and his tarnished cuirass had seen better days; his morion hung perilously on the back of his curly head, and on his sunburned forehead the hair was plastered in sweaty rings. Surrounded by tall, handsome men, he still was an attractive figure.

Damn him, thought Essex.

As for Lord Howard, he was weary to the point of collapse. Right up to the heart of the city, stopping for naught, he had led his men. At his age and in the sandy heat, body armor was torture. Unsteadily he walked to a leather chair and sank into it. He and Essex leveled each other with steady eyes. The energy of Essex and his desire to proceed with the attack on the merchant fleet, now, on the very heels of the capture of the town, when all were near dead with fatigue, excited Howard's grudging admiration. The general, if impetuous, was a true soldier. For his part, Essex was touched at sight of the elderly admiral, battered but intrepid. In the face of such superb endurance, such stout, steely courage, his own impatience filled him with shame.

With a slight gesture of acknowledgment he turned to give orders for supper; they all stood in need of hot food.

That night he laid himself down in a charming little room with an arched window set in pierced stone. He stood by the delicate twisted columns and gazed out at the midsummer moon that rose in all its romantic beauty over the bay. The gentle night air touched his forehead and happy pictures filled his mind. The Queen and her pleasure at his return; the people receiving him as he rode in triumph through the streets.

Joseph came and unbuckled him. Off with the cuirass and the long military boots. He stretched and groaned. "Ah, that's a relief, Joseph. The damned thing's been cutting into me all day." He threw his servant a sharp, half-humorous glance. "Speaking of cuts, where did you get that welt on your face?"

Stooping to pick up the gear, Joseph grunted. Essex laughed. "A wench, Joseph?" he teased. "Where was your hand, my lad? Not in her pocket, that I'll warrant. Here!" he tossed a gold piece. "Plaster it with that. But leave the women alone; that's the order and mind you don't forget it. I shouldn't like to stretch your neck."

Still silent, Joseph took his red welt and his gold piece and shuffled off with the Earl's gear. Essex sighed loudly and flung back on his bed. His eye wandered about the room and he made mental notes of the things he meant to have packed in his chests. The finely tooled leather hangings, certainly; the old credenza with the fat candles, though it looked a bit bulky, was well carved. Perhaps they would find room for it in one of the victualing caravels. He would take the image of the Virgin, so exquisitely tinted, to Frances.

Yawning, he reached for his small pocket Caesar and began to read his favorite passage, the wonderful account of the expedition against the Helvetii. But the candles flickered, his flesh was heavy, and his mind was whirling with the events of a full-packed day. Reaction set in and he closed his eyes. Into the still room the soft night air stole about his quiet bed.

Tiptoeing clumsily, Joseph came in with a great net, which he flung over his master's bed, pulling it taut against the mosquitoes.

Down on the shore, where the English camp lay sprawled and silent, uneasy fires flickered, and the surf at low tide hushed softly on the shoal. There the tired men also slept.

And the city lay wrapped in quiet and tense with despair.

During the next fortnight, between the capture of Cadiz and their departure for home, Essex knew all the diverse emotions of joy, excitement, hatred, fury, and resignation. While they occupied and sacked Cadiz, he lived a small lifetime, and, looking at his face in the glass, he thought he could trace new lines and shadows and even a tinge of gray in the curling hair at his temples.

To begin with, they lost the merchant fleet.

The Spanish offered two million ducats to ransom their vessels, but Howard, determined to leave nothing of military value in Spanish hands that he could rend away from them, refused. It was in vain that Essex pleaded and stormed. Howard was obstinate.

That night Essex tossed restlessly beneath his net, staring up at the beamed ceiling. The thought of those ships lying snugly deep in the water, bulging with treasure, was maddening enough; but the two million ducats that would have filled English coffers was unbearable. Since Howard would not accept the ransom and was in no hurry, apparently, to take the ships, he determined that he himself would run down the bay with his own small force and make sure of them in his own way.

It was not to be. He awoke next morning to a smell of smoke, and plunged out of bed, tearing through his mosquito gauze, dragging it after him. He rubbed blurred eyes. Across at Port Royal billowed a cloud of smoke. For once Medina Sidonia had the drop on the English. He had fired the lot. Like something demented, Essex bawled for a courier and dispatched a force of vessels racing across the bay. But they could do nothing. The treasure ships were blackened wrecks, and this time the smile, though bleak, was on the faces of the Spanish.

As if this were not calamity enough, they lost the galleys, too. While the English and the Dutch were romping about Cadiz, collecting gold and jewels, Clifford and his men had been sent off to hold a fortress. Enraged at missing the fun in Cadiz, they now left their post and rushed to be in at the sack at Port Royal. This was what the Spanish galleys awaited. Their captains upped anchor, and, praising their saints for English greed that grasped at a phantom while losing a reality, slipped down the tide.

In a black rage of despair, Essex shut himself in his room. Howard, aboard the *Ark,* was ill and lay there, wanting only peace and physic.

Meanwhile the sack of Cadiz proceeded. *Carretas* loaded so carelessly that they spilled their contents with every jolt, groaned on their wooden wheels, as they lumbered down the causeway, driven by English soldiers perched on piles of sacks. All day long the lazy donkeys and slothful oxen carried the loot winding down to the water front, or, their way blocked, stood twitching against the flies, while confusion choked the streets, and their drivers yelled and threatened each other. All was noisy dirt and disorder. Well-loved fragments of Spanish life dripped from the sacks of the looters and were snatched out of the mud by the people. A crushed silver candlestick lay beside a single little gold embroidered slipper; a really fine pearl rolled like a drop of milk into the rich blackness of a muddy rut, and a woman dashed under the hoofs to redeem it.

"Dios! They will kill you!" Her husband dragged her wailing back from the prize which the next wheel ground into the ooze.

Sailors empty-armed, hands pressed tight over a secret store in rubies and pearls taken from goldsmiths, walked warily; private adventurers, gentlemen on fine horses, rode with piles of books and small chests on their saddles. In a steady stream the treasure of Cadiz poured down to the sea and the English ships.

Next day the gentlefolk left with their body servants for safe-conduct to St. Mary. The English commanders had given strict orders touching the safety of the civil population, and the English soldiery stood about and gaped at the young *hidalgos* walking proudly with their trusted attendants; the princely yellow-skinned churchmen, theatrical in their violet and scarlet; and the pale *señoritas,* swathed in black lace.

Among the crowd down at the water gate stood John Donne, gentleman adventurer, poet, and musician. Weary of London stinks and London women, he had joined Essex down at Plymouth, eager for what he could get out of the expedition. At sight of the scrambling Spanish, their clothes bulky with hidden wealth, panic in their black eyes, he smiled sardonically.

In the heart of the congestion here, Essex and Howard hovered, keeping a sharp eye on their men, who pressed ever closer, mouths watering at sight of so much beauty and glitter. Essex jerked forward as a heavy buccaneer jostled him. The great redbearded fellow was straining after an elfin girl who walked in the protective custody of her *duenna,* a sort of elderly witch. As she tried to shield the girl from the hot stares of the men, she showed her yellow teeth in a snarl.

"Zounds!" swore the red fellow with the large cod-piece. "What an armful to take to bed!" His fellows roared and clapped him on the back.

"The old she-wolf would eat you afterward, be sure of that," they jibed. But they knew he did not mean the *duenna.*

"A pox on this edict that prevents a private gentleman from getting his hands on a girl and her gold. What do my lords think we came out here for?" The redbeard spat into the mud at Essex's feet.

Instantly Essex turned, hand haughtily on his hilt. "Let no enemy of England say we are lacking in chivalry to such as these," he said stiffly. A soft laugh puffed past Donne's lips. He loved Essex when he was sententious.

In a cloud of musk and amber the girl floated by followed by a disdainful *duchesa,* her wrinkled neck blazing with canary diamonds, stepping high in carved red heels. Nostrils flaring at sight of the conquerors, she raised her head in the fine lace, and as she did so, slipped on the wet steps. The arm of Essex shot out, but with a stare of hate, she swept past him into the boat.

Essex shrugged, and Donne murmured, "Women."

The commanders bowed to the venerable Bishop of Cuzco, captured by the soldiers but instantly freed without ransom, on the orders of Essex.

"We came not to make war on churchmen," he pointed out. "Nor do we sail our ships for gold or riches. Our sole aim is to revenge the dishonorable practices of the enemy and to defend the honor of England."

"*Gracias, señor,*" said the Bishop. Then, in good English, "I thank you, my lord." But at sight of the booty moving slowly but inexorably down to shore he lifted his brows, then spoke encouragingly to his priests and departed on his way to St. Mary.

On the whole, Essex and Howard felt well satisfied with the sack of the city. There had been little violence, only a few fellows had been hanged for mishandling of women and aged, and for the most part the soldiers remained orderly. In view of this, and the great bulk of booty that was filling the ships, the two commanders relaxed into a friendly ease and ate their meals together in the cordial company of their officers and each other.

But this amity was not to last for long. In fact there were exactly two days of peace for Essex and Howard; then the slender thread of agreement broke, and they were at daggers drawn again.

Sitting in council aboard Howard's flagship, they were interrupted by an excited messenger with news of a great fleet of carracks and other treasure ships, sighted as they made for the Azores. No doubt they were putting in for water and victuals before completing the last lap of the journey. A Spanish fleet homing from the New World! The men's hearts leaped.

Howard, his elderly cheeks flat and haggard, drew a deep breath. "This is indeed welcome news. Ralegh, you and Lord Thomas Howard shall await these ships at the Islands, while we start home with the sick and as much of the booty as we can manage."

"Home!" cried Essex. "Home, my lord? With the job but half done?"

"And why not?" Howard was instantly cold.

"Why not? It is my fixed intention to remain here as Governor of Cadiz until the treasure is secured from these returning ships and a base is established from which we can harry the King of Spain." Essex's flush was rising.

Howard dropped his hand on the arm of his chair. "And I absolutely refuse to return without you, my lord."

By now Essex's face was flaming. It was always the same, he thought, as he felt rage mounting inside him. Howard seemed to take a particular delight in balking him at every end and turn. There was the loss of the merchant ships, as well as the galleys, and now, this.

Words trembled on his lips, but he pushed back his chair and rose. There would be no solution to this problem, for neither would give way. Both were obdurate. Howard knew better than to return to Elizabeth without him; and he himself intended to stay here in Cadiz to finish carving out a career already too long weakened by his long stay at Court.

Their officers would attempt to resolve the difficulty between them, but it would be useless. They were deadlocked.

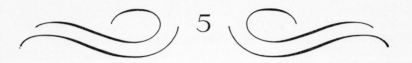

Homeward

*I*t was Henry Cuffe who finally talked him into giving way. Over his papers, Essex sat late into the night, giving ear to the counsels of his secretary. With Howard in this mood there was nothing to be done, and Cuffe therefore urged the Earl to depart with the Lord Admiral, in advance of Ralegh, and thus protect himself on home ground. About midnight Essex made up his mind to go home with the fleet.

Cuffe was invaluable. By the light of a pierced stone lantern he sat writing an important, nay, a fateful document. It was titled *A True Relation of the Action at Cadiz the 21st June under the Earl of Essex and the Lord Admiral to be sent to a Gentleman of the Court from One who Served There in Good Place.* In it he set forth the noble and valorous part played by his patron, thus hoping to steal a march on the Earl's enemies, who would lose no time in coloring their own account of the enterprise to their own benefit and the possible undoing of the Earl.

There were some tricky things to explain, the secretary pointed out, and eyewitness reports of the bravery and skill of the Earl of Essex in the capture of the galleons and the taking of Cadiz would scarcely balance the sad tale of the treasure ships fired at Port Royal and the loss of the galleys. Under the probing questions of Elizabeth, the only coup that Medina Sidonia was able to bring off would take the form of a major victory.

"I cannot believe she will bite at me for that," said Essex uneasily, his arm flung over his chairback. "Ah, she'll have to be pleased, I'll have her approval, and then, to hell with my enemies!" Cuffe picked up his pen. "Get on with the report and I will correct it. But—" here he paused, "after that, what then, Cuffe?"

Cuffe looked up from the quill he was mending, a shrewd gleam in his eye. "Let me take it, my lord, when Ashley and the others go before you on the homeward way, and I'll see it delivered straightway to Essex House. Reynolds shall transcribe it, and to it we will append initials, anyone's, just so the account purports not to come from your lordship. Ashley shall help, Greville shall carry it to some good printer, and we shall see that it gets into the hands of those who have your lordship's weal at heart."

Slowly Essex grinned at his secretary. "By God, Cuffe, I shall raise your wages," he said.

At the thought of Ralegh and the rest who hated him, of the confounding of their black schemes, the hot joy surged in him. For a moment he gloated. Then the inevitable reaction set in, and his elation declined. Secretly he was weary to death of the plots, the constant vigilant planning, the cruel disappointments, the plucking back on a slippery hill. He listened to the pen of Cuffe, scratching away on his behalf. Curiously he watched, but the bent face told him nothing. Cuffe's brow was knit in thought, the face pale and drawn.

"Enough," suddenly said Essex. "Enough for tonight. Get some supper and to bed, man. You look as barren as I feel." He stretched and sighed. "Home will be a welcome sight, Henry."

The tall, thin clerk rose, closed his inkpot, and stuffed the papers into his pouch. He bowed to Essex, who nodded absently. At the door he turned, his russet eyes glinting. "Your lordship's welfare is mine," he said, and quietly closed the door after him.

Aboard the *Ark* Howard lay with aching head and heavy stomach, and he prayed to get safely home with his crew of firebrands.

Morning broke. It only remained for the English to destroy the town and weigh anchor. The castle and the forts were demolished in crunching bursts of gunpowder, and the tower of the Town House was battered down. It fell in clouds of plaster, scattering its pieces over the street below. On July fourth the firing of all secular buildings commenced.

At sundown Essex walked to the water front. Behind him lay a smouldering city. The last boatload awaited him and as he was rowed out to his ship, smoke stung his eyes. He clambered aboard. Now he leaned against the bulwarks and looked back. A great haze hung over the picturesque towers. Were it not for Philip's chagrin at the loss, it were a pity, he thought, to destroy so charming a city. The trees hung in dead, blackened wisps over the ruined walls and all the birds had long since left. Raped and bleeding, Cadiz lay in the sunset, conquered, possessed, and abandoned.

Essex sighed. How he should have liked to govern it, building up a smart garrison, holding it proudly against all comers, sending out his brave lads to harry Spanish shipping, while he sat on the southernmost tip of Philip's land, like a great glittering gadfly. But even in the midst of his disappointment he took heart from the comfortable knowledge that English military skill had once more been proved, English chivalry had been upheld, and the Queen's coffers should be heavier by a round sum, if not the goodly one she expected. Had it not been for the men they had lost, and the initial disaster of the treasure ships, the expedition might have been one of those happy adventures that add luster to an already illustrious career. The *Due Repulse* was moving out of the harbor. With another sigh Essex turned into his cabin.

He looked at his dirty face, smoke-begrimed and drawn. "Water, Joseph!" he called, and Joseph hobbled in with a pewter measure that he had been keeping hot. As a convenience during the days of activity, Essex had grown a beard. "I'll leave it on," he decided. He thought it added a certain dignity to his appearance as a campaigner. Only—what would Gloriana say? He cocked a questioning eye at his servant.

Joseph knew. "Let your lordship sit down," said he. "I'll trim it to the smallest edge on your lordship's chin."

He went early to bed, but sleep would not come, and about an hour after midnight he rose and climbed to the afterdeck. There was no moon and the sky was serenely deep blue, picked out with tiny gold stars. All about were the shadowy forms of ships, swimming slowly, great ghostly bulks slipping by in the dark. The air was soft with the breathless hush that precedes the summer dawn.

He lifted his head and his thoughts soared up, up into the empyrean. He felt a sense of unreality, as if he hung, suspended, somewhere between sea and sky. He gazed up at the magnificent dome of heaven.

What was he doing here, his feet barely touching this small heaving speck of wood? Giddy with staring upward, he clutched the rail to steady himself.

He did not doubt that there was a God who counted the hairs of his head. In some inscrutable way, God had decreed that he would live through this venture, that others should die. Did they even now stand to the accounting of their lives? And life—it was only a brief sojourn in this earthly place, a short time of honor, of glory, of suffering, the soul driven by some spirit dwelling within the breast to urge one onward.

John Donne, poet-adventurer, would say that life was all expression of self, a sponge to be squeezed dry of sensation, then thrown away with a shrug. Ah, but Donne, like himself and all of them, was young. That Pole Copernicus, though, he had been young when he said an astounding thing. Man, living man, was but an atom in the scheme of things. Nay, this could not be. Man was an entity here on earth, living this painful, beautiful life, then leaving it for heaven. If one might believe that, one might find comfort.

Yearningly he fixed his gaze on the blue velvet above and for a moment he floated, disembodied, free, his soul tugging his body into the clouds and beyond, to the realm of the infinite. He trembled in his ecstasy. He clung, quivering, to the rail of his ship that shook beneath him and surged softly onward.

Suddenly the eerie cry of the watch aloft in a nearby crow's nest warned that the *Due Repulse* was riding too close to another ship, and he felt the shift as the helmsman answered.

The spell was broken. Now a desperate weariness assailed him, and he was filled with a nostalgic hunger for something he could not name. Was it a reaching back of the spirit to the days of simple youth, before life became complicated with passions and excitements? His youth was only a shadowy memory, its brief enchantments lost in the more permanent sorrows. Bemused, he went below.

The lamp glowed yellow on the table. Mechanically he sank into a chair. For a while he sat, lulled by the gentle motion of the vessel. Then slowly he took up a quill and commenced to write.

> Happy were he could finish forth his fate
> In some unhaunted desert, where, obscure
> From all society, from love and hate
> Of worldly folk, there should he sleep secure;

Then wake again, and yield God ever praise;
Content with hip and haws, and brambleberry;
In contemplation passing still his days,
And change of holy thoughts to keep him merry;
Who, when he dies, his tomb might be the bush
Where harmless Robin resteth with the thrush;
Happy were he!

For some moments he stared, unseeing at the paper. Then his sight blurred, the quill dropped from his loose fingers, and his chin sank on his breast. His weary face settled into repose.

Early the next morning they dropped anchor and met in Howard's cabin to bid godspeed to Sir Anthony Ashley and some other gentlemen who were to race ahead of them with the first reports of the expedition. Ashley, one of the men whom Essex had knighted, stood near, and he smiled loosely at his benefactor. By his side was Henry Cuffe, a flat pouch strapped to his side. Tucked down in the very bottom under *A True Relation* was a little velvet box. It contained a fine ruby ring, and through the ring was a tiny scroll on which Essex had inscribed: "For the Queen's own fair hand."

He gave his hand and a two-edged smile to Ashley, who imperceptibly nodded. As Cuffe knelt to him, he found opportunity to whisper, "You will be swift and secret? The ring and paper to Greville; trust Ashley." Cuffe nodded, kissed his hand, and climbed down the lines. Both should find their mark as soon as he could contrive.

The Fates willed otherwise.

Essex and Howard went coasting Portugal in light winds that threatened to becalm the entire fleet. With the proximity of Ferrol, and the poor sailing weather, they yielded to the temptation to raid the town. They might have saved themselves the trouble. The Portuguese were cleverer than the Spanish, and by the time the English broke into the town, they had fled, taking their goods with them.

A long-nosed culverin, a few hundred head of cattle and meek-faced sheep provided the sum total of the loot. Essex got one treasure, though: the library of the Bishop Jerome of Osorius. Poring over the beautifully bound books, he whiled away the tedious hours of returning.

From then on it was a race to get home. The fastest vessel reached Plymouth on August sixth, just exactly nine and a half weeks after they set sail on that glorious June day.

6

The Accounting

Essex anchored his squadron four days later in a Plymouth mist. With him he brought the *San Andreas,* haughty but subdued, towering above her captors. A great crowd lined the wharf and as the *Due Repulse,* dripping but beautiful, neared the quay, the cheering mounted to the gray skies. On his high deck Essex stood and waved his hat with its bedraggled plume. His heart beat quickly; how passing sweet were the fruits of victory!

He stepped ashore and was received by a deputation, quietly deferential, and withdrawn in their approval. Something was very wrong. Courteous, though impatient to get to his lodgings, Essex looked restlessly about for Cuffe. The Queen's dispatch he stuffed into his doublet. What in God's name was wrong—had his plans gone awry?

No sign of Howard. He too must have received a welcome that put him behind closed doors. Essex strode up to his private rooms, calling loudly for Cuffe. By a table littered with papers stood Reynolds, his undersecretary, and sitting at it, his long, clever face almost level with the papers, was Anthony Bacon. No one else.

"Congratulations, my lord." Reynolds knelt to Essex's hand. Bacon rose and bowed.

"By Hercules," Essex flung his gloves at Joseph and dropped into a chair, " 'tis good to set foot on English soil and get away from the accursed sun. And where, in the name of ten devils, is Cuffe?"

Reynolds swallowed. "My lord, I received your letters by post, since Cuffe fell ill at Portsmouth. I was prepared to carry out your lordship's instructions, when I received a sharp check from the Lord Archbishop, who had forbidden the printers to set down one word of your account."

"Who blabbed?" said Essex loudly.

Reynolds looked at Bacon, who in turn looked at a long quill turning round and round in his fingers.

"My lord," said Bacon, "it was your good friend Ashley, the one whom you so recently knighted. He told the Queen and Council of your intent, and—" he shrugged, hands turned outward.

"Ashley." Essex repeated the name softly. "Ashley. Well, I'm damned." He rose and took a turn across the room. "So that was why he gave me that sickly smile in the Admiral's cabin. And I thought I had welded him to me with that tap on the shoulder. Do a man a favor and he bites you."

Bacon flushed. His own brother stood to receive favors at Essex's hands. He wondered if the Earl—but Essex was staring at the dispatches that he pulled, all crumpled, from his blouse. Might as well read them and know the worst. This was indeed a different homecoming from the one he and Cuffe had planned. Cuffe stretched out at Portsmouth, with God knew what, and Ashley rushing off to the Queen. What, if anything, had been dropped into Cuffe's wine?

He broke the Queen's seal. An angry flush colored his forehead. This —why, this was worse than the worst! Surprised, was she, that the spoils from the sack had not been carefully preserved to pay the charges of the expedition—they should have searched the ships before permitting them to dock!

And this—he tore open a long epistle from the Privy Council. More of the same, based, it seemed, on Ashley's twisted reporting. Blamed for not intercepting the Indian fleets, were they? Well, God's wounds, whose fault was it they had not done so—and was it his fault that they lost the merchant fleet at Port Royal? He looked up scowling from his reading.

"Bad?" said Bacon, hardly moving his lips.

"Almost as bad as can be." Restlessly he rose again and went to the window. Then he swung round. "And my Lord Archbishop? I thought he was my friend—has he joined the pack, too?"

"Had my Lord Archbishop followed his own desires, he would have joined me in every endeavor to persuade the printers to disobey the Queen's order," replied Bacon. "I myself tried, but though the printers were sympathetic they dared not do it."

"No, no, of course not." Essex was reasonable. But this was not all. They were holding something back. "You have more to tell me?"

Bacon rose and looked at him. "This will sit ill on your lordship, I fear. The day you sailed for home, the Queen made Robert Cecil her Secretary of State."

So. She had done it again. Once more his face was slapped and the whole world was laughing. Everyone knew how warmly he had advanced the claims of his good friend Tom Bodley, who now was disregarded, and that blasted little hunchback was in name, fact, and prestige, now one of the most powerful men in all England. He swallowed convulsively and gripped the table edge.

"Have I anything in my favor at all?"

"There was a general thanksgiving planned throughout the country, to your lordship's advantage, but her Majesty confined it to London."

Essex laughed bleakly. She would do that. "Go on."

"Dr. Barlow, preaching for my Lord Archbishop before Paul's Cross, gave your lordship high praise and full credit for an enviable part in the victory. He was warmly received. He spoke of your lordship's wisdom, justice, and noble carriage in the action."

"The people?" Essex was intent.

"Full support, my lord. And your friends are arranging to have manuscript copies of *A True Relation* made to be distributed here and abroad." Bacon drew his papers to him and picked one up.

But Essex did not hear this last. His mind was busy with an idea, a dangerous thought that lived within the innermost recesses of his brain and only emerged at times like these.

"So the people are with me." It was more a statement than a question.

Reynolds nodded, but Bacon pursed his lips and said nothing. He was thinking that it might be better for his lordship of Essex if the people were less enthusiastic about the Earl and the Cadiz adventure.

He rode up to Greenwich to find himself a hero. Not one of the delirious people who cheered him as he went past thought to give credit to the Lord Admiral, to Ralegh, who, though he had shone in the sea battle, had bungled the matter of the treasure fleet he had been left behind to capture. It was the Lord of Essex who had dealt the hated enemy one more blow, and it was his name they screamed as his escort went chinking past. They forgot he was a general; England's great destiny lay on the sea, and in their eyes he was a master seaman.

The light drizzle that dripped off the brim of his morion down the back of his neck went unheeded as he rode through the warmth of the people with their cries of love. Again and again he lifted his glove in acknowledgment, thrilled momentarily by the worship in the rain-wet faces turned up to him.

Between the towns, riding silently among his men, he had time to think. Then it was that bitterness flowed in and the people's adulation faded to an unreal dream. His brain was reeling with the events of the past few days. Cecil lifted so high, Ashley sunk so low, and—the Queen to be faced. Sickening news had dogged them home. Their straggling ships, anchoring late, brought word that the West Indian fleet had been laden with twenty million ducats! And this they had lost because he could not persuade Howard to allow him to remain on Spanish soil, where the taking of this tremendous treasure would have been for him child's play. He felt as if he had been flung bodily into the laps of his enemies.

Well, at least the people were with him. Again that small prickle shot through his secret being, and his eyes narrowed. He contrasted his official reception, the cold handshakes, the averted eyes, the biting sarcasms of the dispatches, with the warm human cries of the hysterically devoted people of England. Would the day come, perhaps, when he might need the support of these common folk of the land, partisans with him, against—what? The prickle was now a chill that ran right down his spine.

Perhaps, though, Gloriana would be kind . . . perhaps there would be no need of the people.

He arrived at Greenwich and made himself presentable. He stroked his new beard, flicked the lace at his wrists, and strode lightly into the Queen's music room.

In a moss green gown with rose-colored sleeves, she sat among her girls, a quartette of singers clustered about John Bull at the virginals. Gloriana leaned her red head back and softly beat time with her fan to the delicious rhythm of the song.

Then she caught sight of Essex, making his way through the crowd. She stiffened.

"Welcome home, my lord," she called clearly.

From his knees he rose and stood before her. He felt her run her eyes over him from head to foot. He saw her looking at his beard. She fanned herself.

"At this moment we are engaged. You may come to us within the hour and there present your—excuses." She waved her hand; the music continued; he was expected to leave.

For a moment he stared, stupified. God's blood, what did she mean, what excuses? This must be a new name for errors quite beyond his control. Clicking his heels, he bowed and left her.

Panting, raging, almost sobbing with fury, he went down the private hall to his own apartment. He kicked open the door and banged into an inner room. He ground his heel into round scratches on the polished floor. He gripped the stiff brocade at the window as he fought for control.

His first impulse was to take horse for Wanstead and stay there for a year, two, three—an eternity, till she weakened and sent for him. And then he would refuse to come. Illness, household business, foreign affairs—anything should serve to bring this high-stomached bitch to her bony knees.

A rap on the door, and without waiting Charles Blount came swiftly in and put his arm on his friend's shoulder.

"Robin, let it not pierce your heart. She's only playing the haughty game to amuse herself."

"So you've heard already? Christ, how stinks travel in a rathole!"

Blount pressed his arm, but Essex would not be comforted. "They're laughing at me."

"Nay, more of them are with your cause than you think."

"They're laughing with the hunchback."

"If they are, 'tis so low that we who love you do not hear it."

Essex now pressed Blount's hand. "I want to take horse and get out of this clammy charnel house before I catch the plague that rots the hearts of all who stay here."

"Nay, Robin, that's not the course." Blount pushed Essex's shoulder gently back and forth. "That's precisely what the pack wants of you. You can see how much hurt they have tried to do you already."

"But, Christ's wounds, can't *she* see? Where is her sense of justice?

Surely no man could do more than I did at Cadiz, bound hand and foot to an old fool and a strutting adventurer."

"She knows that, Robin," soothed Blount. "But the Queen is—the Queen."

"And well do I know it," muttered Essex. "Why did she give Howard the final say on everything? Had it not been for him, I could have put the time to proper advantage." He threw the crushed brocade back against the wall and put his foot up on the window seat. "Why waste breath, Blount? She's chosen her men. May they all rot together! I'm for home."

"But you can't. How can I make you see that? If you can only contain your soul in patience, your turn will come. After all, you are the favorite—still."

"Aye." Essex was ironical. "A lap dog that cowers under the chair when the mistress is pleased to be wroth. I have little taste for this life on a leash, Blount. I weary of it."

He stared off into space, at nothing. Why tell Bount of that intolerable landing at Plymouth, with the averted eyes of the delegation, the cold handshakes? And the dispatches—Holy God in Heaven! At thought of them the sweat sprang out on him. Hardly in his lodgings at Plymouth, the pack was worrying at him.

Blount was pouring wine. "Drink this, Robin."

He took it, holding it loosely, not attempting to lift it to his mouth. The misery of it all held him tight. Never a single soft word from Gloriana, a word for him alone, as always there had been before. Cuffe's untimely illness, and the complete collapse of all his plans. He shivered.

"If this were all, but it isn't," he said miserably. She's made Cecil her Secretary. He's nearly top dog now."

Blount nodded. It was, indeed, a cruel blow to the Essex hopes Again he tried to soothe his friend.

"Did they tell you, Robin, that Dr. Barlow preached——"

"I know, I know," Essex interrupted.

"The people are with you," went on Blount.

Essex made a pettish move. At this moment he doubted the power of the people, or anyone else, save these clever, inexorable figures here at Court, their hands so firmly on the reins.

"Don't give your enemies their joy, Robert," Blount was pleading now. "Stay and stick it out." He paused for his words to sink in.

Slowly Essex drank the wine, then set the glass down with a decisive click. "I'll stay. They've not driven me mad yet."

"Good man," Blount's anxious face broke into a smile.

Essex returned the smile, though wanly. "My good angel, Charlie. Get me Joseph, will you?"

His anger had now passed, but he felt cold and nauseated, and his head ached.

A wet cloth on his forehead and a half-hour flat on his back somewhat restored him, and punctually to the hour he presented himself.

Opposite Gloriana sat her new Secretary. The point of his neatly trimmed beard pricked into the delicate narrow ruff of an expensive-looking black suit, threaded with gold. There was no sign of Burghley.

If Essex expected a supercilious smile from Cecil, he was disappointed, for the Secretary's face was blank. As for the Queen, despite rose-colored sleeves, she looked pale and thin.

He stood at the table, undecided. Would he have to kneel throughout the interview?

"Sit down, my lord," invited Elizabeth. "It is of no use my pretending that I am satisfied or even overly pleased with the results of this expedition. I am full of discontent."

"Your Majesty's share of the spoils, I presume?" his own tone was dry.

"That—and certain other matters."

"Madam, had my advice been taken in weighty affairs, the Crown's portion would have been considerably greater."

"Indeed. Well, whatever the wrangling between you and your officers, it has cost me a pretty penny. Where, may I ask, is the fifty thousand pounds I so trustingly laid out for this voyage? I did this, my lord, at your behest." She sniffed. "In future, I shall serve my own ends. It will be better for England."

"Your Grace, I took Cadiz and all that was in it. It was my intention to lay the spoils of that city at your Grace's feet. But fate willed otherwise."

Elizabeth laughed nastily. "Fate, my lord? That is an old name for the poorest of poor judgment. Why were not the spoils of the city collected in orderly fashion, under supervision, and strictly apportioned?"

"Your Grace is pleased to forget that we had many gentlemen adventurers whose right to the spoils was guaranteed ere we set sail from Plymouth."

"So now I am to finance all the swashbucklers in Christendom in their pirating affairs! God's blood, my lord, you will have to think of a better excuse than that!"

Essex choked down his wrath. He had promised himself to keep his temper. When would that velvet humpback open *his* trap? Was it not time he said something? Cecil cleared his throat. Ah!

"We are attempting," he said, "to appoint commissioners who will seek out those spoils that are the rightful property of the Crown, and obtain them either by exchange or purchase."

"Indeed." It was now the Earl's turn to be sarcastic. "And do you anticipate any real success in this bargaining project?"

"We are still in debt, my lord," was the biting reminder, "for seaman's wages. Whatever your lordship's fair promises to the gentleman volunteers, we stand obligated to the sailors in the matter of five thousand pounds."

At further mention of money the Queen's ill temper sparkled.

"It seems that everyone is to make a fortune out of this except myself. Why did I allow myself to be persuaded when all the time I knew how it would be?" She rested her head on her hand and drew in her breath.

Suddenly the petulance went out of Essex. He saw her for a tired old woman, querulous and disappointed, her mind poisoned against him by the slow insidious injections of his enemies. She wanted nothing for herself, of that he felt sure. Her one and only object was England—his England—and hers. He thought of her brilliant attainments and her overweening love for her country. She was still a great Queen. His heart softened.

"Madam," he said quietly, "would that your Grace might have seen your fleet sail out of Plymouth on that fair June day. Would that you might have been at Cadiz when we despoiled that flower of Spanish cities. We have done grievous hurt to the King of Spain, on land as well as on sea. And we have brought no shame to England."

"I am less interested in glory than in the balance sheet, my lord. Those are fine words, but they do not pay my debts. What of them?" Her tone was dry now, but she was beginning to be mollified.

"Madam, destruction is rarely profitable in terms of money. We have added luster to your Majesty's fair name, and we have taught those Spanish a lesson or two in chivalry. As for the money, my own purse is sadly drained, as are those of the gentlemen who commanded with me."

She tapped her fan gently on her chair and nodded.

"We have brought home ships to the value of many thousands of pounds and his Majesty of Spain may find that some of them will take sail against him, for they are excellent new fighters. If we are little the richer, your Grace may be assured that he is infinitely the poorer for our venture."

Cecil was frowning. The threatened storm was passing and he did not like it. The thunder should rumble some more. He tapped his papers on the edge of the table and returned to the attack.

"It seems, my lord, that there were some sixty-seven gentlemen knighted. Was it necessary, then, in view of the misfortunes of the expedition, to knight so many?"

Essex glared at the little man who sat so imperturbably opposite him. He ran his eyes over the crooked figure.

"If the Secretary had ever seen service in the field," his tones were acid, "he would understand the peculiar virtues of valor and the certain necessity of rewarding that valor."

It was the same as when they were boys together, and Cecil twitted him about his dancing lessons. But this time the cruel shot went home. Cecil's lips tightened and he said no more. But he would willingly wait long to rejoice at the downfall of the Earl of Essex. There was one last clap of thunder as the storm retreated into the distance.

"I have had no satisfactory explanation of why the treasure fleet returning from the Indies was not waited for by the lot of you." Elizabeth's words were clipped. "Twenty million ducats is a considerable sum, my lord."

Essex was eager. "Had my urgent advice been taken, Madam, those ships might even now be in English harbors. But I was overruled at every turn. As for the fleet at Port Royal, I wished to accept Medina's ransom of two million ducats, but my Lord Admiral preferred to wait until it was too late and the Spanish had fired the ships." At the memory of his humiliations he bit his lip. "I wished to remain on Spanish soil, to establish your Majesty's rule there, but again I was prevented."

"Your liver was too hot and my Lord Admiral's not hot enough," she mused. Then she shot him a sharp glance. "However, there was nothing said about establishing a base at Cadiz when you set forth. Had I wished to harass Philip on his own ground, I should have sent someone else."

A slow smile touched Cecil's lips. From her eye-corner, Elizabeth caught it.

"At the same time, if it can be proved that your better advice was systematically disregarded, someone shall pay."

Cecil's smile froze and a slightly foolish look remained. Royal investigations at this time would be neither comfortable nor convenient. He began to gather his papers and by the time the Queen motioned him away with her head, he was ready to depart. Bowing to the air between the Queen and the courtier, he withdrew.

The door closed and silence fell. Then a smile broke over Elizabeth's pale face.

"Come here, Robin." She patted her skirt and he knelt beside her. She stroked his cheek, turned his face up, and looked lovingly down into it. "How brown you are! Your beard," she traced its curly edge with the delicate tip of one white finger. "I like it. Makes you look older." She drew in her breath sharply. She should not have said that.

He laid his head against her velvet sleeve and closed his eyes, while she went on softly stroking his hair. "You Devereux, tactless, undisciplined! Why do I love you?" She dropped her hand to his throat. "And all you do is play the fool. Even I can get on with Howard; why can't you?"

"Puffed-up poker of a man," he grumbled into her shoulder.

At this apt description of her Lord Admiral she shook with silent laughter. "He used to be your hero. Remember?" Ah, but that was long ago. Now he fell to playing with the ends of her girdle chain, and as she looked down on the long eyelashes her smile grew fatuous.

He felt her staring at him. "Why are you so unkind to me?" he asked.

"My love, I am not unkind. You irritate me. You are such a fool. Do you not perceive your enemies' bent? Even little Cecil is after your blood. That was a cruel dig of yours, Robin."

"Cecil!" He raised his flushed face. "Why did you give him the Secretaryship? You knew I favored Bodley."

She shook him softly by the ears. "Robin, Robin, when will you ever stop trying to pick my ministers? We'll give Bodley something else." She tittered. "Give him that nice little library you brought back from Ferrol. I'm told he is something of a scholar. And now, for God's sake, let there be peace between us."

She bent toward him, and when he would have kissed her white uncovered bosom, she raised his head and laid her lips tenderly on his.

In his arms she danced that night, and he tried not to see that he held only the shriveling husk of the Gloriana that once was. In spite of the Queen's feverish attempts to be merry, she could not hide her sallow neck, nor mask with scent her decaying breath. He did not dance with any of her ladies; but he was conscious that there were many white throats about, and too many palpitating little bosoms.

Katherine Fytton was back at Court. Secure in her favorite's devotion, Gloriana did not scruple now to surround herself with pretty women. It was eight long years since Katherine had knelt before the fireplace in that little card room at Somerset House, a rosebud of sixteen summers. Now she was a devastating woman, ripened into beauty that teased every man who came within pinching distance of her round limbs.

She had not forgotten Essex; indeed, who could forget him? Nor had she remained faithful to her memory of him. She had consoled herself with many a lusty-legged lad about the Court, bedding with them as the fancy struck her. Content then, she waited, knowing in her woman's heart that one day Essex would find her irresistible. Now, it seemed, the moment was at hand.

From across the hall her practiced eye invited him. She was easily the most beautiful woman there, with her chestnut mane, more ruddy than his own curly thatch, and her white, dazzling throat. He contrived to get near her. The Queen's back turned, he stepped from behind the arras and seized her by the shoulder.

Despite her assurance Katherine gave a little nervous start. This *was* the favorite and the English ax was sharp, even if these no longer were the days of bluff King Hal. Elizabeth could be a little mad at times. She would have to be very clever. She slipped from his grasp.

"Later, my lord," she whispered. With a burning blue glance she slid sideways from the room.

Gloriana kept Essex at cards till he could no longer stifle his yawns. "Go you to bed, my zany," she snapped. "I'll see you on the morrow."

But he was careful to escort her to bed, kissing the long white hands. One deep look from his green eyes he gave her, and at that she forgave him and prodded him gently in the neck.

"Robin," she said.

Then she walked wearily into her bedchamber. If she was minded of those days when he played cards with her till dawn, returning to his apartments only when morning birds sang, she did not admit it, even to herself.

Essex let himself out through a private door and sped to his own rooms. He passed a window embrasure and from its curtains came a soft whisper.

"My lord!" It was Katherine, the clear whites of her eyes glittering in the dark. "With me!"

She led him down a hall to a door he had never before noticed. Drawing from her bodice a key, she noiselessly turned it in the lock, pushed open the door, and drew him in after her.

"Don't you think I was clever to steal this key?" she giggled.

He took it from her and locked the door from the inside. They were in a small unused bedchamber. There was no fire in the grate, but the summer night was kind, and a soft white moon came in through the mullioned window, touching the silver on their clothes.

"You've been here before," he said.

"Sh!" She touched his lips with her fingers. "Never mind that. We can stay here for a little while, perhaps an hour or two. You can get back to your rooms quite easily."

"But what about you, my sweet?" He pushed her low bodice off her shoulders. "Take this cursed ruff off. It's in my way."

"Never mind about me." She laughed softly. She unhooked the narrow little ruff that she wore on her bare neck and tossed it aside. "There. Is that better?"

His kiss on her throat burned like fire. He was pushing her gently toward the bed.

"Wait!"

Lithely she turned and twisted herself out of her clothes until she lay, a pale glimmer on the dark coverlid. With a sigh that was half a groan, he threw himself down and twined his legs about hers.

Before dawn they parted, he to sleep soundly, she to gloat over her victory and to plan their next meeting.

If the Queen suspected, during the next few weeks, that the Earl was having an intrigue with one of her women, she gave no sign. For she had caused to be embroidered on her bed hangings a new motto. She leaned her head against the carving on her chair, while through half-closed eyes she regarded the device that bloomed on the arras above her head.

Among the flowers and leaves it stood out, plainly green and blue, with flecks of gold.

Video et taceo: I see and am silent.

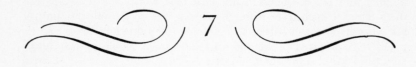

Earl Marshal

A stormy year passed. Torrential rains and wilder winds made a fitting accompaniment for the furious tempests that eddied about Gloriana and the Earl. On the side of the Queen stood the Council, ranged to help her keep the national irons hot in the fires of Ireland, France, and Spain. And on the side of the Earl were his partisans, the war party, eager for spoils, for adventure, for power.

Elizabeth, torn between state and sword, kept her head regally high. Her personal griefs were borne in private. There was the loss of Lord Burgh in Ireland, as well as that of young Norris, both in that fatal country. Feeling old and care-worn, Gloriana took up her pen to write to her friend, Norris' mother, her "dearest own Crow."

She saw Robert Cecil fade and wither under the stunning loss of Lady Cecil, while his father grew ever more feeble with the passing months.

And there was Essex.

His ambition soared ever higher and called him forth once again to the high seas. On fire to take ship once again to Spain, he suspended his wrangling with Cecil and Ralegh and so pleased Gloriana that, against her better judgment, she signed his patent to go to the Azores. Once again, with Blount and a crew of fellow hotheads, he set sail from Plymouth, Ralegh in the company.

It was a heavy responsibility and the first time he had been in absolute command, with no older hand to check wildness; and neither he nor Ralegh was fitted for the task. They returned in October, with little plunder and few prisoners. And what was worse, the feud between them flared to such fever flame that Essex was near using the limit of his authority to court-martial Ralegh for insubordination.

"Were he my friend," he told his followers, "I should execute him."

In this state of mind the two generals came home, preceded as usual by twisted reports, calculated to color the Queen's mind against her favorite. She set her jaw. "Never will I send my fleet out of the Channel again," she snarled to Burghley.

That was bad enough. But when Essex learned that in his absence Lord Howard of Effingham, his old disliked brother officer, had been created Earl of Nottingham, his rage boiled. The Lord Admiral cited afresh for gallantry at time of the Armada and, more especially, at Cadiz!

"Now," he complained to Cuffe, "this investiture throws the shadow over my own exploits. Why, God's blood, this will put him to take precedence over me, Robert Devereux, a Plantagenet, and if truth be known, closer to the throne——"

"Caution, my lord," reminded Cuffe softly, "caution."

Essex flung down to Chartley where he stayed so long that Gloriana began to be seriously alarmed. He refused to come up to Whitehall for the Accession Day celebrations, pleading his old malady; he was even absent on Christmas.

When she could stand it no longer, the Queen wrote him a gentle letter, offering to make him Earl Marshal of all England. With this glittering bait she lured him back to Court.

The ceremony was brief and colorful. Surrounded by his new attendants, Essex looked magnificent in his Earl's regalia, his front blazing with orders, and the last, most gorgeous of all, winking in its nest of new diamonds on his breast. Only the Cecils noted that Gloriana looked somewhat grim.

"You see!" Exultation carried Essex to Bacon's study. "I have directly challenged her, and what has happened? She has yielded and I have my wish. God's blood, all you have to do, Francis, is bully her a little, and she knuckles under. She's only a woman, after all."

But Bacon shook his head and applied himself anew to his work; he was copying his new manuscript: Ten Essays, and a group of *Twelve Sacred Meditations in Latin.*

"The new year looks welcome, Bacon. I'm thirty and it's time I was sighting my goal. Faith, and I get no younger with the years."

"Your goal, Robert?" queried Bacon languidly, laying down his pen. He thought of the Queen's middle sixties and sighed.

"My goal," repeated Essex. "That, Francis, I have not confessed, even to myself."

"You skate on thin ice," murmured Bacon, bending once more to his task.

"The Queen is what—sixty-five?" persisted Essex. "She, too, grows no younger. And it is my firm belief that she grows weaker with her age. Would she, think you, have so complied with my stepfather?"

"Never," agreed Bacon. Then he leaned back in his seat, the pen dangling from his nervous hand. "But, Robert, you are not to think that the Queen bestows this honor on you because she grows old and feeble. It is because she is a woman that she does it. Never forget that."

"Am I likely to?" laughed Essex. "Have I not said as much?"

"The Queen acts on the instinct of the moment, Essex. For that you must ever be prepared. Do not push her too far."

Essex shrugged and lapsed into silence, while the other bent back to his work. It was strange, he thought, how his feeling for his mistress had changed. Once she was his exciting royal idol, knelt to and adored; now she was an aging tyrannical creature that he bore with in resigned tolerance.

Moodily he rode away from Bacon's place and turned his horse's head for London. There awaited his friends and followers, indeed. But whereas at the beginning of his fame they had been young noblemen whose prime interest was adventure and the glory of England, now they were careless hotheads, disgruntled gamblers, who knew only reckless disregard for law and order.

At their head he went forward to his destiny.

And all the while Gloriana, only half comprehending what was happening to her favorite, continued her incessant slaving over State business.

Although nearly ten years had elapsed since the crashing victory against the Spanish Armada, they had been years of constant vigilance.

France and the Netherlands must maintain their newly won independence from Spanish aggression; Philip's generals were a constant menace. The Queen sent regiments under the great Veres, paid, thank God, by the Dutch, to keep her honor green in the field against Spanish infantry. To an extent this freed the slim war budget for the horrid business of Ireland.

At the moment there was the nagging business of the new French Ambassador, who had come to persuade her to take a stand, something she abhorred, either in favor of joining France in peace negotiations with Spain, or in going on with the war. Finally, on the last day of the old year, she consented to receive him.

She was gracious as he knelt to her hand. She was wearing a fair gown of peach-colored cloth of silver, opening on an underrobe of white, richly embroidered in pale tints. M. de Maisse stared at the summer display on an old lady in the dead of winter.

The Queen walked restlessly about during the interview and as she did so, spread open her gown with her long hands, so that it gaped to the waist. De Maisse averted his eyes; she did not take note of his embarrassment. To avoid his mention of his mission she discoursed on one of her favorite subjects, the villainy of the Spanish King.

"I say to you, *monsieur,* that he is a cruel, proud, and wicked prince, one that would not scruple to poison his own sister, so let her look to herself, lest he make away with her by this means." Then she spread open her undergown, so that her shirt of lawn showed clearly to the astounded Frenchman. "I have no doubt," she proceeded, "that at your master's Court, you have heard many things through Spanish lips to my disadvantage."

"There have been divers things averred, Madam," replied De Maisse carefully, "but your friends do not believe them."

"What!" cried she. "Is it possible that you do not believe I fill skins with Catholics for my dogs to tear? Why, even the Lord Cardinal Cosmo sent a servant in disguise to witness one of my Papist massacres! I am reputed to cause the death of one hundred and five Papist women in one house," here her eyes gleamed wickedly, "when the most that ever enters this house at one time, by my permission, is two!"

Her maids and gentlemen, standing about the chamber, snickered.

"God is my witness," she continued, "that I have never allowed ill to be done to any Catholic for faith in his religion, save when they attempted the State. I wish," now she was thoroughly warmed to her subject, "I wish that the inside of my heart were in a picture and that picture at Rome, for all to see that it is pure and free from aught to them save friendship."

"Madam," interposed De Maisse, mindful of his errand, "can your Grace tell me of your intentions to my country, touching the matter of peace with Spain?"

"Master Ambassador," replied Gloriana, "you will say of all these tales that I am telling you that they are mere gullery. You think I am playing for time, do you not?" She laughed gaily. "See what it is to have to do with old women, such as I am." Then, at his troubled look, she relented. "I am between Scylla and Charybdis, *monsieur*."

Indeed, she spoke truth. On the one side was Cecil, with quill and paper, peacefully pressing for settlement with the ancient enemy; on the other, sword in hand, the battle light in his eyes, stood Essex.

"I know," she resumed, "that the matter you treat of is of greater importance than any since I came to the Crown thirty-nine years before."

She then complained about the heat from the fire and pressed open her shift still further, so that the stupefied Ambassador truly did not know where to look. If she were aware of his paralysis, she gave no sign but merely said, "I shall arrange for you to present your case before the Council."

Gasping inwardly at the strange behavior of England's mighty prince, De Maisse now took his departure, going straight to his own rooms, where he lost no time in committing his curious experience to paper.

The Queen and Council now resolved to send commissioners to Paris and bethought themselves to entrust the mission to Robert Cecil. Essex did not know whether he was pleased or annoyed. While he hated his enemy to have so responsible an honor, he rejoiced over the absence of the watchful little Secretary from Gloriana's side.

Despite Bacon's repeated warnings he pressed forward to greater and greater heights. In order that no faintest suspicion of the Cecil faction be aroused, he accordingly feigned a sudden friendliness for Ralegh and the Secretary, and pretending a desire to give Cecil a good send-off to France, he swallowed down his distaste and gave a supper for them at Essex House.

A brilliant gathering sat down to the Earl's great carved table in his dining hall. Near the host sat his beautiful mother, vivacious in green velvet that lent youth to her sparkling eyes, making her incongruous marriage with the younger Blount seem entirely right. Lady Essex sat quietly at the foot of the board and dispensed hospitality with all the distinguished grace of her dead father. If her heart was heavy, Frances Devereux did not show by the faintest shadow in her dark eyes that she was not happy.

For some time now she had been painfully aware that her husband was no longer in love with her. His amorous little affairs with the Queen's maids had waxed and waned, and she had tried to shut the knowledge of them out of her heart. Looking back over her marriage with Essex, she now could smile at her simplicity in thinking to bind him to her with a love as steady and pure-burning as that which lighted the lives of her parents.

She now was uneasy at the thought that he was temporarily free of all attachments, being in that dangerous state when he might fall desperately and unreasoningly in love with any one of the fascinating women that hung about the Court. Slender figures dipped and swayed expertly in the languor of the dance, while soft eyes burned silent messages into those of their partners. These same beauties were unafraid of the bright morning sun that shone full in their faces as they mounted their horses to the gallop, feathers sweeping over glossy curls, long skirts floating away from little feet. They sent their white fingers gliding over the ivory keys of the virginals or sat with lute ribbons drooping over their shoulders while they drew from silver strings the songs of France and Italy.

With a curious insight, born of her love, Frances knew that someday Robert Devereux would give to someone the love that had never been hers or even the Queen's. But—till then she was still his wife and the mother of his three sons, one of whom they had put into the grave. There was that tie between them of birth and death, which nothing could ever dissolve. With that she had to console herself.

A great burst of laughter drew her back to the scene about her. Halfway down the table, flanked by the handsome Charles Blount and John Rutland, sat Penelope. It was she whom they were teasing. Her fair hair glowed silver-gilt in the candlelight, her blondeness thrown up by the richness of her violet robe. Near them sat Ralegh, with his love, the dark and sinister Elizabeth Throckmorten, a figure whose Florentine elegance outshone all the other beauties in the room.

Ruddy with wine, Essex sat at the head and leaned back in his chair. He grinned loosely at Cecil, whose abstemious glass was only half-empty. In mourning for his wife, the Secretary struck the only somber note at the table.

"Come, there," called Essex. "Sir Robert, you put our cellar to shame! Is not the wine to your liking?"

Cecil smiled and observed that the guinea fowl were excellent, the best he had tasted that season. He quietly drank his wine and allowed the servant to refill his glass. He had no intention of letting Essex make a mark of him in this house.

Blount here hastily interposed a remark about the weather, always a safe topic among the English, and Essex's attention was, for the moment, diverted. Lady Essex now created a small excitement by signaling to the serving boys to bring in the *pièce de résistance* of the supper. This was a magnificent marchpane in all manner of natural shapes of birds, beasts, and flowers, tinted to the most delicate shades.

The ladies clasped their scented hands and Cecil smiled in superior fashion at this grandiloquent gesture of the Devereux. The busy little pages, brave in the colors of the house, poured fresh wine into the cups.

"Ah, glorious sack!" suddenly cried Rutland, who had had too much of the sugary drink. "It drives the vapors from the brain, makes the tongue utter ex-excellent wit, warms the blood, ill-illumines the c-countenance, and—" here he nudged Penelope with his silken elbow, "makes the men all hot and swollen for conquest!"

"Enough," growled Blount. Penelope only smiled sleepily and popped a marchpane cherry into her red mouth.

Rutland seized a fresh flask from a server. "Take a bottle by the neck an' a woman by the waist!" he sniggered.

Cecil's lip lifted on his white teeth. Already he was regretting that he had come. How could an Earl of the Realm endure such rowdies! Fastidiously he wiped his lips with his crested napkin.

Here Lady Essex rose and the party dispersed to the outer hall where the Lord Admiral's Players waited to present two pieces, John Dekker's *The Triplicity of Cuckolds,* which called forth loud laughs from the gallants; and the other, a polite little masque by Francis Bacon, dedicated to Gloriana and the Earl. This latter made the Earl's friends merry and pleased; but on the faces of Ralegh and Cecil appeared covert sneers.

During the masque Essex prayed the Secretary to come to his small cabinet where they might be private for a few moments. Surfeited with the broad witticisms of the players, who took free liberties with Bacon's little piece, Cecil, nothing loath, rose and followed his host silently down the passage.

The door behind them, Essex said, "So you are for Dieppe at the week's end, Sir Robert?" The other inclined his head. "I shall pray for your safe return."

"My thanks."

"It is blustery weather," went on Essex. "I beg of you to have a care to your health."

"I shall take every care, I thank you, my lord," replied Cecil softly.

"It would seem," said Essex, "that God has at last disposed our minds to love and kindness. I wish to assure you that I shall do no hurt to your cause in your absence; nothing shall befall that shall be a prejudice or offensive to you."

They exchanged level looks. No trace of a smile crossed either face.

"I hope, my lord," said Cecil, "that we shall never forget that nothing is so dear to us as her Majesty's service." He played a moment with the gold chain about his neck. "God knows I have never desired anything other than kindly intercourse with your lordship."

"Nor I," replied the Earl.

The Secretary held out his hand as a hint that he would be going. "I do not keep late hours, my lord," he said.

With solemn faces they parted.

Essex stood a while in the shadows of his little room. He would do what he could for himself while Cecil was absent, and should a storm send the Secretary to the bottom of the Channel, it would be all the same to him.

Then he snuffed the candles and rejoined his guests.

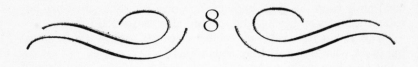

Pamela

So Cecil crossed the Channel and Essex took his place at the Queen's elbow. Assiduous in his attendance, he pleased Gloriana so that she showed her delight, and it was almost like old times. He decided to broach a subject that for some time had been close to his heart. Early one snowy morning he presented himself at the door of the Queen's dressing room.

"Come in, come in!" called Elizabeth hoarsely. "This accursed weather has put a frog in me throat, but I slept like a top last night." She held out her arms to the twin bracelets of cat's eyes. Lifting her wrists to the light, she admired the jewels.

"Your Grace," began Essex, rising from his knees, "I have a small request to make of you, and on this I pray you to listen and be generous."

"Hey-day! Am I not always generous? You make me sound like an ogre. Well, spit it out, lad, what is it?" Her good night had made her affable.

Essex threw up his head. This was going to be easy. "I have a mother, your Grace."

"So you have, Robin, so you have. Didst think I believed you to have sprung full-fledged from the brow of Jove?" She cackled at her own wit. "And you wish me to receive the Countess, is that it?"

She now held out her long hand to Mistress Pamela Bridges, on her knees beside her, engaged in trimming the royal nails.

"That it is, Madam." Essex had his eye on the girl, a newcomer, whose dark eyes flashed as bright as her tiny glittering scissors.

"Hum!" Gloriana marked the direction of his eye and snatched her hand away from the girl. "Enough. You may go." She rested her untrimmed fingers on her hip and scowled after the bowing maid.

"Well, Robin, have your lady mother come to Court. It will be amusing to see what the years have done to her."

She kept him chatting at her side till she was sure the maid Pamela was safe in the Coffer Chamber, where her girls consorted, and whither the gentlemen of the Court might not trespass. Then she let him go to the Council meeting.

But Mistress Bridges had not gone to the Coffer Chamber. She had no desire to go back among those chattering girls, with their sly looks and their gossip. The outer room here was deserted save for the guard and a page or two who pushed past her and disappeared. It was too early in the morning for the antechamber crowd. Here she might stay for a while, quiet and unnoticed. As for the Queen, she would require no attendance for some time, now the Earl was with her.

She knelt in the embrasure of a window and looked out at the falling snow. Idly she lingered there, entranced by the soft whiteness without. New to the Court, there were times when she felt she must get her breath. Gazing out of a window calmed her, took her back to her beloved Surrey. She had come to Court to please her ambitious mother, once a Lady of the Bedchamber; but she had not come willingly. She missed her meadows and the hum of her father's bee garden. She longed for the wet wind that would be whipping the frozen fields outside her father's land and the forest where she and he used to ride. All there would be lovely, white silence.

This vivid life into which she had suddenly been flung bewildered her. She was not yet sure she liked it at all. The young men who pursued her did not frighten her or throw her into that fluttering panic of pleasure that constantly agitated the Queen's maids. They only wearied and annoyed her, and unlike the other girls, no one of them disturbed her dreams. Now she had seen the renowned Devereux. She wrinkled her smooth brow as she considered the Lord of Essex. He was both impressive and disturbing, of that there was no doubt. But she thought the girls were very silly over him, especially Katherine Fytton, who said he took her breath right away.

A door behind her opened, and the guard softly grounded his arms on the tiled floor. The Earl was leaving the Queen early. She shrank behind the curtain. But he must have caught sight of her gown, for her delicate nostrils quivered at the near scent of musk. He was standing at her very shoulder. In the pit of her stomach fluttered a small nervous tremor. She tried to remain very still.

"It snows, Mistress," remarked Essex, as if he, too, were absorbed in the white spectacle without.

"Indeed, yes, my lord." She spoke so low that he must bend his tall head to hear. She would like to leave, but to push past him would be awkward. Why had she stayed? He twisted round inquiringly to her face.

"I am Essex," he offered.

Now she must turn, with a silken rustle, to face him. Under the little sleeve rolls her shoulders were very straight. Her hand, which she gave him, was slim and tawny. "Oh, yes, I know. I am Pamela Bridges."

Intending to be merely formal, he raised her fingers to his lips. He was unprepared for the strange thrill that shot through him at the soft coolness. "You are but lately come?"

"Last week, my lord. This morning was my first attendance." Gently she drew her hand away. "My home is in Surrey."

He put his tingling fingers up to the little fluted ruff at his throat. "Ah, Surrey. Beautiful. No wonder you have not the London look."

At that she smiled. He thought she looked elfin, with her pointed chin and strange, tawny-colored skin. "It is indeed beautiful," she murmured.

"You are homesick," he said gently, "nor can I blame you."

"I had Christmas at home before I left. I cannot complain." She drew a tremulous breath. "They tell me I missed a merry time here."

He grimaced. "You missed a power of noise and a sad stomach from stuffing with sickly riches, that is all. Your holiday in the country was far better, I warrant."

"You have a rare understanding, my lord, even if you are—forgive me—somewhat cynical." Against the pallid brown of her skin, her pale red lips were smooth. He gazed at her, trying to determine what it was the girl had that made her so different from all the others. She was not beautiful in a professional way, but there was something arresting about her. She reminded him of the Greek figures in his mother's garden. Frances, his wife, had caught him with her definitive air of breeding, but this girl was Diana, with the look of a shy fawn in her dark glances.

"And now I must leave you, my lord," she said. She had been at Court long enough to know she could not stay there. Without even a curtsey, she turned quickly away and slipped from the room.

He stood, immobile, a tall dark figure in blue, a man rooted to the spot on which he stood. God! What was this that had come over him? A quiet country girl, with a freshness that even the rich Court gown could not smother, had stepped across his path. A pair of dark eyes, slanting at the corners with a touch of woodland wildness, had looked candidly into his. A soft laugh like the voice of his ferny brook down at Wanstead had quivered delicately in the warm air of a Queen's palace chamber. Of a sudden he felt light as a bubble, young, boylike, subtly excited as if standing on the brink of adventure.

A girl's high laugh broke into his stillness. He turned to find the merry eyes of Katherine Fytton, brimming with delicious spite. She had been hidden behind the brocades of the next window, curled cosily into its deep shadows, to hear and see and be amused.

"Charming!" she cried, as she threw her head back with her old trick of showing a pearly throat and bosom. "What a touching little scene! So our country cousin is homesick!"

Now she was so close to him that, had he liked, he could have seized her round the throat as he did once before.

"Spying again, Kat?" said he lightly. "Do you make it your only business these days?"

"Oh come, Robin! Spying's our business, as well you know. Suppose I were to tell you that the little——"

Swift as thought, he wheeled upon her and laid a hand on her mouth. He did not know what she was about to say, but all at once he felt that the Queen's new maid must be protected. She must not fall victim to the clutch and drag of a jealous waiting woman. Her tender flesh would be rent by the sharp white teeth of this passionate vixen who even now was biting into his hand. He loosened the pressure on her mouth and slid his hand down into her willing bosom.

As he pressed her back behind the curtain, she caught her breath excitedly and, pushing him from her, pulled up her bodice.

"Mad I may be, but not even my enemies call me stupid, my lord," she laughed. "Here." She dropped into his hand a small shoulder knot of velvet. "Give this to the page called Geoffrey, he's the little new one with yellow hair, and he'll bring you to me tonight."

She smiled mockingly upon him, and then she too was gone.

He waited for her to close the door, then quickly he unlatched the window and raised his hand to fling the ribband into the icy blast. But —Pamela! He threw back his hand, stuffed the trifle into his doublet, and left.

Next day the Earl's mother arrived at Whitehall and waited in the privy gallery for the Queen to pass. For two mortal hours, the proud Countess of Leicester, Lady Blount, stood in the drafty passage, her fur cloak clutched about her. Her face grew ever whiter, as she waited, her lips tight and thin. At last word came.

Gloriana had decided to remain in her own apartments. She had sent for John Bull and now they were playing the spinet.

Biting back tears of rage, the Countess returned to her son's house, and Gloriana played and sang till late in the afternoon, when she issued forth to take dinner at Cecil House with Lord Burghley.

On the following day Lady Blount swallowed family pride and came again to the gallery. This time she sat playing cards with her daughter. She was told, "Her Grace is closeted with dispatches from Sir Robert Cecil. She will be busy till far into the night."

To the surprise of everyone, Lettice Knollys came on the third day. But her Majesty had a bad cold and could not leave her quarters.

February stretched its chilly length between the two ladies. Essex was preoccupied. He was pursuing the elusive Pamela, whose company he had enjoyed but three times alone since their first meeting. Always on tiptoe for flight, the most she gave him was perhaps a dozen words, a wistful look from tilted eyes. But it was enough to set his blood pounding, to disturb his nights. At last he was in love.

As for his mother, she humbly begged leave to entertain the Queen at dinner on March the first; Gloriana was graciously pleased to accept. A great bustle in her son's house ensued, and on the evening of a cold, blustery day, Lady Blount stood at the head of the stairs in Essex House, a rich jewel in her hand. There she waited.

Back at Whitehall, the royal coach rumbled into the courtyard. Upstairs, dressed in furs, the Queen stood before the fire, a set jaw on her and a dangerous flash in her eye. She took two steps to the door, then summoned her Steward.

"There's a high wind and I shall have toothache. I have decided to remain indoors today."

Cuffe told Lady Blount that her royal guest was not coming. With an oath the Countess threw the jewel onto the floor and flounced upstairs to her room. Cuffe buttoned his cloak and went back to Whitehall to find his master. He found Essex lying on his bed, white with a sick headache.

"God's death," groaned Essex, turning out of the covers and beginning to struggle into a bedrobe. "I shall bid fair to go crazy yet with these two."

He staggered to the door and went slippering down his private staircase to Gloriana. He found her, standing woodenly in the center of her room. Pale and handsome in his furred robe, he faced her accusingly. Then the high words flew, and in his pain and disgust he flung out of the presence and back to his bed.

Gloriana was elated. She laughed and chucked her little page Darby under the chin. She called to her dog and made him sit up for sweets. She had the maids in to sing to her, and the new girl, a maid with a half-startled look in her slanting brown eyes, sang a country song of the Surrey woods.

For several hours her mood held. Then she began remembering the face of Essex when he stormed out of her presence. Had she gone too far? Perhaps the little farce was played out. She had always intended someday to receive the Countess; it had amused her to torment Essex. The pleased smile vanished and her eyes became cold little stones of fear. Even a queen could not compel love, and if once he turned from her—she snatched a paper and wrote a note.

"Another victory, Joseph! Bring water and wine. I shall dress."

Heedless of his jumping head, intoxicated once more with success, he called for lights and supper, and with a few friends spent a merry evening.

A few days later he was again fortunate. Coming from the Queen, he found Pamela alone in the corridor.

"My lord?" There was the enchanting tilt at the eye-corners.

"What gentle fortune smiles upon me tonight?" He smiled into her brown eyes with their clear glancing whites.

"Gentle fortune?" She laughed up at him. "Can my Lord of Essex be anything but fortunate?"

"How little you know. Pamela, Pamela, if only I could——"

She touched him on the arm. "Should your lordship care to see something? Follow me; we must not talk here." Rustling past him, she went down the corridor to the small cabinet at the end, and, entranced, he followed.

Inside, she took from her pouch a little box, which she opened and handed to him. Within was a portrait in little, a man whose sad, scholarly eyes were exactly the shade of her own. "My father," she said. "He promised it for my name day, and this morning it came." Her voice held a note he had not heard before.

"You love him very much, don't you?"

She took the box and held it a moment to her breast, then slipped it away. "Yes," she said simply, "more than anything in the world. With him life was sweet."

"Sweet," he echoed. "Ah, Pamela, 'tis you who are sweet." He took her hand and turned the soft little palm to his hot cheek. His eyes burned. "Pamela, could you not love me a little?"

Her pale brown skin glowed, and against it her eyes were as bright as his. For an instant he felt her hand turn and curl against his face. Then she drew it away. "I could find it easy to love you, my lord, but —" her voice trailed away to a whisper, "I must not allow myself to do it."

But now he was bold. He had brushed off some of her shyness. He drew her to him. "Oh, Pam, darling, be kind. Say you will love me."

She was startled. "You must let me go, my lord." Leaning away from him, she stiffened in his arms. "No, please, you must loose me."

But he drew her ever closer, gently, insistently, till at last she could bear it no longer, and she melted, all her resistance gone. Then she clung to him. "Oh, my lord!" she whispered.

"Pam, my darling, my dearest one." Softly he kissed her cheeks, her eyes, her lips, murmuring against the velvet. "Love, love, do you know how much I love you?"

"No, no," she breathed. " 'Tis I who love you." She pushed him away a little, then sighed. "And yet—I cannot help myself."

Again he strained her to him, with kisses and endearments. "When—when—?" he begged.

"So soon as I can contrive." She smiled mistily at him and departed.

But days passed before she could manage a meeting. Then she passed him in the Queen's audience chamber, close enough to drop into his hand a small object. He thrust it into his blouse, but from its feel he knew it to be her most precious possession, the miniature of her father. Safe behind his own door, he unclasped the face and found the tiny scrap of paper. She would meet him tonight.

Burning and shivering as if he had the ague, he went like a boy to the meeting. She was waiting for him and for a long time he held her to him and they did not speak.

"Adorable one," he muttered against her throat. "Say you love me. Say it."

She said it.

"And what is the measure of your love?" he persisted.

"Why, I love thee twice as much as yesterday and half as much as I shall love tomorrow—Robin," the word was new and shy to her.

He took her little pointed chin between his thumb and finger. "Art a poet, my Pam?" he teased. "Now, which of your lovers said that to you? Nay, do not reply. I know I am the first."

"And the last," she whispered.

Later when she lay in his arms and all eased, he stretched his length beside her, he turned on his side to look searchingly into her eyes.

"My Pam, I cannot wed you, the time for that is lost, but I can give you my heart. Those others must be content with my duty. My heart is yours, you are first in my loves."

She nodded. "That I shall cherish. That shall be my secret glory, love."

He looked at her, heart-searchingly. She was the dark maiden for whom he had waited. "Do you think we shall always love like this?"

"No, Robin," she said calmly. Then, at his questioning look, "because you are man and I am woman. For a woman there is one love, for a man, many."

"You did not hear what I said. I have given you my heart to keep, Pamela. I have loved before, 'tis true, but never like this. I shall never feel for another what I feel for you."

He believed what he said, and for once he was right. He never did.

9

The Quarrel

*E*ssex took his lady mother on his arm to Gloriana, who not only held out her hand to be kissed but raised the Countess from her knees and embraced her. The two proud ladies chatted, eyes veiled, each reading the other's thoughts as if in a glass.

When Lady Blount had retired, all smiles and sugary reconciliation, Gloriana called for water. "Wash me!" she cried. "Wash me! This is a honey that cloys and sticks to the fingers. By my faith, 'tis too rich for my poor stomach."

A week later she snubbed the Countess in public. The wound broke open afresh; it seemed that the Queen was resolved to carry her hate for Leicester's widow into the grave. With a tart remark to a friend, that lady went down into the country, there to sit and bide her time till her own hatred should flower within the bosom of her son.

March dragged by, with Essex in the dumps. He was depressed by the Queen's treatment of his mother. To make matters worse, Pamela was called home by the illness of her mother. All at once he could not bear the Court.

After a fresh falling out with Elizabeth, he left in a black and sulky mood. He took horse and went off to Wanstead with a few friends.

There he sank into a melancholy that he could not shake. It was not that the falling out with the Queen had been so serious. His nights were disturbed by a strange feeling of foreboding, a nagging un-named fear of what might come.

There was gay company about him, and the silvery laughter of Eliz-abeth Vernon as she sported in the garden with young Southampton. Blount came with his quiet charm, to lie at Penelope's feet, and the friendly voices were warm with love. None of this, not even the lovely spring weather, dispelled his depression.

As for Gloriana, she too was half-ill of grief and worry. She was heartsick at his coldness, and she was gravely upset by the failure of Cecil's mission to France. She wrote Essex a broken little letter which would have stirred a harder heart than his.

Always sentimental, he forgave her and returned to London.

April was bright blue that year, with clear, high skies, and May came, filling the hedgerows with white, fragrant blossom. A warm June suc-ceeded, and Essex relaxed into the healing atmosphere about him. He and Elizabeth made merry together. They spent much time out of doors, which both of them loved. Courteous and happy in each other's society, they avoided sore subjects and gave themselves up to pleasure.

Pamela was there, too, and the lovers' sweet secret was still their own. Stolen hours of enchantment kept him in good spirits, as he poured into the tender ears of his mistress his hopes and plans. Pamela was a perfect companion, discreet and passionate, with a bright, untouched mind that glittered in the sparks from his own. It was a rare liaison.

So the time passed pleasantly enough until July came.

The Queen had summoned an informal conference in the Privy Chamber. Lord Burgh was dead some months now, and Ireland was without a Lord Deputy. It was necessary to appoint someone to that turbulent country. The ministers gathered. Arriving with Essex was Howard, the new Earl of Nottingham, an irritating sight, and Robert Cecil, ailing since his return from France. Behind them was the quiet Windebank, Clerk to the Signet.

The gentlemen disposed themselves about a large table and turned to the head, where Elizabeth sat, her face set and expressionless. Cecil opened the discussion.

"My lords," began his precise tones, "the matter of a Lord Deputy to Ireland is of serious and pressing concern, and it is to determine a successor to Lord Burgh that we are met today."

Sententious idiot, thought Essex, why doesn't he get on with it?

"I favor Sir William Knollys," Elizabeth's high voice cut in harshly. "He is a man of substance and good sense who will do as well as anyone has done in that accursed land."

Essex scowled afresh. His mother's brother was one of his strongest adherents here at Court. This doubtless was some of Cecil's work, the entering wedge of a campaign to divest him of his followers, one by one. Getting rid of his uncle Knollys would be a good stroke.

"An excellent choice, your Majesty," approved the new Earl of Nottingham pompously. "I heartily agree that Sir William will serve us to good account against Tyrone."

"And I say he will not!" declared Essex loudly. "Why not send Sir George Carew? He is a far abler man than my uncle."

"Carew!" cried Elizabeth. "Have you lost your wits, Essex? He cannot hold a candle to Knollys either in ability or experience."

"My uncle is getting ripe with years, Madam. If the stinks of Ireland finished off Burgh so quickly, methinks we shall be put to it to appoint another deputy too soon."

"Can it be," insinuated Cecil gently, "that the Earl fears to lose a kinsman in the service of England?"

"La, la," shrugged Gloriana. "A better death is not to be found on this globe. If Knollys goes to Ireland and perishes," she threw out her hands, "it is the will of God."

"It would seem, Master Secretary, that you are very free with my relatives," began Essex bitterly.

"Come, enough of this." Elizabeth's voice was sharp. "I take it, then, that we are in accord to send Sir William as our Deputy?"

"I am not in accord!" cried Essex. "I still say the choice is poor. Let Sir George Carew go to Ireland to the stinks and bogs."

"He shall not go," decided Elizabeth.

"Give me one good reason why you refuse to grant me this," insisted Essex.

Elizabeth rose and glared at her favorite. "I say he shall not go. Is not that enough?"

"No, by God!" cried Essex, now thoroughly beside himself. "It is like everything else. I am checked in all my counsels. I warn you that the Spaniard is not to be trusted; what then? You turn me the deaf ear, and you send Cecil to seek overtures of friendship with our archenemy. I——"

The Queen turned to her Keeper of the Signet. "Windebank," she said, disregarding the outburst of the Earl, "Master Secretary will prepare the patent and, as soon as it is signed by me, give it the Signet and deliver it to Sir William."

Essex's temper was by now white-hot. He was so near the Queen that he could reach out and touch the gold lace on her arm. "So you disregard me entirely?" he exclaimed.

She turned now and looked right at him. Her face was a mask of scorn. "Don't be ridiculous, Essex. You forget yourself."

All the contempt of which he was capable now flew to the surface. He stared back, his quivering lip lifted in a snarl. "Faugh!" he spat, and turned on his heel, presenting his back to her.

She gasped. "You—impudent—" she reached out and dealt him a resounding box on the ear. "Take that! To the devil with you!"

Instantly he whirled on her, his hand clapped to his sword. "By the most sacred blood of Christ, this is an outrage! I will not put up with it! I would not have borne it from your father, let alone——"

Lord Howard pressed him back. "My lord," he said in a low shaken voice. "My lord."

With another sneer Essex banged from the room, slamming the door behind him.

There was an appalled silence. Gloriana stood like a statue, every line of her face and gown frozen into immobility.

By evening he was gone. She let him go. They waited for her to send them to fetch him to the Tower, but she kept her lips tightly folded. She plunged into a mountain of work and buried herself behind sheaves of papers. In their former quarrels she had sought solace in music. Now a tune maddened her. She began a laborious translation of *Plutarch's Lives*.

Her face grew whiter day by day and wearing the mask, she hunted, she played, she worked. She kept her thoughts locked behind those still lips, confiding in no one.

Then occurred a small diversion. The Polish Ambassador came to town, with an elegant suite, and threw intelligent London into a flutter. So learned a gentleman had not graced the city since the days of Erasmus. Elizabeth decided to receive him in state. In her hall at Richmond, under a cloth-of-gold canopy, she sat, blazing in satin and jewels, her brilliant Court flashing about her in a thousand glittering facets. In the heart of this prismatic splendor she sat, like a phoenix bird spreading its fabulous plumage, and she gave a gracious if unsmiling welcome to the envoy.

Surrounded by his foreign-looking gentlemen, the Ambassador came gravely into the hall. There was a high-bred distinction in his face and figure, and the two tall, commanding personages faced each other. Elizabeth extended her fingers to be kissed. The Polish gentleman then swept his black velvet behind him, so that the gold embroidery on the heavy folds caught the light. He retired some ten paces from the throne. He cleared his throat. The Court and Gloriana settled themselves to hear a fulsome oration, praising in set phrases the puissance of England's great sovereign, and offering promises of peace from his country to hers.

There were no praises, there were no promises. There was, instead, in polished Latin, a round defiance and a sharp calling to account. England's Gloriana, it seemed, had overstepped her rights as a European monarch; she had presumed to despoil Poland's merchants and subjects of all quality in this, her mad and savage quarrel with the King of Spain; she had ignored all petitions and letters; she had taken it upon herself to assume superiority over all other princes; and, finally, if she did nothing to amend these grievous wrongs, the Polish King would take it upon himself to correct them.

All this in Latin. Few men in the room had followed the rolling periods of the address to its close. With a haughty smile the Ambassador concluded and threw back his head to note the effect of his outburst on the English Queen.

Not one word had been lost on her. As the oration proceeded, the phoenix became a pale, red-crowned basilisk, with narrowed eyes and set jaw. There was a pause. Making sure that he was through, Gloriana leaped to her feet.

*"Expectavi orationem, mihi vero querelam adduxisti!"** she roared.

The amazed Pole's mouth dropped apart. Extemporaneous Latin! His own speech had been carefully transcribed and committed to memory and rehearsed with his secretary in private. He had expected to strike Elizabeth of England dumb with his learning, so that she would be embarrassed and might even put off her own reply till one of her scholars could compose it for her. But this! What was she? A mixture of royal lion, goddess, omniscient muse of learning, all in one? The

---

* I have awaited the message (but) you have indeed brought me complaint.

royal eye flashed fire, the royal voice thundered on, while the Latin poured forth in a torrent. She answered every complaint in round and sturdy defiance.

Another pause. English faces were blazing with delight. The Poles looked glum. Gloriana sat down. Still leaning toward the envoy, she continued, this time in French.

"Master Ambassador, I perceive you have read many books to fortify your arguments, yet I am apt to believe that your eye has not lighted on the chapter that prescribes the form to be used between kings and princes."

Her eyes darted over her Court, and her mouth twitched. She threw back her shoulders in their pearled puffs. "For the particulars of your negotiation, we will appoint some of our Council to confer with you, to see upon what ground this clamor of yours hath its foundation."

His velvet tail between his aristocratic legs, the Lord Ambassador of Poland withdrew to collect his shattered nerves and to furbish up his wits and decide how soon he could escape out of this terrible country.

And Gloriana looked at her lords and grinned.

"By God's death, sirs, I have been enforced this day to scour up my old Latin which hath lain long rusting."

For the first time since the quarrel she felt lighter at heart.

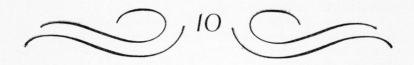

Farewell Burghley

Lord Burghley was dying. The great minister had been ailing since the new year. His body wearied him and he could rest nowhere. They had made him a special chair in which he could recline or be carried about, but he found little ease in it or in his bed.

In the middle of July he attended a Council meeting; and when it was done, he tottered out on the arm of his son. He went to Cecil House, where for the last time, he took to his bed.

Elizabeth was distracted. She, too, was ailing, but hers was a sickness of the spirit. No peaceful falling into death for her; only racking, sleepless nights and heavy days, full of pain. She roused herself to take coach and ride to Cecil House to see the aged sufferer.

They showed her into his bedchamber, where he lay, white and frail, propped up on pillows to ease his breathing.

"Majesty," he said feebly, "I regret that I cannot receive you as I should."

"My old friend," Elizabeth restrained her tears with difficulty, "my old friend, do not speak." She sank into a chair at the bedside and signed for the waiting woman to leave them. "Alas, Burghley, this is a heavy thing for me. What, what shall I ever do without you?"

The ghost of a smile flitted across the old face. "Madam, you will manage."

"Verily, I shall manage, but in what case, my lord?"

She patted the hand that lay, dry and nerveless, on the coverlid. A knock on the door and one of the Lord Treasurer's daughters entered with a small basin. " 'Tis some warm milk, your Grace. His stomach will not tolerate anything else."

"Give it me." The Queen took it. "Here, my lord, drink this. Nay," at his averted face, "I command it. 'Twill give you strength." She spooned the milk into his drooping mouth, gently scraping the drops from the stubbly old chin.

"It distresses me that your Grace shall see me like this," he murmured. "My barber——"

"Tut, man, dost think I never saw unshaven chin before?"

Silence fell upon both. He was dozing now, and she was remembering the countless times that Leicester had fallen into a drunken slumber across her threshold, to waken in the morning, sodden and stubbly with need of a razor.

She looked tenderly at the old man. It touched her that he should concern himself with etiquette when death waited at his elbow. Her eyes still on him, she pushed the basin at his daughter.

He stirred and moaned a little. He opened his eyes. The only sleep for him now came in little catnaps that refreshed him for no more than a moment or two. He moved his lips; he was trying to say something. She leaned over him.

"Robert—full instructions—good son, will serve your Grace well—Mendoza, send him away—dangerous—must watch Navarre—must watch—must—" he was incoherent.

Gloriana's tears fell unheeded on his pillow. With fading breath he was trying to serve her—to serve England's needs. Mendoza! He had been their worry of ten years ago, now was no more than a memory. The dying man was slipping back into his past, and hers. He thought he was sitting opposite her at the table.

She could not longer bear to see him, a frail old husk, waiting for the breath of eternity to blow him into the grave. She rose and called the nurse. Drawing her hood about her face, she left, tall and pale, shivering privately at the imminent approach of death.

Burghley sank rapidly, but remained clearheaded all next day. At about eight of the evening he opened his eyes and said distinctly, "The Lord be praised. The time is come."

Then in gasping whispers he blessed them all. "Farewell," he murmured. "Love God, and—" he took a labored breath, "and love one another."

There was a long silence, broken only by the subdued sobs of the women. Robert Cecil, his face white as the sheet under his father's chin, sat holding the cold hand in his.

Suddenly the blue eyes opened once again. There was a momentary gleam, like a fire that leaps before it dies away forever.

"God save the Queen," said Burghley, and the light went out.

They brought the tidings as she sat among her maids and a few of her gentlemen. The light fell softly on them as they leaned against the chairs, listening to one of the girls reading the Twenty-third Psalm.

"Yea, though I walk through the valley of the shadow of death, I will fear no evil, for Thou are with me—" there was a hurried tapping at the door. Hunsdon came swiftly in and knelt to the Queen.

She looked at him, scowling away her tears. "Over?"

He bowed his head. She went very pale, her heavy eyes strangely bright.

"Let not the bells begin till dawn," she said. "His family must have some sleep. I command them to go to bed."

She rose and stood, one hand on the back of her chair. "It is a heavy loss, my lords and ladies, a heavy loss."

Then she walked slowly from the room.

Elizabeth grieved deeply for Burghley. He had taken into the grave with him more than any of the others. Never again would she look up impatiently from her papers to see his mild, intelligent blue eyes fixed on her in alert readiness. Never again would they walk in one of the many gardens that had been privy to their talks. He had been serious, grave, not given to jokes; sometimes he had smiled painfully at her sallies and rough jibes. But his life had been pure and gentle, his devotion unswerving, his judgment sound as a bell. She wondered how to endure life without him.

When Mary Tudor had died and Elizabeth excitedly assumed the Crown, she sent for Burghley, then Sir William Cecil.

"This judgment I have of you," she said, "that you will not be corrupted with any manner of gift, and that you will be faithful to the state, and that without respect of my private will, you will give me that counsel that you think best."

This from a young Queen of twenty-five to the man she had chosen to be her trusted councilor, then in the prime of his years. From that day their fortunes had been irretrievably linked. And now he was gone. Her sense of loss was overwhelming. Sighing heavily, she made Robert Cecil his successor. And, secretly, she wondered how, without Burghley, she could cope with Essex.

She now received a letter from Essex, full of lamentations and grieved cries of resignation at her treatment of him. She was too far sunk in misery over Burghley to feel more than a slight irritation at him. She read the letter again.

Madam,
When I think how I have preferred your beauty above all other things, and received no pleasure in life but by the impulse of your favor toward me, I wonder at myself what cause there would be to make me absent myself one day from you. But when I remember that your Majesty hath, by the intolerable wrong done both me and yourself, not only broken all the laws of affection, but done against the honor of your sex . . .

She flung the letter to the floor and set her foot upon it. How dare he write to her thus? Her anger mounted. She snatched it up again.

. . . I was never too proud till your Majesty sought to make me too base. . . . and now since my destiny is no better, my despair shall be as my love was, without repentance. . . .

She sent for Killigrew and charged him to approach the Earl without delay. "Tell his lordship," she said, "that I look for a better answer from him of submission, else he shall not again be admitted to our presence."

Essex replied. He explained that he was ill in his bed of a bad cold, but with her Majesty's permission he would attend the funeral of the Lord Treasurer.

All England felt the loss of Lord Burghley; why, he was as familiar to them as their Queen. He had helped to raise England to her proud place on the sea, and his wise hand had guided her into the paths of prosperity. His day had seen the rise of country squire and merchant seaman, and for a generation he had dispersed English tax money for English good. It was a crippling loss.

 219

London buried Burghley with magnificent pageantry. Hundreds followed the catafalque to the cathedral, and the heavens wept appropriately, with a light August rain that wetted the black plumes on the hearse and draggled the sad garments of the mourners. Amid the sorrowful tolling of bells they carried the old statesman to his rest.

Pale and dramatic in his black clothes, Essex wept with the rest. He had never loved this man, put *in loco parentis* to him, but the afflicting melancholy of the scene weighed down his spirits and brought back, as from the distant past, the memory of his father's end. He pressed his kerchief to his eyes and gazed at nothing.

"Does he grieve for Burghley or for sorrow at his own misfortunes?" murmured Ralegh to his nearest neighbor.

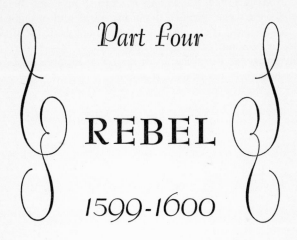

Part Four

REBEL

1599-1600

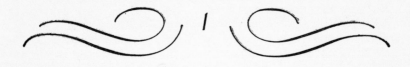

The Trap

*L*ondon had scarcely dried its tears for Burghley when news of a terrible disaster in Ireland descended. Marching on to the relief of the fort on the Blackwater, Sir Henry Bagenal and his powerful army had been wiped out. Northern Ireland lay prostrate at the mercy of Tyrone and his rebels. The Council was paralyzed.

It was the same as always. This Tyrone had always been able to strike terror to stout English hearts. Men now spoke of him as King of Ireland, so powerful had he become. He was surely in league with James of Scotland, and it was said that he had even offered that worthy the crown of Ireland. A strong Catholic monarchy of *two* lands, strategically adjacent to England would please the Holy Father, who was said actually to have ordered a crown made for the Earl Tyrone's coronation as Prince Regnant under James. A fine conspiracy right on England's very doorstep!

And so the fantastic rumors persisted. The next was no rumor.

Irish, hitherto loyal to the Queen, were now tumbling to Tyrone's standard, and the Cahirs, O'Briens, Barrys, and Roches had joined forces with Ownie O'Moore, Tyrone's dread lieutenant, and the lot of them were ravaging the land for the great rebel. Hugh O'Neill, Earl of

Tyrone, was a large figure in the land, with his Irish birth and his English education, and his sworn determination was to drive the English, bag and baggage, out of his country. He was a great soldier, perhaps the greatest of his day, and he had a plausible tongue and a wicked, wily brain that made him greased lightning and slippery work to handle.

And now he had struck another heavy blow for Irish freedom at a time when England could ill afford to suffer it.

"The worst of it," mourned Elizabeth to Cecil, "the worst of it is that this heavy news will brighten the deathbed of that Spanish devil."

For Philip of Spain was indeed dying. Elizabeth's greatest friend had entered the grave and her greatest enemy was fast preparing to follow him.

High in his fetid room in the Escorial, Philip lay loathsomely rotting away. His deathroom was the small oratory from which he could see, with fading eyes, the high altar, the sacred table on which was spread his spiritual food. All day long the solemn minor chanting of the monks and boys below rose to him, with the heavy incense and the waxen breath of great slender tapers. In this odor of sanctity he lay, surrounded by shaven priests and high churchmen.

His body was covered with running sores and over him hung a stench so great as to make attendance on him a penance for his doctors. Clutching the long ivory cross, by means of which his father had entered the next world, Philip listened with a crucified smile to the ceaseless prayers that floated about his couch.

But the smile brightened when they told him the good news from Ireland. He would continue to send troops to aid the Irish rebels against the heretic Queen. God was good, their cause prospered. He laid upon his weeping son the solemn injunction to uphold the true religion and to continue the fight against England.

At daybreak of September thirteenth, the last fluttering breath passed his blue lips, and his putrid corpse was lifted into a leaden shirt and placed in its coffin. The news flew to England. Gloriana was devout in her thanks to God. As for the son, the new King of Spain, she dismissed him with a flick of her hand.

"I have no fear," she told her ministers, "of a youth who was twelve years learning his alphabet." She sat back and enjoyed the details of Philip's last hours. "I wonder he had no fear to enter the next world," she marveled. "Had I lived so wicked a life, I should have been terrified."

When told that he had literally been eaten alive by lice on his bed, she laughed merrily. "God grant me no further ambition than to be eaten by worms when I am dead!"

Essex, whose cold had moved down to his chest after Burghley's funeral, was now lying at his London house. The Queen, really worried, sent her doctor with Fulke Greville to see what could be done. Ungraciously Essex permitted their ministrations. They bled him of about a pint of blood and left him to recover.

A day later he staggered from his bed and sat down by the window. Below lay the garden, stretching green and varicolored down to the water-steps. From his high position on the third floor he could see the polyglot panorama that was Tudor London.

Situated at the bend of the river, Essex House commanded a sweep both up and down the Thames. Gloomily he stared at Arundel House and thought of Tom Seymour, the boy king's gay young uncle, who for folly had lost his head on Tower Hill. But Tom had played his cards so badly, almost as badly as his brother, the sour Lord Protector of young Edward VI; for he forgot that his place was *behind* the throne and not *on* it. The ax had ended all that. Essex sank his chin on his fist and considered. Where had these men lost the way?

A flash of color caught his eye. It was the royal standard flapping in the stiff river breeze that swept over Somerset House. There, though she hated the place, Elizabeth lingered, frozen into static grief over Burghley. Ah, Somserset House, the past, and a little lad of nine, stumbling in his new green shoes after another Earl of Essex! The river of his life had flowed strongly since that day—but where? He was now Earl Marshal of England, but he was also weighted down with debt and hagridden for fear of the future. His great scheme was taking shape within the secret recesses of his thinking, and he was terrified of it.

It had begun to haunt his dreams, and during the days it came at unexpected moments to torment him. When he looked at Elizabeth, alone on her seat of state, he saw that other shadowy seat where a man might sit. The time was ripening for a man of birth and breeding to wear the Crown and carry the jeweled burden of rulership. With all his heart he wanted to be that man, and yet—what would it bring?

The Queen had made the first friendly move in sending her physician, and so he pocketed his pride and decided to return. At the end of a week he felt well enough to have himself announced, and Elizabeth received him. It had been two months since the appalling scene of the quarrel. In silence they faced each other. Then he went forward.

"Are you recovered, my lord?" Her tones were brittle.

"Quite. I thank your Majesty and the good offices of your Grace's physician."

"Good. I presume you attend Council on the morrow? There is heavy news from Ireland."

Since the day was so fine she invited him to accompany her on a short excursion down the river, and he gravely inclined his head. She rested her hand on his arm and they chatted impersonally. Both were wary and courteous.

The sun shone gaily, the river glittered in the afternoon light, and the Queen's maids were merry. Half a dozen barges with fluttering silken pennons glided about them, and the Queen's musicians made sweet music with flute and viol. They passed beneath the arches of the Bridge with their dancing water patterns.

Neither Elizabeth nor Essex was easy. Outwardly exquisite in politeness, but little remained of the old hardy comradeship, when they had joked and teased each other. Now the busy minds ticked off the inward thoughts. Her sudden yielding had touched off no vanity in him this time; instead, he felt a strange declining in pride, an uneasiness tinged faintly with disgust. And she, of course, she knew what he felt. The Italian blood in her sensed all the subtleties of his reflection behind those candid-appearing eyes. There was still defiance in him, and she shuddered to think what he would try next.

Black news from Ireland continued to cast a gloom over Court and Council. Horrible outrages and violences were reported, with the rebels growing ever stronger. A man was caught by them and flogged on his stomach till his bowels hung out; English land-owners were found, sightless, wandering over the countryside, their tongues torn away. There was still no Lord Deputy in Ireland, for Knollys had not gone after all. Things were rapidly rising to the climax. Something had to be done.

The familiar scene was again enacted. Once more, the same little group met to determine England's most pressing problem.

Gloriana pulled down her bodice with a firm, decisive twitch. "My lords, Spain and France are for the nonce laid quiet. It is time to throw our weight into this affair. I shall send my largest army into Ireland with Mountjoy as Lord Lieutenant."

Essex objected. "I think, with your permission, Madam, that Blount is hardly suitable. He is my friend, one whom I love well, but I cannot see where his experience in the wars would fit him for such a responsibility. His estates are mean, his followers few, and I know of my own observation that he would rather draw a book from his pocket than draw from his scabbard a sword."

He spoke without heat. He had promised Pamela that this time he would not lose his temper; besides, he was learning that words spoken in heat cause only bitterness.

"Perhaps," said Cecil, "the Earl will tell us whom he favors."

"I have no choice as yet, Master Secretary. I only object to Mountjoy for the reasons I have stated."

"The reasons are scarcely valid," said Elizabeth. "Lord Mountjoy strikes me as an excellent man for the job."

"But, Madam," persisted Essex, "the country of Ireland presents peculiar problems such as are likely to confound one so new to them. These Irish rebels cannot be treated with even as we would treat the Spanish."

"And what would you do, my lord?" The Earl of Cumberland leaned toward Essex, his clever pointed face screwed into a question.

"I? I have no experience of Ireland. Ask those who have been there. I only believe that were I to take onto myself the subduing of such a band of cutthroat clods, I would use methods special to the case." Essex then sat back.

"And what makes you suppose that Mountjoy cannot do so?" said Elizabeth.

"He is not the man!" cried Essex violently. Then in a calmer tone, "I recommend that to Ireland be sent some prime man of the nobility who is strong in power, honor, wealth, in favor with military men, and who has been the general of an army." He looked round the table.

"It would seem," said Cecil softly, "that the Earl has described himself."

"And if I have?"

"Then it is your wish to go to this God-forsaken land?" inquired Elizabeth.

"Madam, it is not my wish. There are others who can qualify to my description. I have no desire to leave England at this time." He looked straight at Cecil. But the Secretary sat with downcast eyes, apparently absorbed in his fingernails. The meeting broke up; nothing had been decided.

Essex was now on the horns of the dilemma. He did not want to go to Ireland, indeed, it was far from his thoughts, with his affairs here at home in so precarious a state. His presence was essential to his fortunes. And there was Pamela—the very thought of parting from her cost him a heart twinge. However, on the other hand, Ireland beckoned with a strange, lurking fascination. There may be a stroke to be performed that might lead to greater glory than he had as yet imagined.

He was playing with the dangerous idea, bolstered by a still more fantastic notion. His followers had told him that if Tyrone were to hear of the possibility of the Earl of Essex's coming to subdue him, that tough rebel would be only too glad to make terms with the English. Ah, then, who should dare breathe on the shining name of Essex, to tarnish it? If by his very reputation he could send the boldest insurrectionist cowering to the surrender, what might not be his for the asking? The idea enchanted him.

Even Bacon subscribed to it. "But, take care, my lord," he warned, "that you do not pass from dissimulation to verity."

Essex would take care. He would stop short of actually accepting the post; ah yes, he would take care he was not saddled with any lousy expedition to a country that blasted and killed men by the hundreds. He would manage things his own way this time.

So he continued to oppose the appointment of Mountjoy and let it be known that he himself did not positively decline the dubious honor of becoming the Queen's Deputy to Ireland. Long and loudly, in and out of Council, he talked against his friend's going and advanced his heated theories of how to subdue Hugh O'Neill, Earl of Tyrone, the Irish cause of the Queen's distemper.

The Queen grew frightened. She now veered round and said that if Mountjoy was not to go to Ireland, neither should Essex. She would do as she originally intended; Knollys should go and that should end the matter.

Instantly Essex was inflamed. What matter that he never had really intended to go to Ireland? He lost his head. Knollys, of all people! Did the Queen intend to reopen that old sore? He stormed and raved.

"Madam, I declare that my uncle shall not go to Ireland, even if I have to go to that accursed land myself."

Elizabeth smiled bleakly. It was the old recurring pattern. Opposition always aroused in Essex an insane determination to win, win, at all costs. The thing that Bacon had feared came to pass; Essex passed from dissimulation to verity. He plunged fatally into the trap set for him by his enemies.

In the background Cecil went quietly and methodically about his business. He stroked his silky dark beard and observed to his friend Ralegh that if his lordship was so besotted on the Irish problem, he had better get there himself, and that right speedily. With expert skill he guided the Earl's destiny, and Essex, thinking himself at the helm of his own fate, never felt the firmer hand on the tiller.

It was done. He was authorized to proceed to Ireland, there to bring about the speedy subjection of Tyrone and to return to England with the rebel earl's complete submission for the future.

He was in a state of shivering elation. He had triumphed. He stood in the twilight room and the candles were being brought, and he failed to see the angry tears in Elizabeth's eyes and the satisfied smiles on the faces of his enemies. He had won. It was enough.

He raced off to Bacon and together they stood in the pantry of Essex House and drank their beer.

"Field rations!" he cried as he filled their horn cups and raised his to the toast. "The Queen—and Essex!" He drank, setting down the cup with a grin, and again he did not see the warning shadow in the cold eyes of his friend.

He brushed aside the all too familiar admonitions and objections and plunged into the business of getting ready.

Twelfth Night came and still arrangements were not complete. Elizabeth pushed away official business and gave a grand party for visiting dignitaries at Greenwich. She appeared gorgeous in a primrose-colored robe of raised Italian velvet, embossed with Tudor roses, all outlined with pearls and centered with rubies. Her bone-lace ruff rose in elfin wings from her still-white bosom, which she covered with interlaced pearls and rubies. Her white hands lay on her farthingale like fringe and her pale cheeks glowed with a momentary renascence of her auburn youth. Never had she seemed so much the goddess as when she came stepping smartly into the hall, her floating sleeves whipping softly against her skirts in clouds of perfume.

In a high flush she danced, sprightly as ever, and she displayed for everyone's admiration the exquisite little trifle given her by the Danish Ambassador. It was a round watch, a rare novelty, the lids in Italian blue enamel, the whole set about with fine pearls.

Discoursing sweetly, the Earl and the Queen took hands and danced. The years rolled away, and it was as if they had never quarreled. Essex was again twenty-one, Master of her Horse, the adored and adoring favorite. Gloriana was again the excited happy mistress, smiling fondly on her laughing young cavalier.

She thought of that time he first had bent on her his glance, a silver arrow that pierced her virgin bosom and stuck quivering into her heart, there to agitate her with a thousand titillations.

Affectionately she leaned on his shoulder. "I would you were not going, Robin."

"Would I were not, your Grace."

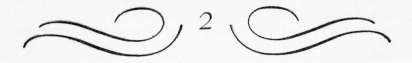

Mistress and Queen

The snowdrops were beginning to raise their fair heads above the frozen ground as Essex rode down into Surrey to see Pamela and his new son. He had missed her more than he thought it possible to miss any woman. Even his preoccupations with the Irish affair did not fill those dusky afternoons and late nights when they had talked and loved.

Late in the spring of the previous year the slim brown girl told him she was to bear his child. But still she remained, her face a little pinched and a growing look of strain in her young eyes. The alert fawn had become a wary creature. It was now time to leave the scene of growing danger for the quiet haven of the country.

According she asked and obtained permission to withdraw to her home in the south. Gloriana had other matters to disturb her peace than the possible defection of a maid-of-honor. Pamela clung dry-eyed to her lover, then went quietly off into oblivion. Now she had her child and her eager letter summoned him to her side.

He clucked to his horse and sped down the frosty lanes at a gallop, Joseph panting behind him. The winter sun was struggling through the gray sky when he flung reins to the servant and ran, two at a time, up the wide steps of the house. He took his chilled bones into the hall and there stood Pamela, pale and charming, one slim brown hand on the newel post at the foot of the staircase.

"My Pam!" His arms enclosed her slenderness.

"Come," she smiled and, taking his hand, led him up the shallow stairs to the nursery.

The newest Devereux had been washed and tidied for the arrival of his noble father. Pamela stood by while he bent his height over the hooded cradle. A baby smell of warmth, and a pair of blue eyes, already turning hazel, were all he could make out. He reached into the crib.

"For God's love!" The nurse exclaimed in horror. "My lord, you'll drop him!" She elbowed him back and slid her hands expertly under the tiny frame.

Essex grimaced at Pamela who laughed and said, "It's all right, Robin. She bullies me, too."

The nurse now placed the baby in his father's arms, curved to cradle the tender little body. The parents bent over the child's face, framed tightly in a lace cap, tied under the indefinite chin. Essex felt a strange mixture of love and regret stir in him. He would have given a good deal to legalize his union with Pamela, all the more now there was a child.

"Oh, look!" cried Pamela, with a little break in her voice. "He's got your nose. There's a little bump in it."

Essex smiled tremulously at the mite that his body, with hers, had made. "He's a Devereux, that much is sure. Pity he can't have the name. But he shall have a title. Shall we call him Walter?"

He shook the tiny crumpled hand back and forth. The child began to whimper and he handed it back to the nurse. He followed Pamela down the corridor to her little boudoir.

She sank onto a seat and leaned, lightly poised, against the window. "I could be stronger," she smiled apologetically, "but I'll soon be all right."

He looked anxiously at her, his eyebrows raised in a rueful line. Then without speaking, he took her hands, kissed them and held them against his neck.

A tap at the door and in came Lady Bridges. Essex rose to his long length and kissed her hand. Watchfully she smiled on her daughter and the Earl, and excused the absence of her husband, who was in the north on business. She was sorry. Soon she left the lovers to themselves and a little silence fell between them. Pamela avoided the subject of her father, who had left to miss Robert's visit, for he was bitterly hurt by this connection she had formed. She sighed gently.

Essex smiled at her. "I can't stay, Pam. We're working night and day, and unless I mistake, I'm for sea at the end of the month." He waited for her to say she wished he were not going.

But all she replied was, "It's a great opportunity for you, Robin." She held his fine, large hands in hers.

"I hope so, beloved," he sighed. "Sometimes, though, I wish—" he broke off, his lips against the velvet over her breast.

Gently she pressed his face against her. "No, my Robin, you wish no such thing. Lolling in a garden all your days? It's no sort of life for you. Stuffy ministers, and the Queen's women?" With a quick, birdlike movement she kissed him.

He slipped to his knees, his arms around her tiny waist. He gave a loving groan. "Oh, Pam, there's no one like you."

"No one" included his mother, who persisted in her sharp chatter against the Irish adventure; Frances, with her mournful eyes, dark and tear-brimmed at his talk of leaving England; and Bacon, whose cold analytical arguments depressed him so that he avoided his old friend.

"My Robin," she drew a fluttering breath and slid her fragile palm once more against his. "How proud I am of you!"

Gratefulness brimmed in his eyes. How perfect, how undemanding she was! "If only we might have all of life together, if I had not to snatch these secret moments with you," he complained.

She shook her head gravely, her fawn's eyes glinting in the firelight. "Don't, Robin. Don't covet more than the gods can give. We can never be happier than we are now. I know it."

But he continued to sigh at life's inequality. Why could they not have met so that he could have made her his own before the world, holding her slender hand in his, proudly, as became a lord with his wedded lady?

"I must tell you, dearest, something that my father taught me when I was a little girl. I was crying for a thing that my heart fancied, and I suppose I could not have it. I forget all but my father's face and his words. 'Come here, my little Pamela,' he said. He put two red apples on the table. 'Look here,' he said, placing one at one end of the table and the other down at the foot. 'There, my child, lie those things that you may have; here lie those that you may not have. And here,' he said, placing his hand exactly in the middle, 'lies your happiness.' Then he gave me one of the apples and told me to read to him.

I did not understand his words at the time, but often since I have thought of them. And now I think I know what he meant." She was silent for a little space. Then softly, "Do you see what I mean, Robin?"

He turned then to her as a man might turn to a goddess he adored. She unbuttoned her kirtle so that his cheek lay against her full breast.

"Pam," he murmured. She stroked his hair and forehead while he listened to the gentle beat of her heart.

The afternoon shadows were beginning to lengthen when she walked down with him to the avenue of pleached trees that scarcely showed buds on their satiny stems. He held her to him and kissed her eyelids.

From behind a brick wall Joseph now appeared leading the horses. In the chill air Pamela shivered and her lover drew the hood closer round her little pointed face. "I shall think of you in the green vales of Ireland," he promised. "I'll be back before young Walter cuts his first tooth."

She smiled brightly, but her eyes sparkled with drops. On his horse now, he looked down at her, his face full of tenderness. She put a small brown hand on his shoe. "You'll come back safe?" she whispered.

He nodded, then went laughing out at the gate. She stood there, one hand braced against the cold red bricks of the wall, gazing after the two galloping figures that shrank into smallness before her eyes. Suddenly the Earl reined in his horse and wheeled. He waved his hat to her, and at the sight her vision dimmed. Shaking with the cold, she turned back up the avenue.

The Earl reached his house at midnight to find a number of his friends gathered in his private cabinet. They were shouting with laughter at sight of one of the young lords, a sixteen-year-old spratling they were teaching to smoke. They had given him a long-stemmed tobacco ladle, and at his manful puffing they yelled with joy.

"By God," roared Malcolm Malby, an old follower of the Devereux, "it's coming out of his ears, gentles, that I swear. Let's strip him and see if it's coming out of his—" he looked up to see the Earl scowling in the doorway.

Essex strode up to the table. In a single glance his angry eye took in the scene. So this was how they spent their time in his absence. With all that was to be done, they came here to carouse with his servants. He shot a baleful look at Cuffe and Reynolds, who made themselves scarce.

In exasperation he sighed. "Gentlemen, I am weary from a long ride and would fain sleep. Such of you," he looked sourly round, "as are unable to proceed are most welcome to what remains of the night here."

At this point the youngster, who had been getting steadily greener in the face, retched loudly and vomited his supper onto the floor. Essex's mouth twitched.

Sir Malcolm Malby, Baron Ferrers, rose, swaying to his feet, his dark, clever face flushed and drunken. "My lord thinks we are an eyesore about the place," he sneered. "He objects to our revels as—" here he hiccoughed and waved his arm vaguely at the heaving boy, "unseemly for the times."

"Shut your drunken head, Malby," said Essex shortly. He turned away. "I'm for bed."

"He's for bed!" cried Malby. "A cold bed for him this night. Pity the little Bridges is not here to warm it." He sniggered and winked at the others.

In a trice Essex had his fingers twisted in Malby's collar. "Ape drunk, swine drunk, goat drunk—whatever it is you are, you'll watch your tongue!" He flung Malby aside. "I cannot fight a soused pig. Put your empty pate under some cold water, and when you are sober, you may apologize." He stamped out.

From under lowering brows Malby watched him go. "In-deed!" He buckled into a chair. He was not so drunk that he did not know what had been said before the others, and he did not love the Earl for it. It appeared that perhaps Essex had a new enemy.

His days were now dizzily crowded with preparation, the nights uneasy with recapitulation of plans and with secret niggling doubts. Cuffe, Wootton, and Reynolds were worked to the limit, sitting hunched over papers until far into the night; Adam Baxter, down at the harbor of Hillbree, was slaving happily aboard the *Popinjay* that lay ready to take his master across from the west coast; and Joseph, up to his neck in the Earl's clothes and armor, hobbled about like a small crooked shadow.

Painfully upon the anxious seat sat Gloriana, watching with shrewd eyes the frenzied movements of the Earl. She was worried for him and for her army, the largest she had ever sent into Ireland. She and Cecil had long talks; at his suggestion she denied the Earl nothing he asked. She even freed Southampton from the Tower where she had sent him for seducing and secretly marrying Elizabeth Vernon, that he might cross the sea with Essex.

"With so desperate an undertaking at hand," said Cecil, "we should do everything to make smooth the way for the Lord Lieutenant." His tone was bland, his face empty.

The Queen looked coldly at him. The way was to be made easy, so as to make failure the more inexcusable. Heavily she sighed and rested her red head on her hand. "You want him to fail."

Up went his eyebrows. "Madam?"

"Oh, go away, Cecil, go away from me."

Bowing, he took his departure.

So the tortuous preparations dragged on to the end of February.

Then one afternoon, when for the moment, her mind was free of doubts, she received a severe shock. Ralegh sent her a present of a fair book entitled *The First Part of the Life and Reign of King Henry IV, Extending to the End of the First Year of his Reign.* The volume was elegantly bound and within, historical fact was prettily disposed among the wit and imagination of Hayward, the young law doctor who had written it.

Elizabeth turned the book over in her long hands, admiring the binding. She then opened it at the middle and idly read a few lines here and there. She riffled the pages back to the title and dedication.

Here she started. So this was why Ralegh had sent the book, and not because he knew she loved fine things. The piece was addressed, in a high-flown burst of compliment, to her Earl Marshal, the most High and Worshipful Lord of Essex.

So! She furbished up her memory of English history of two hundred years back. There had been a revolution; this Henry IV was a usurper, son of a younger son, who bolstered a slender claim to the throne, shoved aside an anointed king, and exchanged the name of Bolingbroke for Henry. The deposed King Richard II died in prison. A pretty tale to set before a reigning monarch.

With set jaw and eyes fixed on the page in angry fascination, she read the sugary dedication. Her hand clenched on the folds of her skirt.

". . . not only precepts but lively patterns, both for private direction and for affairs of state."

Christ's blood, was Essex then likened to Bolingbroke, and was she —but no! She rose, the book dropping to the floor, and rang her little silver bell.

"Get Bacon!"

He came, so clerkly polite and pale that she thought him looking more and more like his cousin Cecil. She shot him a sharp glance.

"That's a smart suit you're wearing, Master Bacon. Your purse must be fat these days."

He bowed, his brain seething with dark thoughts. Had she summoned him only to bait him with her unkindness? She pointed to the floor; he stooped and retrieved the book.

"You have read it?"

He inclined his head and stood, the book in one hand, the other resting on the high back of a chair, the very image of respectful attention. Smug scholar, she thought.

"Your opinion?"

Bacon shrugged slightly, then thrust out his lips. "Your Majesty refers, I presume, to the dedication? It seems to me to be relatively harmless."

"Relatively? What is that? Don't tell me, Bacon, that you miss what the man is driving at." Harmless, indeed. She sniffed scornfully.

"I see, perhaps, some ill-advised sentiment, Madam, but, with your Grace's permission, nothing more." Bacon was as soothing as his cold nature would permit.

Elizabeth rubbed her chin with a forefinger. Then, leaning forward in her chair, she fixed her eyes on him. "And your friend, Essex, what does he see in this? Only some ill-advised sentiment?" She smiled bitterly. "Does he fancy himself a Bolingbroke with his puny little Boleyn claim to cousinship with royalty?"

Bacon stood very still. A cold breeze swept warningly over him.

"Who is this man," she demanded harshly, "this second earl of his father's house, to look so high?"

Bacon could now smell danger for all of them. To steady himself he took a deep breath.

"Madam, the Earl of Essex is innocent in this matter. I know his heart and can testify to the truth that it is his dearest wish to serve your Grace in all things."

She stared at him. "God grant you are right."

There would be no revolution in her time, by Heaven, not while she could bend her mind and her energy to the preventing of it. She had given her life to the maintenance of peace within her realm that English peasant and English peer might sleep secure of nights. She had done what was needful, no matter what the cost.

She plucked restlessly at her stomacher. Then her eye lighted again on the book, lying slim and inoffensive on the crimson table cover. She sank down.

"This Hayward—think you, Master Bacon, that he is treasonable? The rack, perhaps?"

Relief flooded Bacon. She had turned her attention from the danger point. "Not a traitor, Madam, though possibly a felon."

"Felon? How so?"

"Because, Madam, he has stolen so many passages from Tacitus." A cold gleam sparkled in Bacon's eye.

Upset as she was, Elizabeth managed a sour smile. "I did not invite you here for merriment, Master. Treason or felony, this knave shall lodge tonight in the Tower. Council shall pass judgment on him."

She dismissed him and called for her horse. A swift gallop might take away the terrible thought that had suddenly thrust itself into her mind.

John Harington, her godson and a privileged person about her palaces, bustled in to see her. Since the death of Burghley, he had taken it to himself to worry about the Queen's rash disregard of her health.

"Madam, it is frost without, and your Grace's chest being delicate——"

"My chest! It's not my chest that's delicate in your mind, Harington! When I'm too old to ride in the frost, you can wrap me in a winding sheet and call for the sexton. Maids, to your horses!"

The graceful little cavalcade clattered down the frozen path and swirled under the bare trees of the distant park.

March came in with winds that howled about the palace at Richmond, and rattled the casements of Elizabeth's little chamber. She sat, tapping her lips with a quill, the patents for Ireland spread out on a table before her.

"I don't like it, Cecil," she said for the twentieth time as she brushed her lips with the feather, reddening it with her rouge. "I don't like it. I'm not easy in my mind about this at all." She pulled a large paper toward her. "It's a wild, undisciplined land they go to, and I am told this Tyrone means to force us to a costly war. I have no stomach for it."

Cecil was thinking of the paradox of sending a son to fight an Irish rebel who had learned his soldiering under that son's father, the first Earl of Essex, a good man who had found Ireland little enough to his liking.

Elizabeth dipped her quill. "Ah, well, this rebellious O'Neill must be subdued once and for all. To serve in our army and then take arms against us! 'Tis not to be borne." She signed the patents in her square writing, handling the pen painfully, for her rheumatic thumbs were hurting her.

She held the paper off at arm's length, scowling at it before she flung it skittering down the polished surface. "I cannot write so fair a hand as I used to, Cecil; my chirography was once the envy of Europe."

Her boast was a true one. Cecil had seen copies of her younger writing, a miracle of illuminated design with the garland of her signature standing out in fanciful tracery at the foot of an exquisitely spaced page.

Heavily silent, she sat on, while Cecil scratched away at his work. A little dog crouched by the footstool and hunted in its curly coat for fleas.

A grounding of arms outside the door. Elizabeth looked up, her heart leaping. It was Essex, back from a two-day errand.

Swiftly he came in and knelt, his heart swelling rebelliously under the striped silk of his blouse. Gloriana received him with kindness; how could she do otherwise, when the mere sight of him after a short absence could so bring the breath fluttering into her chest?

She had resolutely pushed into the back of her mind that book with its disturbing dedication. Perhaps Bacon was right, and Essex was innocent. At any rate, that she should discuss it with him was her farthest thought. So long as fatal words remained unspoken, their sting was partly drawn. One could affect not to know; one could wait and arm against possible danger. She would watch and remain silent.

She forced her mind to Ireland and what lay ahead of them both.

"Robert," she said earnestly, laying her hand on his shoulder and looking into his face. It wore a sober expression at her use of his name, for he was always either "Robin" when she was fond, "my lord" when she was formal, and "Essex" when she was furious. He was never "Robert" to her, ever. Whatever it was, she was feeling it deeply, and for the moment so was he.

"Robert, I place upon you a solemn charge. I have caused it to be said that you are chosen for this task because of faith, valor, and extraordinary merit. God grant you uphold me in this."

"I shall, Madam."

She leaned back in her chair. "On your arrival you will assemble the Council of Ireland and learn the state of affairs. From what I know of them, they're a poor lot, who blow with the wind. Pick the brains of the men who know the country, and learn of them the ways to circumvent the Tyrone. Do not underrate him, he is no ragged horseboy. And do not take it to yourself to make rash decisions without weighing all the elements."

Her sententious instructions irked him. His solemnity was gone, and only impatience was there, impatience that must be curbed until there was distance between them. Already the Council had loaded him with admonitions and minute directions. Why must she always—His mind wandered, and he watched absently the flash of her ringed fingers as they stabbed the air.

Suddenly she broke off. "Are you listening, my lord?"

He turned his eyes to her face and smiled. She stopped in mid-air and sighed, letting her hand fall heavily to her lap. That smile, she thought despairingly, that nose—they will be the death of me. Aloud she said, "All right, all right. I take it, then, that you listen with your ears if not with your mind."

He took her hand and kissed the tips of her fingers. A shiver of dubious delight shot through her. She drew her hand away. "Get up. You make me nervous, kneeling there as if you were on hot coppers."

He obeyed and folded his hands on the table's edge, like a boy about to con his lessons for an indulgent tutor.

"Robin, now Robin, listen to me. Don't go slapping penniless heroes on the shoulder for knighthoods. We are not meet to keep all the brave men of England." Again she leaned back. "And don't go into leaping contests with Tyrone. Remember that he is your enemy and mine."

He flushed and, glancing at Cecil, saw that the Secretary was apparently absorbed in his papers. His little tilt at Noyon with Henry of Navarre was never to die, though its memory was eight years old.

Now Gloriana looked at him with something of the old tenderness. Forgotten were all their bitter quarrels; forgotten were his proud pretensions to a ruler's rank. Almost she believed she loved him as well as ever.

She sent Cecil away and they sat for a long time, talking as of old. Elizabeth was happier than she had been for years; Essex was almost reconciled to the submission forced on him.

Before he left her, he obtained a document, important enough to be buttoned carefully into an inside pocket. It was a license to return to the Queen's presence at any time as he should find cause, leaving two Lords Justice in Ireland. With this assurance he felt happy and content.

That he had stepped squarely into the trap of his enemies' contriving never occurred to him. Even if he failed in Ireland, he could always come back to charm his mistress out of her discontent.

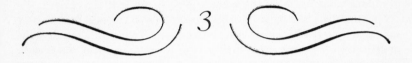

3

Irish Grave

$\mathcal{T}$he Earl made his farewells to his family, spending a few dutiful days with his mother and his wife. Late into the night he lay, with Frances by his side, talking, giving her instructions, should he fail to return. With her heart like lead she listened.

Then he sent the ladies down into the country that he might have elbow room for his departure.

On the eve of his going, he wrote a passionate good-by to Pamela and sent her a ruby and pearl brooch in the shape of a heart. Within was his portrait in little, delicately drawn by Master Hilliard. The packet arrived, but Pamela, in bed with a bad chest, was too ill to take notice of it, even when her mother laid it on the coverlid beside her. On the day of the Earl's visit she had taken a chill in the avenue.

Essex went in the morning to Whitehall to make his formal adieux to Elizabeth. Like the day, she was gloomy. The black mood was on her, and some of her wretchedness communicated itself to him. With cold lips he kissed her, and with colder heart he left.

From a window on the second floor, she watched his departure. Bacon and Cecil stood at her back, and below, in the courtyard, was a great turmoil of noise and confusion. It eddied about the tall figure on the black stallion.

With a sinking feeling she realized that he could afford neither to fail nor to succeed.

For Essex himself there was only a feeling of newness and confusion. All passed kaleidoscopically before his eye. The people screamed and cheered him as they stood ankle deep in mud, their shoes hanging from their necks. Late winter rains kept the streets foul, and above the skies were threatening. Tower Bridge loomed darkly before him, then disappeared in the distance behind.

At Islington the skies opened and drenched them all, and on he jogged, dimly aware that his city escort had now fallen away and his own cornet of horse was moving up close about him. Images, doubts, fears, all swirled raggedly about in his mind, and familiar objects upon the landscape looked strange. Although there was no sun to dazzle him, he had trouble with his eyes, which he rubbed now and then, to clear his vision. He splashed into the muddy streets of Bromley and climbed to his lodging with a jumping headache pounding at every step.

Letters were in from Ireland, speeding east to meet his westward way. The same laconic accounts, but between the lines he could read the bloody tale of mutilations and the savagery of wild men. He spent a poor night with his head, as he pressed his clenched fist to his temple and groaned.

But next day he forged on till the ancient towers of Chester appeared on the horizon. He rode between Christopher Blount, his mother's latest husband, whom he insisted of having as Master of his Horse, and his old friend Southampton. Elizabeth had forbidden the taking of both young men, but he had overruled. As usual, she was angry with both bridegrooms, more especially with Southampton, who had stolen a march on her with his midnight marriage to the mother of his baby son. Despite his experience as Marshal of the Army in the Cadiz venture, Christopher Blount was, in her estimation, young and untried for this greater hazard. She had warned Essex of this, but he tossed aside her objections, and with Cecil to advise, she let him have his way.

But Essex knew none of the little Secretray's dark design in this and thought only how he had bent Elizabeth to his will. Now, as he rode between the two, he felt his spirits rise. His headache was better and his vision cleared.

"Better than the Tower?" he grinned at Southampton, who colored slightly and nodded, smiling. The baby had his mouth and the lovely hair and eyes of the little Vernon. But there had been laughter at Court and the short, uncomfortable sojourn in the Tower to remind him that Gloriana was still his mistress.

Inside the brown-and-white checkered Chester Inn they sat before blazing fires and toasted numb fingers and toes. As he drank from a hot tankard, Essex's teeth suddenly chattered, but he shook off the chill and signed the letter he had dictated to the Queen.

At Beaumaris the Welsh rain beat upon them all and the wind from Ireland blew unceasingly. Essex shook with fever and stalked feebly about his inn, cursing the weather and the expedition.

"A fit foretaste of the moist, rotten country to which we go," he confided to Cuffe. "I had a natural antipathy against this service, but *jacta est alea;* I go in the best cause."

Cuffe looked up from his papers. *Jacta est alea;* the die was indeed cast, and like Caesar at the Rubicon, they faced a fateful future. He made a wry face at the table and went on with his work.

A terrible crossing brought them to Dublin on the fourteenth of April. The holds were black with groaning men who lay below in a foul stench of vomit and cursed feebly the tormenting sea. Wrapped in a drenching mist, late in the afternoon, they approached the harbor. Near to Essex, who braced himself on his wet quarter-deck, was Baxter, on hand for last-minute errands.

"Not much like Spain, eh?" said Essex grimly to his servant.

Baxter shook his head. A man's worst foe at Cadiz was the mosquito or the Spanish languor. This was all different, forbidding, dank, and sodden.

They glided along, and suddenly out of the semigloom of the deep fog a great shape loomed, her sharp and menacing bow pointed dead on their port side. It was the *Charell,* deep-loaded, wallowing as she plowed toward them, lost in the mist, headed now for their towering belly. A few moments and they would be ripped open like a stuck pig.

"God's blood!" roared Essex.

A hoarse screech from his captain, and a violent shudder of the creaking vessel as it swung sharp to starboard to miss the danger. The smaller galleon passed abaft them, her beak grazing their stern with a jarring shock that threw some to the deck. Over the side went a man to inspect the damage. A few tense moments before he came up, gasping and grinning. No harm. Some broken panes and a gash or two in her planking, was all. The *Popinjay* was safe.

Essex groaned with relief. The *Charell* had been deeply loaded with the Queen's pay treasure. What if she and her load had gone to the bottom? Perhaps God was on their side, after all.

With cries and rattling of blocks the English settled to their moorings. Brave in glittering body armor and silk cloak, Essex emerged from his cabin. Joined by his gallants at the ship's side, he and his whole company went clanking ashore to the horses. About five of the evening they rode down into Dublin.

It was a phantom city that awaited them, with the short spring twilight and the fog rolling in again from the bay, to shroud all in ghostly and unpleasant mystery. They left the vague outlines that were buildings on the quay. The loyal folk of Leinster came out of their low-roofed houses to stare at the all too familiar spectacle of a new deputation from England. The Earl and his men returned their curious looks as frankly; black hair and blue eyes, evidences of Celtic blood, were here in abundance. Despite his weariness, Essex felt a faint thrill of interest in this strange, terrible land to which his fortune had brought him.

They slowed at the moat of the castle and he looked up at the squat tower keep and the delicate Gothic chapel. Then over the bridge they went, to clatter under the portcullis in true knightly style, and the new Lord Lieutenant stiffly dismounted and held out his hand to the Lord Clerk of the Irish Council, who advanced to receive him. Boots clanking on stone floors, a bustle of people, curious servitors, pressed against eye and ear as they were led into inner halls. The outer apartments had not been used, they informed him, since medieval days.

They crossed the great hall, and here a steward advanced, bowing. "Would my lord be pleased to come this way to his apartments?"

But Essex hung back, smiling at his hosts.

"I have a fancy to lie in Red Hugh's Tower," he said. "I trust your lordships will not think me overromantic in this."

"Red Hugh's Tower!" The Irishman raised sandy brows in astonishment and shrugged at his fellows. " 'Tis a dreary climb, your lordship, the rooms cold and dirty, being unused——"

"I am used to roughing it, my lord," said Essex shortly. He did not care for the soft jaw and slack mouth of the other. "I pray you, show me the way."

"As you will, my lord." Disapproval, even contempt, was plain in the

Irishman's voice. He led the way for the bewitched fool who had come to make trouble for them all. They climbed to the tower rooms of Hugh O'Donnell, the young Irish firebrand who had endured captivity at English hands, only to escape with the sons of Shane O'Neill on Christmas Eve of '91.

A creaking door gave onto a fairly small room with a circular wall in which was set a window that looked right out over the front gate of the keep.

"Well, by God!" exclaimed Essex, "if at any time of my life, I must endure shackles, let it be in such a sweet eagle's nest as this!"

He strode to the window, peering down at the sheer below. "Sure it is I should not care to creep through a slimy privy chute into the snow, risking my neck on a silken rope." He turned to grin at the Clerk. "Gave you all the slip, quite neatly, eh?" The Clerk looked glum. Essex lightly smote him on the back, and he started back, chin drawn in in offended distaste. "Buck up," Essex rallied. "I am here and your worries may rest for the time."

The Clerk bowed and mumbled something in his ginger-colored beard. Then he drew down his mouth tightly and led his little knot of gentlemen from the room. They took with them a poor impression of the new governor.

But Essex whistled under his breath as he inspected his quarters. The rooms were high enough up from the noise of the courtyard to give precious quiet. A good fire was lighted, and a blazing torch or two stuck into the rusty wall brackets lit up the place with rude comfort. In the inner room was a solid enough pallet, hard and soldierly, and when Joseph had spread his woolen coverlids on it, he thought his bed fit for a king.

"Joseph!" he called. "Bring me something hot. I sup here tonight."

Joseph pattered into the warm circle of the fire. He stared round-eyed. "Here, my lord? Not with the great company below?"

"There is no great company below, Joseph," said Essex tiredly. "There are only men, and feeble ones at that."

He held out his legs and Joseph tugged off the boots and put velvet shoes on the long feet. Essex put his leg against the wall and let the warmth of the fire creep over him. He leaned back in the high old chair they had lugged upstairs for his comfort.

He had no intention of hanging about the necks of these Anglo-Irish at first throw. He would sit here alone and snuff up the Irish air and get his bearings. Then he would lay a course with his new companions.

They brought him meat seethed in a little bowl. It was smoking hot with pepper that brought the tears to his eyes. Contentedly he sat and dined before the fire. His officers and secretaries came and knocked, but all they saw were Joseph's bow legs and a corner of the commander's shoulder. His meal finished, Essex took a heavy cloak from Joseph's methodical peg on the wall and went down his little stone corridor, past the halberdier who stood guard at the bend. He doubled back.

"My man, lead me to the battlements."

The man shouldered his long-poled ax and tramped up the worn steps and down the winding hall to a heavy bolt-studded door. With one end of his pole he pushed it open, then stood aside.

Essex stepped out onto the stone flooring of the roof and walked across to the nearest crenel, where he rested his hand and, leaning through the large slit, looked out over the city.

The fog had lifted and a few murky lights struggled onto the night air. Far on the outskirts of the town winked the thousand lights of the camp. Immediately below him, so near that he could have tossed a pebble onto its steep roof, nestled the Gothic chapel he had noted on his arrival. Suddenly the air became brighter as the moon found an opening between the banks of dark fluff and was now shining palely down, her silvery disc lightly veiled by torn translucent fragments of cloud. The light flowed onto the chapel roof over the delicate small spires that thrust slender fingers into the air atop each buttress.

Again that strange feeling swept over him. Once more he felt the sense of remoteness as when he stood high on his *Due Repulse,* homeward bound from Cadiz. There was something unearthly about being up here alone, standing as it were on the very pinnacle of the gray old city.

At this moment he stood astride his destiny. There could be no going back now, nor did he desire it. There was only going forward. He did not fear his future, for he did not shrink from a premonition of possible failure. Indeed, tonight he was emotionless, drained of fear, empty of elation. He felt himself here in Ireland, it was true, but as yet, he had not donned the mantle of his calling. The Queen's Deputy . . . he had not realized it.

He was bemused, and like a sleepwalker he went back through the studded door to his tower rooms.

But with the sun, rising next morning over Dublin, came reality. As he went through the ceremony that bestowed on him the Sword of

State, Essex felt every inch the Lord Lieutenant. They placed the robe on his shoulders, and he kissed the Sword and the Book.

Did a tiny shudder crawl down his backbone at the memory of Lord Burgh, lying dead, two months unburied in the deeps of this very castle? He shook the thought from him. God's blood, many men had laid down their lives in Ireland, but that did not mean—he braced himself and strode among his lords into the Audience Hall for his first Council meeting.

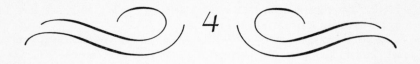

Friends and Foes

$\mathcal{T}$hey took the measure of one another. The lords were thinking that Essex had the cut of a soldier, but their knowledge of him had not convinced them that he was a prudent organizer. More gifted men than he had failed at this tough piece of work. No, by the saints, they did not believe that this tall, handsome young man, in the flush of his prime, possessed the talents necessary for the successful administration of a Lord Lieutenant of Ireland.

Essex was thinking, too. Here was a clutch of stubborn, ineffectual, feeble-witted men. They fingered their rosaries, Catholic, most of them, they agitated their whiskers in endless debate, they spent their time in internal dissension while Tyrone spread his impudent forces about them. Pah!

He asked for a report as to the strength of enemy forces. It seemed there were in all nearly eighteen thousand rebels under arms, and a good half of them in Ulster.

"Very well," decided Essex briskly, "I propose an immediate attack upon Tyrone, for so soon as we can bring this proud ox to his knees, so can we cause the rest to knuckle under to our desires."

Derision touched the tight smiles that flitted across the faces of the Irish earls. Apparently this newly come know-all was thinking to stride into their midst and scoop up Tyrone with one hand. Holy Mother Mary, had he not heard that the great O'Neill was one part devil, one part leprechaun, and one part cobweb shadow that melted into a mocking laugh when a man tried to put a good steel blade through his guts?

"An attack is easier imagined than accomplished, my lord," said the Clerk. "To embark upon that, much cattle are needed, and such few as we have are scarce worth the eating."

Excuses—evasions! A quick answer leaped to the lips of Essex, but was killed unborn by the interruption of the Earl of Kildare.

"There is no local transport available to carry the army, even were it to fare on dry rations, which is precious poor fighting fodder, for we understand that the transport horses are not yet here from England."

Essex shifted irritably in his chair. Checks, obstacles, when would it end? Why could they not start clean and strong on this campaign? He envisioned the crawling carts, loaded with powder, match, and arms, held up by bad weather on the Chester Road, where they must be dispatched across the blasted Irish Sea. Silently he cursed Elizabeth's penury that held back full equipment at the very outset.

"I suggest, my lord, that we await June or early July for the attack on Tyrone, for we can then destroy Ulster corn and cows to the great embarrassment of the O'Neill." This from Lord Dunsany, a Colonel of Horse, who knew what it was to fight with starving troops. "When the grass is up and the cattle fattening, and O'Neill's harvest ready to be taken and spoiled, we can strike to some account."

A murmur of assent ran round the board. To Essex the plan seemed reasonable enough. As for the Irish lords, they were well satisfied with the way things began going. Munster and Leinster, those territories nearer home, ought first to be cleaned of the rebels. A disquieting thought that the English might thus spend their strength and find themselves too depleted for the larger task that was to come held no more weight in their minds than a thistledown.

For the Irish minds conceived that a substantial gain in the central and southern counties might induce that pinching woman at Whitehall to loosen up her stores of men and horse. And as for Tyrone, the north of Ireland was still the north, remote from them, with the O'Neill safe in his Dungannan. With their own garrisons stout and secure here at home, so that no galloping enemy hoofs came to disturb their sleep, Tyrone, for all of them, could stay in his stronghold forever.

All this, snug and quiet, in Irish minds. The pale golden afternoon sun came in on them as round their table they completed plans. Essex agreed to march south.

Spies took the word that the new Lord Lieutenant was intentioned to aid the loyal earls first, and Hugh O'Neill grinned joyously in his great red beard.

"Right into our broth pot he jumps, to be stirred up with the other English calamities," he chuckled. "Faith, I'm thinking that if he's to diddle the O'Neill, he'll need to be a greater man than his father before him, and *he* the great man, indeed! Many's the night we two have sat, cheek by jowl at the campfire, and him teaching me all I ever knew of soldiering."

It was the cream of the jest to the Earl of Tyrone that the son of his old commander should now take arms against him. No sentimentalist, Tyrone felt not the smallest twinge of remorse that he should thus be forced to meet the younger Essex in the field. He had long since divorced himself from England, where under the benign wing of the great Sir Henry Sidney he grew up with young Philip and learned at the knee of the Earl of Leicester.

He threw his weight around and straddled in the ruddy glow of his fire. "I'll not kill him," he declared to his kerns and gallowglasses who stood about admiringly. "I'll just brand me name on his rump and send him to that white witch he serves, for her to deal with him. From what I've heard of late, and from what I've seen with these two eyes, she's the one can do it."

The Irish rebels roared. Ah, the Tyrone was the great boy, and it was altogether fitting and proper that they should go through red-hot fire for him, if necessary. Their idol sat himself down at his table before a whole roasted kid, served to him on a great pewter dish, and called for his minstrels. With the wild skirling of his pipers and the sweet twang of the strings in his ears, he ate his outdoor meal. He was amply content to wait until the Devereux, his knightly enemy, had worn himself out ministering to the plight of the loyal earls.

All unknowing, the Earl of Essex climbed to his eyrie to send news of the plans to London.

"We shall write at once for an immediate advance on reinforcements," he told Cuffe.

"But, my lord, these are not officially due till July."

"Blast it, Cuffe, do you think I know not my own business in this thing?" grumbled Essex peevishly. "We cannot proceed without supplies and that's the straight of it."

Two hours bent over a table cramped his long muscles, and he sighed and stretched. Then he took hat and cloak and went down to the yard. "Blow up my cornet!"

Thumbs hooked in his belt, he lounged in the stone archway, while the trumpeter called the assembly of his escort troop. They would all take a ride through the countryside.

The fluttering capes and bright feathers of his little company swept through the town and out of the southern gate. These horsemen of his were not the brave gold and silver lads of the Cadiz expedition, but hard-faced, hard-living gentlemen pirates, desperate for success, gamblers with death.

Proudly riding at the head of the cornet was Baxter, raised to the rank of cavalry officer and guidon of his master's colors. The pennant now whipped bravely behind him as he led the way into the brisk afternoon wind. At the rear of the column rode Malcolm Malby, his brow creased in a sulky frown. He was still nursing a sullen wrath against the Earl, although the apology for the drunken vulgarity at Essex House had never been offered. Essex, apparently, had forgotten the incident; not so Malby. He bore along with his dull anger a resentment at the Earl's recognition of the common seaman, Baxter. The promotion to the cavalry stuck in Malby's gills; along with his native sense, Essex was fast losing his sense of propriety so to single out a common hind for attention and favor.

They rode through incredibly green country, dazzling enough to hurt the eyes. Skirting the bay, they struck off through the lush meadows that followed the contour of softly swelling downs, keeping the coastline on their left as they rode south. They galloped up Killiney Hill and drew rein. There before them stretched the whole beauteous prospect; to the north the magnificent sweep of Dublin Bay and to the west the gentle Vale of Shanganagh.

Essex sat in silence. Then he spoke to the rider at his side. "Ah, Malby, what a fair country, a bright green jewel in England's crown. I had not heard rightly of the beauties of this land. If only our duty were over and we might tarry to enjoy the heavenly delights of such a place." He looked off in the direction of the rocky coastline, where the sea sparkled coldly in the dipping sun.

He did not see the sneer that Malby hid behind his glove. Briskly they galloped back to the castle.

A restless week followed in which they lay about, impatient for the news from home. Without endorsement from the Queen and Council they dared not proceed. Then the letters arrived. The attack plan was approved; Essex could go into Leinster and Munster. But supplies, not yet due, were withheld. It was the first serious check.

A private letter to Essex lashed him still more. Elizabeth wrote flatly countermanding his appointment of young Southampton as General of his Horse. The disobedience of Wriothesly with Elizabeth Vernon still rankled. Gloriana was tart. She ordered Southampton home with the first wind so that she might deal fitly with him.

"Deal fitly? Body of God, have you not served out your time already for this rash attachment?" Essex cursed afresh and threw the letter from him. It fluttered to the floor. "You shall not go home, by Christ's death," he vowed.

The two Earls left the room and the letter lay forgotten. Malcolm Malby, a silent witness to the scene, picked it up, looked quickly about him, then thrust the paper inside his doublet. The Queen's letter, lying under the muddy boots of her gentlemen!

May the ninth was set for the companies to leave Dublin, but Essex was loath to set forth without additional supplies and men. Sickness and some desertion were thinning his ranks. He looked about him; what local voluntaries were available?

"My Lord Lieutenant," deprecated the Lord Clerk, "it is ill work depending on any support from such as these. They have forsaken their own homes; they have lost strong castles, sometimes without striking so much as a single blow. And besides," he threw out his hands, "they are so scattered that it would be a waste of time to attempt to find them."

"And if we were to find them," drawled Lord Dunkelling, "what good to provide them with arms? They are but indifferent fighters."

"So much for that, then." Essex was curt. "Gentlemen, we shall proceed in such case as we find ourselves. I shall send letters to London, advancing our condition, and may God strengthen our arms for victory."

The letters were written and sealed, and Cuffe took them away as he left. Still Essex was not satisfied. The letters were too official, too formal. Surely there must be something he could say to touch her. He sat on in his little room, staring at the ink and sand before him, his brain wearily busy with words. The light flickered on his tired face. Leaning against the mantel, one arm shielding his face from the fire, Malby stood, warily watching. Suddenly, as Essex struck the table with his fist, he jumped.

"Odds blood! It's not strong enough! I've got to make her see."

He seized a paper and poured words onto it. As in France, now he was ardent and eloquent. His loving mistress, whose heart and good will he prized above rubies, could not so mistrust her devoted servant. Had they not agreed to trust one another? What was life to him, if he had not her love and confidence? With all the passion of a lover he wrote, pouring himself out as if pleading for a kind word or an infinite favor. Smiling, Malby watched him.

Eagerly the pen scratched on. Then he was done. He dashed the sand over the wet ink and shook it onto the floor. With shaking hand he folded and sealed, then looked up, his face flushed and his eyes haggard.

"If this doesn't move her, Malby, I'm lost. I've signed it with my blood. Find Cuffe, will you, and tell him to get it off tonight."

With feline grace Malby lounged forward and took the letter. Without a word he went softly from the room, down the corridor, whisking round the bend of the tower wall. Instead of seeking Cuffe, he turned his steps to the studded door at the top of the little flight of steps that led to the battlements. Out on the platform he wasted no time. Tearing the letter into fragments, he balled them in his fist, hurled them far below to the glimmering moat, then noiselessly vanished into the black.

At dawn the next day Adam Baxter emerged yawning from his tent into the wet courtyard to await the Earl. They were to speed the van of the army that was already up for departure from Dublin. An old trooper tightened the girths of the Earl's horse as it restlessly moved on the cobbles. His grizzled beard was dripping with moisture and he growled to himself as he jerked the straps.

"Transport and baggage animals will have to come back tomorrow and will be to do again."

"It's a caterpillar way to move troops," agreed another fellow. He flung saddle and bridle onto Southampton's roan that skittered to and fro in her nervousness. Baxter at the head of Saladin fiercely resented the criticism of his lord. If they must use the baggage transport over and over again, sending it doubling back to fetch the rear, he would not lay the blame on the Earl.

Now Essex and his gentlemen appeared, their breaths white on the morning air. Quickly they rode out to the confusion of three thousand men, carts, and animals. Essex spurred forward and soon lost himself in the swirling melee.

"Body o' God!" A sweaty-faced captain swore loudly behind Baxter, who jerked his horse aside out of the way of a rumbling cannon. A lathered cart horse struggled beneath the whip as the Irish mud held the heavy wheels. The panting columns of pikemen, sweating heavily, marched with the harquebusiers and the mousquetiers, worst off of all. A slight lad staggered past, all cumbered with his bandoleer and bullet bag. He had lost his long iron rest that he would need before he could fire.

A long blast split the air and made the horses dance. Miraculously the crooked lines resolved themselves into a semblance of order and set off up the hill, winding over the brow to disappear into the west.

"They'll get as far as Naas, then they have orders to make camp, and the animals must return to Dublin for a fresh load." Essex was despairing.

"Finely handicapped," groaned Blount.

"We shall soon see Maryborough," said Danvers soothingly. He patted his sturdy bay. "They are in sad need of provisioning and garrison. That will be our start."

But Essex sat like a statue, watching the line as it wound away from him.

One more day he lingered in the castle, writing and pacing his tower rooms. Long before dawn he was up, drinking hot broth against the cold ride ahead, and then, with the residue of his arms, he swept along the twenty miles to Naas.

At word that there was no resistance from Naas, he was cynical. "They throw open the doors in return for food."

He stayed the night and got an early start next day for Kilrush. Again half the force must remain behind that the transport animals might once more double back.

Through glorious country they followed the old Norman road that sweeps from Dublin down to Kilkenny and thence along the Valley of the Nore to Waterford. Kildare and Leix rolled off to the blue horizon on either side the line, in rich wooded land that lay like a lovely woman under the soft eyes of a lover.

"A beautiful country, but its breath is foul," observed Essex.

They stopped to survey a ruined church near a half-burned village.

Bones and skulls of dead lying in the grass under their horses' feet were what was left of those who had died there in the open, slain by murder or famine. Standing guard over the remains, the grim cromlechs, crooked stone reminders of ancient Druid days, reared their stark lines to the sky.

Lord Grey, a man with a huge, thoughtful brow, joined Essex as they moved away. "A sorry affair for England, my lord, this four years' war."

Essex nodded. He thought of Lord Grey's brother, a fine, promising figure of a man, marked for honors and lost in the fever fogs of this deceptive land. Frontiers were but dim marks at the forest's edge; the enemy, like locusts waiting to swoop down, fell destructively on food and crops. Stout soldiers, used to the open marshes of Flanders and the northern meadows of France, were bewildered, hoodwinked into wearing themselves out fighting the men who were no more substantial than the mists that wrapped the dales and fields. Baffled, they gave up.

Shifting his weight in the saddle, Essex drew a deep breath and turned to Grey. "I allow myself the hope that with the subjection of the castle forts in the south and west, we may gather enough might to force submission from Tyrone."

Surely his father's old lieutenant could not be too fearful a man to be reckoned with!

They followed the lovely wind of the Barrow until they reached Athny, where the feeble garrison came straggling out to welcome them. Under the shadow of the fort they bivouacked for the night.

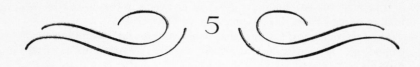

Ten-day Triumph

The morning sun dried mist-dampened clothes and raised drooping spirits, and shortly before noon they emerged from a forest clump to see Carlow, a larger fortress than any they had yet encountered, looming up on the landscape. A brave sight it was, with its round loose-stone towers and flanking prayer shafts.

"Aye," remarked Grey to Essex. They drew their horses to a walk. "There you have the heart and core of Ireland. See those towers? They were built in the days of King Cormac and old St. Patrick, and the lovers, Naisi and Deirdre."

"Ah," smiled Essex, "you have a taste for the wild lore. I must admit, though, it's a picturesque sight."

Now the white flag of surrender went up, lying limply against the staff in the still air, and Essex and his men went thundering over the bridge into the yard of the fort. The English were welcome, for it appeared the Irish garrison stood in need of help against the marauding roamers of the neighborhood.

"Marauding roamers!" cried Essex. "Would that *we* might get a glimpse of them. Boucher!" to his Master of Ordnance, "you will plant such strength as we can afford here, while we get on to Maryborough. We spend more time upon the journey than I like." Curtly he acknowledged the fort commander's salute.

Impatiently the English took horse and rode on past the Rock of Dunamase, a huge pile starting up into the air to the old Norman castle that crowned it.

"Five days out of Dublin, and we see no rebels in this infested country," remarked Essex. "Gentlemen, I am disappointed."

They were nearing Castle Reban when a scout on a steaming horse panted up. "My lords, there is a force of rebels gathered about a half-mile distant, around the brow of yon hill."

Essex reined in and the thick lines behind him drew to a lumbering stop. "What do they number?"

"So near as we could imagine, not more than a hundred or so, my lord."

"Then it's more like to be two hundred," put in Southampton, over on the left. "There'll be a second layer of them in the trees behind the front."

"Take your force and clear them out," ordered Essex. "I've no fancy for arrows in our backs when we proceed to the castle."

Southampton gave his bugler the sound advance, and his small body of foot and cavalry plunged joyously forward to the turn of the road. Lord Grey, with a reserve troop of horse, galloped well behind Southampton's dust. Beneath his brows his eyes burned fanatically. Perhaps now he could strike the first blow to avenge his brother.

Essex and a few officers took stand on a grassy elevation where they could view the pretty little skirmish in the dale below. Southampton pressed the rebels, tall fellows with pikes, hair in their eyes, and rags on their backs, up to the woods. There they broke and ran. Whereupon Grey, with a wild yell, clapped spurs to his horse, shouted to his troop, and led the chase into the dark recesses of the miniature forest.

In about thirty minutes he was back, sheepishly ahead of his men, who had lathered their horses to no avail. The rebels had spread to cover, where horses could not follow, and were swallowed up in the bushes and trees. It was an old Irish trick.

Southampton, fretting about among his men, was white with rage. "You forget yourself, Grey," he cried cuttingly. "You were under no orders to pursue those knaves into a possible ambush!" He wheeled and galloped angrily to report all clear to the Earl.

The Englishmen now proceeded slowly in the direction of Maryborough. And now an emergency arose.

Riding just ahead of the Earl's cornet, Baxter suddenly stiffened and half turned. Shifting his pennant, he gestured with his free arm toward the bend of a low, swelling hill. But a shout from another part of the column revealed that some of the rest had seen the flash of the sun on a helmet. On the left, a scout burst from a thicket and came sharply up to the salute. He was excited. A considerable force of Irish, under heavy arms and apparently well organized, had been seen working its way to a vantage point forward where it seemed certain they would attack the lines and the convoy.

The lines halted. They were just south of Cashel Pass and it was a good two miles to the fort at Maryborough. The leaders dismounted and gathered about a large rock.

The Earl of Ormonde, newly joined with his contingent the evening before, now rode up. "Aye, there, my lords," he called cheerfully, as he swung himself down. "It looks as if we were to have a go at them, after all."

"Good." Essex was brief. "Do you take them for the attack, Ormonde?"

"Oh, to be sure." The other snipped off the words. "I think they purpose setting on us at the entrance to the pass when the wayfare is choked with men and beasts. At least," he gave a delighted grin, "'tis what I would do, were I the rampin' rebels."

"And I," agreed Essex.

Lord Kildare, the dashing Irishman with the cleft chin, now coughed behind his gauntlet. "If your lordships are not minded to engage them at this point, I could guide you to a detour on the eastward side of the mountain. Like a book I know this country."

Southampton, who had removed his helmet to wipe his brow, muttered into the steel basin before putting it back. He did not like the Earl of Kildare with his fleering ways and his shady reputation.

But Essex had no intention of bypassing the enemy. "This rabble must be taught that the Queen's armies go where they please. We shall force the pass."

Kildare shrugged.

Reconnaissance scouts were sent to learn the condition of the surrounding region. The pass proved to be sure, but with dense woods on either side, and behind them a hill and a bog disposed on right and left.

Essex whistled through his teeth and tapped them with his dagger hilt. He considered the going; it would not be easy, but this was all to his liking. Now the scouts reported that at the further end the rebels had dug trenches where they would await the opportune time to fall on the English.

"We shall foil that plan." Essex beckoned to his officers and they clustered together, heads bent and shoulders quiet. Essex stood, thumbs locked in his belt, his face beneath the peaked morion young and animated. This was egg-and-pie to him. The knot dissolved and each man ran to his mount and swung to the saddle, turning his horse's head round. The trumpet pealed urgently, and the English stiffened to the job, then fell back into lines and slogged forward.

There was a good fight. These rebels were not the ragged rabble of the Castle Reban meadow, but well-disciplined, well-armed troops, trained in guerrilla warfare by the great Ownie O'Moore himself.

With a wild shout the English advance guard got cleanly through and after them jangled the cavalry. All burst into open country. Then came the convoy. This was what the Irish awaited, and the yells were all Irish now, and outlandish oaths split the air. The battle closed. A wild confusion of flashing blades and waving arms, bodies locked together, breast to breast, while the taut legs strove to wind themselves about the adversary and fell him to the ground. The Earl's flank guards now flew into the fray and blood splashed down onto the green grass and reddened the clear waters of the ford.

Essex was a fury that spurred his horse from one end of the lines to the other, now at the vanguard, now at the rear. Once he sprang to the ground to cut his way to one of his captains who was in difficulty. When he panted back, he found Baxter holding Saladin, who plunged as he tried to crash into the melee of carts and men. The former seaman had a deep gash over one eye and he laughed as he dashed aside the blood with the back of his hand. The two men, equal now in the fight, exchanged grins. Rank was forgotten; they were a couple of soldiers with the glorious fog of battle upon them. Essex tore off his shoulder sash and flung it to his servant.

"Tie up your noggin with that, and mind what you run against next time!"

Still laughing, he clapped spurs to his black and dashed off to the rear. There the gallowglasses were slashing away at the defenders of some of the heaviest carts.

But despite the savage onslaught of the enemy, the English pushed doggedly through. Maddened by their failure to disable the line, the Irish doubled their attack. The rear guard took a terrific mauling and bled freely. Gay feathers, hacked from English hats by keen Irish blades, fluttered onto the ground, where they lay like flowers on the green sward. The English dead were heavier here, but for every one who went down, snatching at the grass, one tall Irishman went also, and their blood mingled.

Then it was over. Down at the far front of the pass the convoy pulled itself together and marched off. Behind them lay the dead, arms outflung and faces to the soft blue sky. The late-afternoon breeze came up and ruffled the verdant grasses.

The English panted into Maryborough and drew to a halt. Close behind the Earl was Baxter, the heavy folds of his pennant whipping back into his face. He fed and watered the horses, his own Lass and Saladin, then joined his mates in the meadow beside the fort. They squatted, complaining, about a campfire. They were tired and hungry and they also were chagrined that the Irish should have so cut them up back there in the pass. A grizzled veteran was staring with disgust at the bit of cheese that he held.

"Body o' God!" he swore. "It stinks worse than the sink holes o' Spain on a hot day. How is a man to eat this muck, much less fight on it?" He flung the offending chunk into the fire, where it sizzled and sent up a foul little stench.

"Why poison us wi' it?" cried Baxter, forking out the cheese and flicking it away into the grass. He sat down and fumbled in his knapsack for some dried meat. Someone passed him a leather bottle of sour beer and he took a long swig, grimacing at the taste.

A youth with a pale unwholesome face now joined the others. "I wish I never come," he whined, "that I do. What wi' sick belly on ship and the shakes and shivers I get o' nights, I'm fair full of this errand, I am. I want to go 'ome!"

"Ye'll not see home this side o' Christmas, and happen not then," said the elderly soldier. "Ye'll more than likely lay your bones in the good green earth o' Ireland afore this is done."

"I'm hearing there's a power o' sick back in Dublin city," put in another trooper who up to now had not stopped his stolid munching and staring into the fire. "Barefooted they are on the wet streets and straining to get across to Wales."

"I had words wi' one o' Bagenal's men back there," said the pale-faced boy. "Death and terror he says there is, and nothing else for us. An Irish dirk in the back on a dark night, or Irish fever to dry up man's blood." He heaved a shuddering sigh and buried his head on his arms.

"Aye," now spoke the veteran sarcastically. "And I suppose he invited ye to desert, now?"

The boy did not reply. Baxter looked gloomily at them all. He too had heard wild stories in the Dublin streets. Some of his fellows had disappeared when told they would have to fight their paymasters to get their money. Some had actually gone over to the rebels themselves, fired with stories of Hugh O'Neill and his gallowglasses and the Irish girls that lived in the north country outside the Pale and lay in the meadows for the taking.

Inside the fort the Lord Lieutenant sat and listened to grim reports. His forces were thinning and like the men, his captains were depressed. Not only were the forces diminishing, but those that remained were being badly treated.

"How is that?" inquired the Earl.

A captain stepped forward, one hand thrust through his belt. The beer, it seemed, was giving out, and some of the men had drunk the water from the river and were down with fever. A shipload of cheese ready to be loaded into the carts was found to stink so that it could not be approached, much less eaten.

"The meat?"

"Christ's blood, my lord, the beeves are not of the good quality that went to Cadiz three years back, and some are actually rotted."

"Now may God blast that thieving sutler in Chester who sold us bad goods for fair. When I return, I will see him hanged for cheating the Queen's officers!" Essex spat at the fire and kicked the logs with his boot heel. He turned to his officers. "Do what you can, my captains. We shall win, in spite of devil's work on all hands. Do what you can."

In a dim little hole in the wall he went to his bed. Before turning in, he wrote in his journal, holding it close to the sputtering candle.

May 16, 1599. This day did we arrive at Maryborough by God's Grace safe and with few losses at the rebels hands. Our men suffer for want of food and there is much sickness among them. But our hearts are staunch and by the help of Almighty God we shall win a victory such as will kindle a fire of thanksgiving in English hearts.

In two days he was away from the fort and bound for Kilkenny. At dusk he rode beside the Earl of Ormonde, whose capital it was. They passed under the shadow of the great keep and its walls gave back the welcoming shouts of the people. Ormonde took his visitor at once into the long gallery where a blaze crackled in the hooded fireplace and there were high-backed chairs drawn up out of the draft.

But the cheering of the crowd continued until Essex walked to the far end of the gallery and showed himself at the triple-arched window. The cheering grew frantic.

"God save your lordship! God preserve your Honor!" A dense gathering of people was drawn up and all carried long green sticks and bunches of sweet herbs tied to the top, or clutched stiff rushes which they waved like a forest of green lances.

Essex bowed and smiled and bowed again. "Why, this is a royal welcome, indeed!" Excited at the adulation, he felt better than at any time since his landing. Back before the fire he discussed his further moves with Ormonde. Between sips of the hot ale that Joseph brought him, he mentioned Waterford and Castle Cahir.

Castle Cahir! Ormonde raised an eyebrow. "If you can take Cahir from the rebels," he said doubtfully, "all loyal Ireland will bless you."

"I take it, then, you think we have a job to do," grinned Essex. "A castle on a river island. Marry, man, we took Cadiz, this will be child's play."

He was sure of himself. They would establish Cahir as a stronghold here in the south, and Munster could then feel secure enough to give him additional men and supplies for the great march north to Tyrone.

That night the English lords were pleasantly diverted from thoughts of war and bloodshed by Irish songs and dances, and a minstrel with a Tara harp sang a wild lament from the tongue and heart of Brian Boru's own bard.

Essex leaned back in his seat and let his thoughts wander. The leaping shadows cast a weird pattern on the old stone walls and the torchlight guttered in the brackets. It touched up the old scarlet hangings and glanced over the Irish Earl's jewels that flashed at his throat and breast. But for all its elegance of Gothic vaulting and trefoil tracery, there was something wild and elemental about the life even in the cultivated castle of an Anglo-Irish earl. Essex felt it stirring in his own blood.

The minstrel swept his fingers across his little harp and sang.

Oh, where, Kincora, is Brian the Great?
And where is the beauty that once was thine?
Oh, where are the princes and nobles that sate
At the feast in thy halls, and drank the red wine?
Where, O Kincora?

Aye, where indeed? Essex thought of Tara, that ancient glory ground of Irish thanes, and Cormac, who built the Banqueting Hall of the Kings, and Grania, the Princess, running away on her bridal eve with Dermott O'Duibhne, when all the time she was promised to Fionn, the mighty captain. The fugitives vanished into the wild secret wastes of Ireland away from the wrath of the ravished bridegroom.

Now the magic was strong within him, and he felt a strange love for this green island, and his imagination thrilled to the tales he remembered from his childhood, tales of the leprechaun that hides the crock of gold and the Banshee Woman who wails her weird *caoine* for the dead.

The lights sank and only the fire glow and the fitful streaming torches of the dancers lit the scene. A woman with a white skin and blazing hair threw herself in and out of her partner's arms. As he watched them melt into a last frantic embrace, Essex thought of Milesius, whose land was Scotia and whose hair was a flaming beacon in the land. The woman must be a descendant of his. Strange, fascinating people, these Irish.

With her way of looking, the woman disturbed him, so like Katherine Fytton, so unlike his dear, shy Pamela. Ah, there was a twinge. No letters since his departure, and weeks had wasted since she stood in the windy avenue and kissed him farewell. Suddenly, in this alien place, the longing for her was a sharp pain.

Brooding, he went to his bed, high in Kilkenny Castle. In the dark he lay and thought of home. His mind, tired but busy with the weight of his way, now so uncertain, held him and would not let sleep come. He sighed and turned over, and was suddenly aware of someone in his room. It was not Joseph. This was a slender shadow that came without a word and slid into the bed beside him. Wordlessly the woman writhed into his arms, and as he clutched her to him, he felt a great wiry mass of hair, which even in the dark he knew to be flaming, golden red.

When she left him, drowsy and relaxed, he sank into a dream. He thought he was crossing a great black bog, while a spirit like a will-'o-the-wisp curved a white finger to lure him on.

Letters from London now caught up with him. He ripped them open and read, feeling the hot blood rise in his head as he ran his eyes down the precise writing of Cecil. Gloriana was displeased. She disapproved of this triumphal progress into the south. When was he turning north to Tyrone? Had he forgotten the object of his journey? He was commanded to right-about-face and get into the business for which his royal mistress had sent a gigantic army into Ireland.

He stared at the square signature that sprawled above the wax. He exploded.

"Now of all the infernal, incalculable riddles! Is this the answer to my last letter? I wrote my love, I pleaded for reinforcements, and for supplies. I—agh!" he kicked a chair out of his way.

Cuffe wondered to what letter his master made reference. But he forebore to speak.

"You saw the letters authorizing my march into the south. Unqualified approval—and now—I am rebuked for my disobedience."

"There is justice in your lordship's position. Shall we not write to draw this to her Majesty's attention?"

"Justice! When knew you justice to keep company with princes? And this one a fleering weathervane of a woman!" He flung himself down and thrust his clenched hand against his teeth.

It was morning of the next day before he could bring himself to put words to paper. He wrote a panting, passionate letter, full of reproaches and protestations. Then, restless for action, he rode out to the camp.

The May morning was cool with a clear blue sky and the hills looking greener than ever. Like an ugly blot on a fair velvet carpet, the English camp huddled on the level common that stretched between low hills. Discontent and unrest were brewing in the dirty alleys between the tents, and the Earl and his riders found disease and misery lying sprawled with the men on damp straw pallets.

At sight of their commander, tall and auburn on his black charger, they took heart, and the ones that could walk rallied smartly to the muster call. Those that lay ill of the flux gave their breeches to those, who, through wear or tear, had suffered the loss of their nether garments. Soon the camp was agitated with excitement and the carts were packed and lashed over with canvas, while horses came neighing to the line and the men laughed once more at the prospect of real combat. Cast down as he was by the reports he received at Maryborough, Essex himself grew lighter as he saw that the body of the men remained sound; the spirit, somewhat dampened by long marches and inaction, still good.

A crowd of old- and new-style soldiers was gathered about two fellows, red in the face and spitting at each other. On foot now, Essex edged out from between sheltering tents to listen.

"Thou geck!" cried one of the two, a stout gray forester in a green jacket. "How canst thou say the longbow is doomed to perdition? Can your clumsy firestick there shoot at a mark of two hundred and forty yards?" He thrust his crimson face up to that of the other, a harquebusier, whose heavy weapon was cocked over his shoulder, to the imminent risk of the nose immediately behind him.

"By the pigs!" he cried, giving his weapon a slight shove into the air. "Thou art witless. I do not fear to let me enemy come within spitting distance of me. Tell me, goose-brain, canst thou fire fifty good shots in the space of an hour, and each one a messenger of death?"

The men roared. "Go it, harquebusier!" The bowman breathed short and his eyes bulged.

"Fifty shots! Crumb and pie!" he sneered. "Fifty shots! Half a sheaf of arrows can I loose while thou art fumbling with that iron pipe of thine!"

"And half those fly wide o' the mark!"

"What! Dost think I cannot hit the clout every time I fly?" The bowman shook his fist under the other's long nose. The crowd yelled for a fight. "Pish! Have I not seen thee and others like thee staggering at sundown under the weight of that thing that cuts a groove in thy shoulder, whilst I and my comrade go merrily past with our good bows no more than a feather at our backs?"

The men now cheered the archer.

The harquebusier spat accurately between the feet of the fellow next him and a grin cut across his dirty face. "Aye, ye can cheer, but wait till the next fight and it be raining. Then where will ye be, fizz-pots? Bowstrings slack and arrows dropping their fletchings into your hands."

This stung the stout bowman, for if there is a tender spot in an archer, it is a taunt at his weapon. He slept with his bow warm and dry against his body, his bowstrings well waxed and lovingly coiled in a waterproof pouch. "I'll think of ye then, when I'm nocking and letting fly six to the dozen whilst the Queen's fire-shooters are struggling with bullets jammed in their pipes."

"Ha! Ha!" yelled the men, slapping each other in their joy. "By cock-and-pie, that's the way, Oxley!"

"Knotty pates!" The tall harquebusier called after them as they moved away, "with thy bowels turning to water, we shall see who is the better fighter!"

It was well known that to do good work an archer must be in the pink of condition, well fed and untired, since his whole body went into the discharging of his weapon. A man fagged with a long march or weakened with the flux would make but a second-rate bowman. Whereas, a harquebusier, weak or not, could blaze away with a high score of hits. His fighting took less effort.

Essex and his servant backed into the shadows and mounted. They walked their horses between rows of empty tents. Essex felt warm and happy. Smiling he turned to Baxter. "Well, Adam, would you say the round went to the harquebusier?"

"It would seem so, my lord," grinned Baxter.

Essex galloped ahead. Brave lads! He prayed God to grant them their chance at the enemy while their bowels still held out.

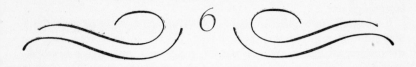

6

Castle Cahir

On the morning of the twentieth they struck out on the southern road and forged into the glittering green country, bound for the coast and Waterford. Essex was still feeling the elation of the previous day, and at the prospect of a good fight his heart beat fast. One rousing victory and the men would be restored.

This, then, would be the last lap of his progress through forts and castles. With a part of his army based at Waterford, and Cahir once more in English hands, he could turn north to the serious business of subduing Tyrone.

He roused himself sufficiently to jest with his officers and to laugh at the wit of his Irish comrades. He rode close to Dunkellin and lent his ear to the soothing rise and fall of the warm, running brogue. The May day had turned sultry and it seemed as if summer was at last with them. With dry weather, he exulted, their chances in this dripping overgrown country would be considerably better.

Under a great clump of oaks they stopped to water their horses in a quiet stream. They were all sweating a little in their saddles, and steel-chested bodies drooped over the beasts as they stretched long necks to the cool water. The sun dappled the shining coats in little round discs. The pleasant Irish voice of Dunkellin rambled on.

"Henry Plantagenet, aye, he was the one. It was here in the south that he came after getting the submission of the chiefs. And got it he did, and them all lined up in their cloaks and golden brooches. He had a son, John. Maybe ye'll be rememberin' him?" His brown eyes laughed into the Earl's green ones.

"I will, indeed," smiled Essex, softly slapping the dust from his glove against his horse's dustier mane.

"Ah," went on Dunkellin, leaning with both hands on his pommel, "this John must have been the graceless scamp, a regular windy one, for he plucked the beards of the haughty chieftains and swore that when he was king he would return and take their land clean away from them. Aye, he said he would take it, by Hook or by Crook!"

Essex now slapped the glove hard against his boot, and his grin was hearty. Hook and Crook were two of the most famous landmarks in all Ireland. This was a story for which he had a fine relish, with its hidden barb and its clever play on words. He leaned over to look at his horse, still sucking up the water smoothly through velvet muzzles.

"Aye," put in Kildare, whose bay splashed lazily down stream to join them under the dappled light. "That same John later signed for English freedom at the points of his barons' daggers, did he not?"

Essex raised a quizzical eyebrow. Then to Baxter, apologetically at his stirrup: "Yes?"

"My lord, let not Saladin fill his belly with the cold water. He'll chill himself."

"Right you are. Come, lad, out of it!" He leaned over the shining ebony neck, then wheeled his mount away from the tempting drink.

Behind him was the mocking light in the eye of Kildare, who looked across at Malby. Kildare was lukewarm in this venture, for he had once thought to make a private peace with Tyrone. Now, with quiet malice, he saw how Essex spent his strength in marching south.

He had a favorable opportunity later in the afternoon to speak to Malby. Together the two strolled casually into the lee of a covered military wagon, and Malby affected to be looking beneath the canvas for something.

The Earl of Kildare, chewing on a straw, broke the quiet, for they were well out of the sound of the camp across the meadow. "We continue to march south, Malby."

"Aye."

"By all good military procedure, we should be marching north."

"Aye." The Englishman did not intend to tip his hand yet.

"It is well past the middle of May—" Kildare cocked an eyebrow at the other.

"And, if it is?" Malby was still wary.

"I think you have little love for my lord of Essex, Malby."

"That's as may be."

"I'm also thinking you came with him to Ireland to pay off an old score—and not against the Tyrone." Kildare smiled, his eyes sharp.

"As to Tyrone," said Malby quietly, "he is going to win, my lord. You know that?"

"I believe it to be possible. And then—" he paused delicately.

"And then, where will the loyal earls be, my lord?"

Kildare shrugged. "I think I can abide an English defeat, Sir Malcolm."

"Ah," smiled Malby.

He knew now that Kildare was an informer, who kept Tyrone supplied with bits from the council table and other secret scraps, and with this he would buy safety when the bottom should drop out of the English campaign. "You have an ingenious taste for business, my lord Kildare," he said softly. "Perhaps I can assist you."

"'Twas in my mind," began Kildare, but broke off, as a jangling warned of the approach of a trooper. They strolled off, Malby with the trooper, while Kildare still loitered near the wagons. He would send the good news north that Tyrone had gained a new ally, one close to the Earl, who could keep the O'Neill informed of the very thoughts of his English enemy.

Down to Waterford they went, slowly and clumsily, their carts creaking and complaining, their cannon rumbling along in the slack marshy mud of the roads. They kept on to the very tip of County Kilkenny, where at last they sighted Waterford, spreading itself proudly in the sun. It clung to the southern bank of the Suir, which, with its two sister rivers, meets the harbor and tumbles thence into the sea.

The English army tightened its belt, squared its shoulders, and went clanking down to the water front. There lay the shipping, motley and still, and across on the other side rose the gray walls of Waterford with the round green hills at their back. And dominating the landscape was old Reginald's Tower, built by the hardy Danes over six hundred years before, still stout and strong enough to hold many prisoners in its dark belly.

The cavalry, led by the commander with his officers, thundered sedately over the ancient paved bridge through open gates into the town, and hard behind came the pikemen, who, at a sharp command from their captain, now shouldered their weapons and jogged along in close formation.

By dusk the great bonfires were lit in the streets, while a yelling torchlight procession screamed for the Lord Lieutenant to come out of the Tower and show himself.

Amid the smoke and sizzle of cooking fires at one end of the hall they sat down to their meal. Huge sides of beef and mutton twirled on the jacks before blazes of wood and turf, and there was abundance of fresh cow milk, a luxury to the English. Butter and cheese, too, and thin, delicious oatcakes baked on hot stones and hung over beams to crisp.

And among the ashes, mumbling bits of meat between her gums, crouched the inevitable beggar. Wild and wispy was her hair, and she was bent nearly double with her age. Once she looked up from her muttering, the red glare of the fire in her eyes, and through the steamy murk she saw, far down at the end of the board, the Lord Lieutenant as he laughed and talked with the Governor. Then she got up out of her ashes and shuffled through the crowd of servers and retainers, till she was halfway down the candle-lit board.

"Now then, old 'un, be off!" Adam Baxter, in attendance on his lord, warned her in a low voice. But the beggar put out a skinny claw and shoved him strongly aside. He followed. "Be off wi' ye!"

"What is it?" Essex looked up.

"Ah, by the saints," smiled the Governor as he played with his silver brooch. " 'Tis the old shuler; she wants to tell your Worship's fortune. Let her, it may prove amusing."

The shuler pushed her dirty claw against his shoulder. For a few seconds she stared down into his face, her eyes, under the long shaggy brows, sharp and canny. All of a sudden she let out an unearthly eldrich cry that made him jump and sent his men leaping to their feet.

"Blood!" she screeched. "I see blood, and it runs in a stream down to your knees. Aye, God be good to your soul." Mumbling now, she turned away.

Essex laughed, a little pale under his tan. "And is this your idea of amusement, my Lord Governor? It's well I am not squeamish—but—hand me that joint, I pray you. I'll need something to take the taste of that out of my mouth."

To the relief of the embarrassed governor, he applied himself once more to his dinner and appeared to forget all about the weird old creature.

But late that night, out of the dark, came the ancient crone face to chill his blood. The Irish reverenced these horrible old gargoyles. Had they, then, the second sight? He sighed and turned on his bed.

Up at dawn, under strict orders to push on, the army roused itself to the march. Under their steep-pitched roofs, the citizens of Waterford awoke from sleep to hear the clopping of cavalry horses on the cobblestones.

"The Lord Lieutenant rises early," they mumbled sleepily before they settled down for another forty winks.

There was a twenty-mile march for the army and soon the pikemen reversed their weapons, holding the steel heads and trailing long butts on the ground. The cursing, sweating crews manhandled their cannon and culverin on their platforms as the horses dragged them over the long weary way.

For nearly ten miles they followed the Suir, a long confusion of men, horses, and wheels. Like a great unclean snail, they smeared the landscape with a slimy trail, leaving a trampled track strewn with bits of leather, scraps of chain, empty casks, horse manure, and human ordure. At the halfway mark a halt was called. Men and animals rested.

A bugle tugged them to their feet, and they struck sharply off to the west, cutting across a wedge of land that lay within the curve of the river. Toward evening they halted once more, and their leaders mounted a small grassy rise. They had reached the water again, and there below them lay Castle Cahir, lofty and solid on a little green islet, joined to the southern bank by a narrow bridge. The bridgehead was well guarded, and from where he sat Essex could see the glint of the setting sun on the sentry who paced the tiny battlements. Despite the fact that the rebel Cahir was himself a prisoner in Dublin, his island fort was still stoutly held.

The prospect of a sharp encounter was good. To the west of the castle lay a thick wooded area, and round two sides of the turreted building itself were thick-walled courtyards. Just within one of these, on the bridge side, so they saw it plainly, was a small orchard huddling up to the sheer southern walls.

Essex drew his officers about him. "We shall try first for a surrender, and failing that, use our cannon. If the rebels remain obdurate, we shall wait for cover of darkness, then force a way through the outer gate and take the orchard. That will bring us right under the walls for a close attack."

The plan was good. All fell out as he had foreseen. The advance courier, sent across the bridge with a surrender demand, got an arrow through his throat and fell choking into the river.

"So that is it," said Essex, with a gleam of grim joy. "The knaves want a fight."

Beneath the crazy glare of torches the English toiled like mad devils to bring up their field pieces, and when morning broke they were ready. In the dawn they stripped the canvas from their cannon.

The first shot, booming over the water, struck true, and debris crashed into the orchard. The English shouted and fussily cleaned their cannon for the next shot. But the rebels took advantage of the slight lull to send a shower of arrows pattering back and there was agony and blood and a hurried carrying of victims behind trees.

Now the ready cannon roared again. This time the ball fell short, and at the same time the undercarriage collapsed and the smoking muzzle subsided at a crazy angle. The cannon would be of no further use that day, and despite the horrible cursing of the captain it would be up to the lighter gun to batter the enemy.

"What in hell is keeping that culverin?" The high voice of Essex rang out furiously.

The culverin fired bravely enough, small peppering shots that riddled the wall but did no great damage. Feverishly the men worked at the reloading; the gun jammed, and again the cursing did no good. Essex groaned and gnawed his lip. Soon however, it was cleared and worked well, its crew keeping up a steady batter at the castle, until when evening fell, they had fired fifty rounds.

"Stop!" called Essex. "You waste your powder. "We'll parley in my tent."

Around a smoky light the officers gathered, tough fighters, veterans of the French and Cadiz expeditions. Essex decided that Brett and Chamberlain, both hardened campaigners, should take three hundred men and force the gate, take the orchard, so that the guns and machinery might be safe to move up to beat and scale the walls.

"The devils are going to resist, thank God!" he said, as he gave the two brown captains a white smile. Nearly dead with fatigue, he was enjoying every blow of the fight.

While the advance party crept across the bridge under cover of the dark, the men on shore collected their ladders and scaffolds, while the chief petarryer worked at his petards, fashioning them carefully so that the catapult would not set them off before they landed among the enemy.

The Irish guessed what was afoot and now and then sent wild arrows into the dark about the bridge; a few found marks but most of the three hundred men got across, to batter at the gate with a long, stout pole. With a crash it gave way, and a hellish uproar broke loose as assaulters clashed with defenders. Those on shore could make out little as they waited with beating hearts for the outcome.

Captain Brett presently came back to report the orchard taken. But the cost had been high; one hundred and eight men lay before the southern wall of Castle Cahir.

Another torch-lit night of labor, men dropping in their tracks, to sleep off dead exhaustion, while the mad scramble of work went on about them. By morning the cannon and the culverin had been drawn up closer to the castle and most of the siege machinery dragged across the bridge, to sit under cover of the orchard. All had gone well.

All day, through what seemed endless time to the men on shore, the guns battered steadily at the broken walls. Toward the end of the afternoon, the guns still banging away, Essex summoned two of his lieutenants to his tent. Through the camp a small ripple of excitement passed. Something was up and they longed to be in it.

Soon the news spread. A night sally! Everyone craved to go, but only a small force was selected. Eyes glittering with excitement, the little body crept softly across the bridge through thick darkness, while Essex, nervy and restless, stood straining after them. He took a quilted jerkin from Baxter and huddled it about his shoulders. Minutes dragged and it grew colder. Men blew softly on numb fingers, but none slept. The little camp was tense with waiting.

At last! A sudden scuffle, a wild shouting, and the night was once more split with another steely clash. Streaming torches held by the rebels cast moving light on the scene, and the men on shore danced with impatience.

"God's blood, I should be there!" cried Essex.

"Ah, look!" cried Grey.

A few ragged two's and three's burst from the gate, silhouettes in the light of the flaming cressets. After them came the English, screaming their disappointment as the Irish plunged into the river, and swimming into the night, escaped with their skins.

It was over. Men walked about, a few torches flashed in the orchard, the captains were within the fortress, and Castle Cahir was in English hands.

"God be thanked, we have at last done something," said Essex, as he unbuckled his sword and handed it to Joseph.

Next morning he rode across the river. As he approached the outer yard, a stench met him. The two-day corpses, already puffing, lay where they had fallen, strewn in disorder under the early sun. Holding his scarf to his face, Essex jerked his head at a captain.

"By my faith," drawled Malby, "this Irish odor likes me not."

Essex shot him a disapproving scowl. "We have English dead here, too," he said. To the captain, "Get them under ground—all."

Parties with mattocks and spades set to work to dig long trenches in the orchard, and the dead, English and Irish alike, were dragged by the heels to be tumbled into their moist, earthy beds. Baxter stooped, took a stiffened arm, and turned the body over. It was the pale-faced youth who had whined round the campfire about going home. He swallowed and turned away.

Inside the castle, Essex stalked about the men of the garrison, who awaited him in chains. Scowling they stood, some ruddy like the O'Neill, some black, and some bright-headed people like those of the north. All wore the same look of uncowed defiance, their eyes full of hate.

First minded to hang them from the donjon of their castle, Essex relented and sent them instead to Waterford, to be lodged beneath the waters of the Suir.

His brief pleasure was dampened by horrible news from Wicklow. The Irish had actually routed one of her Majesty's troops, under Sir Henry Harington, and a detachment of them, led by a young lieutenant —Essex's face flamed—fled at their leader's heels. Bitter, bitter disgrace.

He raised eyes of steel to the courier who stood, stocky and well muscled in striped trunks and tarnished cuirass before him. "Well?"

The man moistened his lips. "My lord, Sir Henry led us forth by the Ranelagh River, where he had intelligence of a large force of rebels assembled there. We were hopelessly outnumbered. We camped, but we were harassed by night attacks and many casualties."

"Casualties are the order of battle. Were there no stout hearts among you?"

"The horse troops fought bravely, my lord, in attempt to cover the retreat, but they were cut to pieces."

"And you call yourselves Englishmen," said Essex softly. A sick, choking rage mounted in him. His eyes went cruel. "Guard! Hang me this fellow in chains. No man lives to bring me such news. By the thumbs, and at dawn finish him off with the rope."

The soldier's chin moved, but with no other sign, he followed his guard. Outside, they paused. The young halberdier was nonplused. There was but one other guard outside the apartment, and he could not be spared.

"Now, what i' the devil's to be done wi' this?" Plainly the job was beyond him. "Here," to the other guard, "do ye watch him, whilst I take off belt." He leaned his weapon against the stone wall and unbuckled his broad leathern waist belt. He passed it through the prisoner's at the back and gave it a twist. "Put your hands behind ye now, and no tricks," he growled, and the courier obeyed. The young halberdier trussed him up tightly with the belt, pulling it through the buckle so that it left a foot or so of the end free. Then he reached for his longpoled ax. Still grasping the prisoner's leash, he gave him a prod.

"Now, march, an' be in no hurry, unless ye've a fancy to run to your death." In this clumsy fashion he conveyed his prisoner through the corridor and down a fanlike set of steps leading to a narrow pass between the double walls of a thick round tower. Here the prisoner, cleverer than his gaoler, saw his chance.

Cumbered with his charge and his long ax, and the extreme narrowness of the passage, the guard was at a disadvantage. It was no work for the other to aim a fierce kick backward at his shins, jerk the belt from his astonished hand, and show a clean pair of heels round the bend of the tower.

After him went the halberdier, his weapon banging against the walls that got in his way, but it was no use. Scratching his head, he stopped. Then he shrugged. "Aye, 'tis poor work stringing up Englishmen when so many rebels be spoiling for the rope." He glanced fearfully over his shoulder for fear of a witness to his bungling. Then he took himself off to the cook house, there to lie until other matters drove from the Earl's mind his anger at the courier.

But already Essex had forgotten him. He was busy arranging for the disposal of the Wicklow cowards who were to be held in chains till his return. On his table lay another letter. It was from London, and now he forced himself to open it.

The Queen declared herself grieved, nay, incensed, at her Lord Lieutenant. Was it meet and proper that she should receive no word from his hand for three weeks; why should her Deputy allow others to convey to his Sovereign news of his movements in Ireland? She demanded an immediate reply, an assurance that Essex was marching north with all haste to the subduing of Tyrone.

"Cuffe!"

But in answer to his roar, Malby entered. Cuffe was taken with a vomiting spell; Sir Malcolm prayed permission to serve the Lord Lieutenant. Essex grunted and drew a clean sheet toward him.

Once again he wrote his love and obedience. For now, as he wrote, he saw the pale face and red hair of his mistress, clear and familiar, and felt the silky caress of her perfumed hands. He swallowed the lump of pity in his throat and applied himself to write with all the art at his command.

Over his signature, he looked unsmiling into the dark face bent upon him. "Once more, Malby, I send my love and duty, and small gain it will be to me. Get that off, like a good man, will you?"

Softly, so softly, Malby went down the passage to the nearest outer window. Making sure he was alone, he sent the little packet plunging to the muddy river bottom, where its inky protestations would soon be washed away in the quiet flow to the sea.

"Go," he whispered, "go to join the others."

Essex sat on now and let the murky thoughts trail through his mind. The disgrace at Wicklow nagged at him, and the Queen's strange behavior, declaring she had not received letters most certainly dispatched, was puzzling. Would Cecil dare to withhold his letters? Would he?

The bag from London contained one other letter. He picked it up. The writing was strange. He turned it over. The seal was cleanly stamped into dark wax, and he tilted it to the candle light. An oak cluster, leaves and acorns. Pamela!

Quickly now, he broke it open, read the unfamiliar writing from the lady down in Surrey.

Then the words all ran together and he grew deathly cold. Pamela had died of the chill on her chest.

The Shadows Gather

$\mathcal{P}$ale and composed, the Wicklow captain who had run with his men stood before the tribunal at Dublin and heard his sentence. For cowardice in the face of the enemy he was condemned to death. He was a slight young man with a thatch of curls, and as Essex turned his stony face, equally pale, upon him, he thought sadly how immature the boyish officer was for such responsibility. He forgot that at less than twenty he himself had served under Leicester in the Low Countries.

"Done." He ordered a priest to be brought to the prisoner. The roll of the other officers who had not forsaken their posts was read.

"Still," said the Clerk of the Council, "they did nothing about those men whom they commanded, and who behaved with so pitiable a weakness on this occasion."

Essex looked at the sandy little man who had received him on his arrival in Dublin. He liked him no better now. "Cashiered," he said briefly.

"But, my Lord Lieutenant——"

"It is enough!" cried Essex. The Clerk bowed his ginger-colored head. Council agreed that a reduction in rank was sufficient punishment for officers who had stood their posts but who had not punished the desertion of their men.

The private soldiers, those who had run away, were condemned to be hanged.

That night Essex could not sleep. Now it all rolled in on him, the bitterness, the sick longing, the numb, bruised feeling whenever he thought of Pamela, and the disappointment at the defection of his own men. He was stung by the disgrace, the intolerable necessity of having to court-martial his soldiers, and by the look in Irish eyes as he did it.

After the paralyzing shock of the letter from Lady Bridges, he had tortuously returned to Dublin. There were bitter milestones along the way. Limerick and Crumme, each with its unsatisfactory conferences with southern earls. There was the green and rocky coast of Ballingar and Enniscorthy, where the rebels had once more had the better of them, as they stayed in ambush.

There was the galling knowledge that with his force shrunk to a mere twelve hundred men, he dare not engage the Irish here and must by-pass the lurking force. He dragged his army like a great snail up the coast to the mountain of Groghan-Kinshelagh, where at last he forced the will-o'-the-wisps into the open for a good cut-and-thrust encounter. They took a few prisoners, who, he sighed, would now have to be fed.

The same night he was taken with violent pains in his bowels and, despite the skill of Joseph and the others, had to be carried into Dublin in a sling. There he submitted to the bitter infusions of the doctor and the ministrations of Joseph with the closestool.

Now it was early July, and still they were tied up in the capital, awaiting re-enforcements and supplies. On his bed Essex groaned softly and threw back the blankets.

From somewhere in the courtyard came the sound of a man's singing. It was a sweet enough voice, and as the singer came to the pauses, he filled in with a softly tuned lute.

> "The wind doth blow today, my love,
>   And a few small drops of rain;
> I never had but one true love,
>   In the cold grave she was lain."

On the night air the words came clearly. Essex felt his heart swell. He put out his hand to close the window, but the voice stopped him.

" 'Tis down in yonder garden green,
    Love, where we used to walk,
The finest flower that e'er was seen
    Is withered to a stalk.

The stalk is withered dry, my love,
    So will your hearts decay;
So make yourself content, my love,
    Till God calls you away."

The song died on the breeze, and after it, softly, the echo. Sharp memory pierced his breast. Just as when the sorrow of his father rolled in on him, so now he put his head down on his arm and wept.

Next morning was beautiful, with the Wicklow and Dublin mountains shining in the sun. Gorse and heather, waist high, clothed the low hills, and if a man were to mount the highest of them, he might see, faint and blue on the clear horizon, the coast of Wales.

In grim silence Essex with his staff rode out to the camp. It seemed incredible that on this fair morning men were to die the death of cowards. There stood Harington's company, huddled together, surrounded by the pacing guard.

Essex called Boucher. "We shall execute one in ten." His lips were tight.

"But—" began Boucher.

"God's blood, Boucher, what are you made of? One in ten, I said. Have them lined up at the muster."

He sat rigid while the ranks, now ordered, stood stout and straight, in full armor. About every tenth man hung the fetid odor of death. A short command, and the doomed soldiers stepped forward, faces set, eyes ahead. The first one was a tall youngster, like the young captain, with eyes that once were merry. Now his face was stiff in lines of determined bravery, his upper lip trembling and slightly beaded with sweat.

Sickened, Essex wheeled suddenly away out of earshot of the drums. Despising himself for the weakness, he still could not help it. God damn Harington, who lay in the custody of the Provost Marshal, awaiting the Queen's pleasure. He felt his head throbbing, his stomach turning over and over, as suddenly the drums began.

That night he was ill, but he propped his head on his hand and wrote a sick, feverish letter to the Queen. What did his royal mistress mean by saying that for three weeks she had received no word from him?

It reached Elizabeth at Nonesuch, where the Court was enjoying the first really warm day of summer. A scented breeze came in off the garden to where she sat, cold, cold, her high forehead damp with sudden moisture.

Over the tops of his eyelids, Cecil watched her. She was in a proper temper this time as she read and muttered and scratched viciously at her reply to her Lord Deputy. She pushed the inkstand so hastily that it overturned onto the cloth. The Secretary rang for a servant and wordlessly gestured for the mess to be cleaned up. Elizabeth did not appear to see it as now she leaned back and twirled her quill angrily.

"Three months! And what has he done?" Cecil shrugged, and instantly she turned the lightning onto him. "Fool! You would have him go. Now, what?"

"Majesty, the Lord Lieutenant has taken two important strongholds in the south."

"The south—pah! My men have always been able to blast a way into Ireland with English cannon. 'Tis nothing!"

She flung him the letter. With pursed lips he read it. God, what excoriation! She had left nothing unsaid that could further wound him. Pitilessly, she held up to the light the proceedings of the past three months. She went over every foot of the ground. To the problems she brought every crumb of her rough masculine logic. Cecil saw and marveled. She showed up the weaknesses of her army's position in Ireland; she probed deep and then salted the wound with her last few words:

. . . and on you, my lord, I lay the weight of this failure. The fault lieth with you and you alone. How can you further waste English lives and English gold? Is your army sick? We are forced to wonder why our Lord Deputy did not act when the bowels of his army were sound. Winter is coming, you say? We would remind you that this is July. Is there then no time of the year that is satisfactory to the Lord of Essex? We await your Council's opinion of the matter. . . .

Silently he handed it back. He would give his hope of further glory to see the Lord Lieutenant's face when he read it.

But that pleasure was Henry Cuffe's, who found it no pleasure to see the incredulous anger with which Essex received the Queen's latest word. He read, then halfway through, crumpled the paper in strong hands and the ecstasy of temper, while he raged about the room. Termagent! What a bitch to write such filthy poison to the first Earl of England! How dare she! Then—how could she?

Cuffe got up and closed the door. Hysterically, Essex flung himself down and wrote that he would not stir from Dublin until reenforcements arrived.

At home the enemies smiled in their silky beards and marveled politely that the Lord Lieutenant tarried so long in Dublin. Was it fear of the O'Neill, was it a woman, or—in a whisper—was it that Essex was waiting to be crowned King of Ireland?

The letter from Ireland reached Elizabeth in a barricaded London. They were in the midst of another Spanish scare. Elizabeth shrugged contemptuously. "We have them regularly, my lords; I am not afeared."

But the people were panic-stricken. The principal streets were chained and barricaded, and the exodus with children and goods into the country was wholesale. Down at Tilbury armed men swarmed, flocking to the colors.

"Hah!" sniffed their Queen. "I rode at Tilbury in a breastplate in '88, but I'm done with that sort of thing." She wrote to Essex. "The ninny, clamoring for men at such a time."

Undismayed as she was by threats of Spanish violence, she nevertheless was not sanguine enough to ship men out of her country. She wrote for a few minutes, then threw the pen from aching fingers.

"I cannot," shortly to Cecil. "Write what I say."

Hand at her hip, she stalked back and forth, swishing her violet skirts at the turn. Essex was to march north immediately on pain of instant recall. He was to set about the job for which he had been sent. A fancy military progress, indeed! Who sent him to Ireland for that! Time, high time, to stop this glittering dalliance and attempt Tyrone. Tyrone, the Golden Calf of Ireland, preserved without loss or taint within his sanctuary, to the rejoicing of those base rebels who had defied their rightful ruler!

Cecil looked up.

"Well?"

"Madam, the thought came to me . . . suppose the Earl become desperate and do return to plead his cause?"

"In such a case . . . in such a case I would not see him." Then, with a sharp look, "Think you he will attempt such brazen effrontery?"

"Madam, your Grace knows the Earl."

Aye, indeed, she also knew something Cecil did not know. It was that she had given the Earl permit to return to her, should extreme circumstances warrant it. How much did this clever little crooked man really guess?

"Add this. The Earl is expressly forbidden to return at this time, no matter what the provocation."

She could not allow a return at so dangerous a time for England, and besides—this last she kept to herself—she had no desire to see him just now. He would win her over, and this time she must be armed against him. However she softened the thrust by permitting the departure of two thousand men. "Although," she remarked to her ministers, "it cuts me to the quick so to spend our strength."

In her fantastic garden she walked with Francis Bacon. About them the doves cooed and brooded busily in the sun and flapped in and out of their cote.

"Bacon, you pass for a clever man and a friend of the Lord Lieutenant of Ireland."

Essex! What was coming? Bacon paced on, his nerves stretched and alert.

"What is your opinion, Master Bacon, on the affairs of Ireland?" Covertly she eyed him. "What think you of the Earl's proceedings?"

Staggered, Bacon kept his head. He was no minister, high in the affairs of the country, to be consulted. Perhaps this was a trap, and all of them, friends of Essex, were to be caught in this web of the Earl's spinning. He had heard talk of treason; Essex was conducting the Irish campaign in what appeared to be a highhanded manner. He felt a small panic rising in him as he delayed his reply. Elizabeth waited. It was as if she knew his secret thought.

"Well, Master, have you then no opinion?"

Now Bacon pulled himself together. "Madam, if the Earl were to shine here in your Court as a courtier *par excellence,* brilliant as my Lord of Leicester, then were he in his natural element."

She waved her fan and a cloud of sweet perfume enveloped him. He blinked.

"Well?"

"But, Madam, your Grace has put arms and power into his hand, and this may prove a kind of temptation to him to behave cumbersome and unruly."

Ah, the didactic approach to life! These philosophers. She stared at him, her black eyes unblinking in the strong sunlight. Overhead the doves cooed gently.

"Go on, you interest me."

"If—if I might suggest," said Bacon, with a rare stammer, "that your Grace might bring the Earl of Essex near to you and hold him here with some high honor, that is, if your Grace's affairs will permit—I should think it would be good." He returned her gaze directly.

"I thank you, Master Bacon, for your candor."

She waved him away and he left her alone by her little grass plot. She looked unseeing at the broad flower bands of color. With a silken flapping, the doves flew down and waddled about on their pink-toed feet. Beauty and color and soft summer sunshine were all about her, but she shivered with cold and apprehension.

So that was it. By giving him what he demanded, she had put into his hands the dread instruments of treason. What a fool she had been ever to listen to him on matters of policy! How much better to have sent the gentle, long-headed Mountjoy into Ireland. Unruly and cumbersome, eh? Aye, that was what Essex had ever been, right from the first, right from the time when she first had gazed into those fascinating green eyes and loved him with her whole heart. What a handful he had been and how she had gloried in ruling him!

But this—this was different. This was not one of their petty little quarrels over royal favor. Ah, no. This was an offense against something that was greater than she. It was the deadly crime that no man might commit and live. No, no, she could not think he would attempt so dread a thing as to wrest away her throne. She breathed a prayer for him to pause on the brink and draw back, ere it was too late.

She stiffened her neck in the fine Dutch gauze and walked quickly up the path. All at once her eyes were blind with tears, through which the variegated hues of her garden swam in a blurred curtain of color, but she blinked them back. No one should know how she suffered.

She swept into her music room. She played, she forced her stiff lips to a smile, she threw over her velvet shoulder a rough jest, and all the while her heart ached and ached.

Henry Cuffe arrived in London, the bog mud still sticking to his boot soles. He made straight for the Council. There he painted a gloomy picture.

Gloriana sent for him—an unprecedented honor. She had a hunger to talk with one who had lately been with the Lord Lieutenant.

"And how is it with your master?" She kept her head high, but her lips trembled.

Cuffe told a blunt story. With cold despair clutching at her, she heard him in silence. She looked curiously at the tall scribe; he had been with Essex, close to him, privy to his bosom thoughts. She opened her lips to ask—then closed them. She would show no personal interest, give no comfort to a disobedient fool.

Into his hands she put a small packet of letters. "You will take these. And you may assure the Lord Deputy that my eye is upon him."

With hands rigidly clenched on the arms of her chair, she watched his bowing departure.

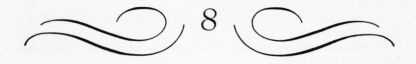

8

Tyrone

$\mathcal{C}$uffe arrived back in Dublin to find that the good weather still held, and Essex, against the advice of friends and Council, eager to start into Ulster without waiting for the re-enforcements. It was moving onto September, and with the fall of the leaves the fogs and rains would begin, and Ireland would become once more a wet, green marsh.

"Ah, Cuffe!" He greeted the glum face of his Secretary with the same wary concern that had been the Queen's.

"My lord." Cuffe dropped to one knee and kissed the Earl's hand. A vague foreboding filled him as he noted the fine drawn look and the somber eye of the commander.

Essex read the letters quietly, his brow clouding over, his lip caught beneath his teeth.

"Christ!"

Cuffe held his peace. He knew that the Earl had come across Mount-joy's letter, and he guessed the bad news it contained. Cecil had been given the Mastership of the Wards, a plum that Essex had marked for himself, for he was desperate for money. He sent for Blount and South-ampton.

"Your brother Charles," he said to Blount, "writes me that the hunchback has the Wards. And this, while I am here, doing the dirty work in this accursed country. I shall cross over into England at once."

They were silent, in appalled dismay. Go to England now!

"God's death, my very life is being sapped from me at home, and I here abroad in the field." He scraped back his chair. "I say I shall go into England at the head of my army!"

The silence was now desperate. "But—" stammered Blount, "this is civil war!"

"It is, indeed," echoed Southampton. "It cannot be, Robert." Then his puckered brow smoothed. "I have it! Why not take a picked force of tried followers and surprise the Queen at Nonesuch? Once in your power——"

Essex laughed bitterly. He had veered back again. "A picked force of tried followers, didst say? I doubt it there are twenty men who really hold me in that esteem." He rested his head on his arm and leaned against the mantel. Moodily he stared at his feet.

"There are hundreds who would die for you," began Southampton eagerly. Essex raised his bent head and a wry smile of amused sarcasm curled his lip. "Are there? Why, then, there is Henry here," motioning to the writing Cuffe, "and my guidone, Adam Baxter, and you, my two good friends. Nay," he shook his head, "I even believe my letters are intercepted. Someone close to me is tampering with my dispatches. That is how royally I am served, my lords."

No reply. Cuffe, as befitted a servant, was quiet. Essex now sighed heavily. "I am wild. Forget my words, get you to bed, and we will set off for Ulster as soon as may be."

Late into the night he sat, reading and pondering over his other letters. One letter in particular he read earnestly several times. It was from Bacon and it contained an account of the lawyer's talk with the Queen by the dovecote, and between the lines Essex read that he had lost one of his oldest friends.

One thing he was determined on. He would show the world that even a Queen might not order his life for him, nay, not even if he died for it!

He was in a fever to be off. The troops were slow in arriving from England, and the year was growing older. Whatever was to be done must be done quickly.

Then out of the west came horrible news. Sir Conyers Clifford, his old friend of the Cadiz expedition, sent to the relief of O'Connor Sligo, had been killed. It had been thought to create a diversion by sending Clifford to the aid of Sligo, beleaguered in the northwest, giving room for Essex to penetrate into Ulster. Now Clifford, with Ratcliffe his colonel, had been found face downward in a bog, their foot force completely routed. Again the English turned tail and were shot down by their maddened officers.

Frantic with rage and sorrow, Essex could not talk. For a long time he stood at his window, reliving that day in France when Clifford, chosen because of his closeness to the commander, came to tell him of Walter's death. Now both were gone. Never again would he stand with his old comrade in arms, to hear the Queen's instructions, never again exchange a bawdy jest with the veteran as they stood together in the fight. And Ratcliffe—Mary's only and adored brother—this would kill the Queen's maid.

He eased his pain by knighting fifty-nine brave men. In public ceremony he stood among their bared heads and tapped them. If he recalled Gloriana's parting injunction concerning the wholesale rewarding, he shook it from his mind. So long as he could wield the flat of a sword, just men should be recognized. Besides—someday he might have need of them.

Resignedly he shaped his final course for the north and Tyrone. He set off for Navan, which was to be the rendezvous for all the troops. Up to ancient Kells they rode, near to the old abandoned monastery of St. Columbkill. They galloped up a hill and drew rein. There, in a flat hollow, lay Navan. The afternoon cast long shadows in their wake as they cantered gently down the meadow up to the old round walls. It was a primitive affair, indeed, with a sod wall for stockade, and in the center of the circular enclosure, the fort itself, squatting low on the land.

They went in to great peat fires with smoke that stung the nostrils. There they would sit and keep Tyrone out of the Pale. They unbuckled and made camp and Essex spent the next four days in restless reconnoitering for winter quarters. They could not abide in this tumble-hole.

He found a site and they dug in.

Hardly were they settled when word came that Tyrone was at hand. Essex dashed to his hilltop and there he had his first glimpse of the force itself. Only a mile and a half away the gleaming tops of the helmets caught the sun as the Irish force moved on the other side of the river.

Essex took cover under the frowning walls of half-ruined Ardolph, his men drawn up in loose battle formation. Field camp must now be made, and foraging parties were sent in search of wood. Soon blue tendrils curled above English campfires, while beyond the wood and river, mostly hidden by the trees, moved Tyrone.

After a quiet night, with only the soft tread of the sentry to wake the weary soldier, they were early stirring and off for the clear country near Louth. He would force Tyrone into the open if it were the last thing either one of them did.

Off went the English, and like a shadow, the other side his screen of cavalry scouts, went Tyrone. His army, its outline blurred, seemed to be about twice that of the Earl.

Essex dared not attack. Short-handed as yet, he knew Tyrone had the drop on him as well as the superior numbers. He sat in his tent and pondered.

There was a sudden flurry of galloping hoofs and the quick challenge rang out. The English had a visitor. Henry Hagen, Constable of Tyrone's Castle Dungannon, came in on safe-conduct with a message from Tyrone. The rebel desired a parley.

"Tell your commander that I cannot parley with him; but I will be at the head of my troops tomorrow morning, on yonder hill." Essex pointed to a rounded rise between the two camps. The Constable saluted and left.

In fine style he sallied forth next morning, riding easily at the head of his force, the refreshing autumn air bringing the red blood into his pale cheeks. He began to feel light again. Perhaps, after all, things would be well and point to an easy victory. All would be put right at once.

The English drew up in position, sun glinting on steel, feathers blowing busily in the breeze, where Tyrone could get a good look at them. The woods remained quiet.

Essex fidgeted in his saddle. This was intolerable. They would take the next hill and try for sight of Tyrone.

Ah! There they were, Tyrone's guard of horse, also brave in fluttering capes and glistening steel bodies. At a signal the Irish capes spread and scattered, and Essex rose in his stirrups.

"After 'em, lads!"

Like the wind the English gave chase till they were on Tyrone's very heels, and the Irish then turned. Steel clashed on steel, and there was cut and thrust, a great banging of weapons, and then one of the rebel captains cried out in a loud voice.

"Arrah! My master the O'Neill desires not to fight! He wishes speech with the Lord Lieutenant!"

He had ridden to the English fringe to cry out his message, and instantly three foot soldiers pulled him down. They dragged him before Boucher, who rode near. The man repeated his strange message that Tryone would speak with the Lord of Essex, but not between the two armies.

They rushed to Essex. What were these Irish devils up to now? Essex pondered the request, convinced that Tyrone's strength was not so great as he had supposed, and that perhaps the rebel had decided to submit. Small wonder, with winter coming on, that he had no stomach for a continuous brush with the Queen's armies.

He was further convinced when next morning the Lord Constable again appeared, with Tyrone's submission and his desire for the Queen's mercy.

"My master begs that the Lord Lieutenant will hear him," began Hagan. "He begs leave to wait upon the English commander at the ford of Bellaclynthe."

Essex raised his brows. "The ford . . . ?"

" 'Tis on the right hand by the way to Drumconagh."

Triumph tinged the smiles of the English. Had the sight of good troops led by English gentlemen brought the O'Neill so soon to the surrender? But Essex did not smile.

"How do I know that your master has not treachery in his heart?"

Now the Irishman's brows went up. "Treachery, my lord commander?"

"Aye. Irish dirks often land in English backs."

"If they present them, my lord," murmured Hagan.

Ah, the Irish wit. Essex knew *touché* when he felt it. His eye gleamed. He sent word by Hagan that if it was in his mind to meet the Lord Tyrone, it should be on the morrow, at the appointed place. He was not at all sure he would be going. He would first send someone to look the place over, making sure there was no ambush in the mind of the Irish.

While he awaited the return of Blount and Danvers, he lounged in the doorway of his tent and watched the business of the camp. Through the stockade came couriers on lathered mounts. They brought evil tidings. Having cut to pieces Clifford and Ratcliffe, O'Donnell was now marching with great numbers to join Tyrone. Essex wrinkled his brow. Scouts, like his own, must have carried similar news to Tyrone. Then why, with superior numbers and heavy re-enforcements on the way, was Tyrone begging for a parley? Here was a poser.

"Slippery devil," he said to Southampton. "It's a trick, Henry. I shan't go."

Now Blount and Danvers came back. "Yes, Robert," said Blount, "we've talked with him, great red beard that he is. It's an open place. There will be no foul play, at the ford, that is."

But there was something rank-smelling about the whole enterprise. He passed a bad night and did not fall into a dead sleep until about an hour before dawn. Joseph had to shake him hard to wake him. Feeling drugged, he sat up on the edge of his camp bed and yawned heavily.

He decided to go to Tyrone, and, moving still as if in a dream, he rode out of his camp. To the last day in his life he knew he would remember this morning. The snap of autumn was in the air, and the sweet scent of the gorse made fragrant the yellowed ground on either side the path. They rode in silence, Essex staring ahead. What in the name of all the little devils did Tyrone want? Slantwise, the others eyed their commander and wondered the same thing.

Under a clump of trees they passed, stooping to avoid low branches, and the column rounded a bend into the open and rode up to the meeting place. A ford gleamed coldly, and there on the further bank a little group of officers in Irish costume clustered, faces turned toward the English. On a slight rise behind them was a fair, ordered company of kerns and gallowglasses dressed in motley array of heavy jerkins and body armor. The cavalry sat on black horses with dark breechans for saddles, thorn pricks in their brogues for spurs, and their long hair blew in the morning breeze.

A magnificent chestnut now detached itself from the little group of officers, and its rider took it into the water up to its red belly. There he waited.

Essex and his companions were also on a rise, backed by precisely glinting lines. Then the commander went alone to the edge of the stream and out on a spit of hard ground into the center of the little stream. Twenty paces apart, the two earls faced each other.

With a flourish Tyrone doffed his helmet. "My Lord Lieutenant, I offer my humble duty." His voice was full and round with the good warm Irish music in it.

Essex bent his long body forward, then stared at the other. Like a sleepwalker he slowly uncovered, placing his morion on his saddle. The two horses stood rigid, ebony statue facing the chestnut one.

The O'Neill was splendidly attired. Over a crimson and gold coat he wore a fine damascened breastplate, a present, Essex opined, from that Spanish devil. Down the front streamed his beard, a flaming waterfall, and his sharp eyes gleamed green and blue, like the hills and lakes of his country. The great breadth of his shoulders could not be disguised by the gaudy lined cloak that billowed back from them.

"We meet at last, my lord," said Essex. Then he could have bitten off his tongue. He had never intended to use gentle words with this rogue and murderer. He was vaguely uncomfortable; something was wrong.

"Aye, that we do," replied Tyrone quickly. "And too long it has been that I've not given myself the honor of laying eyes on the greatest sword in all England—and Ireland, for that matter," he finished generously. Like butter the words rolled off his tongue.

Automatically Essex bowed again. "I thank your lordship."

Tyrone laughed, throwing back his head to show perfect teeth, slightly flecked with milky spots. "Arrah! And how like your father ye are! Many's the time I have sat with him, and he the greatest man in all green Ireland. Bitter the day we should come to arms, you and I, for to me the Lord of Essex was my guardian angel, and I his other son."

His other son! Essex felt his back stiffen.

"I would now," went on Tyrone with an ingratiating smile, "that her Majesty had sent anyone here but the son of my old friend. 'Tis like fighting one's own flesh and blood."

Ah—this from the man who had murdered his own cousin, whose baby days had been steeped in the bloody deeds of his kin, who butchered their own with reckless impunity.

"Let us come to the point, my Lord Tyrone," said Essex curtly. "I am here at your Lordship's request. What's to be done?"

"Ah, now, and ye have the head for business, my lord. Sure, and I never meant to become a rebel against the gracious Queen's Majesty, my dread and well-beloved sovereign."

Then what of Bagenal, treacherously ambushed and cut to pieces only a few months back, and now Clifford and Ratcliffe, and all the hundreds of English who had laid their bones in the dank Irish mold? "But you *are* a rebel, my lord," said Essex proudly.

Tyrone turned persuasive. "Let me explain, my lord. Surely it is not unknown to your lordship that I wedded the sister of Sir Henry Bagenal, and because I took into my house two other noble ladies, she did object. She forsook me and went wittering to her brother." Here he shrugged and waved his helmet. "And did I not hang the golden gauds in her ears, and did I not give her women to lace her little shoes and comb the black hair of her?" He paused.

Essex blinked. What was this? The domestic difficulties of the O'Neill fit subject for a parley!

"I am listening."

"Then what did the Council do? Before I had the chance to put my grievance before them, they proclaimed me traitor, me, Hugh O'Neill, a black traitor, when as all the world knows," here his voice sank, "I had naught in my heart save love for my mistress and desire to serve her sweetly in fealty and worship." Now there were actually tears in the little blue eyes.

"And what of all this?" Essex was feeling more and more bewildered at this theatrical display of wounded feeling.

"You are the first Lord Deputy into whose hands I dare put my life," went on Tyrone plaintively. "And now the love I bear your honorable father, and the love I bear your honorable name and fame in all the world, emboldens me to approach your lordship that you do beg for me the Queen's gracious mercy."

All this rolled onto the morning air like the sonorous notes of an organ. His speech concluded, Tyrone sat now with bowed red head, his eyes modestly on the water where his horse stood.

Essex's head was whirling. "So I am to sue the Queen for mercy to your lordship?"

Tyrone smiled up into the eyes of the Englishman. "You are the only man to whom I would have spoken so freely, for you are the only man I can trust," he said candidly. "Your Lordship has the fine heart of a gentleman and so can understand my feelings."

It was a masterly stroke. The O'Neill had touched the other upon his most sensitive spot. Above all other virtues Essex prized loyalty, and the mention of his father, together with Tyrone's protestations of love for Elizabeth, had found their mark. The Irishman had guessed cleverly that the son of Walter Devereux, one-time Lord Commander of Ireland, would not be able to withstand an appeal to his gentlemanly nature.

"I cannot tell," he said slowly.

"Ah, now," Tyrone's voice was soft, "would I be giving the lie to the son of Walter Devereux?"

Essex looked steadily at him.

"Now, by my hand," cried the other, "I swear that ever after I will be a most true and loyal servant, and during my life I, nor none of my followers, shall hold up hand against your lordship."

"Ever after—what?"

"I was thinking," said Tyrone easily, "that perhaps we could conclude a truce, with commissioners from both sides to agree on terms."

Essex winced. A truce! "I do not know," he said doubtfully.

"Now, be thinking on what I have said, and then we shall join together in some agreement that is to the advantage of both sides." There was a delicate pause. "Shall I be sending commissioners to you in the morning? If you are not agreeable, you have but to say the word, and I shall be content to continue the war. But it will cut me to the heart to shed blood where none is needed."

How pat the words came off! The Tyrone had conned well the lesson he had set himself. Silence fell between them, and the black stood still, but the chestnut, chilled in the water, moved with a soft swish of the flow against its thighs.

"Agreed," suddenly said Essex. "Send your men to me tomorrow."

Tyrone grinned and clapped his morion on his fiery head. "I bid your lordship farewell—and good sailing!"

He wheeled and splashed back to his men. Essex remained where he was, while the Irish galloped up the hill, their banner of a red hand on a white ground bellying out suddenly at their head. Then he returned to his men.

"He offers his submission," he reported gloomily. "We are to be approached in the morning to sign a truce."

They returned and Essex strode in silence to his tent. He closed the flap and sat down to think. He stared at the canvas walls and drew his brows together. Was this then to be the end? Had the O'Neill won, after all? He sat on his camp bed and leaned his arms on his knees, and the position eased the cramp in his stomach.

This was the worst of all the bad things that had befallen him. Gloriana's tempers, even their great quarrel of last year, were baby play, compared to this. He was forced with a momentous decision, and he did not know what to do.

How could he believe Tyrone sincere, when he had behaved all this while like a wily fox, enticing Englishmen to the chasing of him, leading them to torment and ignominious defeat? He thought of those little eyes full of tears, the soft, persuasive flattery. Pah! He spat between his feet and groaned perplexedly.

He *had* to decide. Then—what the devil did Tyrone mean by wishing him good sailing? Did he then calculate that Essex and his force would return to England, leaving him victoriously in possession of the land—was that it? He sent for Danvers and Southampton and together they sat talking till late in the afternoon.

"If Tyrone offers his submission and ceases this nagging warfare, 'twill be the same as if we had beaten him in the field," soothed Danvers.

"Aye, but not the same as if we took him in chains to London."

"But if he become once more a loyal subject, furthering her Majesty's interests here in Ireland, what is lost?"

" 'Tis a bloodless victory for him if we sign this truce," protested Essex. "I doubt if this will sit well on the stomachs of the Council at home."

Southampton had been fidgeting and grumpily silent. Now he burst out.

"To hell with the Council and all such high-stomached fellows! My ears are sick of hearing of their tender feelings. Had they seen fit to support us, we should not now be dickering with Tyrone for a truce or aught save a good dose of English steel!"

It was true, thought Essex sadly. Ever since their ill-fated landing in April, they had been systematically thwarted and checked, so that they had been forced to move with damaging caution. Silently now he cursed himself for listening to the Irish Council. It was no better than the one in London, for it too was concerned only with immediate advantage. He hated himself for being persuaded to the Leinster and Munster campaigns when, as now he realized, he should have been engaging Tyrone in Ulster. The worst of all, though, was the sure knowledge that Tyrone knew and relished all this. That was the salt on the wound.

"I fear we are too weak for him," he said slowly.

"Then why should he desire a truce?" cried Danvers.

Essex shook his head. "That I know not."

"To spare the effusion of English blood, we should sign," persisted Danvers.

"Is English honor now to be sold to spare English blood?" Essex felt a bitter twinge.

"Our captains are in low spirits and Tyrone's cunning trenches are death traps for brave men." Danvers was obstinate. "I counsel your lordship to sign."

"I am ready and willing to meet Tyrone in the open field, weak as we are," said Essex. He hesitated and glanced at Southampton.

"These ambushes," went on Danvers, as if he had not heard, "it is sheer murder sending men into that infested country."

Essex stood up. He felt unbearably goaded. He gave orders for his officers to gather.

The old familiar scene. Bearded faces above little rolled collars, negligible gold chains dangling with orders, field uniforms and gleaming breastplates catching light from candles stuck in overhead rings. Eyes —hooded, veiled, steady under level brows, flashing with youth's impetuosity; eyes—wearied and red-rimmed holding now a hint of desperation—a dozen pairs of eyes, Irish and English, all bent on the tall commander at the table's head.

It was the same. Some with Danvers were for an easy truce and a quick return home. Some were for fighting it out, let the cost be what it may. Southampton kept his thoughts to himself; he was for signing, then returning home under arms, to seize the power and make right their decision by force.

Danvers kept boring in on them. "Winter will soon be upon us, and little can be done then. We shall lie freezing till the spring and then likely have to face a truce. I am for signing."

"And you, Sir Christopher?" Essex turned to young Blount.

"My Lord Lieutenant, 'tis a hard choice. But I am for fighting, for that was our charge, and I feel assured Tyrone, for reasons of his own, is not wishful to meet us in the field."

Southampton moodily kicked the table leg, his eye lighted by a sullen glare. Essex turned to him. It was not like his friend to show a sulky face for so long. Southampton jerked his shoulder.

"Christ's blood, I say sign, sign, and if the Council does not—" here he broke off. Danvers had trod heavily on his foot.

Again Essex shook his head. He was well used to the sudden excitements of Southampton. Then he rose.

"Gentlemen, I thank you for your counsels. I shall sleep on it. Have Constable and Sentleger with Wootton stand in readiness to meet Tyrone's commissioners, should I so decide."

Council broke up. Southampton lingered, but Essex would talk no more of the matter. "Come, Henry, let us take a walk." The two young men wrapped their long bodies in cloaks and slipped out into the dewy evening air.

But Essex was not refreshed. He sighed wearily as he threw his cloak to Joseph and sank down on his bed. The pleasant walk about the meadows had done him no good. He still had his problem, with which he would have to wrestle all night.

In his heart he knew that if he signed the truce, he had lost and was as good as ruined. On the other hand, there were the men to be thought of, all those lives to be thrown to the bogs and wastes of this blasted country, and Tyrone, growing ever stronger in the north, until, like a lion, he might be able to hold out for years.

And then, creeping on fainthearted feet, the little niggling thought: perhaps Tyrone was honest in the matter and meant a true submission.

What to do? Toward dawn, worn out with turning the same thoughts over and over in his mind, he slipped to his knees at his pallet. "O God," he groaned despairingly, "show me what to do. Grant me the ineffable grace of Thy wisdom and lead me into the light, for it is indeed dark about me."

He buried his face in his arms and listened to the dull thudding of his heart. Then, stiff and cramped, he rose and went to the door of his tent. There was a faint pink flush in the east; the day was at hand.

He breathed deeply. He would take the chance on Tyrone—and on the Queen. He sent Cuffe to tell the commissioners to come to him with the morning bugle.

The fair weather held, although the languorous autumn warmth had turned to a sharp cold. Under a sky now crimson with sunrise, the Irish and the English met at a large rock out in a meadow between the two camps. The rebels were led by Conn O'Neill, the natural son of Tyrone by one of his mistresses. The young man had his mother's black hair and his father's sharp blue eyes. With bared heads he and his men respectfully awaited the approach of the English, at whose head rode young Southampton and Sir William Constable. It was a good surrender scene; the only thing lacking was the prisoner.

The truce was concluded. Cessation of arms for six weeks, to be renewed thereafter every six weeks till May Day, and only to be broken after a fortnight's warning on either side. Tyrone's son came forward and held out his brawny arm, Southampton his thin browned hand.

They clasped and O'Neill dropped lightly on his knee and touched the other's hand to his brow.

"The oath of Hugh O'Neill, Earl of Tyrone, on this," he said.

Southampton stepped back and saluted. "The word of Robert Devereux, Earl of Essex, Lord Lieutenant of Ireland on this."

Then all drew their swords and there was a grand flash skyward. "God save the Queen!"

It was over. Tyrone had won. His commissioners went posting back to Castle Dungannon where he had retired to await them. He was sure of the Lord of Essex, and he strode out to the courtyard and pulled Conn off his horse.

"It's great work ye've done this day for Ireland, my lad," he grinned.

Arm about his son's shoulder, he led the way into the great dark hall where his officers were gathered, glinting in gold and steel brooches and body plates. There was great pouring of Irish beer and cups were raised to the O'Neill, who stood, flushed and glorious, at the head of his board. His family had once held the kingship of all Ireland for six hundred years, and now he, their uncrowned king, stood the proudest man of them all this day. His red beard glittered in the smoky torchlight and the glow of victory was upon him.

"And mind ye all," he thundered, "when we lie in the dust o' Drumlane, 'twill not be the English lion that drinks our blood!"

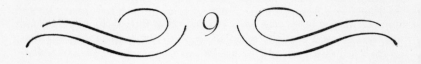

Return

$\mathcal{E}$ssex and his company bade farewell to Dublin on a dark morning with a late September drizzle creeping down their backs, just as when they left London in the previous spring. Up through the lush green lands of County Meath they rode, past high hedges and low stone walls and ragged herds of Irish cattle, standing patient in the rain. They traversed the Boyne Valley and came into the fabled land of Tara.

At last they sighted the great Cross of Muirdach, carved with the Crucifixion and other holy objects, standing up seventeen feet high on the landscape; and then they knew they were but five miles from Drogheda, where their ship awaited them. They put their horses to the gallop and approached the massive road that led them up to the walled town, once the stronghold of the Danes. The swallows were wheeling about the towers, half-minded to fly south, yet loath to leave the fair green country of Louth and Meath.

Essex watched them, strong and fearless, and he envied them their free flight through the air. He had a mad desire to take wings himself and fly, far away from the haunts of man and his sorrows. The cool, salty breeze now mingled with the damp-laden air and made the heather tremble about his horse's feet. Gulls came screaming in from shore, and suddenly, before them was the sea, sullen, flecked with white, gray under a gray sky.

There was no need to delay. Essex went aboard immediately and stood grimly on his quarter-deck. The wind rose and took them out of the harbor. As he had stood on his *Due Repulse,* watching the walls of Cadiz recede into smoky distance, now he watched green Ireland fall astern. Regret, regret, always regret. Would he ever feel light and free again? Aye, perhaps. But now there was bad and bloody business afoot, for which he had no relish.

For he had taken the step. The great resolution had at last formed in his shrinking mind, and there was to be no turning back. He was going home without permit, with nothing but that secret document she had given him, which, lost in the fury of the present fiasco, he knew she would now repudiate. He was going home with nothing but failure to present, that he knew. But he was going to burst in on Elizabeth with the full challenging force of his personality. Face to face, he would find out from her why she had sent him no loving letters, why she had tied his hands, why she had forced him to ignominy before his enemies.

He had tried courtiership, soldiering, statecraft, all to no avail. He was past thirty, and the time had come at last for them to have it out, once and for all. So now, with a skeleton force to secure him from arrest, he was on his way. The die was indeed cast.

The crossing was comparatively smooth, with little sickness below decks, and in more rain they landed on a dripping Welsh coast. Six days from the time he took ship at Dublin, Essex and his little troop trotted within sight of the spires of London.

The few days aboard, and the ten-mile ride down the river to Nonesuch combined to hold his desperate hand. He decided to leave his men on the far side of the river, taking with him a mere handful to confront Elizabeth. Early in the morning they cantered through Westminster, leaving their horses at the ferry. With six of his gentlemen Essex was rowed across at Lambeth.

But they had been recognized. A gentleman, on his way to the palace, clapped heels to his horse and raced to Nonesuch, fairly falling off his mount to run inside to Cecil.

"Sir Robert! Sir Robert!" He burst in on the Secretary's breakfast. "The Earl of Essex has returned. He is even now on the bridle path with a company of six gentlemen."

Cecil looked up calmly from his porridge. "Six, did you say?"

"Aye. Will you not send word to the Queen?"

Cecil spooned up his porridge delicately. He touched his lips with a napkin. "No, he said quietly, "no."

A quarter of an hour later there was another flurry in the courtyard, and seven steaming horses were taken by the ostlers, while Essex and his friends hurried under the shallow arch past the halberdiers. No one remarked anything unusual in the appearance of a few mud-splashed men, eyes sunken in their heads with weariness. The presence of the Earl was sufficient guarantee. It was assumed that the Queen had sent for her Lord Lieutenant to come posthaste to her.

In the hall Essex spoke softly to his followers. "You take the front staircase. Go up quietly. Give me time to get up the other way and meet me at the Queen's chamber door. Be ready."

He tore up the private stairway that he knew so well. On the landing he stopped for a moment to get his breath and ease the pounding in his throat. For a moment he felt deadly ill. He leaned on the wall, and then the giddiness passed, and a light feeling returned. He was going to Gloriana. What else mattered? She was only a woman and—he bounded down the corridor and past the guard, who started as he went by. The six were there. Motioning to them to remain quiet, he listened a moment, his ear at the door. Through the thick carved panels came a murmur of sound.

Without stopping to consider what he was doing, he pushed it open and stood, hand on the knob, his face alight with eagerness.

A startled cry from one of the maids, and Gloriana, standing among her tirewomen, turned. She stood there in early-morning disarray, gray hair hanging in loose hanks about her thin face, a soft, shapeless robe flung over her night rail. Her haggard cheeks were drawn with sleep and her lips were pale and sunken.

She gasped. She could not believe—yes, yes, it was he. Then as she realized how she looked, a quick throb darted through her.

The Earl stood at the door, splashed as he was to the hips with mud, a two-day stubble on his chin, his doublet stained and crumpled. At his side swung his great sword.

Leaving the door ajar, he came swiftly forward and sank on one knee. He took the Queen's hands and held them to his lips. But she was staring at an ominous little tangle of steel-clad men who lingered by the door.

"Essex!"

Then, recovering, "Robin!" she said, and made her voice soft with pleasure. "Robin, it's you!"

He rose and now he looked at her. Appalled at what he saw, he did not betray himself. Gloriana now was smiling, lips pressed tight over her teeth. But—she was smiling, and her eyes were gracious. The door closed.

"Robin," she continued, "I am enchanted to see you. And how like you, my dusty knight, to come bounding into my bedroom before I am presentable for the day."

"You are yourself, my Queen." He tried his old smile. "The other does not matter. Say you forgive me."

"For what, my Robin?"

Mechanically conscious of her staring women, of her own shocking appearance, of those armed men behind her closed door, her one thought was to get rid of him, and quickly. There was something else, too. How many men lurked about her palace—and her guard—had they disarmed her guard?

Again the tight smile. "What is it—for what am I to forgive you?"

"For my hasty return. You gave me leave to come, you know."

"Well do I know. But, Robin, could you not wait till we were both clothed?" She shook her gray head at him. Then, casually, "Have you given orders for your men to be fed?"

"My men!" He laughed. "There were only those six that you saw. I came alone."

Alone! Her eyes grew keen. "Then, lad, let me finish dressing, and do you go and wash. You are not pretty, my lord."

Tall as she was, even without her heels, he towered above her. She reached up and pinched his ear. He laughed again and, bowing, left her.

Outside in the corridor he clapped Southampton on the back. "See how easy it was? By God, I have suffered much storms and trouble abroad, but it is worth it to find so sweet a calm at home."

He dressed carefully, and in black, striped with silver, he descended the great staircase into a perfumed bevy of lords and ladies. They flocked about him, avid to learn of his experiences in Ireland. He was now the hero adventurer on whose word all hung flatteringly. All the Court knew that he had forced the Queen's bedchamber, and that she had tolerated it. There were smirks and little shivers of delight from the girls.

He drew an eager throng about him at the long table in the dining hall and he entertained them with tales of unsung heroes, and of the dark tarns and wild fens of Ireland, and of the bright-haired Milesians who had danced for him at Castle Kilkenny. He boasted of his meeting with the O'Neill, and he never saw the polite sneers of Cecil and Ralegh, who, with Lord Howard and a few others, ate apart at their own table.

He was riding the crest of his little wave, and his senses delighted in the soft adulation and frank eulogies of his listeners. He was too in love with his success to smell the trouble that was brewing for him in the upper rooms of the palace.

Then the Queen sent for him and they had an hour in which to chat of the affairs of the green kingdom. Keenly she listened to his account and was strangely silent on the subject of his meeting at Bellaclynthe Ford with Tyrone. Feeling a vague dissatisfaction, he left her.

The girls fluttered their long lashes at him and the music of John Bull and his minstrels rose on the air, and with it his good spirits rose to a pitch of delight. Ah, but it was good to be home at last and out of that accursed country. He forgot to miss Pamela. He looked about for Mary Ratcliffe; he would like to say something about her brother. But Mary was keeping her room.

The Queen and her Secretary were not of the gay company that supped below stairs. All day long Gloriana had denied herself to the Court. It was as if the blow to her pride inflicted by Essex had, for the time being, laid her low. She could not face her Court—not yet. Again she sent for Essex. The message interrupted his cards by the fire; he raised his handsome brows and left.

He found Gloriana no longer warm. She was seated before her fire, and at his entrance she rose. She swept across to the table, gathering her oyster-colored skirts to sit at its head. She motioned him to a chair.

"Now, perhaps, Robert, you will tell me exactly why you have returned."

His eyes widened. "I have returned, Madam, because I could no longer bear the separation." He almost believed what he was saying.

"No, Robert, no. I am an old woman, but I am not so stupid as to believe that."

"Did I not come straight to your Grace's chamber?"

"You did."

That was a thing she would never forget or forgive. That he had dared to force her room, seeing her as no other man had ever seen her, not even Leicester, shocked her severely. Now, in her paint and flaming wig, her slim height nobly clad in pale gray satin, she was once more the goddess. But he had peeped at her, unjeweled and unfortified. No, she should not forget it.

She broke the silence. "Shall I tell you why you have returned to me? It is because you have failed in Ireland and you wanted to cut short your enemies, that you might plead your cause in your own way."

He swallowed. "Possibly."

"No, surely! And now I shall tell you what you ought to have done, my lord. I could have told you that to trust this traitor Tyrone on his oath is to trust the devil on his religion."

"Madam, had you talked with him, as I did at Bellaclynthe, you could not have doubted his fealty." No matter what his own doubts, he must not let her guess that he had not acted in perfect assurance.

"No?" returned Elizabeth dryly. "I would not trust him if he were to swear on the head of his son and that son in our hands. You should have given him no talk till he stood in chains before you. I did not send you to make terms with these rascals."

His head flew up. "This was not your Grace's manner to me this morning. I thought——"

She brushed his thought aside. "And those fifty-nine knights! Think you, my lord, that this was well done? It has always been a sore point between us."

"I rewarded those that merited it."

"The glory of England should be reward enough for a brave man. Look at me! I serve England, and I look for no other reward than the loves of my people."

"You are the Queen, though."

"Aye, that I am, though you seem to forget it." She rose threateningly over him. "Learn, my lord, that even if I am Queen, there are things from which I cannot save you."

Between them throbbed a tense silence. They glared at each other, hearts beating angrily.

"There is another thing you will be required to answer to the Council. Why, in Christ's name, did you turn south? Did not your common sense, your soldier's mind, tell you to march north?"

"For that, I had your Grace's permission and the full approval of the Council of Ireland." She should not push that off on him, when it had been with her full knowledge and consent that he had gone south.

"Council? Pish! I presume you refer to that lot of shortsighted dotards who style themselves the Lords of Ireland? What do they know of military strategy? Where was your instinct, my lord?"

"I followed instructions." He was stubborn.

"Instructions, is it? Now, as to that, my permit, as you say, I have this to state. I have lived among princes and when one of them counsels aught that is to the injury of the realm, it is the subject's duty to disobey. Your tactics, my lord, may be sound, but I see you are no strategist."

The subject's duty to disobey! He had had enough of that. He stared ferociously at her, the blood rising in his cheeks. Of all the contrary, infernal turncoats! Too choked with rage to form words, had he thought of any, he could only swallow. Unaware of his rising rage, she went on.

"And there is another thing—the letters I wrote, full of my concern and love for you. I cannot say I received the same from you."

Now he found words. Springing to his feet, he cried, "I did write, by God! I wrote, early and late! I sent my love, over and over. By all that's holy, 'twas not until lately that I was too heartsick——"

"You wrote? Then, what——?"

"Someone tampered with our letters."

It was her turn to stare. "Do you know who did this thing?"

"I do not."

He was bitter, defeated, cut to the quick, as always, by treachery.

"Before God," said Elizabeth in a shaking voice, "before God, if I find out who did this knavish thing, I will make of him an example to make London ring." Her bosom heaved. "It seems, my lord, that we are at cross-purposes. Still," she sighed, "whatever our private differences, the facts still remain, and they are bitter."

Challengingly they faced. In her countenance were lines of contempt and grief. "We are defeated, the laughingstock of Europe, outdone by an Irish rebel. How does that sound to you, my lord?" He felt, rather than saw her dreadful look. "Your members of the Council await you in the Chamber. Go to them." She turned away sharply. "I shall not see you again—tonight."

She swished her fan toward her, her face averted. For the space of a moment he regarded that narrow back, then he left the room.

The small group of Councilors heard his story in stiff silence. When he had finished, they leaned forward and shot their close questions at him. By a strong effort he kept his temper.

He left a room in which the air was heavy with unspoken thoughts. Weary to the bone, his heart uneasy and sad, he climbed the stairs to bed. He gave his body to Joseph, who undressed him and brought his old robe. Wrapped in the familiar folds, he sat down to warm himself. Small chills coursed his backbone and the sockets of his eyes ached as if from long riding in the face of the sun.

There was a knock at the door. God, no one tonight. He was too tired. But Joseph took a paper from someone who left. Essex held it to the candlelight. Robert Cecil's hand.

The Earl of Essex is commanded to keep to his chamber.

And scrawled below it, in square, characteristic letters, the name he had seen a hundred times.

For a moment he could not move, then he rushed to tear open the door. Two halberdiers instantly slanted their weapons crosswise before him. He closed the door and leaned against it, a rigid figure with a face of stone.

He was a prisoner.

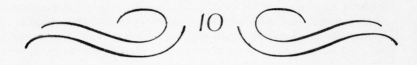

Royal Prisoner

*H*e sat and stared out of the coach window at nothing. The Queen had not seen him again. For two days he had endured the horror of the locked door, and then came word that the Earl Marshal was to submit himself to the custody of the Lord Keeper. Without ceremony he was bundled into a coach and they set off for York House.

The Lord Keeper Egerton was discomfited. Barking orders at his staff, he flew about his house. He did not want Essex as his guarded guest. There would be men-at-arms in the upper corridors, making love to the maids and tramping his smooth floors with their great boots. Worst of all, there was Lady Egerton, who lay in her last sickness, and the house was already tense with doctors and bed-women. Essex was a dangerous prisoner, with his suspicious friends and the heady uproar in which he lived.

Hardly had the hasty preparations been made when the prisoner himself stalked into the lower hall. At sight of the burly guards Egerton groaned. But he conducted Essex civilly enough to the third floor and said he hoped his lordship would find his quarters comfortable.

Essex grunted. "Depends upon the length of my stay." He surveyed the walls of the room. "I fear I shall tire soon enough of the tapestries of this fair little retreat." He turned away to stare out of the window.

Egerton shrugged and left. Already the long gallery was occupied by the Queen's guard.

Within the room Essex did not stir. He remained gazing into the garden below, and at the sound of the key in the lock behind him, his lip twitched.

And so began his polite imprisonment. Day after day it continued. His appetite failed and he began to droop. They brought him savory foods, but his stomach, delicate always when nerves possessed him, rebelled, and he could eat nothing. His eyes continued to ache and a slow fever burned in his veins. Wakeful white nights he spent staring into the stuffy darkness of the sealed chamber, too dispirited to call Joseph or to light himself a candle for reading.

At last he sent for Egerton. "My Lord Keeper, I would that you have Lady Essex brought to me." It had been so long since he had had the comfort of Frances; Ireland and the Queen's wrath stretched between them so that he hardly knew he had a wife.

A troubled frown puckered Egerton's brow. The prisoner's request embarrassed him. "I shall convey your lordship's wishes to her Majesty," he said. Then he hastily excused himself, lest he be burdened with more petitions.

In silence Gloriana received the message. She sent back no reply.

Then with the urgent longing of the caged beast, he became wildly restless. For hours he paced up and down his room, hands locked behind him, brows fixed in distress. This then ceased and faded to a lethargy, and he lay on his bed for hours, where he had flung himself, caring for nothing, reading nothing, seeing no one. To the few who were allowed access to him, he denied himself.

And then came a day, late in November, when a feeble wintry sun was struggling to light up his room. His door was unlocked, and there in a long brown velvet cloak stood Frances, hesitating in the shadows. Her pale face, faintly flushed with cold, stood out clear against the darkness of the walls, and her hair hung in damp little tendrils from out her hood.

There was the silence of a single heartbeat between them. Then she ran forward to his arms. With sick, feverish eyes he looked at her, putting back her hood, holding her head in both his hands.

"Fran," he said gently, and kissed her.

Her eyes sparkled with tears she would not let fall. She unclasped the frog at her throat and threw back her cloak. He drew off her gloves and held her soft palms to his cheeks.

"It's like wine and sweet music to see you," he said.

Her smile was tremulous. "They wouldn't let me come to you before. I explained that in my letters."

His mouth tightened, but he clenched his teeth on telling her that the letters had not reached him. He could not wound her with that.

"I would have had you here the first day."

She laughed a little now. "With my Lady Egerton so ill, and you, my lord, a guest here, it would have been hard having me and the midwives in the house."

He looked incredulous. "No!"

"Yes," she smiled. "A little girl, born these three weeks. I am just out of my bed."

So he had left her with child. She must have known for weeks before he left her in the spring. Why had she not told him? If only he had known this, it might have put heart into him all those accursed months. He was romantically moved. Still his faithful wife, she was bearing him children, while he was doing his best to make her a widow.

"We'll call the little one Frances, my love."

He clasped her waist and pressed his face into her lap. It was his old gesture when he was tenderly turned toward the woman who at the moment held his heart. Frances felt its power. She put her hands softly on his hair, dry and lifeless with the fever.

"I fear I make but a poor husband," he whispered.

Again she smiled. She knew how easily he slipped into humility when the mood was on him. She put back the hair from his eyes.

"I love you, Robin," she said quietly. "My life is your life; you know that."

Then she rose and, calling Joseph, began her soft tread about the room, putting things to rights and making his airless prison more comfortable. She had been permitted to bring him nothing, else, she assured him, she would have brought up his maps that he loved so well, and some of his smaller books. He shook his head.

"I shall never more need maps, and I have lost my heart for reading."

Although at sunset she had to leave him, he slept better that night than on any other since his arrival, and the morning sun, streaming in on him, saw him sleeping peacefully, relaxed on his pillows like a boy. At a little before eight he woke and ate a warm meal.

Almost before he was dressed, Frances came. Each day thereafter, she shared his prison cheerfully, while she strove with all her woman's wit to rouse him to some sort of activity. It was no use. The only thing that would help him was word from the Queen and no word came. It began to look as if she had forgotten him. With a sinking heart Frances watched him gradually relapse into his old gloom. The fever returned and by the first days of December he was so weakened that he kept his bed all day and would not let them dress him.

The long train of events now claimed him. The trip from Drogheda, half-sick as he was from dysentery, the headlong plunge through the wet and cold half across England, the climactic disaster at Nonesuch, all converged into a sickness that gained rapidly upon him. He made no more effort to cast it off. His mind and body remained torpid and the doctors declared themselves baffled. They bled him and physicked him, and he grew steadily worse. To change his bed, they lifted his wasted body in sheets; even that much exhausted him.

Frances watched him slipping away, and a great desperation took hold of her. "I shall go to the Queen myself," she told Egerton.

He was aghast. "To the Queen, my lady?"

"I shall. If she will not suffer me to speak to her myself, I shall find an ear into which to pour my tale. Surely," she finished scornfully, "the Earl has some friends left among the Queen's ladies."

Egerton would have nothing to do with it. It was quite bad enough to have the Earl on his hands, without incurring further wrath. He hurried upstairs to his wife's apartments.

Frances dressed herself in black. She took a long time and was careful. She wore only the plainest of gowns and no jewels save the wedding band and the locket containing the miniatures of her two boys. She pulled the black hood of her cape over her hair and left the house by the water-stairs. That way she would be more private.

With only one attendant she entered the great vaulted hall, shortly before noon, to find the usual crowd of idlers, hanging about the fire-places and stairways. She hesitated. Where should she go? She wondered if there were a single person here at Court to help her. Mechanically she walked up the wide stairway to the upper corridor. Then her steps quickened as she remembered Lady Cobham, Mistress of the Robes, who used to be her good friend in the days of her widowhood. She walked down the long hall to the Coffer Chamber and went in.

A light buzzing came from a knot of girls gathered about someone in the center of the room. They did not see the quiet black-clad figure just within the doorway, waiting to be spoken to.

"I told you not to go near her today!" cried one of them. Then Frances heard the sound of a girl's sobs.

"She hit me with the mirror. How was I to know she won't have one of the damned things about her?"

Frances knew the voice, petulant, with a little husky tempting note in it. It was Kat Fytton who was sobbing pettishly, her self-pity fed by the girls who crowded about her. The circle now parted and she saw Kat, one hand to her flushed cheek.

"It's a shame," said a red-haired girl violently.

"Sh!" warned another, who caught sight of Frances, silently witnessing the scene.

"My Lady Essex!" cried Penelope Wingfield. The others stared curiously, while Katherine continued to sniffle and blow her little nose. She herself had no mind to talk to Lady Essex, who must know that she had been the Earl's mistress. But, God's death, why was the woman in black! She caught her breath. Was the Earl——

Swiftly she approached Frances, her temper quenched in fearful curiosity. "Is—my lord——?"

"No," replied Frances shortly. She turned to Penelope. "I desire to see Lady Cobham. Can you tell me where to find her?"

Penelope shook her head doubtfully. "It's likely she's with the Queen. Her Grace is fussy these days with her clothes, and my lady——"

"Perhaps I can wait here for a little," suggested Frances.

"As you wish," said Penelope indifferently. She had no desire to get herself into trouble, with the Queen like a wildcat, striking out at innocent maids right and left, cursing everyone who crossed her path.

At the noon meal of the maids Lady Cobham appeared. At sight of Frances she held up fat hands. Then she bore the Countess off to her private room. "Come away, child, away from these little tiger cubs. They will scratch you to pieces. Aye, me," she sighed throatily. "Everyone is at the murder point these days, and the Queen like to drive us all off our heads with her megrims."

To the plea of the young woman she listened with pursed lips and hooded eyes. "I can promise you nothing. 'Tis sure her Grace will not see you, nor dare you stay here. Go home, and I will advise with my Lord Cobham and others who are kindly disposed to you both. But, my child, though there is talk here at Court, and many who do think your husband abused, I fear there is no hand strong enough to draw sword in his defense."

"I want no swords drawn in defense; there has been enough of that. All I ask is that someone will tell the Queen how it is with my lord, and ask—nay, *beg* that she find it in her heart to send to him. I would have said, allow him to come to her, but," here she faltered, "he is so weak that the lifting of his eyes is too much for him."

Feeling that she had accomplished nothing, she left. Bitterly she wished she had not even tried. With a sick resignation she returned to York House to relieve the nurse who watched at her husband's bedside.

It was late in the evening, about a week later, that a black boat put off into the river from Whitehall. Within the tiny covered seat sat one who was shrouded in a dark hooded cape, whose face glimmered like a white oval in the deep dusk of the curtains that shut out the damp air. There was no word spoken, and the oars rose and fell with a sharp rhythmic splash, the shafts creaking softly in the rowlocks. The barge drew alongside the stairs of York House.

A gentleman in a tall-crowned hat stepped quietly out onto the wet landing, then turned to assist the woman who stooped to leave her canopied seat. Still in silence, the two figures passed up the steps and melted into the darkness about the house.

The woman pulled her hood about her face; the gentleman murmured a word to the servant who appeared in the hall. He bowed and the two ascended to the third floor. There they paused and the woman put back her hood. Elizabeth had come to see for herself how it was with the Earl of Essex.

The gentleman put aside the long arras that hung over the door and the Queen passed into the sickroom. A small rushlight burned on the bedside table and a nurse in a nunlike coif sat nearby. At sight of the Queen she rose and stared, curtseying.

Elizabeth never saw her. She walked to the bed and put back the curtains. Essex lay on his back, his thin profile resting against the pillow. The flesh had fallen away from him, so that it was a very death mask that she saw, the fine bones of the skull barely overlaid with the ivory skin. The face had been shaved, but a light auburn fringe straggled above the mouth; the eyes were closed and sunk deep in the head. The hair, still richly chestnut, lay in a dry, ragged tangle on the neck, where a faint pulse throbbed thinly. The Earl's great shoulders rested outside the covers and from the cuffs of his white robe protruded his emaciated wrists and his beautiful tapering hands.

For a long time she stared down at him. He did not move nor make any sign that he knew that she was there. Then she turned and raised her eyebrows at the nurse, who shook her head.

"Madam, his lordship lies like this by the hour when the fever is not upon him, " she whispered.

Elizabeth moved back from the bed. The curtain fell from her hand. In her own face there was no vestige of color, and her thin cheeks seemed also to have fallen in.

"I should scarcely have known him," she said.

Softly as she came, she left the house. She had seen for herself. He was dying. She gave orders that her doctors, all eight of them, attend him night and day.

Early on the morning of the tenth of December, the bells of old St. Paul's began throwing their sorrowful showers of sound into the frozen air. Word had come to the Dean that the Earl of Essex was sinking and could not last the night. He would be dead at dawn. The Dean forthwith hastened to give orders for the bell-ringers to climb to the icy tower to wake the morning with their melancholy tolling.

But the fact was that the Earl, though deadly ill, was not dead. He lay on his prisoner's bed and barely stirred the air with his feeble breathing. Though his body was wasted to the bone, his persistent heart beat on and refused to permit escape to the impatient spirit that clamored for release.

The worthy Dr. Richard Vaughan, Bishop of London, assured of the Earl's dying, came to condole with the bereaved wife. Attended by his priest and two servers, he swept up the staircase, his episcopal robes raising a fine dust as he panted up to the third floor. Then adjusting his short cape and twisting his amethyst ring, he motioned to the priest to push open the sickroom door.

There was a sound of subdued weeping. The sick man, his eyes open, lay back on his pillows. Kneeling in a small group at the foot of the bed were Southampton, Cuffe, the Steward Meyrick, and a little apart, as befitted, Adam Baxter and Joseph. In a moment of lucidity Essex had asked for them to be brought in. Frances, a strained, compassionate figure, leaned over the wraith in the bed, and her tears, unheeded, fell onto the coverlet.

Essex was barely conscious but had strength to mutter. To those about him it was the rally before the end. At sound of his visitors he moved his head slightly to one side and saw Vaughan, face pale under his flat cap. The cleric moved to the bedside, holding back his long black stole as he leaned over the Earl. He was amazed to find the man alive.

"How is it with you, my lord?"

He must find out whether or not to stop those tolling bells. If the Earl were going to live, it would be foolish——

Essex regarded him languidly. So they had sent for Vaughan—he must be very bad. "My Lord Bishop," he breathed faintly, "I fear I am for the long journey."

The Bishop raised a fleshy hand to his collar. "I trust not."

Essex let out his scant breath in a light sigh. "My life is lived out," he gasped, "what am I—to live so long—in such misery?" He panted a little. "I pray you—read the prayers." He looked infinitely weary.

Vaughan stood looking down at the bed. He knew the Earl wanted the prayers for the dying. Though he could not actually believe the man to be at the last, he dared not refuse his request. He slipped off his outer cloak and dropped it into the hands of the priest, who signed to the servers to begin preparations for administering extreme unction.

Frances crumpled to the ground and hid her face against the lace edge of the bedcover. Joseph, a crooked little shadow of grief, crouched back in the shadows, while the others gazed dolefully at the inert shape on the pillows. The room was dark, paneled to the ceiling with glossy recessed squares, but now it was softly lighted at the window by the strong whiteness of the falling snow. No curtains hung from the massive bedposts, for Essex complained that he could not breathe with them about him, and the spare body under the embroidered cover looked as if reclining on its bier. The silence became oppressive.

They lighted candles and began the solemn service. With a lightness astonishing in one so heavy, Vaughan got to his plump knees and began the prayer for the dying.

"O Father of mercies, God of all comfort, our only help in time of need, we fly unto Thee for succour in behalf of this, Thy servant, here lying in great weakness of body. . . ." The smooth voice droned on through prayer after prayer. The only other sound was the soft clicking of Southampton's rosary as he said his own prayers for the repose of his friend's soul. Then the Bishop arose, and his place was taken by a priest. Essex remained ghastly still. They anointed him with holy oil and brushed his lips with the wine. They continued their exhortation of the Almighty. The snow swirled on past the window.

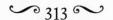

Essex had not moved. He seemed now to be dozing. He was still alive when the Bishop finally departed, leaving his assistant to continue the supplication of heaven. Orders were given to stop the bells, and as night fell, they told the Queen that the Earl was still breathing.

Morning broke. Alive and slightly better, he was fully conscious. They told him that Elizabeth had been to see him a few nights before, and a tiny thread of color crept along his cheekbones.

He mended rapidly. His constitution, sound at the core, came to his help, and gradually he threw off the terrible lassitude that had assailed him ever since his return from Ireland. The news that Elizabeth had finally relented enough to come to see him, although secretly, was his tonic. On that he daily fed, and from it he gained strength.

John Harington, arrived from Ireland, found him sitting in a chair before the fire, talking with a few friends. He strode into the room, the Wicklow disgrace lightly falling from his shoulders, and clanked across the bare floor, to drop on his knee at Essex's side.

"John!" Essex kept his hand on the other's shoulder and looked into his face. "When did you arrive?"

"Last night."

"Have you seen——?"

The other shook his head. "Not yet. I'm told I'm in disgrace." Disgrace for the favorite godson. Was it Wicklow still?

"Yes, it seems I paid a visit to Tyrone and behaved like an English gentleman to him and his sons."

At mention of the rebel's name Essex winced, as if someone had pressed a painful bruise. Then he recovered himself. "Did you now?" He leaned back. "Tell me."

"I had the curiosity to see the O'Neill in his lair, as it were, and since arms were sheathed between us, I saw no harm in a little friendly meal at the fern table." Harington's eye kindled. "Robert, 'twas a sight. There they were, the red-bearded one and his sons, two children of good towardly spirit, and all dressed up in velvet and gold lace. A sight, I do assure you."

Essex half closed his eyes and gazed off into space, as if a vision of the merry scene rose before him.

"We dined off the fat of the land, and then, odd's-fish-my-skin, if Tyrone didn't take a fancy for me to read to them. I gave them some of my *Arioso*. Tyrone is putting his boys to the learning that he himself lacked as a young one. Ah, but the older lad especially took my eye. There's good blood there, Robert. To him I presented the book with a wish that the boy might come to our own Cambridge and learn the sweet ways of English lore."

"Aye." Then Essex sighed and shook off his trance. "When are you for Court?"

"I must present myself as soon as may be. The Queen may refuse to see me, but at least I make my devoir."

Essex nodded. Then he looked straight at Harington. "What if I ask you to speak for me, John?"

Harington looked troubled. Here was a delicate matter. It is true, Essex had made him a knight, but, as he put it to a friend with whom he had ridden up from Wales, he had no desire to be wracked on the Essex coast.

"You have been familiar to her from your youth, John. She bears you no malice. She will listen to you."

Harington stared into the fire and did not answer.

"God's blood!" Essex burst out with his old flashing heat. "Go to her and take the time of her mood. If luck is against us all, then keep silent. Come now, that's fair enough."

Harington presented himself at Court. Gloriana received him in a black-and-green-shot gown. It had a high collar and she had a high mood to match the frame of lace that towered behind her quivering head. Hardly had Harington dropped to his knees when she began of him.

"God's son! It is time you present yourself for the wigging that you so richly deserve! Do I hear aright that you have broken bread with that rebellious bull calf, and actually consorted with his sons—do I?"

Thankful that he had not committed himself to Essex, Harington breathed a hasty prayer to his guardian angel, ducked his head, and murmured something about his own loyalty and Tyrone's pacific attitude to the English.

"Speak up!" she thundered. "Cease that damned mumbling! Tell me in good round English what you have been up to, and at once, do you hear?"

He glanced fearfully up. "Madam—I visited the Earl of Tyrone and dined with him at his castle. At that time he assured me of his duty and his solemn intentions touching the peace that my Lord of Essex——"

"God's blood! I am no Queen! The Lord of Essex now! And that's another pair of boots—who gave the Lord of Essex command to return to me? I did send him on other business!"

At the mere mention of the Earl's name she was beside herself. Now that he no longer stood in danger of death, she poured forth all the vicious, excited rage that had been dammed up, awaiting his recovery. Eyes starting from her scarlet face, she towered over the luckless Harington, seizing him by the belt. She shook it back and forth till the clasp gave way and the strap came loose in her furious hand. She flung it at him and turned away, her fist clenched in the stiff folds of her gown. She rustled up and down and gasped for breath. Then she whirled round on the kneeling man.

"What have I to do with you? You are a poet—an idle knave—and Essex worse!" But her tone, less furious now, gave him courage. He had seen her like this before.

"Madam," he ventured, "whatever the mistakes of the past, the fighting in Ireland is, for the nonce, quieted, and your Majesty's honor preserved."

At that her wild, hysterical laughter rang through the room. "My honor preserved! With a truce that doth smell to all the corners of Europe. There speaks the statesman, indeed."

She laughed again, but less scornfully. She fingered a miniature of Burghley that hung from her girdle, and sentimentally she gazed at the likeness of her dead minister.

"Ah, Burghley, how ye would wince and spread that white painful smile of yours if ye could but hear these babes in the wood. Thank God ye are out of it, as soon I shall be, bless heaven!"

She bade Harington rise and she herself swept to a seat at her desk and took up a pen. She tried to go on with the copying of a fine manuscript, a job she had set herself for the quieting of her nerves, but her hand still trembled, and she gave it up. She leaned back in her seat and looked curiously at the man beside her. His eyes were blue as chips of lapiz in his brown face. After all, she liked him.

"Tell me about Tyrone," she said unexpectedly. "What doth he resemble? I seem to recall a man somewhat tall and of a reddish hue who hung about the Court with Lord Sidney and Leicester. But then—there were so many like him. Tell me."

"Ah, Madam," said he eagerly, "he is a chieftain of flesh and substance, tall and broad, and red, like your Grace. His eye flashes with the azure of his Irish skies and lakes, and he brings all men to his smile.

With what charm such a master makes them love him, I know not; but if he bid them come, they come; if go, they go; if he say do this, they do it."

"Great merit in that," said she sarcastically. "Perhaps you'll be telling me that he puts some Irish spell on them."

"That I cannot say," replied the poet. "But I do know his guard is for the most part made up of beardless boys, without shirts, who wade in the frosty rivers as familiarly as water spaniels."

"Hum," said Gloriana, thinking of her own guard, brave in spangles. "Go home, Harington. I've seen enough of ye for one day."

Harington melted thankfully away.

"Him and his azure skies and lakes," she muttered irritably. "Azure, my foot! He'd have me believe, I trow, that Tyrone bewitched Essex into this damned truce."

She sent for Bacon. Since their conversation of the previous summer, she had seen him only occasionally. It took her a long time to forgive him for so lacerating her feelings with regard to Essex, but in the end the clever penetrating intellect of the man won her over.

Bacon came eagerly to the call. He would talk freely with his royal mistress. No pang of remorse twisted him as he contemplated a further turning of his back on an old friend; he could no longer afford the luxury of the Earl's regard. Essex was a dangerous man to know these days, and Bacon did not mean to be cut short in his prime. He had seen too many others suffer for their attachments. True, Gloriana would not live much longer, for she was sixty-seven, and it was plain that this affair of Essex was killing her. Bacon would play his cards very carefully, keeping a sharp eye about him.

They spoke of Essex. Bacon, now at ease upon the subject, suggested that the Queen solve her difficult position by sending him back to Ireland. She glared at him as if he had lost his wits.

"Essex! Ireland! Whensoever I send Essex back into Ireland, I will marry you, Master Bacon." She snorted through her thin nose. "No, no! Enough and to spare of that. I have another deputy for Ireland."

Bacon retreated. He had made a tactical error. "Perhaps it would be wiser to keep him here," he agreed smoothly.

"Here he will remain," declared Elizabeth firmly, "till he do make his case before Star Chamber."

So! It had come about. A lightning flash of memory throbbed through Bacon of that cold day before his fire, when Essex was for going to France and spoke so lightly of his queen and of her throne.

"Majesty," he dared, "not a public prosecution, I beg you. The Earl has many friends, and besides, his delinquencies might be difficult to prove."

She regarded him disagreeably. "Upon my soul, you do take to yourself a heavy load of opinion."

Angrily she dismissed him. But in her heart she knew him to be right.

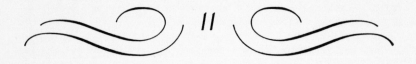

Release

Gradually Gloriana gave in. Spring came to the country. It was Easter-tide. On Maundy Thursday, while the poor of the city were symbol-ically being fed, Essex went home to his house on the river. His guards went with him. With a sigh of relief Egerton saw him go, and the maids mounted to the third story to clear out the room that had pris-oned him for so long.

Gloriana had sent out delicate tendrils to take the mettle of the people with regard to Essex.

"What are they saying in the City?" she asked Cecil carefully.

Cecil hesitated. "There are numerous stories, Madam."

"That I am aware, you crook-backed fool!" She was instantly irri-tated. "I asked you, what is being said. Christ's bones, can I never get a straight answer to my question?"

"There is a wave of popular feeling in the Earl's favor. Many there are who believed him abused."

"I thought as much. What if I release him?"

"Without trial, Madam?"

"I said release. Naturally without trial."

"Then will the people say all the more that his lordship has been wrongly imprisoned."

"It is not as if he were within the Tower."

"He is within four walls, Madam."

"Aye." She closed her eyes and thought of her own youth, when Mary had shut her up, yes, by God, in the Tower. How she had beaten her spirit up against the bars! She swallowed.

"Let him walk in the garden," she directed.

They sent Mountjoy down to Essex House to bear the tidings. He walked in on the prisoner, bringing the cold air of the chilly day in his clothes. The slender branches of a tall elm tapped in the wind at the casement.

"God be thanked you seem once more yourself, Robert." Essex smiled wanly and moved his thin legs under the robe. "Robert, I lie awake of night, conjuring as to your future."

"My future!" Essex was bleak. " 'Tis finished, Charles."

Mountjoy rallied him. "In faith, I have seen you many times like this. Come, man, out of the doldrums. There's work for all of us, you especially."

"I am a ruined man, retired to oblivion."

"That is unlike you. Her Grace has begun to pity you for her harshness. I am bidden to tell your guards you may walk in the garden."

A bitter snort of laughter escaped Essex. "So I am to promenade in the garden, am I? Generous mistress!"

"It's the entering wedge, Robert. Can you not see? She will give in, but only by degrees. God's death, man, you know her better than any of us."

"Aye."

"Now attend to me." Blount hitched his chair closer. "I have met with Danvers and Southampton, for there is much need to deny the slander that you have aimed at the Crown."

"So they say that, do they?"

"That they do. You do not think, do you, that while you have lain in your bed, your enemies have been idle?"

Essex shook his head.

Blount went on. "I have dispatched a message to Edinburgh urging the King of Scots to press his claim to succession on the death of the Queen."

"A Scottish king on England's throne."

"Better than a Spaniard, Robert. The King of Scots is to assemble a large force on the border, just to make good his demand, and I shall muster four or five thousand and bring them across the Irish Sea into Wales. I warrant that we shall soon get a declaration from Whitehall that will lay forever that old bogey of Essex as King of England."

But Essex was no longer listening. The words "across the Irish Sea" had stuck in his mind, and he fixed his accusing gaze on the other. So Mountjoy was going to succeed him in Ireland. He would be Lord Lieutenant, after all! They leveled looks. Each read the other's thoughts.

"I wish you joy of your venture," said Essex icily.

"Robert, well do you know that I have never sought the Irish appointment. I even begged to be excused; I have ample reason for wishing to remain at home."

Between them lay the unspoken thoughts that rose from their long intimacy of friendship. Penelope—ah, the parting from her would go sore. And the Queen's command—Essex suddenly smiled. The old mercurial flash! Of course Mountjoy would serve him in Ireland, better even than here. He was cordial again.

"Forgive me, Charles. My confinement has made me crabbed. I am not fit company for man or beast. You are welcome to the bogs and fogs. God grant you escape better than I did."

He had left his honor on a green field in County Meath and the memory galled him.

Gloriana made up her mind. She would heal this sore that bruised it continually. Accordingly she gave orders for Essex to be heard in Star Chamber, temporarily convened at York House.

The judges arrived, grave and portly, all eighteen of them, to assemble in the Lord Keeper Egerton's library. Round the massive oaken table, its legs tortured into the bulbous Tudor grotesquerie, they sat. Velvet and soft-leather shoon rested on the long stretcher beneath, and on the table top, among the papers relating to the Lord Essex Expedition to Ireland, rested the white, blue-blooded hands.

Among the company sat Bacon. Like the others', his face showed nothing of what he was thinking. Like the others, he was ill-informed of the reasons for the Earl's miserable failure. To the suggestion that the Queen and the Council by any slight defection might have contributed to this failure, shoulders were politely shrugged. They were not met to pass judgment on Queen or Council. They were met to censure the Earl of Essex, whose fiasco in Ireland had put them all into a cruel dilemma.

He came in, tall and pale, elegantly dressed in soft gray worked with gold. The return to the house where he had spent so many bitter weeks had shaken his nerve. But he was steadfast. His agitation showed only when he played with the Italian stiletto on the fretted belt chain or drew out his yellow kerchief to wipe his fingers.

He was commanded to kneel. He did so, steadying himself on fever-weak knees as he went down. His crimes were now enumerated. The disobedience over Southampton; the fatal march to the south; the indiscriminate knighting of men; the shameful peace with Tyrone; the forbidden return with armed men.

Essex shifted his weight to one knee. Here the Archbishop, a man of God, suggested in a whisper that the accused might be allowed a cushion for his aching bones. Essex thanked them cynically and slipped the little velvet pad beneath his knees. The relief was agonizing.

Coke, his fine nose elevated to a fastidious angle, now launched into a windy commentary. All was high sound and pious intention. Essex studied the egg-and-dart beveling on the table edge, and ignored the Attorney's thrust. But the last one he could not ignore. It was a deadly blow.

"And there is little doubt in my mind but that the Lord of Essex fully intended joining forces with Tyrone in rebellion against our true government."

His chin went up as if struck. In a daze he saw the Attorney gather his robes to sit, and he heard the command addressed to him to rise. His bones hurt him sharply as he dragged himself up, his head whirling from Coke's abominable accusation.

They continued the examination. Essex grew steadily whiter, until at last, with a soft groan, he reeled against the table. Again the Archbishop intervened. Essex was allowed to lean against the table. He prayed that God would spare him the humiliation of fainting.

Now Bacon rose. All this time he had been studiously avoiding the sick eye of the prisoner.

"First, honorable judges, I wish to lay aside any bond of affection or duty that I have ever owed to the Lord of Essex. There comes a time when private feelings must give way to those of nobler import, those of love and duty that are owed the realm."

He cleared his throat, his voice dry and husky as the rustle of a snake across a rough floor.

Essex now stared. Bacon produced a passionate letter written by Essex to Egerton after the Queen had boxed his ears and the Lord Keeper attempted to lay the quarrel between them. This Bacon read. As he read, the letter lost nothing of his smarting denunciation. No, no, it cannot be; this is a dream, a nightmare, thought Essex.

It was no dream. His own words rang out clearly in the room. "Cannot princes err? Cannot subjects suffer? Is an earthly power or authority infinite?"

Here in this quiet place the words sounded violent, revolutionary. Essex glared at the court. The judges sat silent, their faces set in shocked and rigid lines. Ah, the desiccated Solomons, could they not feel for a man in the heat of his injury? Had they never been lashed into white-hot fury of righteous anger?

But—and now rolled over him a feeling of deathly sickness. He had trusted Egerton, yes, and Bacon. This was the result. A light sweat broke over him and black spots swam before his eyes. They brought him a stool and blindly he sank down, folding his long legs under him. He had been standing and kneeling close to three hours.

Bacon laid down the letter. Now he picked up a book. God's death, what now?

It was Hayward's book with its damning dedication. What—what was this—no more than just another book addressed to him. Lord, there were many of these, more than a man had time to notice. Ah, the dedication! Treasonable, was it? They would stop at nothing to drag him to perdition. He looked at Bacon; but this man was a stranger to him, someone he no longer knew.

At last they allowed him to speak. He slipped to his knees and, for one fleeting second, rested his head on his folded hands. Then he raised it.

"First, gentlemen, let me say that since her Majesty has graciously been pleased to spare me the humiliation of a public trial, I had not expected to say anything. Had I come prepared to speak in my own behalf, I could say naught but this: I have never swerved in my loyal intention to my Queen and my country. I have left it to go to a place full of sickness and misery, and I have endured the rigors of military life when I would fain have been at home with my family." A pause. "All this I have gladly undertaken in the advancement of my country's glory."

Some of the lords, remembering the Earl's panting eagerness to fight abroad, were not impressed. But in the eye of more than one susceptible judge a tear glistened. Essex ran his finger round the inside of his ruff and went on.

He felt deadly weak, but he must give his categorical denial of these abominable charges. Full explanations were what he desired most to give, but as he unfolded his defense, he saw how the court fidgeted. Ah then, had they come armed against his innocence? So it seemed. It was time to play his trump card. Fumbling within his doublet, he brought out the Queen's patent.

"As to my disobedience in returning to her Grace unbidden—" he flung the letter to the table where it skittered among the nervous hands of his judges. A mild hubbub arose—they were put about by so unexpected a disclosure. Coke rose hastily and cut him short. Ignoring the letter, he proceeded to the censure. How well the criminal record was related—how eagerly the judges corroborated and agreed! At length they let him go. A carriage awaited to take him home.

The stairs of his house seemed long and steep. It was all he could do to get upstairs and hide himself behind closed doors. He drank the wine that Joseph gave him and fully dressed, fell onto his bed.

When they described the scene to Elizabeth, she went very pale and her mouth quivered.

To Egerton she said, "There will be more talk that we have dealt harshly with my lord. I would that this thing had not happened." Then she fell silent. Suddenly her voice was loud. "I shall release him. He has suffered enough. Take the guard away from Essex House. He is to come and go at will."

Softly she beat her hands together and walked about her rooms at Whitehall. This crisis on her very doorstep kept her unwillingly in London, though her soul yearned for Rylands or Richmond. Oh, for one hour with my father, she thought, he would know what to do with this damned thing.

Pacing the gallery, she stopped to stare at him, as he straddled under a delicate arch, his pale family grouped about him. There he stood, a brilliant, compelling figure, mouth set, eyes staring coldly ahead. She shuddered and her very soul recoiled. How well she knew that dreadful vengeance! No nonsense, if a man stood before him, armed friends at his back, he would have known what to do.

And even in her shuddering, so did she. Her father's daughter after all, she clenched her will to be a true Tudor. Grimly she concentrated on the picture of Essex, in mud and sweat, dominatingly before her— those men at her door. . . . She clapped her hands.

"The guard to remain on the Earl of Essex."

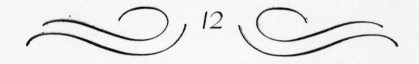

Disaster

The summer wore on. Relieved at long last of his guard, Essex went down into the country. He walked about his gardens among the ripening fruit and the falling leaves, and for long hours he stood on the leads of his house, looking up at the twisted rose-colored chimneys or gazing out over the distant horizon. His strength returned to him, food lost its feverish taste, and life, though tinged with somber hues, seemed more worth the living.

Although Gloriana had relented enough to permit him his freedom, he was not allowed to approach her. He still did not know the exact state of her feelings. Constantly he thought of seeing her again. If only he could lay eyes on her, he could then discover what was in her heart for him.

Frances was with him and the children played about him on the lawns, running among the bright formal flower beds, shouting under the oaks. Baby Frances was getting her first pearly teeth, and when her father lifted her up to his face, she smiled on him. Young Robert, his heir, was growing a tall pale lad, shut up all day long with a tutor, as he himself was at ten years old. His stepdaughter Elizabeth Sidney, a tiny-breasted maiden of sixteen, already betrothed to the sprig of a neighboring manor, was busy preparing to be wed in the autumn. All was going well with everyone within the household, except himself.

On a bright August morning he and Cuffe were playing tennis. He laughed to think how three months earlier he would have swooned in the heat, much less been able to run a ball on a hard court. Now they stood in the shade of a horse chestnut and wiped the sweat off their necks while they drank cold whey from brown earthen jugs.

"Your lordship improves."

"Aye, Cuffe. Now if I could be assured of the sweet wines farm, I should rest easy for the time."

It would soon be Michaelmas, and his right to farm the custom from sweet wines would run out. Ever since the gilded days of the Armada he had enjoyed the income from this valuable commodity. It had been his financial backbone.

"The wolf will gnaw at my door for a certainty, should the Queen not renew my patent."

But he spoke with a certain lightness, for he could not believe that after so many years Elizabeth would take from him his main means of support.

With veiled anxiety Cuffe eyed his master. It would be like Gloriana to take this means of further chastising the Earl. Always touchy herself where money was concerned, she whipped those who offended her with a little golden flail.

In a fever of tormented expectation, Essex awaited the outcome of the issue. He dated everything up to the end of September. The early days of October would decide his fate.

"If your lordship's fortunes are not increased . . ." suggested Cuffe.

"That being the case, Cuffe, I shall bury myself forever in the country and forget how ambition led me to shine as the bright star I have been."

Again he spoke with a lightsomeness he did not feel. In his secret heart he knew if the patent were not renewed, his life would be over; he thought he would rather be dead than have this happen to him.

He wound the restless skein of his energy into a ball by writing to the Queen. Pathetic, impassioned, he begged that she discipline him, but not ruin him. He beseeched leave to come to Court. ". . . if only to kiss that fair correcting hand and display my confidence in Gloriana's royal word. . . ."

The Queen read the letters. If she was moved by them, those about her knew it not. She folded her thin lips together and kept her head high.

Insensible to remorse, Bacon inscribed to Essex a letter. Essex read it once, twice. How coldly intellectualism dictated the academic explanation! Between the measured lines of careful script it was easily apparent that Bacon knew on which side his bread was spread. And this . . . was this pity?

> . . . for as I was ever sorry that your lordship should ever fly with waxen wings, doubting Icarus' fortune, so for the growing up of your own feathers, especially ostrich's or any other's save of a bird of prey, no man shall be more glad.

So Bacon was sorry, was he, to see his old friend choose the way of Icarus, to fly too near the sun! Would he have rejoiced, then, to see fair white wings springing from the Earl's shoulders, to bear him aloft to fame and fortune? Ostrich's feathers . . . fine to see, but too feeble by far to bear aloft the great bird body. Essex seized his pen.

> . . . I never flew with other wings than desire to merit, and confidence in my Sovereign's favor; and when one of these wings failed me, I would light nowhere but at my Sovereign's feet, though she suffered me to be bruised with my fall.

This Bacon showed to the Queen. At the last words her heart throbbed. She spent a sleepless night, and next morning, through her chamberlain, commanded Bacon to avoid her.

Essex took long rides with only Adam Baxter for attendant. There was healing in the sweet English countryside and he basked in the warm sun of the meadows. One day the two rode past a thatched cottage and turned into a field high with moonpennies and scarlet poppies. They ate a frugal meal of bread and cheese and drank from a leather bottle that Baxter unslung from his saddle.

Essex lay on his back in the feathery bloom of the field and gazed up through the lacy living curtain to the blue sky. He pulled a straw from his mouth and tossed it away.

"Adam, you're a simple enough fellow. What is it in a man makes him struggle to get preferment? Now, here we are in this sweet spot. What more could man desire than what is here?"

Squatting on his heels, Baxter looked at the distant horizon and the yearning for the sea was in his eyes. "I cannot say, my Lord. I only know we have to follow what's in us, willy-nilly."

"By God," said Essex softly, "that's it. You're right, Adam." Then he sat up and looked curiously at his servant, seeing him clearly for the first time, unobscured by circumstance. "But you, Adam, you are for the sea, 'twas what you told me that first time I saw you down at Plymouth. Why, then, do you say—ah!"

He broke off. The other was looking straight at him, his eyes steady and somber. Adam Baxter had forsaken the sea for what was stronger in him, for love of his master.

Essex got to his feet. There was a small ache in his throat, and with no more words he turned and mounted Saladin. The other fell in behind.

They had ridden far and the full disc of the harvest moon was making a glory of the heavens when they turned into the park at Wanstead.

"Good night, Adam, and—my thanks." Essex walked tiredly into his house. There was no sign of a courier from London.

The nerves of all at Wanstead were on the stretch. Everyone in the Earl's household knew what the renewal of the sweet wines lease meant to him and to all of them. Essex now hung about the house, loath to miss the courier who at any moment might come clacketing into the courtyard with the welcome news. Friends rode down from the city and the house was loud with denunciations of Bacon and Cecil and the Ralegh faction. They urged the Earl to move.

Southampton was impatient. "Odds-fish my skin! There are hundreds who wait your words, Essex! My purse is open to you; why hesitate?"

Essex shook his head. He would do nothing till the matter of the sweet wines was cleared up. A false move now might ruin all.

"The hell with it!" growled Southampton, now really angry. He stamped out of the house. "We will seek gayer company," he told his men as they turned their horses back to London. He would leave the Earl to his gloomy procrastination.

As for Essex, he called to Cuffe and went into his writing cabinet, there to compose more letters to Whitehall. Striding about the small room, he dictated to a fidgeting secretary another pleading appeal to the Queen.

Suddenly Cuffe threw down the pen, exasperation for once mastering caution. Long illness and long service had drawn the two men close. In his weakness and preoccupation Essex tolerated from his dependants what sometimes amounted to incivility. But this time Cuffe overstepped the mark.

"Good God, my lord, is this to be the meat you feed the Queen? Why do you not assert yourself? Are you not Lord Marshal of all England, far fitter to rule than an elderly woman, whose day is done, and whose mind is one turmoil of indecision?"

Essex stared. "You forget yourself, Henry," he said coldly.

"On the contrary, I remember myself." A fanatic light glowed in Cuffe's pale blue eyes. "I remember myself, and all of us who have lain at your lordship's feet, no matter what the mud through which you have been pleased to wade." At Essex's stupefied silence he gathered courage. "You have shown yourself to be low-spirited in this affair, nay, fainthearted, and you have relied on men of slender and weak judgment, instead of drawing to you men of stout heart and enforcing your demands with iron."

Now Essex found his voice. He roared. "By God's passion! I will not stand this from a servant. You look above yourself, my man. Henceforth you are none of mine. You are free of my service from this moment. Now, get out!"

Cuffe stood like a stone, his bloodless lips quivering. So this was the end of a lifetime of service. All the best years of his life poured out at the Earl's feet—for this. He turned on his heel and left.

Essex clapped his hands. "Fetch Meyrick!"

Sir Gelly Meyrick, his Steward, hurried in, his round face full of trouble. He had seen Cuffe getting together his belongings, and heard his side of the story.

Essex, still pale, now had his voice under command. "Meyrick, I have this day dismissed that impudent pen-pusher. Strike his blasted name off my books."

Meyrick hesitated, then bowed and left. In his small office he took down the books of the Earl's household. He turned the yellow pages and sought among the fine script for the date of Cuffe's entrance into the service of the Devereux. Why, God's blood, the man had been secretary to the Earl since before the Armada! Meyrick leaned back in his chair and toyed absently with his long clay pipe. What a tremendous store of information must reside within the wily brain of Cuffe; what secrets must be his! He took a paper and wrote:

To Master Henry Cuffe, Secretary to the most noble Lord of Essex:
I pray you to repose and to take no new service until I can resolve the

present difficulty between my lord and you. Be assured that my heart is yours in this matter, and that the welfare of my lord is also deeply touched in this.

G. Meyrick

At the Manor of Wanstead on September 3, 1600.

Essex whiled away the long September twilights with cards, at which his mother and sister joined him. In the absence of Mountjoy, Penelope, still the lovely velvet charmer, rested her black eyes on young Southampton, whose wife was with her mother. She flirted lazily with him, while her mother looked on and forbore to scold, and her brother, glad to have his friend once more with him, did not even notice. Frances sat at her tapestry frame and a slight smile hovered about her lips. Expecting another child, she was glad the astrologers had predicted another boy. A new son would divert her husband.

And still no decision on the sweet wines. More frantically now, Essex wrote, coming out openly to beg that his substance might not be cut from him. In the absence of Cuffe, Reynolds wrote from his dictation, and he missed the long spare frame of his old secretary bending over the table.

The letters reached the Queen. "Hum," she commented to Bacon, whom she had lately admitted to her presence once more, "my lord of Essex has written me some very dutiful letters and I have been moved by them; but what I took for abundance of heart, I find only to be a suit for the farm of sweet wines."

Bacon fixed his eyes on Anne Boleyn's ornate little clock on the farther wall and said nothing. Silence these days was much the better part of wisdom.

Then came one letter that touched her heart's core. It was so moving, so pitiful, that she could no longer bear it. To the devil with it all! If indeed the Earl were pining, languishing, despairing, as he said, she would amend it without delay.

"Go fetch him to me," she said to Harington.

At the message his heart leaped. The blood beat in his head and suddenly he felt light as air. It was over; she had given in. He had won!

He laughed aloud and snapped his fingers at the dogs, at the children. He clasped Frances round her thickening waist and strained her to him. He teased Elizabeth Sidney about her approaching nuptials. He was gay and young again; he rode the rosy clouds of triumph. Once again he had won!

Then with a group of his disgruntled noblemen he took horse for London. They did not share their leader's ebullience of spirit. Behind his back they muttered in their beards. Danvers rode his gray close to young Sandys, whose father headed the troop with Harington and the Earl. Danvers was among the disappointed ones.

"This is not what we planned," he said in a low voice to Sandys. "We shall never line our pockets if things turn this way."

"No. I was all for taking arms. This is what comes of writing letters. Let my lord become once more the flunkey, and then, what of us."

"Aye." Danvers was glum.

But the happy Earl, oblivious of their glares and murmured complaints, rode forward to the longed-for meeting. The purple Michaelmas daisies were feathering in the hedges and as they rode past the front of an estate, their nostrils were suddenly full of the overpowering scent of wallflowers that clothed with living velvet the low stone wall. Did Essex think of that other dreamlike ride when he went to meet Tyrone? If he did, it all seemed years ago. They paused on the brow of a hill to see London shimmering in the autumn haze, its massed spires and towers piercing the pale blue sky. With a shout, Essex shot forward to the river road and Whitehall.

He tarried long enough to put his dress in order, then bounded, two at a time, like a boy, up the Queen's private staircase. In his hand he held a spray of heliotrope daisies.

He went in and found her dressed in yellow, powdered with sequins. She stood by her chair, the tip of one long finger pressed against its arm; to conceal the shaking of her other hand she held a small ivory book.

They gazed at each other and the bitter year that had divided them rolled away. Still holding the spray of flowers, he sank onto his knees and lifted her dress to his lips.

At first she could not speak. She looked at the drooping auburn head, the broad bowed shoulders. A choking rose in her throat, but she swallowed it down. She bent and lifted the flowers from his hand and held them to her face. They smelled of the sweet outdoors.

"How is it, my lord, in the country?" He had come from the fragrant places while she was a prisoner within her gray walls and spires.

"It is a desert where you are not, Madam." His eyes were on the tip of shoe that showed beneath her gown. "I am humble before your Grace's goodness of heart. It is more than I deserve."

"It is," she agreed.

Still the silver-tongued courtier. How could she tell if his heart were true? Was this not another of his glittering tricks to worm his way back into her graces? Ah, but if it were, how well he knew the way to her heart!

"Robert, you write so fair a letter that a woman is hard put to it to withstand you."

She felt rather than saw the winning smile that crossed his face. He raised his eyes to her hand that trembled still against the arm of her chair. Now she could see the lines of pain about the mouth, the fascinating green eyes, shadowed with a new strange caution, the smooth brow creased into an anxious line. Ah, he had suffered and, Christ's blood, so had she!

She put her hand on his shoulder. "God knows, Essex, I have held for you naught but love in my heart till your wild, willful ways drove out that sweet blossom and planted bitter rue in its place." She pushed him slightly back, and now he looked at her.

The white face had become more masklike than ever, the spots of rouge standing out like the last haggard bloom of the dying rose. The eyes were filmed with sorrow, the lips compressed, the gestures jerky. The flaming silk of the wig screamed her age, and for all their fretful glitter, her elaborate spangles could not divert the eye from the withered skin and sagging throat. Unable to bear his appraisal, she moved restlessly aside.

The old inexplicable riddle was there again. What did he really feel for her? She had to know—nay, she would know. The Tudor in her resolved to put him, once and for all, to the test. She would discover the answer to this tormenting nightmare of uncertainty.

"Tell me, Robert, why you were so anxious to come to me?"

"To pay my duty, and to learn from your Grace's own lips that I am forgiven, and to assure you——"

"Robert," she took the plunge, "if I were not to renew the farm of sweet wines, would your love and duty to me be the same?"

He caught his breath, looked up, startled. Not renew! Did she not realize, then, that he would be ruined? He would have to sell his homes, dismiss his staff, live like a private gentleman, he the Lord Marshal of all England! Not renew!

Her hawk's eye had caught the quick dismay that flashed across his face. So that was really it. He had come only to make sure his financial future, and she, no longer the adored mistress, was but a barren old woman. Rage flared in her.

"Get out!" she screamed. "Out, out! Let the sight of you trouble me no more! Well do I know that I am only your golden dolly!"

Mouth open, he rose hastily, took a step toward her. With the strength of an old madwoman she thrust him back.

"Begone, begone!"

Sobbing and panting, she sank into a chair and beat on the arm of it. Misery, misery!

He went rigidly down the steps, looking not to right or left. Joseph and Baxter still stood by the horses he had left but moments before. Where the others were, he neither knew nor cared. He mounted and turned his horse's head up the river.

To Chartley he went, for he could not face his family with this new failure. There he stayed, stunned, paralyzed by this worst disaster of all. Danvers rode down to see him.

"I bring good news, Robert. The Queen has spoken of you and the sweet wines."

Again with this man, he stood under another tree, this time a great oak, but their topic the same. Moodily he pushed about the leaves with his toe, not looking up from the ground.

"Humph! If her Grace has indeed spoken of me, 'twould be to assure whoever heard her that I should not have the farm of the wines. I can do naught these days to please her."

"Nay, my lord, it was to me she spoke, and with her old smile. While she did not actually say you should have the wines, at least she said the matter was as yet undecided."

At that he raised his head and for a long time gazed off into the distance. Then, "I cannot believe she will cut me off, Danvers. *I cannot believe it.*"

The two men went into the house.

Hope renewed even faintly, Essex forced himself to ride abroad every day, that he might nurse the chance of finding a messenger from Court upon his return. At least if he were away all day, he could not positively know the worst. But each night, ere dusk, unable to bear the suspense any longer, he put his horse to the gallop, the last mile a heart-thudding expectation.

Twice a rider came in from Wanstead, once late in the evening when he had gone to bed. The sharp rise of breathless presumption was only equaled by the agonizing declension of spirit as each messenger proved not to be the one for whom his taut nerves stretched into an eternity of waiting.

And so a slow month crawled along.

Then the blow fell. The messenger came, the letter was snatched and torn tremblingly open. Gloriana announced that henceforth the revenue from the sale of sweet wines would be reserved for the Crown. Essex was a ruined man.

It was over, the long misery of not knowing. The last flame of his attachment to her flickered out and the embers grew cold. It was an icy fire of hate that burned in him now, and he swore that if making her pay cost him his life, the death would come sweet. He sent for Cuffe and offered him double pay to pocket his feelings and return. Essex had need once more of the wily brain and calm nerves of his old servant.

He flung caution to the winds. In his first frenzy he stalked among his excited friends at Wanstead and raved. Among the strange, reckless band, no tongue was more caustic than his, no vow more wild, no shaking denunciation of the Queen and the government too strong.

"The Queen!" he cried bitterly. "Pah! Her conditions are as crooked as her carcass!"

A great shout of derisive mirth roared wildly up to the high ceiling of the hall where he and his cronies were gathered about the fire. Sitting on the settle in the shadows, his fine eyebrows raised, was Malcolm Malby. He still hung about the Devereux, but Ralegh's gold, payment for services rendered, lay in his pouch. He hoped to play his cards so well that Robert Cecil, the Queen's Secretary, would find use for his talents.

In a small room high up in one of the towers of Nonesuch, Katherine Fytton sat before a mirror. She pinched a little color into her pale cheeks and touched her lips with coralline salve. She was meeting Malby, and at the thought that he came from Essex, her heart, under the black velvet bodice, gave a great jump.

The years had taken something of the presumption from Katherine. Almost entirely gone was the dashing air, the fire and color of youth. Within, the heart was reckless and rebellious as ever, and ever truer to her youth, for, on it she bore the mark of Robert Devereux. It would be with her to her grave. She would go on giving herself to men who were near him, who had his trick of the eye or turn of the head. Till she was old, she would go on deluding herself that once again she lay in his arms, that the man who pressed her to him in the darkness was Essex, who for that brief, beautiful time had been her lover.

Oh, Essex! How sadly short was that time when he came from Spain into her open arms. With all the mad passion of a love long denied she had adored him. She could have held him, too, had that bitch Pamela Bridges not stepped across his path. After he became infatuated with the Surrey girl, he had eyes for no other woman, and now that she was dead, it seemed that he never would forget her.

Katherine's slender connection with the Devereux household was through Malby, and it was from his supercilious lips that she gathered her scraps of information. She lived in a misery of moods, alternating between despair, then rage and thwarted love, and worst of all, to fear —fear for Essex. She knew that she was expected to drop intelligence gleaned from Malby into the right ear. He had need of her, for through his connection with the Essex party, he was in bad odor. But so far her hands were clean; not one scrap of news of the Devereux faction had gone from her.

She rose and, with a small sigh, went off to meet her latest unloved lover.

She found him in a state of quiet triumph. He now had something to pass on that might amply repay all his old grudges against Essex. For this he had waited, and now the fish had come right to his net.

Behind a locked door they faced each other. He, tall, dark, saturnine, with a sarcastic droop to his lip, and she, scarcely able to conceal a painful eagerness that rose in her throat, shutting off her breath, so that she panted a little.

Malby smiled. He knew she did not love him, that she permitted him her favors only in return for news of Essex. This he fed her in small, thin morsels, keeping her always starved and half-frantic. He observed the rise of her bosom and her short breathing.

"Dare I hope that you are overcome at sight of me, my Katherine?"

"I—I am always glad to see you, Malcolm." She forced herself to speak calmly. Would he begin to speak of Essex before the love-making, or would she have to endure the hateful travesty until, satisfied, he would begin his round of gossip? She hid her trembling hands in her long skirts and raised herself in the chair to look at him.

"You are glad to see me, my dear, because I come from him." Never before had they dragged their secret intent to the open light. At her startled look he went on, "No, no, do not deny it. I am not exactly a fool."

She let her head droop.

"Very well," went on the drawling voice. "We shall speak of him. And when we have finished, you shall carry the interesting intelligence to Lady Worcester. Her husband will know what to do."

"No, no!" she cried. "I will do nothing to hurt him."

Malby filled a little cup with wine, drank it slowly, and carefully set it down again. Then he flicked the lace at his wrist. "Yet he has hurt you, and grievously."

"That is a matter between the Earl and me." She spoke with difficulty.

"Then I can only assume that you do not know what he says of you." The dark eyes were on her now, and she shivered with apprehension.

"What do you mean?"

He looked at her, his head bent to one side, his voice fluid with pity. "I mean that the Earl has boasted on more than one occasion of your favors, of your devotion, so much so, that only last night, at wine with us all, he promised you to Cuffe, as a small reward for loyal service."

In fascinated horror she stared at him, her face against the black velvet, chalk-white.

"My lord declares that you would do anything he asks—even that." His eyes glittered and held her, trancelike, and between them the hateful words were still warm on the air, forcing themselves into her brain, till she could have shrieked.

"It is not true! It is not true! You cannot prove so monstrous a thing."

Sadly he shook his head. "Would that everything were as easy, my dear." His hand now caressed her shaking shoulder. "There are half a dozen men who rode with me to town tonight, any one of which——"

"No!" She pressed cold hands to her eyelids. "Let me think. I want to think."

Like a stone she sat, while warily he watched her. He did not intend she should sit thinking long, till her reason told her that this thing could not be, and she believed what she wished to believe. Also, she might demand proof, and it would be tiresome to have to bribe someone to a lie. For another minute he watched her, a cold, still, beautiful statue with burnished hair, as she sat before him in her rich gown.

"Do not let it upset you, my Katherine. He is not worthy of a second thought. He is like that with all—even with me, who offered him my heart's blood. However, you are fortunate."

She broke her silence. "How fortunate?"

"You can strike back at such a rogue. You can make him wish he had never known you, much less—flouted you."

It was the right word. She flushed as she remembered, aye yes, the dozens of times he had done just that, in lesser ways, teasing and tormenting her, daring her with Pamela, deliberately flicking her on the raw of her passion for him. She caught her lip under a tooth.

"Give me some wine."

When she had drunk, she rose. The color had come back into her lips and her eyes flashed coldly. "What is it you wish me to do, Malcolm?"

He told her.

Eyes narrowed, she listened. Then as he finished, he sat back, while she came toward him. Sinking onto his knee, she offered him her red mouth and pressed his hand to her swelling breast.

The word reached Egerton. Mindful of the Earl's surliness when under his surveillance, the worthy Lord Keeper deemed it his duty to tell her Majesty what her erstwhile favorite was saying down at Wanstead. Katherine saw him making for the Queen's cabinet, and her intuition told her what he meant to do. To her tower room she fled, locking the door, to lie shaking on her bed. Her hour of triumph should have been high; it was ashes in her mouth.

"Her conditions are as crooked as her carcass!" The horrible words were spoken. In silent incredulous pain, Elizabeth heard them. Into her drawn face came a look of anguish. Like Katherine, like all the women to whom Essex had been tender, she felt at first only a shocked disbelief.

"Are you sure?" Her lips were like clay. "Are you sure?"

"Sir Malcolm Malby is here, Majesty, he will corroborate——"

A violent shudder shook her. "No."

None should come to gaze upon her wound. She would cover it up, hide it from the world, this mortal hurt he had dealt her. She had seen Essex in rages, she knew what his dreadful tongue could do. She had heard him on the subject of others who had aroused in him so fierce an enmity. She knew, she knew it was true. It had the ring of authenticity.

She crouched by the fire and in her eyes was a look of death. "Let him venture to touch my scepter," she said in a shaking voice to Cecil, "and I'll have his head."

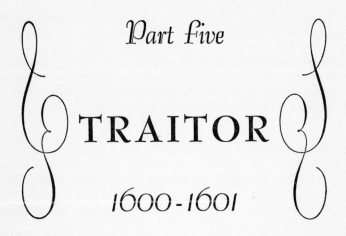

Part Five

TRAITOR

1600-1601

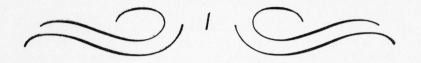

The Tree of Treason

*I*t was a restless throng that eddied about the Earl and ministered to his madness. The dissatisfied minority rallied to his support. They were men of property who grumbled at heavy taxes that were ruining them and complained of corruption in high places. The matter of the sweet wines, curiously enough, had opened the whole aching sore of Crown grants to favorites.

The Puritans, men of religion, fired by fantastic evidences of venery in the Anglican clergy, were for the Earl of Essex, under whom they sought liberty of teaching and opinion. The Catholics pinned their hopes on men of their faith, who were among the Earl's best friends. The young men, who had neither faith nor politics, flocked to him, for in their revolt against the old school they saw in the romantic figure of Essex their great white hope of a new era.

The soldiers still worshiped him as their legendary hero and gave to him a greater devotion than that enjoyed by any former general. He even had friends at Court among those who truly pitied him his consistent ill fortune and who did not see that his difficulties were the inevitable outcome of his own nature. In their eyes the tragic failure of so promising a young man was due, not to his own defects, but rather to the villainy of his enemies.

The seeds of treason grew and flourished. Already the plant was above ground and putting out leaves. When it blossomed, all hell would burst over England; when it fruited, some would feast. Would the fruit be sweet or bitter—would it go down easily or set the teeth on edge?

Everything depended on Essex. What would he do?

The malcontents now gathered at Essex House and the Earl sat with them of nights and listened to their wild talk. He rested his chin on his breast and thrust out his lower lip. They babbled on about Cecil and his faction. They told him the Secretary was working for a Spanish succession. His imagination rose again; the old anti-Spanish obsession took hold of his mind.

"You are right," he told them. "On the Queen's death, the Crown will be offered to the Infanta. I see it all clearly."

He believed he was correct. Hell's fire, look about and see how Cecil and his intimates had feathered the nest to their advantage. Buckhurst and Howard, bosom friends of the little Secretary, held the Treasury and the Navy. Burghley, Cecil's older brother, was Lord President of the North, and Carew, their eager coadjutor, was the new Governor of the Irish Council. On Elizabeth's death these would converge to place the Crown in Spanish hands.

Mountjoy? Ah, there, too, was a bitter open wound. Arriving in Ireland, Mountjoy had briskly set about the business of subduing Tyrone, where he had been miraculously successful. In his success he seemed to have quite forgotten his conversation with the Earl before the fire at York House. He no longer intended to enforce the Scottish claim, and to all of Essex's letters he replied with a veiled obscurity that was maddening, disheartening—sickening. Another old friend had discovered that loyalty to the Earl of Essex was personally dangerous and was withdrawing gently from the perilous proximity.

Excited letters went north from Essex House, urging the King of Scotland to send the Earl of Mar to London to advance his claim to the succession ere it was too late. From the tone of the letters the Scottish earls might have concluded that Elizabeth was on her deathbed, but they cannily kept their heads.

Stuart James sat in his castle at Edinburgh and stroked his ugly chin. Men had had their heads lopped off for jumping too eagerly at that spiked wonder, the English Crown. He thought of his mother, dead under the ax at Fotheringay. Wheest! He would rule England, of that he had no doubt, but he would rule it legitimately, and from the reports of his agents, Gloriana was in good health, and suffered only from bad temper. He knew that on her deathbed she would name her successor, and not before. Any movement in that direction on his part would immediately be construed as treason. No, Stuart James would remain calm. He sent seven careful lines of noncommittal writing to Essex and kept the Earl of Mar at home.

Essex read the seven lines, interpreted them as suited him, and concealed the little paper in a tiny black leather bag he wore within his breast.

Late one night the chief protagonists of the Essex faction met in the library. They sat about the table, for all the world like a Privy Council. Essex was at the head, Southampton at the foot, and ranged on the sides were Danvers, the two Sandys, Christopher Blount; there was also a dark, oily little man, Sir Ferdinando Gorges, whom Essex had picked up on a campaign, who ran ever at his side, like a small, alert jackal.

Like a Privy Council they were indeed, in all save wisdom and reason. The room was ill lighted, and blood and terror lurked in the shadows. Down at one end of the table sat Harington, his face twisted with trouble. He wished fervently that Mountjoy were here to put the drag on the heavy coach that threatened to plunge them into disaster as it careened crazily down the long hill. But Mountjoy was not here. Wild folly held the reins and the road ahead was mired with danger.

Tonight the talk was more violent than ever, and when actual plans for a rebellion developed, Harington, white to the lips, sprang up. "I'll come no more here!" he cried. "I've no desire to spill my blood on Tower Hill!" He rushed from the room.

With an oath Sandys jumped up, hand on his dagger. "Let me follow him and slit his yellow throat," he begged.

"No," restrained Essex. "Let him be. He'll not talk; that I know."

But the Queen's godson did talk, and Elizabeth was well informed of the treason plant that grew in the fertile soil about the great Gothic house at the bend of the river.

Essex cared not. Once more on the crest of a wave of assurance, he did not see how he could fail. Once in the saddle, everything would come right. And he would be greater than ever. He laughed a lot these days and his wild wit matched that of Southampton.

 343

As for Elizabeth, she cared naught either. "They plan a riot," she remarked contemptuously to Cecil. "Let them. We can soon take care of that."

"But, Madam, riots grow to rebellions, and then what?"

"Then, what?" Elizabeth's eyes sparkled. "Why, then, Cecil, I suppose the Tower. Compose yourself, my small Pygmy. There'll be no rebellion here. I have leaped puddles before; I can leap this."

It was Christmas again, and Elizabeth sought relief from her cares in entertainment of the Duke of Brachiano, fresh from Paris. She made an incredibly elegant progress to Blackfriars. In defiance of winter, she favored her usual pale colors, and though the day was overcast and gloomy, she stepped out bravely in a pearl-colored robe, surrounded by her gallants in well-braced silken hose and her ladies in white, yellow, and green, the colors of eternal hope. She went swinging in a litter under a delicately embroidered canopy.

Like the statue of some Eastern potentate she sat, silent and still on her high seat, looking stonily out over the heads of her people, forgetting to smile or to acknowledge their cheers. Scorning to lean against the cushions at her back, she held the "crooked carcass" stiff and straight. Her mouth was set in a bitter line and her eyes were veiled.

She gave a state banquet for the Duke and listened graciously to his compliments. In astounding Italian she replied, and if the Duke were less stunned than the Polish Ambassador by the linguistic dexterity, he was at least impressed, and ventured to say so. She poked her little fork at nothing, not listening, her busy mind full of Essex and what was passing down there at his house.

She danced. Archly she smiled at the Duke. "Tell your lord the King that the Queen of England still rides and dances like a maid!" she cried.

But when the long evening was done, she was ill and strained. Safe in her own apartments, she put a hand to her empty stomach.

"Bring broth."

They brought her the soup. At the first taste she roared out an oath and flung the mess, bowl and all, out the nearest window. "By my soul, the good God sends the food, and the Devil below sends the cook!"

Her harsh voice crashed into silence. Every nerve in her whole thin body was wracked and jangling. Oh, for some palliative to soothe ceaseless pain!

And now at Essex House things were going roughly. The Earl's followers fell out and snatched at each others' throats, each shouting his plan for invading the City. Wearily Essex told them to commit their ideas to paper; but they ranted and wrangled, and listening servants ran with the news. Council was kept advised of every move.

"Ha! 'Tis the pea in the shoe. I have had experience of this thing before," declared Elizabeth. Thirty years ago she had scotched the Earls of the North by the strategy of the unexpected. She would use the same now; she would steal a march by sending for Essex to demand an explanation.

She waited till the time was ripe. The Christmas and Twelfth Night gaieties were over and January wound its slow, cold way to February, which dawned with an early thaw.

Then, suddenly, Elizabeth was in terror. Not for herself and the Court, although here at Whitehall only a skeleton guard protected them. She was terrified for Essex. Well did she know that ardent nature, surrounded as it was by the worst friends that ever a man had. She feared for the day when he would take the fatal step; how swift would be the retribution, how dreadful the end!

Perhaps it would be better to give in on the matter of the sweet wines. It was true, he might get above himself and seek to rule her kingdom—but anything, even that, was better than rebellion and sudden death. Could she live with herself if she allowed him to run onto his doom without raising a finger to stop him?

But—he was so insolent. That last terrible insult on top of everything else—there was no knowing what he might say and do, once he had the whip hand. He had once said to her that men were better fitted to rule than women. He believed that. She had laughed at him then, for that was in the old days when they were free and easy with each other and such talk was only pastime.

This was deadly serious. The time had come to prove those light words to be either true or false. Could she see Essex on the throne, a warmongering hothead, who had so positive a genius for attracting to himself just the wrong sort of men for England's good? Let him rebel, if that were his resolve. Let him take his chance. Aye, let him take her throne—if he could. In the meantime they would make ready.

On the first week in February, Council met in special session. Katherine Fytton, ears strained for any echo that might come from the royal chamber, learned that it had been decided to summon the Earl to make answer to the loud rumors that floated from the windows of his home. Ever since her last revengeful stab at Essex she had been in a torment of regret. Now, to her overstrung imagination, he stood in deadly danger. Positive that this was a plot to get him unguarded and then take him prisoner, she determined to warn him.

She waited till evening, then wrapped in a heavy cloak, a light veil muffling her face, she slipped out by the side entrance and sped to the water-steps. No one saw her go or, if they did, thought her a palace servant going to a lovers' rendezvous. Down at the river landing under cover of the stairs waited a light skiff and the youth who was to row it.

"Good Dick," she breathed.

The lad had been bribed, but to serve such a lady, he would gladly have come for nothing. Katherine thought sadly how she now could command only the devotion of serving boys. She crouched in the stern, a forlorn figure with drooping shoulders, her face a white triangle in the dark frame of her hood. Her icy fingers curled round the handle of a tiny keen dagger that she wore in a velvet sheath at her girdle. She was deadly afraid of the black river with its lurking shadows. Now that the fog was rising, it looked more eerie than ever, and she shuddered to recall whispered tales of terror exchanged with other maids in warm beds, tales of dreadful deeds done under cover of the night.

But thoughts of Essex nerved her to do what she must. Afraid of the river as she was, she was more afraid of not being in time to warn him. Even now they might be on their way to arrest him.

"Oh, hurry, Dick!"

Vaguely, she wished she had worn a mask. No matter, the main thing now was to get to the Earl.

It was not far down the river. The lad sculled strongly against the tide and soon they were down at the bend. With scarcely a splash, they drew alongside the steps. The great mansion looked dark and silent.

"Wait for me here," whispered Katherine.

Tremblingly she ventured her shoe onto the first slippery step and drew herself out of the skiff. A footfall sounded on the other side of the wall. In a cold panic she shrank back. She shook in every limb. She knew she dared not go alone.

"Dick," she gasped.

Noiselessly the youth tied up and scrambled to her side. The two set off for the house that showed dim lights now in the frosty fog. Whoever had been on the other side of the wall had gone so far about his business that they slipped by unseen. They walked on the wet grass for fear of clattering on the brick walk, and Katherine scarcely drew breath till they were safe within the shadow of the ivy-grown walls.

Once there, her heart beat with a new anxiety. Now that she had come, how to get to the Earl? She looked helplessly up at the high walls and the closed casements as she realized that she did not know what next to do.

Suddenly a door from under a small portico opened, and the bright yellow light of a raised lantern cut through the gathering mist and fell full on them, the youth and the girl. Katherine, her eyes wide with fright, gasped again as she saw that the man with the lantern was Malby. She had walked right into the lion's jaws.

For a moment she was paralyzed. Then she rallied. "Oh, Malcolm," she uttered. "I-I have come to find you. I——"

It was no use. Malby, not in his usual urbane mood, was undeceived. A snarl lifted his thin lip and swiftly he was at her side. "In Christ's name, what do you do here? Get back to the river before you are seen!"

For a moment she hesitated. Then she turned away and mechanically walked over the grass, back to the stairs. Blowing out the lantern, Malby followed closely after. When they were once more on the cold landing, he seized her arm so tightly that she gave a smothered cry of pain.

"Fool! I should know better than to trust a woman. You came here to warn him." He gave her arm a shake and his voice was passionate with rage. "Answer me! Isn't that why you came?" Then his voice changed, and at this she was more frightened than ever. "Ah, I thought so. I trow you did not bargain to run against me." He gave a soft, savage laugh.

It was very quiet at the foot of the Essex steps. The river and its banks were swathed in swirling bands of mist. The great houses on the opposite side were menacing gray shapes, broken by the suffused yellow streaks of the lighted windows. To the girl it seemed a nightmarish kind of All Hallows' Eve. With mounting terror she looked about her.

Dare she break away and run screaming back to the house, to the mercy of Essex? But now Malby pushed her before him into the boat. Her chance was gone. He seated himself on the thwart beside her and signed to the boy to cast off. Dumbly the youth obeyed, then clambered in before them to his place at the oars.

In ominous silence they sculled down the river. Katherine felt as if she were in some horrid, soft labyrinth from which there was no escape. Somewhere outside, and here her heart gave a great jump, was Essex, and those who would destroy him because she had failed. Robert Devereux, the only man who had ever mattered to her, would——

God! She did not see the stealthy movement with which Malby drew his dagger and, raising his arm, sank it to the hilt between the boy's shoulders. The lad gave a cry and, before her staring eyes, flung out his arms, and fell sideways out of the boat, pitching them all into the cold moving water.

Katherine's scream was quickly stifled as she went under, but she struck out blindly and hit her hand against something solid, which she convulsively gripped. It was the edge of the boat, swinging heavily back on its little keel. Gasping, the girl clung with all her might to the solid object, while the water pulled and tore at her soaked skirts.

Dick had disappeared. Malby, hair plastered slimily to his round skull, now swam strongly over to her, splashing a good deal and blowing out his breath hoarsely as he came. Not a word had been spoken; it all seemed like some ghastly dream. This could not be happening. But now she caught sight of his face, saw the murder there, and knew he meant to kill her too. She opened her mouth to scream, and as an eddy swept her against the boat, felt something hard at her hip. It was the dagger.

She fumbled for her weapon. With a shudder of cold and apprehension, she set her teeth, for she feared terribly to let go her hold on the boat by even one finger. Now he was beside her, chattering in a set grimace with the cold. Without giving him time to raise his arm from the water, she struck with all her strength at his unguarded throat. To her surprise she hit him. With a kind of gurgle he clutched his neck and sank. At the same instant her fingers, numb and aching, lost their hold, and with a despairing cry, she saw the boat drift out of her reach as the dragging waters pulled her down.

At about the time that Katherine set off in her little skiff to go to her death, a messenger left the Council in a coach. He too, was bound for Essex House, with orders not to return without the Earl.

Some of Essex's friends, Southampton and the rest, had been across the river all afternoon at the play, *Richard the Second*. The performance, ordered by the young Earl, had been in the nature of a lesson to one or two fainthearted members of their band who feared to take sword against the government. Now, as the early darkness was falling about the city, they returned to dine with Essex. They were noisy, flushed, inspired by what they had seen. Their gusts of roaring laughter, as they roistered into the house, filled it with the sudden sound of high voices.

"What did I say?" Southampton laughed at one of them. "Rebellion's an easy dish when the meat is good and the cause is hot and deserving, like the fire that cooks it."

Cup in hand, Malby now lounged forward. "Did they play the piece in its entirety, Wriothesley, even the deposition scene?" He, being absorbed in matters of his own, had not accompanied them. "I seem to recall that particular scene as smelling unpleasantly in certain nostrils."

"Even so, my crony, the players gave the whole piece, and by my orders." Southampton was feeling reckless.

"Ah," murmured Malby, as he filled his cup from a jug on the table. "So the Earl of Southampton orders objectionable treason for the amusement of the playgoers."

"So you style it, Malby."

"No, no, I do not style it thus, my lord. 'Tis the label of the Queen and Cecil. 'Tis they who call it—treasonable. To my mind it is the best part of the play." Narrowly he watched the other.

"Quite," agreed Southampton dryly.

"But," went on the drawling voice, "what of the players, and you, my lord, when the Queen learns that the scene she ordered stricken out be put back into performance?"

Southampton stared unpleasantly at him. "Should you not like to run first with the news?" he sneered. He had never liked Malby, and since the Irish adventure he liked him still less; the fellow smelled of treachery.

"No need." Malby buried his dark face in the cup, drank, sighed, and put the cup on the hob. "The little river breezes will waft the news to Court soon enough."

There was a knocking on the outer door. The messenger from the Council was arrived to see my lord, and at once.

In he came, his face long and serious. He put a gauntleted hand to the cape brooch at his throat, then threw a quick glance about the hall. "Where is my lord?"

Malby jerked his head in the direction of the upper rooms, then, taking a black beaver from a peg, he left the hall. The jealous eye of Southampton watched him depart, then lighted back on the waiting messenger. Together they went upstairs.

But Malby, continuing on his way, turned down a narrow passage, and, helping himself to a lantern that sat on top of a court cupboard, he lit it carefully, then let himself out by the portico. There he came face to face with Katherine Fytton and the youth Dick.

Meanwhile, Southampton, arrived in the upper hall with the messenger, took from him the letter, leaving him leaning against the linen-fold panel, and entered the Earl's chamber. Essex was at supper with Chris Blount. He took the note and held it to the candelabra on the table.

"I am summoned to Court without further delay." Without looking up, he gestured in the direction of the veal pie in the silver dish. "I may not even finish my supper. Shut the door."

Southampton obeyed. Essex held out the letter and he read it. "A plot. On your life, do not go," he urged.

Christopher Blount read over Southampton's shoulder. "Has he read the other letter?" he asked Essex.

Essex handed Southampton another letter that lay beside the silver dish. Rapidly Southampton skimmed it. A friend warned Essex that there was a plot to murder him that very night. The assassins: Ralegh and Cobham.

Southampton whistled. "Cobham! Methought he was your friend."

Essex shrugged. "What man is my friend, Henry?" he said drearily. "Tell the messenger I will not go." He began to pick at his veal pie.

Henry Wriothesley put down the Council's summons, went out, noiselessly closing the door behind him. The messenger still leaned against the wall. Straight at him looked the young Earl.

"His lordship is ill tonight of a cold on his chest."

"Nevertheless, my lord, he must obey the summons."

Southampton beckoned the other to follow him to a small window set in a gable. This he pushed open. The white mist curled up from the river like smoke. The air was dripping and it sank into their lungs like a damp knife.

"It would be death for him to go out into that. Convey his lordship's regrets to the Council." Shutting the window, he looked blandly at the messenger.

"But—my orders—" he began. Then as Southampton made no reply, he turned and went downstairs out to his coach.

He had been told to bring the Earl. But did the Council know how many desperate youngbloods hung about the house of the Earl, ready to throw a messenger, gagged and bound, into a dark cellar room? Let them send a force if they wished to put their commands on the Earl of Essex.

But the Council was by no means ready to give up. In a little over an hour another knocking disturbed the rebels. This time it was none other than Secretary Herbert who came up, his mustache and beard gemmed with the fine moisture of the night, his long cloak hanging in heavy folds about him.

Scarcely waiting to be announced, he strode in on Essex and laid a decisive hand on the table. "The Council awaits your presence, my lord," he said succinctly.

"I have already stated that I do not go abroad tonight."

"And the Council is adamant, my lord." Then Herbert dropped formality. "Do you realize what this will do for you, Essex?"

"I have given the matter but scant thought, Master Secretary," said Essex shortly.

"Let me recommend you to think on it, my lord. The Council awaits."

But Essex was obstinate. "I tell you," he cried, "that I will not go! You can see for yourself that it would be most foolhardy for me to venture forth among my enemies, tonight of all nights."

"Your lordship is afraid? I am to tell them that?"

"Tell them aught that pleases you—or them. Are they gods, that they do order about a free citizen of the realm?" Essex's voice was high and sharp.

"They are the law, my lord." Herbert turned to go.

"The law," sneered Essex. "There be two minds for that, Herbert. At any rate, I do not stir forth tonight." Then he finished rashly, "I have that afoot which requires a whole body in the undertaking."

Gravely the other left.

"Get Danvers and the rest of them," hurried Essex.

They came and by ten o'clock were assembled in that upper room. Essex, dressed in a soft-skin doublet that buttoned to his throat, faced them. The candlelight caught in his russet hair and edged the soft point of his beard with fire. His eye glittered and a high color sat on his cheekbones. Never had he looked more determined; never more the hero of a handsome undertaking. He hooked his fingers in the gold chain on his shoulders and spoke.

"Gentlemen, these messages that we have received tonight are the opening gun of the attack upon our enterprise. Our hats are in the ring. The time is come."

There was silence. Ferdinando Gorges squirmed a little in his seat.

Essex opened his mouth to continue, but Danvers cleared his throat. "I counsel flight, my lord," said he cautiously. "Get you to the coast with a hundred gentlemen, or else to Wales, but put space between yourself and the Council."

Essex glared incredulously at the frightened face before him. Danvers, always the capitulating coward! It was the same in Ireland. What a yellow-belly he was!

"Never have I contemplated flight, as well you know, Danvers. If you fear for your own skin, stay back, but by God, you remain in our custody till all is over."

There was a short pause, while every face looked searchingly at Danvers. "I-I will stay with you, my lord," he said.

"Good. Now, what is to be done, gentlemen?"

"I say, attack the Court tonight," said Sandys hotly. "They will be unawares, and we can push the matter easily."

"No, no," put in his father, an elderly man with a scanty gray beard. "We are not mustered. That would be folly."

"We could get three hundred men within the hour. Would not that be enough?" Essex turned to Gorges, whose charge it was to get the fighting men together.

"I-I think not, my lord," said Gorges, slightly rolling his large brown eyes.

"What is my strength within the City?"

"Oh, that, my lord." Gorges showed his relief. "There is no question of your strength there. One of your strongest supporters is a colonel who commands a thousand men, all ready at a moment's notice."

"Who is this man?" put in Southampton.

"He prefers to remain anonymous till the moment of attack. You can see how that is, my lord," replied Gorges earnestly.

Southampton shrugged and sat back. He did not think much of this oily little man in whom Essex put so much confidence. A thousand men, to be supplied in secret—was it possible? Evidently Essex seemed to think so, for now he was talking animatedly, a spot of color high in each cheek. He looked happy, assured.

He rose. For the space of a long moment he stood looking at them. "At dawn."

With a heavy guard posted around the house, they went to bed. No prowling assassin should put an end to their great tomorrow.

At midnight Essex stood alone in his chamber. The hour had struck. Tomorrow would decide his fate, his desperate future. By tomorrow night he would be high on the crest of victory, or prostrate, in chains at Elizabeth's feet. The final denouement had come sooner than he planned, but now that it had come, he felt only a great relief. All would soon be over.

Frances had long since left him, gone to her own chamber. She and Penelope and his mother were here in the house. That he did not like. He would have preferred them to be down in the country with the children. But they were here, and it could not be helped. Perhaps all would go smoothly, and they would be in no danger. For the first time he was able to think of Pamela's death without the sick twinge of loss, for she was well out of it all. No matter how things turned out tomorrow, her position would have been a difficult one.

Tomorrow. Christ's blood, things must go right, he *must* win! He would win. As he fell off into a doze, his mind was singularly light and clear.

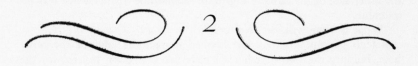

Attack

*E*arly next morning the church bells began to ring, for it was Sunday. Essex House hummed with an air of expectancy, and soon curious small crowds began to gather in the Strand. Mysterious riders came, were stealthily admitted at side entrances through which they slipped like shadows. Then more men, loud and arrogant, began arriving, pushing their way through the townsfolk and gathering noisily in the great courtyard.

Spies hurried to Whitehall to warn Cecil that something was brewing down the river. Cecil remained calm and gave orders. It would be too bad to move too soon; yet fatal to wait too long. In any case, they would let the first blow come from the Earl.

A light skiff put out from the river bank just below Essex House, and was met by another in midstream. In the first was the little Spaniard Gorges, and in the second was the tall figure of Ralegh.

"I have come in answer to your note, Sir Walter," began Gorges nervously.

"You were well advised to come, Sir Ferdinando," replied Ralegh.

Gorges bristled. "I will have you know that I come with full knowledge of my lord and the Earl of Southampton, who wished to kill you," he cried.

"Kill me?" mocked Ralegh, with a flash of his old fun. "I should have brought my men-at-arms."

Gorges flushed. This arrogant captain would have need to laugh on the other side of his face ere nightfall. Meanwhile his insolence was intolerable.

"What is your will, Sir Walter?"

Ralegh put out his foot and hooked it over the edge of the other boat, holding the two together. "I have taken it upon myself, for the sake of our former association, to warn you that it will go ill with you if you are found in the center of a rebellion."

"Ah—so?"

"You were much better off to get back to your charge at Plymouth, which I am told you have deserted. Remain, and tonight you will sleep in the Fleet."

Gorges laughed now. "Tush, Sir Walter. This is no time to talk of prison; get you back to Court, and that with speed, for my lord of Essex hath put himself into a strong guard at his house, and you are likely to have a bloody day of it."

The Sunday chimes floated lightly across the water and made melodious sound about the two men who stood facing each other in their little boats. They were almost alone, for few craft were upon the river at that hour, produce boats being tied up for the day at market landings, and pleasure barges awaiting the warmer afternoon.

Ralegh shifted his foot and the edge of the other boat dipped slightly. "I have liked you, Gorges," he said. "Many's the good game we have shared and many's the bottle we have split. But I tell you, as sure as this day is Sunday, you are marked for doom if you persist in this, and if we meet under arms, I shall not scruple to kill you."

But now Gorges, who had been keeping an uneasy eye on the shore, remarked a boat full of musketeers leaving the Essex stairs, and hastily pushed away from Ralegh.

"Fare you well, Sir Walter," he called out defiantly. "When you sue for clemency, I shall recall this morn."

Ralegh signed for his two men to row him back down the river, and departed, well content with his errand. He had found out what he came to learn, that Essex had a strong guard about him.

Gorges meanwhile made for the water-stairs, where he climbed the slimy treads to the garden. He had not found out what he was sent to learn. He had learned nothing of the Council's intent, and he had given away information to the enemy. The Earl could hardly have sent a poorer emissary.

To the guard at the water gate he murmured the password "Freedom" and bustled up the long walk into the back of the house. More guards challenged him, for at this point Essex was leaving nothing to chance. Within, all was hubbub and confusion. Aroused by a dawn summons, men were coming now in a steady stream through the front door, going straight to the courtyard at the back of the house. There they were made acquainted with the new plot to murder the Earl.

A few women servants scuttled up the stairs with food trays and hot water for the ladies. Frances appeared at the head of the stairs and Essex sent Cuffe up to tell her to stay in her own apartments and to keep the others there too.

The hall floor was foul with the tramp of many wet shoes, for some had come through dewy grass, while others waded the muddy river banks to get to the meeting place. There was a smell of sweat and horses and in the courtyard a wild throng eddied about the tall figure of Essex, who moved among them, incongruous in his damascened breastplate and high-crowned hat. A few of the others wore armor, but for the most part, there was a preponderance of feathered beavers and broadcloth capes. Light dress swords and daggers there were in plenty, but the excited crowd was surely not equipped for a steely struggle.

Everyone yelled at the same time. The din was indescribable. At length Essex mounted the steps of an entrance and pleaded for silence. It was nigh onto ten o'clock and no plan had been settled. He began to speak. But now a new confusion arose. A messenger with a tall ax pushed his way through to Essex and told him there were four gentlemen from the Court demanding immediate entrance and speech with the Earl.

This was something unexpected. What to do? While he hesitated, the uproar began again. He shrugged his shoulders helplessly. "Send them in!" he ordered. "Stay! Use the wicket gate and tell their servants to stay without."

In a moment the Queen's four gentlemen appeared, rich in furs, with golden hat chains on their feathers. The noisy, swaggering mob parted to let them through, then closed behind them. With knotting jaw muscles pulsing in his thin cheeks, Essex watched their approach.

He noted that Egerton, his hateful gaoler, was first, working his way through the fierce-eyed youths with that old look of a bad smell in his nostrils. William Knollys, his old uncle, followed, and at sight of him, his heart turned over. He had no wish to see his uncle hurt. Worcester was behind, that pompous nobleman who had accompanied him on his first trip as prisoner; bringing up the rear was the Lord Chief Justice Popham. The Council could not have sent four men less calculated to bring the Earl of Essex to reason. Head and shoulders above the group that surrounded him, he waited for them in silence.

Egerton stepped lightly in front of the other three and faced him.

"My lord," he began pompously, "we are come from her Majesty to understand the cause of this—this assembly, and to learn from your lordship if you have any cause of grief against any person whatsoever." He paused, and those about him fell silent. Then he raised his heavy voice. "If it be so, these grievances shall be heard and you shall have justice."

"Justice!" retorted Essex so that all about heard him. "Is it justice to plot against a man's life? Is not that grievance enough?" He struck his hand upon the hilt of his sword. "I have been perfidiously dealt with, as your lordships are well aware." Contempt curled his lip. "Why have you come here to learn what all men must know who follow me and my affairs?"

Egerton rolled slightly on his feet and cast a quick glance over his shoulder. He and his companions were completely hemmed in.

"If you have any cause of grief, my lord, you are to declare it," he said, just as if Essex had not already replied to him. "It will be truly related to the Queen and justice shall be done."

Again Essex smote his sword. "It is too late now for the slow wheels of justice!" A bitter smile froze his features.

Egerton cast a helpless look at his companions. "If you are unwilling to state your grievance publicly, let us go to some private spot where you can be heard, my lord."

Over the heads of the Queen's gentlemen, Essex marked how his followers, who did not like this tame business of talk, moved restlessly against one another. Now a push from behind sent some of them sprawling against old Lord Popham, who turned, glaring at the indignity. Ostentatiously he brushed off his cape and hunched it closer about him. The men nearest began to jeer. They were gathered for violence and meant to have it.

"Away, my lord!" One wild young baron reached out as if to push the Lord Keeper aside, but Danvers, his face flushed and discomfited, stopped him.

"By the blood of God!" flared the youngster. But now more cries arose.

"They abuse you!"

"They betray you!"

"Away with them!"

Daggers began to flick out of sheaths. Egerton was sweating. He raised his voice and cried shrilly. "My lord, let us speak with you privately and understand your griefs——"

"Stop their lying mouths!"

"Throw them into the street!"

Desperately Egerton turned round and felt with his heel for the step on which Essex stood. Finding a space, he squeezed himself onto it, and thus raised, he lifted his tall hat and waved it for attention.

"I command you all, upon your allegiance, to lay down your arms and depart!"

The shouting at the front of the crowd died down, and a little group before the Lord Keeper stood still, while a deadly calm fell about them like a cloak. Hands fell away from daggers, eyelids flickered, fierceness melted into a troubled hesitation. To refuse now to lay down arms would constitute treason, and should their efforts fail—a few shivered and drew quietly away.

But those at the back, shoving and pushing against the crowd at the steps, had not heard and now began to shout derisively, "All! All! All!"

Essex had not wavered. His scorn still flashed in his eye and had it not been for his uncle's presence, he would have left the four to take their chance with the angriest of the mob. As it was, he turned suddenly and went into his house, gesturing for them to follow.

After them pressed the crowd, yelling, "Kill them! Kill them! Let us chop them up!"

Egerton almost ran at the Earl's heels. "My lord," he persisted, "let us arbitrate. There is no need for bloodshed."

"Is there not?" Essex, still striding along, flung over his shoulder. "Try telling that to some of my friends out there!"

He stalked on, his face stony, and they pattered after him, dignity gone, a great question in their faces. Outside his library door, Essex stopped. The patient statue in steel, still standing at his post after an all-night vigil, showed a weary face beneath his helmet.

"This guard to be relieved," said Essex shortly to Cuffe who came to the door. Cuffe stood aside, then gestured to the four men. "In here, if you please, my lords."

They went in, an awkward, indeterminate group, hats still on, faces turned toward the Earl.

"Gentlemen, I have conducted you hither to save your lives. It is not my intention to spill blood, but my followers there are impatient. They feel my wrongs even more sharply than I do myself."

"Do we understand, Robert, that we are unable to return to the Council?" said Knollys incredulously.

Essex winced. He was fond of his uncle. Curse it, he had not bargained for this devil's work of Cecil, sending a man's own flesh and blood to treat with him in a thing like this.

"Here you must remain whilst I do go into London and take order with the Mayor and Sheriff for the City. I shall return within the hour. In the meantime my household is at your command."

"This is a serious thing you do, my lord," began Popham.

"I preserve your lordship's life," returned Essex as he stalked from the room.

"Davies!" He beckoned to a thin little man who stood near talking to Cuffe in the passage. "These gentlemen are not to stir from this room. I hold you answerable."

He turned and ran swiftly down the broad stairway and passed straight out into the courtyard.

"Ah!" A mighty shout went up from the tangled mob that now turned its face toward its leader. "To the Court! To the Court!"

"No, my friends!" cried Essex in agitation. "I have given my word to go into the City!"

Naked sword in hand, he walked forward, and a disorderly two hundred surged after him. No one had been told what to do. Carefully detailed plans were now so many words on paper. Where was the midnight planning, the skillful plot to seize Court and Council? What was become of the scheme of the bloodless overturn of the government, that final coup that was to climax their march on the Queen?

Thrown off balance by the sudden arrival of the Queen's gentlemen, Essex now ran into the street, waving his gleaming blade, Sidney's sword, crying, "For the Queen! For the Queen! A plot is laid for my life!"

The mob pushing at his back, he strode on past the front of his own house and those that flanked it. Windows swung back over his head; open-mouthed faces appeared. What was this disturbance in the quiet Sunday streets, led by a man who called one moment for the Queen, and the next for his own life's preservation?

From gutter to gutter the rioters surged while onlookers were pushed back against gabled walls. A small gathering at a street fountain set up a feeble cheering and Essex, still waving his sword and crying out, sped on.

"God save your worship!" The people applauded but remained where they were.

"Come, good people, take arms! Join my cause! Take arms, take arms! For England and for freedom!"

Essex looked expectantly from side to side as he kept moving, ever moving, waiting for the first that lined their path to jump in with them and lead the rest. If they would only move! Once start them melting in with his own men, and the rest would be easy. Why, in Christ's name, did they not rally to his call?

The parade went on and the people let it pass. They even waved their hats and caps, some running before the Earl to cheer him, but then they slipped back into the crowd and watched. No one joined him.

Down past Paul's went Essex, head still high, sword still aloft, and the heart within him growing cold as lead. Men and women now flocked out from the morning sermon; they gaped curiously at him and let him pass. Still walking, Essex turned now to Gorges who was near the head of his company. If the townsfolk would not rally to him, he would have to rely on the military.

"Take me to your colonel who is to produce the thousand men."

Gorges gave back an instant. Then he recovered himself. "He is the Sheriff Smythe," he said hurriedly.

They turned their steps in the direction of Smythe's house, past more staring people; but now the Earl kept a tight-lipped silence, his sword sheathed at his side. He clanked on, his eye fiercely alight, his breath short. At the end of a little street they saw Smythe standing nervous and indecisive at the wicket gate. He waved to them and Essex broke into a light run.

"My lord," cried Smythe, without giving Essex time to say anything. "I hear that your lordship's life is in danger, and I beg of you—I beg of you—the Lord Mayor's house—I have no protection——" But Essex pushed past him and was up the steps into his house without stopping.

Smythe did not follow his visitor but set off at a run round the side of his house, where he snatched up the reins of a waiting horse and galloped away. He had gone to fetch the Lord Mayor.

Essex now sank upon a chair in the Sheriff's hall. His face bore no vestige of color and his whole body was wringing wet with sweat. He looked up, slightly panting, to see Adam Baxter near with a shirt over his arm.

"Good man."

He rose, motioning the servant to follow. Inside a small anteroom, he dragged off breastplate and tunic. He dropped them, streaked with dark sweat, on the floor, where Baxter quietly picked them up while his master changed his soaking shirt.

"I'm thankful for this, Baxter."

The soldier stared at him, a passion of worship in his eyes. How gladly he would die to take away that green look of horror from the Earl's face and the shadow of despair that grew in his eyes.

"I'll find your lordship some food," he said. Soon he returned with a platter of bread and meat. The color had somewhat returned to his master's face, and he now set about eating his food with mechanical relish. The others crowded in on him, Danvers, Blount, Sandys, Southampton. Malby was nowhere to be seen.

"Where are the military that were promised?" cried Southampton.

"Aye, where?" repeated Blount.

"Get Gorges," said Essex, his mouth full of meat.

But Gorges was not to be found. Some said he had gone after my Lord Sheriff, others that he had not been seen since they left Paul's cathedral. By now the room was full of people. Essex thrust the plate at Baxter and climbed onto a stout stool.

"My lord! My lord!" It was the lost Gorges who came running in from the outer hall.

"Well?" shouted Essex, rising on his toes over the heads.

"My lord!" puffed Gorges. "A thing has happened! Lord Thomas Burghley is in from the North and he is riding to all points of the City with a herald and they are saying that your lordship is a traitor, and promising pardon to all who should leave you and depart!"

"Ha!" cried Essex contemptuously. "A herald, forsooth! A herald will do aught for a shilling. Why did I not think of a herald? By now we should have had the City. This is only enemies who employ a trick to destroy me. Here, make way!" He jumped down and pushed his way from the room, a small trickle of men following him.

There was a thick crowd before the house. The roofs dripped with moisture from the river mists, but the men stood their ground on the glistening cobblestones and shouted for the Earl to show himself.

At sight of Essex, someone threw a clod of mud. It struck the house and fell into the Sheriff's grass plot.

"Good people! Good people!" called Essex earnestly. "I am acting for the good of the Queen, the City, and the Crown! Do you want your sweet country betrayed to the Infanta of Spain?"

"No, no!" roared the crowd.

"Then follow me and see justice done!" Essex turned into the street, and they parted to let him pass. None followed.

He now mounted a horse that someone brought forward, and moved out into the center of the street, a tall, desperate figure in the obstinate current that flowed against him. He started forward but drew rein at sight of Sheriff Smythe who returned, spurring his horse to excited speed. At last!

"Yield, my lord!" he shouted. "Yield, or you are lost!"

Essex gasped. "By whose orders?"

"By order of the Lord Mayor!" Smythe drew to a prancing stop. Essex reached out and grasped his bridle and the horse quieted.

"What was that you said?" Then, as Smythe made reply, he stopped him. "Aye, I heard aright. Now, you listen to me. You shall go with me, you and your goodly company, and together we will take the gates. 'Tis the only way for the safety of the City."

"My company!" cried Smythe hoarsely. "Why, God's death, your worship, you are out of your mind! I have no company, naught save an apprentice or two!"

"Aah!" Essex reeled back in the saddle. For a moment he was stunned, as if struck with a heavy stone. "Man, man, ye cannot mean that!" He glared wildly at the Sheriff. No company! The Sheriff shook his head.

"I am betrayed," groaned Essex. Then he turned, quivering, to the other. "Man, if you fear God, love the Queen, or care for religion, look to yourself in this, for by the Lord's most precious blood—" he caught his lip in his teeth, and wheeled away.

The sweat now poured down his face. He started back the way he had come. He had but one thought; to get to Essex House, to get home. Home, home! He trotted up the street, Adam Baxter running lightly at his stirrup.

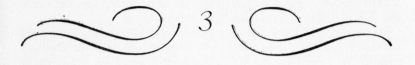

3

Defeat

$\mathcal{D}$own the river Whitehall was a whispering tumult. Wild rumors ran up and down the corridors. The Earl had killed the Lord Mayor and was marching even now upon the palace with a force of two thousand; the Earl had barricaded himself in the Sheriff's house and they were shooting people through the windows; the Earl had sworn to have the Queen's head ere nightfall; the Earl, the Earl——

Elizabeth took longer than usual over her toilette, and if her maids were nervous she pretended not to see it. She had herself completely dressed in amaranth, glared at the purplish pink, declared the sight of it made her sick, and ordered them to dress her in Judas-color.

" 'Twill be appropriate for the occasion," she observed grimly. "A fine scarlet for a traitor's day."

Then when she was painted and powdered and frizzed to her satisfaction and her jewels were disposed about her person so that she felt at home, she picked up her pomander and fan and announced that she would receive the impatient deputation ramping like lions about her antechamber.

Cecil came in, a spot of color in each pale cheek. His quiet complacence was gone.

"Well, Master Cecil, you look perturbed. How goes the rebellion?"

"The reports are—alarming, your Grace." Cecil glanced uneasily at Bacon, who for his part, was standing as if his shoes were on fire.

"Alarming, did you say?" The Queen reached out and took a comfit from a dish on the table. She sucked it reflectively. "Alarming? Pooh, Master Secretary, I am not alarmed."

"Madam," put in Bacon, "Sir William and the others are not yet returned from Essex House and we have it that they are held prisoners."

"Prisoners?" The Queen seemed bent on repeating them in her most irritating fashion. The two men before her knew that she was playing one of her Tudor roles, and while unwillingly they admired her calm, they were exasperated at her inaction.

"You sent four noddies," she continued, sucking loudly at her sweet. "I trow they would not have taken me prisoner!" She gave a short laugh. "These rebels are having a busy Sunday. Four old men! A triumph!"

"If your Grace will issue orders to have the guard doubled——"

"Ah, let it be done if it will ease you, Cecil," she said indifferently. "I suppose you will have roused the countryside so that honest men cannot enjoy their dinners in peace today."

"Madam." Cecil was aggrieved. "We have fortified the surrounding villages and barricaded the road from Charing Cross. We were remiss in our duty if we did less."

Elizabeth looked curiously at him, amusement in her black eyes.

"Little man, the Lord who hath placed me in this seat will preserve me in it. And now I should like my dinner."

Cecil and Bacon went hastily to the Lord Admiral to tell him that the Queen either would or could not bring herself to issue proper orders and that it was up to them to take the lead. Three companies under Howard and Lord Grey were mustered and the noise of their clanking and collecting mounted to Elizabeth's chamber.

She stuck her head out of the window and laughed at them. "What a sight of men for the subduing of a few rebels! Shall I not go with you? I should like to see a rebel show his face then!"

Aye, indeed. They looked up at her and grinned. Old as she was, she was a sight to rouse admiring awe. Red and fierce and regnant she stood, framed in the narrow casement, one long pale hand on either side the wall. Her magnificent crimson sleeves filled the aperture and her front blazed with a carcanet of emeralds and rubies. But it was her face that moved them. White and prideful, full of the strength of England at bay, it was a cavalier defiance that she showed to Essex this day, but it was none the less strong.

"Lend me your helmet to keep the wet from my hair." She laughed down at a young captain who stood near the ivied wall. "I'll come with ye!"

"Madam!" Cecil's worried face appeared at her satin shoulder. "Your Grace cannot be serious; these men are desperate, there is no knowing what they intend."

Pettishly she whirled on him. "Pygmy, do you tell me that you do not know what they intend?" She moved back into the room and the men below saw her no more. "Why, God's blood, I can see what they intend. They mean to take my throne, yea, even that. Man, they want to rule!"

She prodded him in the chest and grinned, showing her blackened teeth. He backed away, a slight smile crossing his pained face. For a moment she thought she saw his father.

"Come, Cecil, furbish up your courage. We are not yet finished. And if it shall make you any easier, I shall remain at home. I did but jest." She walked to the door and turned back at him, her flat farthingale sweeping round her hips. "Tell me when the rebels are in hand and, until then, leave me in peace."

The arras fell behind her. A thrill shot down the spine of the little man. What a woman!

In the library of Essex House four men waited uneasily the return of the Earl.

"Does it not seem to you that this is a wondrous long hour?" Egerton put the question to Popham, who sat, pretending to read from Essex's Homer, all the while keeping his ear strained for alarming noises.

The Lord Chief Justice looked up and laid the book on the table. "Aye," he returned. He had himself pleaded with Davies to let them go, but the Earl's little man was obdurate.

"Your lordships can see that I am under orders," he insisted firmly.

"You had much better take the orders of the Queen's gentlemen," warned Egerton. "The Earl will be deceived, he will not return, and then, what case are you in, who are jailer for the Queen's councilors?"

Davies threw back his head. "The Earl will not be deceived," he said proudly.

"Do you mean to say that the City will rise as the Earl expects?"

argued Knollys. "And that there will be indeed a great effusion of blood?"

"As to that, I cannot say," was the calm reply.

"Spoiling the City by desperate persons!" Knollys shook his gray head. "No good will come of this, Davies. In the end it will be the worse for the Earl and his company."

But Davies was steadfast. He went and sat on the window seat and gazed obstinately out onto the garden below. The river was calm, almost empty of boats, for the day was still dank and uninviting. From the prospect before him, none would suspect that not far away a desperate struggle was being waged. There was a long embarrassed silence. Then Davies rose.

"I-I will fetch the ladies to you, sirs," he offered. "They will be happy to converse with your lordships."

"I pray you, do not disturb them," said Egerton severely. "We have naught to say to them, I am sure."

Out in the city streets the rebellion was rising to the climax. The Lord Mayor had jumped into action. Trained bands, companies of militia, were filing into the square before his house, and the Bishop of London had gathered a force. The Bishop himself walked helplessly about, at sea as to how to marshal the agitated crowd of armed men who were gathered outside his palace. Many of them were his own servants and wore his armor, but now an old weather-beaten captain came forward from the thickest of the throng.

"Ah, Leveson!" cried the Bishop in relief. "Just the man we need!"

Leveson touched his helmet, then turning, barked an order. In almost no time the crowd resolved itself into orderly lines and stood, grim and spiky with harquebuses and pikes, while a few men began chaining the street across. Behind the ponderous links they stood, first the shot, and behind them, the pikes.

"Way there! Way!" Foot soldiers pushed roughly among the idle gazers and moved them off. With their end of the street well blocked, they awaited the rebels who must come this way if they expected to gain the City. The Earl of Cumberland and a small force of stiffly marching men now joined them, and the defense settled into professional pattern, ready to give battle if that was what the rebels wanted.

The noon sun had retired behind gray cloud banks, and the Sunday bells had long since stopped ringing. There was an oppressive hush in the air and over that part of the City hovered a quiet but direful expectancy.

A quickened noise of shouting, horses' hoofs, and Essex and his mob appeared at one end of the short street. They advanced, and when they were within four pikes' length of the chain, they halted. There was little noise now, save an occasional clack as a horse moved on the cobblestones.

"Who commandeth here?" The voice of Essex rang out clearly on the dampened air.

"My Lord of Cumberland!"

Essex's horse now shied a little, and he patted its neck, controlling it to quietness. "I shall offend none, if I am permitted to get through to my house," he offered.

"None have liberty from the Sheriff or the Lord Mayor to pass here," was the steely response.

"I have permit from these officers to pass to my house," shouted Essex. "And I mean so to do!"

"You cannot pass."

Young Sandys, immediately behind Essex, now lost his temper. "The insolent knaves! Shoot! Shoot!"

Almost at once came a deafening report as several of the Earl's men discharged their pistols.

"Fire!" thundered Leveson. A return volley hit the Earl's men.

Essex felt his hat fly off, a bullet hole through the top of the crown. At a choked cry behind him, he turned in the saddle to see Baxter stagger and fall, almost beneath the horse's feet. Blood was pouring from his throat, sliding down the brightness of his breastplate like scarlet honey.

"At them, Blount!"

Essex swung down and slipped to his knees. Baxter lay where he had fallen; he was quite dead, his eyes open, his bare head resting on the wet stones.

"Damn them for a lot of bloody, murdering villains!" Essex half sobbed as he rushed with the others, who by now, were hacking at the chains. A scream, and Christopher Blount was down, a gory slash across his face.

"Caitiff!" he cried up at the man who straddled him. For answer, the other swung up the reverse end of his weapon and dealt Blount a heavy blow on the side of the head. Without a groan, he fainted.

It was no use. They could not get through. Essex, on his horse again, wheeled about, his men with him. They were not followed, Cumberland's force remaining by the chains.

"My lord!" He looked back to see Gorges spurring after him, his face gray with fear. Beyond him, as in a flash, appeared the whole scene. The limp form of Blount being carried off, and Baxter, lying as if grown to the ground, one arm outflung, the other clenched above his head.

Gorges now came up. "My lord, shall I not go back and release the Councilors? I myself will escort them to the Queen."

With a jerk Essex came to his senses. Gorges! The little greasy man. Like an echo came the meaning of his words. "The Lord Chief Justice only is to be released," he ordered curtly.

Gorges nodded and galloped away.

They retraced their steps now and took a roundabout way back to Essex House. The company of rebels, so full of fiery zeal in the morning, was falling away, and it was a pitiful shadow of the morning mob that now, in the gathering dark of late afternoon, returned with their leader.

Essex flung up the stairs. The corridor was empty, even of the guard, and when he banged open his library door, it was to be confronted by only Davies and Cuffe.

"Where are they?" he damanded fiercely.

"Gorges came and said that your lordship's orders were to free them all."

Essex felt another cold chill. "Damn him for a traitor."

What to do now? He gnawed his lip. They had failed miserably in the streets; soon the Queen's men would be upon them. What to do?

"We must barricade the house and hold out as long as possible," he said. "It's that—or surrender at once."

The house flew into action. Guards were roused from the kitchens and outhouses to be posted at all entrances.

"Haste! Haste!" Essex was feverish. "There is no time to lose!"

Books were piled in the windows. "Come," said he to Cuffe. They disappeared into the small study. "Lock the door."

Cuffe did so. Essex was tearing open his private caskets and pouches and he and Cuffe began shaking the contents onto the fire. Fumblingly he pushed his hand inside his blouse and tore from his neck the dangerous little black leather bag. An acrid smoke bellied out into the room and made them cough. At last they stopped.

Essex straightened. "All?"

Cuffe nodded, his face pale and strained. Essex looked at his secretary and he felt his throat tighten.

"Henry," he said hurriedly, "there is not much time. I pray you, slip down to the water gate and get across the river. There is no need for you to fall with me."

Cuffe looked into the face, full of defeat, before him. His lips were trembling as he bent over the last papers and mechanically put them into the writing cupboard.

"I beg of you," insisted the low voice. "Henry, I beg of you."

"My lord," said Cuffe unsteadily, "I once said that your lordship's welfare was mine own. I am yours for good or ill; we fall together."

Essex shook his head wonderingly. "You know what it means—and still——"

Cuffe put out a blind hand, entreating him to have done.

Essex cleared his throat. "I have not merited it, Henry." Cuffe bowed his head.

A violent knocking interrupted them. At once Cuffe turned the key and the door flew open.

"Essex!" It was Southampton, his face crimson with excitement. "They are unloading at the stairs!"

Essex strode to the window. "So soon?" he muttered. There in the early twilight he made out the moving forms at the foot of his garden. Soldiers in the Queen's armor were disembarking and parting at the water gate, marching right and left to surround the house.

"They are here!" called Sandys. He came up the steps with long bounds. "Cumberland, Howard, all of them. And hark!" A low rumbling came to their ears. They were bringing the cannon from the Tower.

The two earls rushed up to the leads and took a hasty survey. A sudden access of fury shook Essex. "To the devil with you!" He waved his sword and ran below.

"My lord! My lord!" It was now Danvers who appeared, sweating and pale. "Sidney is coming. He is at the fountain and desires a parley."

"A parley." Essex was sour. To Southampton, "Go, Henry."

Southampton ran back up to the leads where he could shout at Sir Henry Sidney down in the garden. With three or four harquebusiers, Sidney stood at the fountain that marked the foot of the shallow steps leading onto the long sweep of lawns. The men's torches fluttered in the evening air and gilded Sidney's breastplate.

Inside the house, tension gripped the listeners. They sat or crouched behind piles of books at the windows. Some gritted their teeth, some muttered prayers; all were fear-ridden. They could hear distinctly what went on between the men in the garden and the young man on the roof.

Sidney's clear voice rang out. "My lords, you are commanded to yield!"

"To whom should we yield?" returned Southampton.

"To your adversaries," was the contemptuous answer.

"We shall never surrender to such bloodthirsty rogues; that were to run us into ruin."

"Then surrender to the Queen's mercy."

"That were to confess ourselves guilty!"

Those within heard a louder bawl from Southampton, as if he had cupped his hands about his mouth to make his words carry the further. "But if the Lord Admiral will give us hostages for our safety, we will appear before the Queen."

"And if not?"

"If not," rolled back the answer, "we are every man of us resolved to lose our lives fighting."

The brave words echoed on the air and sent a nervous tremor of anticipation through the listeners inside. There was no further exchange. A step on the stair and Southampton now appeared, flushed, with a kindling eye.

"You have done well, Henry," said Essex.

Aimlessly they walked about for a few moments, awaiting the next move from Cumberland. Sidney returned to the fountain and sent in word that conditions were not to be discussed with the rebels. My Lord Admiral, who did not war with women, would allow the two countesses, Lady Rich, and their women, to come forth unharmed.

"It's a trick!" cried Southampton. "They want us to unbar the door, and then they will rush us."

"No, Henry," decided Essex. "I do not think so. But if they will give us one hour to make all safe after the women have gone, we will accept."

"But——"

"No. Cease, Henry. That is my word."

The Devereux ladies appeared in a little body. They were surrounded by their women, who most of the day had crouched behind locked doors in an ecstasy of terror. Their mistresses were calm.

The two young women came first. They showed no trace of fear, though both were white to the lips. They knew what had befallen their beloved foolhardy one, and to them he was irrevocably sacrificed to his own valor. Frances held her quilted cloak about her as she came proudly down the stairs to her husband. Her head was high; at this moment she was an English soldier's widow.

"Robert—love," she clung to him. "I shall keep the children safe. God preserve you." Her voice broke in a tiny sob, which instantly she smothered against his shoulder.

Essex put his arm tightly about her. "No man was better wived," he said gently. He kissed her hands, then her lips, and gave her to his mother, whose face quivered, though her eyes were bright and dry. He turned and held close to him the perfumed slenderness that was Penelope. Her velvet eyes were misted over but her lips were firm.

Like a sweet cloud, they departed out of his life.

Essex watched them go, then suddenly sat down. He faced the remnants of his followers. "We fight it out now, gentlemen. Let all be made safe after the ladies."

There was dead silence.

He stared at them. So that was it! They were sick of the rebellion; they were for surrender and appeal to the Queen's mercy. They were not as he had imagined, eager for death rather than face defeat. What he had taken for zeal in a holy cause had turned out, now it was uncovered, to be mere lust for power and excitement. Well, God's death, he had given them the excitement—pity he could not give them the power. And so they were for quitting.

Slowly he cast his eyes about the hall. It was one of those unforgettable scenes, like the surrender to Tyrone, the leaving of Cadiz, the dreadful quarrel with Elizabeth. There they were, his feckless followers. Some leaned against the carved post of the staircase, some lounged about the hooded fireplace. A few stood near him, their faces troubled. Danvers, heavy-eyed, and the elder Sandys, quiet and anxious. All looked surfeited, crowded—afraid.

"I take it then, you would have us ask for conditions?"

There was no reply. Only the fire cracked and a man's shoe creaked as he shifted his weight.

Southampton, standing with one foot on a chair, leaned his elbow on his knee and played moodily with a small horn cup, swinging it by the handle from one finger. Back and forth it dangled, catching the light on its metal mountings. Essex watched it. He knew that Southampton, good, loyal friend, was for fighting it out, the only one, besides Cuffe, who would stand by him to a brave death.

He got to his feet. Great circles darkened his eyes and his mouth was etched in lines of stubborn weariness.

"Henry!" Southampton looked sharply up.

"Tell Sidney that we yield on conditions. We are to be dealt with civilly; we are to be fully heard and justly treated." He paused; resignation settled onto his shoulders. "For myself, I would have Master Ashton come to me for my soul's comfort."

Southampton's mouth tightened. For a moment he hesitated. Then he set the little horn cup carefully down on the chair and left the room.

It was ten o'clock at night. Despite all the upset and excitement of the day, the city had gone quietly to bed. But for the small force about Essex House and the busy torches in the garden, there might have been nothing out of the ordinary stirring in London on this Sunday night. Bitterly Essex thought how slight a ripple he had made in the calm current of English life.

Like a tired statue he stood and heard dimly the sound of barricades being torn from his doors and the sharp clop-clop of military boots as the soldiers moved about in the dark outside. The front door was flung open and a cold blast of air rushed into the hall.

In silent dignity the leaders of his rebellion passed by. Handclasps, eyes veiled in regret, and they were gone with their guards. He was nearly alone in the house now, and it was time for him to go. Southampton had left, both men shrinking from the moment of parting, making the briefest of farewells. Essex thought now that he could not walk forward the few necessary steps. A dreadful lassitude had overtaken him and he would gladly have died there in the muddy great hall of his house.

Shaking off his trance, he took his sword slowly from the scabbard and walked steadily forward into the cold torchlight.

He came face to face with Lord Howard. There he stood, the old fellow commander, at whose side he had so often ridden in honor and glory. Stiffly Howard awaited him, and his eyes glistened with emotion. His mouth was clamped tight over those square teeth and he looked gray and ill. Essex handed him Philip Sidney's sword and gently Howard took it.

"My lord," he said with a slight bow.

Essex followed his guard round the house to the back. Through his dark damp-smelling garden he walked, he knew, for the last time. The frogs were croaking down by the river and in the tops of the trees a little night wind stirred. In deadly silence, surrounded now by his guard, he passed down to the water gate and stepped into a waiting barge. They were taking him to Lambeth where the Archbishop would have custody of him for the night.

He was rowed rapidly across and they glided alongside the shallow steps of the episcopal palace. Suddenly he remembered a cold night fourteen years before when he had left Lambeth for the start of the great adventure. Well, this was the end.

The palace was blazing with lights, but otherwise there was small sign of life about the place. Two gleaming sentries stood in the Gothic doorway and they grounded their arms as the Earl stalked past. Of the other members of his party there was no sign.

Only a captain with a small handful of soldiers stood to receive him. The officer saluted and led the way upstairs. Still silent, his heart burning with memories, he mounted in the wake of the steely soldier, whose creaking leather doublet made hideous the velvet quiet of the Archbishop's lofty hall.

Once behind a locked door, he relaxed his stony calm. His features shook and he quivered all over. He drew a long shuddering breath and hid his face in his hands. What a cruel failure! What an end to overtake a man!

At last he raised his head and stepped to the window. He pushed open the leaded casement and gazed out across the river to his house. A few torches moved about his garden, but soon they stopped flitting back and forth like great fireflies, and, one by one, went out. So, thought he, had flickered out his great purpose.

It was very still. He stood a long time at the open window, oblivious of the damp cold. Now, at a slight noise, he started. It was the sound of a footfall, coming down the front of the palace, out on the stones of the river road. The watch was passing on his round.

Out on the air, now frosty with the promise of bitter cold weather, came the ringing cry:

"One hour before twelve of a February night, and a-all's we-ell!"

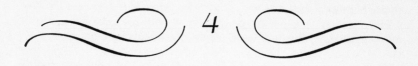

The Tower

*N*ext day they lodged him in a cell overlooking the large courtyard of the Bloody Tower. He bent his tall head under the arch of the tiny entrance to his apartments and passed inside. It was over, and he knew it. Even if he escaped with his life, he was finished.

Wearily he sat down and watched Joseph begin his usual puttering round of the place that was to shelter them.

"Now, where be best place to put . . ." Joseph was muttering to himself as he hung the long cloak on the wall, carried the few changes of clothing into the inner room where his master was to sleep. There were some books, too, and, here Essex smiled, his bootjack. What in the devil's name prompted Joseph to bring that.

He looked about the small chamber. How long it had been since he had lived happily in the spacious kindness of his great houses, a free man, joyously going about the adventure of his life! These little rooms! He had lodged in a good many, of late. A whole apprenticeship of staring out of windows; and a veritable lifetime since he had lain on the grass with one of the Queen's maids, or at the slender feet of Gloriana herself, laughing, jesting—his heaviest thought the fortunes of Bacon or the rig of his new ship!

What had happened to him? What concatenation of horrible circumstances had contrived to lodge him here in this cell, in the Bloody
Tower, a captive under the likely sentence of death—was this where
folly had led him? Aye, he doubted not he would get it this time. He
had forced the hand of his enemies, and of the Queen. They had now no
choice but to kill him.

His rebellion! A negative gesture at best, with his heart but half in it
most of the time, except when he fed himself with false hopes.

They came next day and told him the Queen had ordered a speedy
trial. They spoke of her composure throughout the whole wretched
business, and he smiled sardonically.

"Why, God's death, didst think she would blench? How little you
know her!" Through stiff lips he jested.

At the news that no charges would be pressed against the King of
Scotland, he laughed aloud. "So! They will whitewash Mountjoy, will
they?"

So successful was his old friend in the green country of Ireland that
they could ill afford to dispense with his services; and to bring him
home, charged with an attempt to corrupt the Scottish monarch, would
be most embarrassing at this time. Ah well, Mountjoy had withdrawn
his foot from the fatal brink in the nick of time, and besides he had
salted his safety with successful service to the Queen. Essex did not
begrudge him his life.

Ashton came to attend him and they had long talks. "It seems, Master
Ashton, that my life is to hinge on that short Sunday afternoon walk
through London," he said. But the divine cast down his eyes and advised the Earl to make his peace with God.

"That I shall do," assured Essex.

He spent hours brooding on the events that led up to his failure. Idly,
he wondered what had become of Malby, missing on the last day. Was
he too a traitor?

Then his thoughts sprang ahead to the trial that lay before him; unwillingly, he admitted to himself that he wished the ordeal over. He
knew that he would be allowed no counsel, being already adjudged before his hearing; but he would be allowed to speak in his own defense,
if that meant anything, and he resolved to plead not guilty to the charges
that Cecil and the rest would hurl against him. They would charge him
with conspiracy against Elizabeth's life. He set his lips; he would go to
his death protesting his innocence in that quarter.

"I have acted in defense of my own life as well as in the interests of my country," he told Ashton. "Is that a crime in the sight of God and man?"

But Ashton was cautious. "I have little knowledge of the affairs of state, my lord; my concern is with the soul, and in any case, I do beseech your lordship to confess your sins before God and throw yourself on His divine mercy."

Essex sighed. He did not want to think about God; he wished rather to nerve himself for what was to come to him here on earth. At this point he did not think that God could help him much. The materialistic philosophy of his age was upon him, as he searched in temporal quarters for the help that would not come.

Then his cup of bitterness brimmed over. They told him that Bacon was to act as counsel for the prosecution. "So," he murmured, "the viper will sink his fangs in me again."

It was not enough, what Bacon had done before. The denunciation after Ireland was evidently but the opening gun of an attack that was to continue to the death.

He thought of all the acrimonious struggle with the Queen on Bacon's behalf. It did not seem to him possible that a man could be so base. Ingratitude, that sharpest sting of all—the poet was right. One's own folly one could abide, but treachery, ah, that was misery, indeed.

Ten tingling days in the Tower, and each morning he braced himself to be called to account for his crimes. Then, on the morning of the eighteenth, while February sleet whirled about the grim Tower and rattled against its heavy walls, he and the others were taken from their cells to face their peers. They were to be dragged through the farce of a private trial.

"Of what use will be all this—our lives are forfeit before ever we set foot in this chamber," he thought. But he resolved to answer his enemies roundly.

He and Southampton came in with their guards, separately. Christopher Blount was already there, still pale from his rough encounter with the trooper in the street, the red scar of his cut livid on his face and a great bruise down one side of his head. But he was steadfast, even with a dash of the old jaunty air of happier days.

Over the heads of their peers their eyes met, and they exchanged faint smiles. Essex looked away. How intolerable that he should have brought about the doom of these two young men whose lives were but beginning. Southampton was far too young to die, and now it seemed that Will Shakespeare and the others would have to make merry without the man who loved them.

He tore his thoughts from Wriothesley and glanced round now at his judges. Miserable embodiments of the law! Coke, the Attorney General, with the intellectual sneer, what did he know of a man's desperate purpose? And Bacon—ah, here the sore spot pressed too hard. Essex forced himself to regard the cold countenance, imperturbable above an immaculate ruff. Calmly Bacon returned the look; no color rose in his pale scholar's face. Popham was there, too. No frightened strain of composure on him now, for all he had cringed for his life at Essex House. Safe he was, and on the winning side.

How the scenes of his life repeated themselves. Just so had his judges sat after the Irish fiasco; the difference now was that a man's life lay on the council table. Better for them to be condemned and get it over with.

Why not? But for the people—ah, yes, the people. They would be outraged if one short day's work could so bring a man to the ax. The people must feel right about the matter, come what may. They must be made to see that this Sunday's work was the culmination of eighteen months of carefully conspired plotting; of a design as foul as the one Essex himself unearthed about that famous Dr. Lopez, back in '94.

Ah, yes. Accuse them roundly of treason, easy to prove, carry them through all the tortuous windings of evidential examination, then pronounce sentence and carry it out. With a slight shiver Essex seated himself at one end of the table.

Outside, the sleet continued its staccato assault on the leaded panes, and a searching little draft chilled the feet of the men in the room. Popham gestured for the door to be shut.

A throat was cleared. Coke raised his brows at Sergeant Yelverton, who arose with alacrity to open the case for the Crown. Formal charges, and pious surprise that the two Earls did not blush for shame that they stood upon their trials without confession! Yelverton lowered his eyes and sat down.

Coke rose. In transports of windy oration he discussed the law of treason, as if its dread details were not clear to all present. It was obvious, he pointed out, that Essex, together with his earls, barons, and knights, intended violence on the sacred person of the Queen. The embroidered rhetoric flowed on, until Popham shuffled restlessly.

Poison and peroration. Excited beyond his usual manner, Coke grew rougher, more and more cutting, then abusive. Eyes, resting on the two earls, softened.

Essex sprang up. "Is not a man to take arms against his murderer?"

"Murderer, my lord!" cried Coke. "Confess! Was it not your purpose to take not only the Tower of London but the royal palace and the person of the prince—yea"—shaking a long finger— "and to take away her life?"

"My purpose," retorted Essex, "was such that you, Sir Edward, could neither appreciate nor understand."

"I understand treason and murder, my lord Essex. I understand rash behavior as I see it——"

"Treason and murder!" interrupted Essex. "Aye, there indeed, ought you to be concerned. As the Queen's Attorney, ought you not to look to such matters among people that are much closer to her Grace than it has been my pleasure to be for these many months?"

There was an agitated flutter among the council group. What was this? Across Bacon's face a tight smile crept.

Essex followed up his brief advantage. "I refer to the matter of the Spanish plot to seize the succession!"

Oh—that! Council members relaxed. Everyone knew of the Spanish obsession of the Earl of Essex. If that were all——

"I have it on excellent authority that Mr. Secretary Cecil has said that the Infanta's title to the succession was as good as any others."

Now there was a stunned silence. Cecil pro-Spanish. God in heaven, what next!

Suddenly the curtain over by a wall moved and out stepped the slight form of the Secretary, who all this while had stood concealed there, that he might hear without being seen by the accused. White and agitated, he dropped on one knee before the Lord High Steward.

"Well?" said the officer quietly.

"I beg leave to answer this foul charge, my lord." Cecil's voice slightly trembled.

The Steward looked his surprise. "Surely, Mr. Secretary, you will not take these words of my lord of Essex seriously?"

Cecil, recovering himself, darted an angry look at Essex. "I am stung and roused," he declared, "that the lord of Essex should dare to impugn the honor of one who has ever held the realm in the tenderest esteem."

A sarcastic smile played about Essex's lips. Cecil now launched into a long, suffering oration. He avowed his loyalty to her Majesty, and as he went on, his controlled voice began to rise as high as his high shoulders.

"It is a wolf's head in sheep's clothing that we have here to deal with. I would rather have seen my own soul in heaven and my body at rest than that I should have had to witness so grievous a thing as this treason of my lord of Essex."

Essex's smile seemed carved in granite; as for Southampton, he looked as if all the bad odors of the city of London had risen about him.

"You are very brave today, Master Secretary," said Essex.

"Not brave, my lord, but thankful that you did not take me as fit companion for your humor." Cecil glanced meaningfully at young Southampton. "For had you done so, you would have drawn me too to betray my Sovereign." A slight pause. "And now," he continued, "you shall name the man to whom I said that the Spanish would succeed to our throne. Name him."

"Southampton, will you answer?" Essex turned to his friend.

"The man to whom you said this thing, Master Secretary," said Southampton reluctantly, "is Sir William Knollys, the Earl's own uncle."

Cecil became shrill. "I beg your lordships to send for Sir William, that this thing may be proved."

"Carry the request to the Queen," ordered the Steward.

"No, wait!" cried out Cecil. "I pray you, do not reveal to Sir William the nature of the errand."

Knivett the messenger lingered. "And if her Majesty refuse to permit Sir William to come?"

"Then you shall say to her Majesty that should she prevent this thing, though I will live and die her true servant, I will nevermore serve her as Councilor or Secretary."

At this fantastic message, Knivett raised his brows and departed. They returned to the attack.

Essex was denounced as a hypocrite in that he had professed himself a true believer, yet had consorted with Blount, a notorious Papist.

"He is my stepfather and a good man."

"Then you do admit that you have promised protection to all Papists for his sake?"

"I deny it."

They dragged up his other offenses, one by one, and set them down in the book of treason. By this time, however, Knivett was back with Sir William Knollys.

They repeated the accusation against Cecil. It was a breathless moment. If it could be proved that there was an active pro-Spanish faction at work to give the Crown to the Infanta, the two earls might yet squirm out of the trap. On one side of the balance hung Cecil's reputation and honor; on the other, the lives of Essex and Southampton. What would Knollys say?

Knollys took his time and spoke slowly. His words fell on the silent air like heavy drops of water. "I have never heard Sir Robert Cecil speak any words to the effect that you specify. What he did say was in discussion of a book, Doleman's *Book of the Succession*. He remarked that it was a strange impudence in Doleman to give as equal right in the succession of the Crown to the Infanta of Spain as any other."

A relieved smile flitted across the white face of the Secretary. The judges turned questioningly to Essex. The corner of his lip went down. "All I can say is that the words were reported to me in another sense."

So they were going to save Cecil, were they? Like Mountjoy, he was to be whitewashed because he was valuable to the Crown. So be it.

He rose. Across the supercilious face of the Attorney he drew the lash of his scorn. Coke squirmed, attempted to interrupt, and Essex flayed him. His judges remonstrated, and suddenly he became gentle.

"My Lord Judges," he said, "the interest of the Earl of Southampton and myself is so infinitely greater than that of any man in this room, that we ought to be permitted to answer their charges."

"My lord of Essex," reminded the Lord High Steward stiffly, "it is fitting first for the evidence to be delivered, and then may the prisoners have liberty to speak what they will."

Essex's eye flashed. "I demand my rights and those of my fellows that we be allowed to answer every piece of evidence as it is produced, that there may be no shred against us that is allowed improper weight."

A murmur ran round the board. The peers deemed this reasonable, and Coke and the Steward sourly retreated.

But it was really no good. They brought in Widdington, who repeated second hand that fatal Sunday scene at Essex House. A scornful smile touched the lips of the accused men. Were they to be convicted on hearsay?

Then Popham arose and in a voice quivering with indignation told how he and his three fellows were held prisoner in the paneled library of Essex House at imminent risk of their lives.

At sight of the little man with his short legs and his two chins, Essex almost laughed. "Risk of your lives is truly said, my Lord Justice. I shut you and the others up for your own safety."

Coke put in a disagreeable comment. "Why not then dissolve your company when commanded upon your allegiance?"

What a fool was this! "How could I? My house was surrounded by armed men and this had put my followers into such an ecstasy of fear that I could not suddenly dissolve them. Would you have the London streets run with blood?"

"Nay. But I fancy your lordship would."

Once more the threat of Ralegh against the Earl came up, and this time they summoned the Queen's captain.

Essex cried out. "Ralegh! What booteth it to swear the fox?"

The judges were scandalized. "Your lordship will be pleased to remember that you are here on trial for your life and this is a formal inquiry."

"The latter I question," said Essex bitterly. "The first I am not likely to forget."

In came Ralegh, and at the fixed gaze of Essex he fidgeted. He lightly stroked his mustache, affecting a nonchalance he did not feel. Why, in God's name, had he summoned Gorges that morning? Were it not for that, he would now be on the other side this door, away from this heated atmosphere of treachery and hate.

They pried it out of him, all of it. Essex was appalled. Gorges! He doubted Ralegh's word, till they read him the signed confession of his little greasy lieutenant. God's wounds, what did this mean? They must have wrung it out of him by inches, writing it down between his screams.

Ralegh was excused, and now came in Gorges, pale and lightly sweating, but sound in limb. The man was a traitor! Essex felt another sick qualm. How like to that wretched Gomez d'Avila he was, the little man who had helped them to do Lopez to death.

Now the Lord High Steward fixed his eyes firmly on the shaking Gorges and commanded him to repeat what he had so obligingly told them the day before.

Gorges glanced sideways at his former master, then gulped. "I-I advised the Earl to go and submit himself to the Queen."

"You—what? That is not true! Gorges, I beg of you to speak openly as you know it to be."

Gorges writhed against the table. He cast down his eyes, then rolled them at the judges, for all the world like a frightened dog. "I-I have told all I remember. I-I cannot say," he finished vaguely.

"Sir Ferdinando, you are a gentleman," urged Essex. "I pray you answer me, did you advise me to leave my enterprise?"

"My lord, I think I did," said the unhappy man.

"Nay, nay! This is no time to answer on thinking; these are not things to be forgotten." Straight into the twisted face before him he stared. "Now, on your oath, did you intend so to counsel me?"

Gorges hung his head. "I did," he murmured.

Essex turned to his judges. "My lords, regard Sir Ferdinando, and see if he looks like himself." All eyes were fixed on the little man. No one spoke. Essex waited. God's death, they must be able to see that the man lied in his teeth. It was evident in every line of his face. "There, my lords, there you see the guilt plain on——"

"That will be all, Gorges." The Lord High Steward cut in. "You may go." He turned to the furious Earl. "My lord of Essex, I pray you, command yourself. You will accomplish naught by intimidating witnesses."

Essex bit his lip and his eyes filled. Hard to believe that the man's loyalty to him had really been touched. If only he could have known that Gorges lied under compulsion. That knowledge, however small, would have been balm to his hurt.

Now they began on Southampton. Ingenuous in his defense, Wriothesley vowed that his sword had never been drawn all day, that he knew naught of actual intentions when he presented himself at Essex House on that Sunday morning.

A cold smile ran round the board. The judges deemed it inconceivable that the Earl of Southampton meant that he was in ignorance of the plot that had grown and flowered for the past year. Ah, he *was* cognizant? Then he merely referred to that final fatal uprising, was that it? They pursed their lips.

Southampton looked at Essex, a steadfast anxiety in his eyes. He hoped that the Earl would not think him playing the craven, too. Much as he feared his fate, there was no faltering in his love for the man who for the past two years had dominated him. Firmly planted on his two feet, he stood and faced his judges.

He denounced their enemies, and stubbornly he clung to his passionate defense of the Earl's position, as well as his own. Love, loyalty, and indignation glowed in his young eyes and scorn was in his flaring nostril and quivering lip. His devotion swept like a breath of fresh air through the miasmic atmosphere about them.

All this was too much for Coke. Repeatedly he burst in on Southampton, time and again attempting to trip him. At length the young Earl, his passion spent, turned quietly to him.

"Mr. Attorney, it is the uncivillest thing in the world to interrupt a man when he is speaking for his life." There was an abashed silence. "If in this business I was too far carried away by the love I bear to my Lord of Essex, I confess then, I have offended."

But Coke wrangled on.

The issue faded; it spread to minor exaggerations. Bacon now intervened. The change in climate, from the legal to the emotional, was not to his liking. It was dangerous for the Crown's case. The issue before them was the determining of the exact meaning of the Earl's conduct, and to this he now brought them back.

He carried his few pointed remarks to a deadly close. "Under pretense of danger and assault, the Earl of Essex entered the City of London; but in reality he had no such enemies, no such dangers. His aim and drift was clearly to take the government of the City into his own hands, to alter the form thereof." He turned and leveled on his former friend and patron his unwinking reptilian gaze. "My lord, all whatsoever you have or can say in answer to the charges are but shadows. And therefore methinks it were best for you to confess, not to justify."

Essex opened his mouth, then shut it and swallowed. He had no words to speak his feeling, bitter and sour as it rose within him.

It did not take them long now. They summed up the charges rapidly. It only remained for them to sentence the noble prisoners.

The two earls were duly convicted of high treason, Blount with them. As for their death day, that rested on the Queen's pleasure. They were formally sentenced to die the death of traitors and the ghastly details were carefully read out to them. They remained unmoved.

The court now rose to go. Beer, biscuits, and tobacco were being brought in for the refreshment of the judges who had put in a long, thirsty session. The prisoners moved toward the door where their guards awaited them. They did not speak to one another, and for the last time their eyes met. In those of Essex was a rueful esteem. Both Blount and Wriothesley had stood loyally by him; indeed, Southampton's unswerving loyalty had been the one sweet drop in an otherwise wholly bitter cup. Watching the young man leave, he encountered the somber gaze of old Lord Morley.

He paused. The elderly lord had never been so intimate with him as had the son, now lying in the Fleet, in company with those hundred or more who had been taken on the Sunday. In the old man's face there was no condemnation, only a look of understanding. It was as if, through his personal pain, he could still trace the pattern of the Earl's downfall and feel sympathy for the ruin of a man in whom the seeds of greatness had been so poorly planted.

Sensing this, Essex took courage to speak. "I would entreat your pardon, my lord, in that I have led your son astray and involved him in my own griefs."

Morley inclined his head. "My son was entirely free to choose, sir, and by my faith, I cannot find it in my heart to blame him for his loyalty to your lordship."

Essex flushed faintly. "My thanks," he replied. Then he passed out among his guards.

Back in his cell he felt the terrific letdown as the unbearable tension of the trial was suddenly relieved. As the cord springs back when the arrow flies, so the very soul of the man now recoiled from the knowledge of his fate and all that it implied. He fell prey to acute fears.

With a fascinated horror he regarded the clergyman who kept him company. Here was the mortal reminder of the grace and of what lay beyond. Repent! Repent! Like a death knell rang the words. He must make his peace—with what?

He groaned out a request to fetch the Lords of the Council. To him they came, crowding into his small room till they boxed it up with the judicial atmosphere of the law closing in upon the wretched man.

"I am guilty!" he cried. "My thoughts have been black and my companions have been my doom! *Mea culpa!*"

The gleam in their eyes died. They were witnessing the painful dissolution of a proud man. Embarrassed, they averted their gaze from the sight of white torture and agonized eyes.

"I know my sins," he said. "I know my sins unto her Majesty and to my God. I must confess to you that I am the greatest, the most vilest and most unthankful traitor that has been in all the land."

Ah, yes, he had been all of this. And the others, too! He lashed round on them all, Cuffe, Danvers, even Penelope and Wriothesley.

"Proud spirits, all! Let them be looked to!"

His face was contorted; he looked less than human. He excoriated his stepfather as among the worst. And Mountjoy—yes, there was another traitor. Did they not know his part in the sordid story?

The judges kept their eyes averted.

He subsided, panting into a chair. The wild look faded, and the long hands unclenched. He drooped back into the semblance of his former self.

There was a movement among the lords. If the Earl had finished his confession, they would like to leave.

"My lords!" Essex called them back. "I have but one request." Their eyes gave assent. "Let-let it be private."

"Her Majesty will grant that," assured Popham.

"The day?"

Popham shook his head. "You will await her Majesty's pleasure."

With that they left.

Her Majesty's pleasure! He gazed into the fire and his sick mind rolled the words about. What would that be—and would she expect him to appeal—and if he did appeal, would she——? He set his lips and something of the old look came into his face. Whatever happened he knew that he would not appeal. He could not crawl for mercy; he had cast the die, he would abide the chance.

The burden rolled from his shoulders. He became now almost tranquil, for he had confessed, he had humbled himself before his judges. It only remained for him to die bravely. His disaster, now a bad dream, faded into the blurred yesterdays that were all that remained of immediate memories. Like an old man who feels the quieting air of approaching death about him, he wandered back to the scenes of his youth, reliving boyhood days at Wanstead.

When he stirred his fire his mind suddenly shot back to cold mornings, and Walter, and how they two, blowing on numb fingers, saddled their ponies, wrapped sacking round the hoofs that the groom should not hear their stolen flights. Oh, those days when they could escape their tutor and ride joyously over the odorous meadow paths, their horses swishing among high-growing grasses, what exquisite times they were! Light and free as air, they were sweetly unaware of the dreadful game that lay ahead, to make all their childish pastimes the more longingly remembered.

And now he was come to that cold time of remembering, and the imagined warmth of those distant days could not comfort him for long. Four curly heads pressed against a window, his and Walter's and their two sisters' as they looked out on lantern-lit snow and listened to the Christmas waits, while behind them the great hall was fragrant with the spice of winter greens. He and Penelope watched their chance to slip into the stillroom to search among the mysterious jars on the shelves. Penelope, her red mouth stained with cordial, running with lifted skirts down the passage, hiding from the nurse, giggling with him behind the arras. Heaven, he had not thought of this for years.

And Pamela. Ah, Pamela! The nut-brown maiden, whose remembered dark eyes, vivid velvet, still brought the intolerable ache to his heart. Delicately fine, she was like the gentle people in his family, like his father. How the tall Lord Essex would have loved Pamela.

And now it was the quiet elder Devereux, whose grave face came out of the shadows to him. And he saw a little lad of seven, fascinated by his father's fine gold chain. The child took the chain and hid it in a dark place to fondle in solitude the bright thing, so like a lovely snake. The chain was missed, and suddenly the boy could not look his tall father in the face.

"My son," said the Earl, "bring me the chain."

The child put the jewel into his father's hand. The man placed his hand gently on the boy's shoulder and waited till the shamed eyes climbed to his.

"Lad, never look lower than a man's eyes. You will remember?"

The son remembered and the man's eyes smarted.

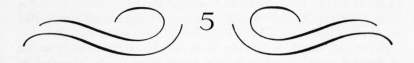

Decision

The cold February evening drew in to a close. Within the colder shadows of her room Elizabeth sat alone and tried to warm herself at the fire. They had told her that all was over. The Earl was guilty and must die. Guilty! Of course she had not doubted it, but hazily, in her hurrying thoughts, she had conceived that there might be some way out of the dreadful dilemma into which Essex had forced her.

Guilty! She stared at the royal arms entwined with her cipher above the arch of the fireplace. The emblem of royalty and all that it implied was for once hateful to her. For she was the instrument of justice; hers must be the hand to sign away his life. In her was embodied the final law, and if she did not pardon him, the law must take its course. It would be easier to drag the symbol from the stone than to change the law. It was, inflexibly, England.

With a sinking heart she realized what all the time she must have known. Even in those first delirious days, when Essex was a young man, celebrating his majority in velvet and laughter, teasing her maids, making daring love to her, setting her gallants by the ears, and snapping his long fingers at her old ministers, even then she felt a presentiment that someday he and she would be each other's doom. And here it was. What had she lived for? Gloriously she had reigned with the loves of her people, but it was nothing to her now.

Well, it was not too late for her to pardon him if she so desired. She would please the people, too, who pitied him in his forlorn misery. No, the people would applaud royal mercy, for was not Essex their idol? Yes, indeed. She twitched in her chair as she thought of what he had said to Mountjoy, boasting that if he were to be pardoned, he would do the same thing over again, and this time with success.

In her quiet room she sat on, alone with her melancholy thoughts. It was true, true, he thought himself more fit to rule than she. He was *not* fit to rule. Had she not seen him, turned this way and that, a prey to those natural defects that now destroyed him? Ah, yes! She knew all about that hysterical outburst in the Tower, the groveling, the breast-beating, the *mea culpa!* Such a man was never to be trusted.

As if to show a shadowy Essex, standing ghostly in the dusk before her, she sprang to her feet. Never beat the breast before one's enemies! She drew in her breath sharply, and her thin nostrils quivered in disdain. Groveling!

Suddenly she felt her age, she felt old, tottering on the brink of some desolate eternity. Whether Essex lived or died, her blow was mortal; woman and queen were slain, the grave made ready to receive them. Suppose Essex lived, and James, the Scottish Stuart, were seated on her throne. With Essex alive and determined, there would be civil war.

War! Her knees buckled and she sank back, fingers pressed against her mouth. And even as she lay there, a tiny thought stabbed her deep with a new dismay. What—what if he sued for pardon? Ah—but would he? She doubted it. Proud, stiff, obstinate, that high spirit would never bend before her. But, the stab persisted, what if he did? Her tired heart jumped with a momentary return of the old thrill. The familiar melting softness crept over her, and she wondered, if he gave the slightest sign, how she could resist sending for him.

Uneasy now, she looked at her hands and twisted her rings. At this moment she was completely inert, her will flexive, ready to flow into the first open channel. Ah well, the next move was clearly up to Essex; let him make up *his* mind. She rang for her women to light her to bed.

Much later in the night, tossing in uneasy slumber, she dreamed she was standing in the garden at Greenwich and her father appeared before her. Down the brick walk he strode as she had seen him dozens of times in life, and she heard distinctly the clack of his heels and saw the split velvet as he came nearer. Large and terrible, he loomed above her. With those glittering eyes he read her heart, he knew her torment.

At her unspoken question he bellowed, "Pluck him out of thy bosom, Bess!"

She commenced to shake. "Pluck him out, I say!" The great voice rumbled on. "A viper! Pluck him out!"

"No! No!" she shrieked. Shuddering from head to foot, she woke.

Essex did not sue for mercy. The days crawled by and a deep silence hung round his little Tower cell. She could not eat—she could not rest; she was wild. Where to turn—dear God, where?

"Destroy him or he will destroy you." Her head was the cold counselor. Essex could not live; it was not right for England that she should let him live. But the heart, all woman, remembered only the old loving —and that he was so young. But, still——

"Rule with the sword—plunge England into a bath of blood," she muttered. "No, he shall not rule."

The Court was beside itself. They brought her Master Thomas Alleyn to read. The famous actor came in and quailed before the white mask that confronted him from beneath the flaming hair. The two eyes were black holes in the head, lost in a net of fine wrinkles and great purple shadows.

He stood before her, book under his arm.

"What have you there?" she asked indifferently.

" 'Tis a fine new edition of Master Marlowe, your Grace, the Lucan's *Pharsalia,* in good blank verse——"

"New! New!" she interrupted violently. "I want naught that is new about me. Give me old things, old faces, old hearts, old loyalties—" her voice broke. "Here!" She plucked from a nearby table a book and flung it at him. "Read me that. Any page will outdo the drivel that lies in your new stuff."

He took the volume and read with dismay the title, *Richard II* by William Shakespeare. Here was something, certainly not old, and, moreover, full of treason. Did she know what she had given him? Apparently not. He glanced fearfully from the book to her, at a loss to know what to do. She looked half-mad. Around her chair the courtiers stood in shrinking silence.

"Read! Don't stand there like a cooked sausage. Read!" She leaned back and closed her eyes. God in heaven, how stiff and sore was her neck.

Alleyn cleared his throat and muttered an inward prayer. He opened the book to the second act. " 'Tis the speech of John of Gaunt, your Grace, from the play, *Richard II* by William Shakespeare."

"Mm," murmured Elizabeth, not listening.

Alleyn began. " 'Methinks I am a prophet new inspired . . .' " His beautiful voice took on dignity as the lines rang sonorously through the quiet room. He motioned a page to bring the candelabra nearer. Elizabeth moved her narrow feet on her little hassock and settled wearily back in her chair. The fellow had a good voice, nay, a fine voice . . .

Suddenly she became intent; she opened her eyes. What was that?

> " 'This royal throne of kings, this scepter'd isle,
> This earth of majesty, this seat of Mars,
> This other Eden, demi-paradise,
> This fortress built by nature for herself
> Against infection and the hand of war,
> This happy breed of men, this little world,
> This precious stone set in the silver sea,
> Which serves it in the office of a wall
> Or as a moat defensive to a house,
> Against the envy of less happier lands,
> This blessed plot, this earth, this realm—this England.' "

"Ah!" Her eyes gleamed. "That is it. That is what I feel. Read it again, Master, read it again." Roused from her lethargy, she moved about the room.

She stood, the candelabra blazing on her; the diamonds on her bosom winked, no brighter than her eyes that glistened strangely. She nodded her jeweled head in time to the gentle cadence of the words.

" 'This blessed plot, this earth, this realm—this England,' " she repeated softly. She turned a pained smile on the actor. "Master, this night you have done me a service, all unaware. My heart was sore with great affliction, but you have brought me ease. I am grateful." She drew from her finger a gold ring set with a great cat's eye, and taking his hand, pressed the jewel into it. He fell on his knees and kissed her sleeve.

Late that night she sat with Cecil in her study, her hand resting on the death warrant. It provided that instead of suffering the extreme atrocity of his punishment, the Earl should be privately beheaded in the precincts of the Tower. It wanted only her signature to make it law. Elizabeth looked steadfastly at her minister, and a great resolve stood in her face. Cecil knew she had made up her mind.

"Cecil, I have lived in a glittering glaze of glory, but it has never blinded me to my England and my people." She paused. "It is more important to me that a weaver have a good dinner than that one of my generals win a great victory over my enemies, if, in the winning, we gain a great territory and the weaver suffer for it."

She mused a while, the papers still unsigned. The words of the great poet had resolved her difficulty. She marveled that the way had seemed so hard. Nothing really mattered, after all, save England. She drew a long, quivering breath. For England, then, she was prepared to sacrifice the one person who had been dearer to her than all the others.

England! Quiet Sunday mornings and yellow fields of wheat. Maypoles and rolling downs and the bells of glorious crooked London. The sweet smell of the meadows—all part of the sacred trust of rulership. Leave Essex on the throne! A hothead, light-mindedly on the holy throne of England! England, with its oaks, its stouthearted seamen . . . and the waves beating on the eternal Cornish coast.

" 'This scepter'd isle . . . this jewel set in the silver sea.' "

And peace, most precious of all; for that, she had lived her life. For England's life, she would now give his. Her people might have cause for discontent now, but under an Essex they would bid fair to perish. Their peace, imperfect as it was, should not be disturbed.

In the end she followed her heart. She signed the warrant.

Finish

*H*e awoke to a deep sense of quiet. There was not a sound and he lay high up in his room, relaxed with the long night's rest. By the grace of exhausted nature he had slept the night through, dimly aware, as he dropped off, of a hammer banging down in the courtyard. Now all was still, the morning cold and clear and, at the window, the red February dawn.

He turned on the bed and stretched. Then the remembering rushed in and he felt the knot in his stomach. He yawned stiffly, with no sense of sleepy satisfaction, only the first fluttering of his nerves, then, sighing, threw off the covers. His day had begun. He walked into the other room and pushed open the window. There was the sky with the glow over the eastern horizon, and through the deep quiet came the high twittering of little birds in flight from the far bank of the river to the trees outside the great walls.

He could not see into the courtyard below, for the abutment of masonry blocked his view. But down there they must be setting the stage. Down there he was to be cut off, cast into outer darkness by the severing of flesh and bone. Down there, on a raised scaffold, all would see folly's final immolation, but they would not like what they saw, of that he was sure. It would be too close to their own frailty for comfort.

Today he would be the principal actor in their drama, for in him the spectacle of fatal struggle would be quickened before their eyes into action—of living, breathing, and dying. Any one of them might at this moment be standing where he now stood, and he could feel how the grim thought must keep them company today. Again he sighed, resisted the desire to yawn, and turned from the window, chilled to the bone. He must dress warmly, he must not shiver. He rang his little bell for Joseph.

He put on a suit of heavy satin quilted with wool and wrapped himself in a long velvet cloak that hung close and warm about him. He took three spoonfuls of the warm stuff in the bowl on the table, then, his stomach revolting, he pushed it away and reached for his little book.

Suddenly he shivered. A bell began to toll, and as the first deep notes struck through him, he could not control the shudder. He shrank into his cloak and resolutely bent his mind to his reading. Frances had sent the book, her quick perception guessing that in John Donne's *Meditations* he might find comfort. This small book was what had become of the gay, cynical young chap who had accompanied him to Cadiz and the Islands. Donne had now turned to religion, as if to find there an alchemy that would transmute his own bitterness into peace.

He turned to a passage that he liked. The solemn, insistent note continued as he read, to the accompaniment of his own funeral dirge.

. . . Perchance he for whom this bell tolls may be so ill as that he knows not it tolls for him . . . and perchance I may think myself so much better than I am, as that they who are about me and see my state, may have caused it to toll for me and I know it not. . . .

He raised his eyes to think, savoring the words. He knew for whom the bell was tolling, no doubt of that, but—did they? Death is the great equality which all must share and none can escape the tolling bell. Ah, yes, they must know the melancholy fact of mortality. He read again.

. . . All Mankind is of one Author and is one volume; when one man dies, one chapter is not torn out of the book, but translated into a better language . . .

Not to be torn violently out of life? Leaving his corruptible parts, he was to be translated into a better language. Was this then the adventure to which the feeble prelude pointed? Well, there was still the getting there—the knot in his stomach tightened and his throat dried.

There was a knock and they entered. They were come for him. He closed the book and stood up; there was no need of words. He bowed to them and reached for his hat, and there stood Joseph with it in his faithful hand. The hat, with its high crown and twisted golden chain was the touch of bravado in his somber costume. He took it, but Joseph now clung to his hand, the bitter tears trickling. Ah, Joseph, good man, this is indeed part of the worst. At the pleading in the eyes, he shook his head.

"No, Joseph, I shall do very well with these gentlemen. 'Tis but a short journey that I make. Stay here and after—after—" impossible to go on, but Joseph knew what to do with the packet on the table. The sobs grew.

"Nay, now——" One's courage was a flimsy thing at best; he must get out of the sight of this terrible grief. "Joseph, my friend." He pressed the quivering shoulder and strode out.

A rattle of steel at the main entrance. There was his guard, a section of partisans drawn up in the outside air. He stepped out into the morning. The cold air smote his lungs and he gasped, then stiffly erect, walked forward.

The priests in their black and white fell in on either side of him and they moved along. There seemed to be a great crowd—too many people. He felt a flash of anger, for they had promised. But they all had to be there, the set official faces. Cumberland, his beard a dark wedge on his miserable face, Hertford and Binden, Compton and old Lord Morley. Morley—ah, the sad morning of his condemnation! Upward of a hundred there must be, and with them Lord Thomas Howard, come in place of his brother, the old companion of the campaigns. No sign of Ralegh.

He set his teeth and strode to the scaffold.

With a final, lingering stroke the bell stopped and the echo died. A sudden deadly ruffle of drums made him start, and then, gripping his cloak about him, he climbed the steps. At the top he looked straight into the face of an ebony man, arms folded, eyes glittering through the slits in his black mask. The medieval headsman. And where—ah yes, the ax. They always thrust that into the straw, out of sight of the condemned. His heart jumped.

Out over the top were the gray walls and in the east a faint glow where angry red now faded to pink. The drums stopped. Deep silence settled. A pair of robins chirped on the wall; the little male preened his rosy breast. Spring was on the way.

They were crowded there on the platform. Why, in God's name, couldn't they make these things handier? Sir John Peyton his jailer, the three clerics, that black fellow, and himself. He backed up, glancing behind to see whose toes he was trapping. Ah, Peyton was stepping forward, clearing his throat. The formal announcement promised to be a long, cold job.

He quivered at the waiting. Oh, for the final relieving stroke. He hugged close his Devereux pride, feeling it form a solid wall between him and them. His cold hands clenched in the suède gloves, crept deeper into the private shelter of his cloak. He fixed his gaze on the gray walls. And the flat voice of Peyton droned on.

The gray walls. Strong for the holding of a prisoner, for the sure encompassing of a morning rendezvous with danger and death. Beyond the walls—beyond—there was misery, too, where *she* lay. What was she thinking and feeling in this last extreme moment? Had she believed him weak enough to send to her? He felt his lips tight against his teeth. No, by heaven, he had held fast against her, even as now he held himself rigid against fear and the showing of fear.

For this was his destiny. No matter how many times he might live, he would spend his time here on earth in the same way, struggling toward the unattained goal. Of course they both knew he'd meant to take her throne, and would try it again. Ever since he became Earl Marshal he had always meant, given the chance, to rule England. So here he was. He had no regret for things done; only that he had failed.

Then suddenly, he thought of the others, to suffer after him. Ah, now, the twinge was sharp. For loyalty, that thing so prized, they were to walk this same dolorous way, and soon. Meyrick, Cuffe, and Davies were to die next week; but Blount and Danvers would lay down their heads before that. Of Southampton, not a word. Perhaps he would be spared to rot in the Tower. Young men all, followers of his standard, now to die beneath it. A passion of sorrow rose in him.

Peyton was finishing, thank God. There was a slight movement and they turned to him. Again his stomach tightened. His hand jerked stiffly up to his hat and a priest took it gently from him. He threw back his head to the sky where the pale blue was turning to white. The freshening air blew softly upon him and the old light feeling suffused him. He took a deep breath and felt relieved. He spoke.

His words came easily, with power, rolling from his lips to reverberate over the heads below. He felt himself fluent, clear, controlled. No use recapitulating past injuries; if what he had done was a sin, then better freely to acknowledge it. If the working out of destiny led to puffed pride, to vanity, and love of this world's pleasure, then so be it. He was proud, he was vain, he was in love with this world he was leaving.

"For her most gracious Majesty, our Queen, I do desire a long and prosperous reign (ah, the crotchety old woman, beckoned by the skinny finger of death) and I do beseech your lordships' charity and understanding, and for the last time I do protest that I have ever meant death or violence to my Sovereign."

No one moved.

"I now beg you all to remember me in your prayers." He paused and looked down on them. There were tears on Howard's weathered cheeks and Clifford's head was in his hands. He looked across at the open windows and there was Ralegh, gripping the sill with white knuckles.

His message was done. He had said it all and now the last hardest job was to do. He turned steadily, with no jerking of the nerves, and wheeled his cloak from his shoulders. He unhooked his ruff and as the chaplains took the garments, one of them bent to his ear. "Be not afraid, my lord. 'Tis swift and painless."

At sight of the doleful face he felt himself grinning. He tapped the lawn shoulder. "I have on divers occasions felt the fear of death, and that in places where death was never so near nor so certain. I cannot say I fancy it."

But the jest was already stale. Earnestly now he said, "Pray God to strengthen me in this great conflict; and let Him not suffer my flesh to have rule over me."

A rustle and the headsman was in the straw at his feet. "I pray thee, my lord, forgive me this thing that I do." The round black head was humble, the figure down-bent. One could feel only pity for such a fellow.

"Thou art welcome to me; I forgive thee. Thou art the minister of justice."

The pain at the pit of his stomach lessened. He knelt, and the days of his boyhood came back to him. Now was the time to resume the old relationship with piety. He began to speak to God. But he had nothing left to say, except to entreat the divine mercy. Ah, yes, there was something else. The old familiar prayer, lisped in babyhood, murmured in chapel with Tom Gray, whispered with Frances, with Penelope, hands softly palm to palm, the old beloved supplication . . . "Our Father, which art in heaven . . ." And down below, far below, it seemed to him, he heard the echo of the trailing voices.

The ceremony had reached its final scene. He rose and began to undo his doublet. The white lawn sleeves lifted, but he shook his head. Ah, Joseph, you are not here. He undid his own buttons, his fingers steady to push the last jet ball through its silken loop. The jacket was off, and he stood before them in a bright waistcoat with long scarlet sleeves. The sun, now fairly up, sent slender bars of light into the yard, and he felt it warm on his hair and down the side of his body.

It was done. All the bright years melted away, and there was only the blank wall. He must go—but she must stay. At least he had that. "When one man dies, one chapter is not torn out of the book . . ." And so, to the better language.

He turned to the headsman. "When I open my arms, thus," he spread them, a scarlet cross against the sky, "strike, and fear not."

He stretched his long body in the straw. The others, signed by the headsman, crept away, and the lone priest crouched, whispering. The stillness was tight. He lay, eyes closed, not blindfolded. Then the scarlet arms flung sideways.

"Executioner, strike home! Come, Lord Jesus, come, Lord Jesus, and receive my soul; into Thy ha——"

The headsman stooped, fumbled a moment with the hair, then lifted the quiet head and showed it to the company.

"God save the Queen!"

Out over the river, a cannon shot boomed.